Murder in Whitechapel:

The Adventure of

The Post Mortem Knife

by

D. A. Joy

Domnall Publishing

Cover illustrations and layout by Kyle R. Joy based on original illustrations from "The Illustrated Police News" in 1888

ISBN-10:0615808840
ISBN-13:978-0615808840

DEDICATION

To Richard Lane

Teacher, Friend and Baker Street Irregular

I think he would like this one.

ACKNOWLEDGMENTS

Two books were invaluable in determining the details and timing of this novel:

"The Complete Jack the Ripper" by Donald Rumbelow is the best description of the Ripper killings with a detailed review of each of the killings and a dispassionate review of the suspects.

"The Annotated Sherlock Holmes" by William S. Baring-Gould serves the same purpose for the Holmes aspect of the novel by justifying the chronology of the Holmes stories, explaining the historical terminology and cross-referencing the historical events of the time period.

Friday, September 7 *The Greek Interpreter*

The ringing of the police bell announced the coming of the carriage from a fair distance. The clatter of hooves and rattle of harness punctuated the speed of the coach to anyone out so late on a warm September's evening. The coach sped into the night, reaching towards the far end of Beckenham.

Sherlock Holmes and Watson sat on one side of the carriage. Holmes' thin, sharp features appeared stern in the pale light, a combination of deep thought and ire lay behind the visage. Watson, shorter and sturdier, showed concern at the night's activities. Across from them sat the young police inspector Gregson, a pleasant young man with good features and dark hair. He displayed only anticipation at the coming adventure. Beside him, the fourth member of the group was Mycroft Holmes, the broader and stouter version of Sherlock whose face bordered on panic as the carriage swayed.

"This is why," the elder Holmes managed above the noise of the bell, "I prefer not to be involved in your exploits!"

The detective was unmoved by the rebuke.

"If you had asked my advice instead of running that foolish note in the paper, we would not be in such dire straights," admonished Sherlock. "I fear the lives of Messrs. Milas and Katrides hang in the balance because of it!"

It was just a few short hours since Sherlock Holmes had heard the tale of Mr. Melas, the Greek interpreter. Melas had been hired under unusual circumstances for a job of translation. He had met a Mr. Paul Katrides, a man who was obviously held against his will. The little interpreter had used his wit and the kidnappers' ignorance of Greek to learn the unfortunate man's story. Melas even identified the perpetrators as Harold Latimer and his associate Kemp, two men well known to Scotland Yard.

Mycroft deduced the cause of the situation and the older brother had placed an ad in an attempt to discover more information. That effort revealed the location of the prisoner, but it also exposed that Mr. Melas had gone to the authorities despite the warning of the kidnappers. Sherlock had come to Mycroft's assistance in the case, but the criminals abducted Mr. Melas in revenge for his betrayal. Holmes was delayed by the legal requirements of obtaining warrants and now raced through the night in an attempt to save the men's lives.

It was after eleven when they arrived at The Myrtles, a large, dark house standing back from the road in its own grounds. They reached the door where Gregson hammered loudly and pulled the bell, but without any success.

"Our birds are flown and the nest empty," concluded Holmes

Gregson considered the heavy oak door before them. "This will not be an easy door to force."

Holmes did not have time for the leisurely pace of the policeman. He slipped away. It took only a few moments to open a ground level window and walk to the door and open it for his friends.

"I found an open window on the side," he divulged.

"I am thankful you are on the side of the force, Mr. Holmes," remarked the inspector. He waved his warrant as he stepped inside. "Under the circumstances, I believe we may enter without an invitation."

Barely had all entered when Holmes raised his hand for silence.

"What is that?"

A low moaning sound came from somewhere above them. Holmes dashed up the stairs with the inspector and Watson at his heels, while his brother Mycroft followed as quickly as his bulk allowed.

The sinister sound came from the middle door on the second level. It was locked, but the key had been left on the outside. Holmes flung open the door and rushed in, but he was out in an instant, gasping for air with his hand to his throat.

"It is charcoal!" he cried. "We must give it time to clear!"

Holmes was still choking when Watson rushed in to grab one of the men. Holmes and Gregson retrieved the other and dragged him into the well ventilated hall, Watson closing the door behind them to seal off the deadly vapors.

The victims were blue lipped and insensible, with swollen faces and protruding eyes. Indeed, so distorted were their features that it was difficult to recognize one of them as their friend, the Greek interpreter. His hands and feet were securely bound, and his face bore the mark of a violent blow. The other was a tall man in the last stage of emaciation. He ceased to moan as they laid him down, and Watson sighed heavily. Their aid had come too late. But Mr. Melas still lived, and in less than an hour, with the aid of ammonia and brandy, they had satisfaction of seeing him open his eyes.

“What is that on his chest?” asked Mycroft, pointing to a piece of paper pinned to the interpreter’s coat.

Holmes ripped the sheet from the coat while Watson ministered to the unconscious man.

"A note!" snorted Holmes. He handed it to Mycroft. "He addresses it to me, but it should be to you!"

Mycroft pulled out his reading glasses and looked at the few lines, mumbling as he did.

"Saw your hand...vows vengeance...has escaped your grasp." He handed the page to Gregson. "It is a good thing this Latimer fellow believes it is you, Sherlock," he announced. "His vow of vengeance will fall in your direction and you are much more used to handling such vendettas than I."

The detective ignored his brother's poor attempt at humor. Watson's efforts had the desired effect and Melas was coughing and coming out of his stupor. When he was able to speak, the little Greek quickly confirmed Holmes' assessment of the evening's events. He had barely reached his rooms after the interview at the Diogenes when Latimer and his friend appeared and bullied the small Greek into their coach. They drove directly to the residence, foregoing the charade of the previous evening. This night, the dialogue was short and brutal. With a pistol to his head, Kratides relented and signed the papers. Melas remembered nothing after the fierce blow struck his head.

"Quick, Gregson! You may yet catch them at the channel!"

The inspector left quickly, but returned in an hour with the sad news that their actions were too late. Latimer and his associate escaped to the continent before the alarm could be spread.

"I am not pleased, Gregson," relayed Holmes as they headed back towards Baker Street. "Had you come immediately, we stood a good change of saving Mr. Katrides life and arresting the perpetrators. Your...*legalities*!" The detective fairly spat the last word.

"Those legalities are necessary, Holmes." Gregson, obviously distraught by the course of events, was not happy at being made the goat. "It is what is required by the crown."

"Yes, of course." Holmes' voice showed he was not convinced. "I will be less inclined to seek official help in the future when lives are at stake in such a fashion."

"Then you run your own risk of being held to account by the law you flaunt, Holmes!" chided the inspector.

The detective snorted. "I shall take that risk if it means saving a life!"

"It has been a long night, Holmes," said Watson in an attempt to ease the tension.

Holmes drummed his fingers on his knee in irritation. They left a shaken and exhausted Melas at his room, then a thoroughly worn out Mycroft at the Diogenes. Finally, the carriage turned onto Baker Street. Holmes was looking forward to breakfast and sleep after the long night's work, but a police coach waiting in front of the residence told him it was not to be.

Saturday, September 8 *Annie Chapman*

"Mr. Holmes, sir," spoke the constable in earnest respect. "There's been…"

The policeman got no further as Holmes' hand shot up, a finger held to his lips.

"No more!" the detective hissed. "I shall find whatever facts I need at the scene of the crime!"

"Holmes," interjected Watson. "It would be nice to have a few minutes to freshen up before heading off on this new adventure!"

Holmes did not consider his appearance: tired, unshaven, hair mussed. A look at the worn continence of his friend, however, proved the need to regroup.

"We shall be ready in ten minutes."

The constable nodded. His job was not to judge this man before him. In typical British fashion, it was to follow orders and "fetch" him to the scene of the crime.

"As you say, sir," returned the policeman. He touched the brim of his helmet. "I will be waiting."

Holmes dismissed him with a casual wave and entered

his residence. Watson was close behind and rubbing his chin. It took longer than the indicated ten minutes, but when they returned, they had shaved and changed to fresh shirts.

"What do you think Lestrade wants?" asked Watson as they walked down the stairs to return to the coach.

"Why Lestrade?" asked Holmes.

Watson paused, and Holmes could see his thought processes as clearly as if he read the other man's mind.

"It is unusual for you to be summoned in such a fashion," explained the doctor. "If one of the detectives needs your advice, they normally appear in person to present the facts. Only Lestrade and Gregson make a habit of calling you in this manner, and Gregson brought us home."

"Masterful deduction, Watson," conceded Holmes.

Without further comment passing between them, they boarded the coach and started off quickly to the east. With bell ringing and the driver whipping up the horses, they proceeded at haste through the quiet, early morning streets of London. The sun had yet to break the horizon and many people were awakened early by the sound of their passing.

Their carriage passed St. Peter's, then St. Andrew's, while they sat in silence. The constable and Holmes were both lost in their own thoughts as they approached the East End. There was no doubt of the destination as they turned onto Aldgate. Watson touched Holmes' leg with his cane.

"Whitechapel, then? " he ventured. "Another prostitute?"

"You *are* in fine form this morning, Watson," he said, confirming the deduction. . "No doubt, though we must await the scene to discover the details."

Whatever good humor was displayed by Holmes disappeared as the detective continued. He pulled out his watch. "We should arrive shortly after 7:30."

He lapsed back into silence with this, and Watson also looked to the surroundings outside the carriage.

"It rained again," he observed, looking at the wet streets. "It has been a miserably wet summer."

The comment did not raise a response from Holmes. It was apparent Watson wanted to force Holmes to continue their minimal conversation, but the detective was clearing his mind, arranging his thoughts to process the scene of murder. The doctor perceived his friend's mood and looked back out the window of the cab to observe their progress.

The carriage turned onto Commercial Street, just where it joined with Whitechapel and Commercial Roads. This was the East End, a place of crime and infamy, and a place Watson had never thought to visit. Though it was still early in the morning, many people moved about the crowded streets and slowed their progress at the sight of the police coach. The looks received from the denizens of the slum showed a loathing of the police and everything associated with them. More than one woman shook a raised fist as they clattered past.

Without visiting Whitechapel, one could not appreciate the appalling conditions tolerated by its inhabitants. The most vile filth and corruption lined the streets. The odor as they passed a slaughter house turned Watson's empty stomach, and he was glad they had not taken time for breakfast. The people were ill-clothed and dirty. Men, coming from their work in the slaughter houses, were covered with the blood and gore of the killing floor. The others they met on the street took no notice of the condition of their clothing as most were dressed no better. Children ran unsupervised, despite the early hour. Even the buildings reflected the fallen state of the society.

The *Times* usually preached in the Sunday edition of the need for some action to be taken in this section of the city. Watson had voiced the opinion more than once that it was a scene more fitting of Calcutta, or one of the lower Indian states, than as part of the center of the Empire. Why these people accepted such a life was beyond him, he had stated. And it was Watson's idle comment from some months past that stirred Holmes from his reverie.

"Because they cannot do otherwise, Watson," observed Holmes, interrupting the doctor's thoughts. He dismissed a protest with the wave of his hand. "Surely, no man can look at such squalid conditions and not turn his mind to why people tolerate them." He gestured beyond the carriage. "Too many of these people make their living on a daily basis, earning barely enough to put some food in their bellies, and buy a bed for the night."

"But, Holmes," Watson protested. "Even such a life does not mean you give up human dignity to live like animals!"

Holmes shook his head sadly. "Too often, that is the price of survival in the East End, Watson. "

The coach stopped, halting short of Hanbury Street with the way blocked by a crowd of humanity. The constable opened the door and stepped down.

"This shall have to do, Mr. Holmes," he said. "We must walk from here." He led off, pressing through the people who were staring at a house surrounded by police. "Word must be out that Jack was at it again."

"Jack?" inquired Holmes.

"A name the locals have conjured, Mr. Holmes. We are unable to trace it to an individual."

The constable forced a path for the detective to the building. They were in the area constructed to house the Spitalfields weavers, but since steam had taken over the looms, the building was long converted to a lodging house. Unlike those where a person could purchase a bed for two or three pence a night, this one was broken into rooms which were more or less permanently held by the residents. Holmes' eyes darted about, trying to take in every detail and process them into a complete picture of the scene.

The men entered the central passage and emerged into a small, enclosed yard at the back. The body of the woman lay at the bottom of three short steps. Lestrade and another inspector looked up at Holmes' appearance.

"Thank you for coming so quickly," greeted Lestrade. He quickly introduced the other man beside him. "This is Inspector Abberline, who is in charge of the case."

Abberline was a sharp contrast to the thin Lestrade. He was a heavy set man with piercing eyes. Whereas Lestrade sported a mustache, Abberline favored a prominent mutton chop beard. The older Abberline's bowler helped to conceal the bald expanse of his head which lay at odds with the luxuriant growth on his face.

Holmes nodded in the inspector's direction. "We are acquainted. My associate, Dr. Watson."

Holmes took a quick moment to consider the chief inspector again while the doctor shook his hand. It had been over a year since their last meeting, but most of what he saw confirmed his recollection. Abberline was of the normal stolid type that populated Scotland Yard. He projected the competence one associated with the police inspectors, the feeling of experience and control in situations of emotion and chaos. But now, Abberline showed he was carrying a heavier load.

"What are the facts, inspector?" asked Holmes. As always, the detective was only interested in crime.

"Witnesses recall seeing a woman matching the victim's description talking to a man on the street shortly before the body was found. We know the time so precisely because one of the landlords swears he was here before 5:30 and the body was absent. Apparently, the *ladies* often use this back court for their gentlemen.," said Abberline in an even voice.

Holmes nodded and proceeded towards the body, but Abberline touched his shoulder. The consulting detective looked up in surprise, but quickly controlled his irritation as the police inspector spoke.

"You may inspect the area, Holmes, but I must ask that anything you find be communicated immediately." Holmes opened his mouth in protest, but Abberline would have none of it. "I know your methods and respect them, Holmes, but too often you keep critical facts to yourself. I cannot allow that, not on this case. Do you understand?"

For the briefest moment, Holmes considered leaving the police to their own devices. He wanted to say this to Abberline, but he refrained. The pressures facing the police from these grizzly crimes were palpable: the mob standing before the building spoke to this in volumes. Holmes nodded his assent to the demand.

"Nothing has been moved?" he asked.

“Not by the police,” stated Lestrade. “I am afraid the area has been very well trod.”

Holmes tapped his foot on the hard surface of the court. “We need not worry about footprints here, Lestrade.” With that, he stepped down to examine the body.

The woman was short and stout. As he always did for Holmes, Watson pulled out a pad and pencil to jot notes about the scene of the crime, as well as record any comments made by his friend.

The woman’s abdomen was torn open and the viscera removed and placed above her right shoulder. Two flaps of skin, apparently cut from the abdomen, were placed at her left shoulder. Holmes knelt to examine the body in his normally detached fashion, but Watson was unable to hold back a comment.

“What sort of vile monster can do such a thing?”

“That is what we are trying to discover, doctor,” stated Abberline flatly, stepping over to Holmes.

The detective move carefully across the body and the area, but had time to ask for an opinion from his friend.

“You have never seen anything like this, Watson?”

The doctor shook his head. “Not since the frontier, Holmes. The Afghan would do that to our soldiers, or something similar, when they were captured alive.”

“It speaks to a great deal of hatred, doesn’t it, doctor?”

“It does,” agreed the physician.

“Similar to the last one, I see,“ observed the private detective. He moved forward slightly to examine her throat. A handkerchief was tied about her neck and

Holmes had to move it to see the viscous wound that lay behind. Her throat was savagely slashed, revealing all the internal tissue down to the backbone itself.

"My God!" The exclamation was torn from Watson at the sight.

"Indeed," agreed Holmes with his dry understatement. "Still, Inspector, that is not what killed her. Notice the area around us. If her throat had been so terribly cut while she was living, blood would have sprayed everywhere. There is only a little here on the fence, so her heart was either stopped or nearly so, when the throat was slashed." He looked to Watson for confirmation, though he could only manage a nod of assent. "No, she was dead before these injuries occurred. That's why there is relatively little blood on the ground." He looked more closely at that ghastly neck wound, then examined her face. "Watson, what do you make of this?'

"Those bruises are most recent," he returned, pointing to marks on her left cheek. "Notice the protruding tongue. Check her eyes, Holmes." He gently opened an eyelid and Watson could see the tiny, burst veins from his vantage point. "Suffocation I would say. Probably strangulation, but you can't see the marks on her throat because it is slashed."

"I would agree," returned the detective. "But notice these other bruises on her face. These are older, surely."

"At least a week," agreed the doctor. "She has had multiple fights from the look of her. One last week, and another with her attacker."

"Undoubtedly."

Holmes sprang to the fence, pulling out his glass as

he did so. He went over a small section in minute detail, producing a tweezers and picking at the surface of the wood.

"See here, Lestrade," he continued, as if the scene where a classroom rather than that of a ghastly murder. "Flecks of blood and flesh. My guess is your murderer shoved her face into the fence, rendering her unconscious and producing the fresh wound we observe. With her senseless, or nearly so, he was able to strangle her without opposition."

Holmes walked around the body, stopping before a number of items laid out at her feet. "Whoa, what is this?"

He knelt again, looking at the odd collection of items. A comb, a piece of muslin, a few coins, and two copper rings were neatly arranged there. "Note the rings and her fingers," he said. "Surely, she had these on and they were removed by the killer. The rest are also personal items. See where her pocket was cut to remove them!" He outlined the jagged edge of material. "A letter, post marked the 28th from Sussex. Probably nothing to do with this business."

Holmes looked at the collection of unrelated objects and shook his head. His mind, a veritable encyclopedia of crime, could find no matching reference; nothing that would explain such an add arrangement of victim and possessions.

"Anything else, Holmes?" prodded Lestrade.

Again, the darting eyes of the detective considered the victim, the scene, and the available evidence. He continued his lecture, as if in a classroom instructing students.

"Her fingers show the presence of at least 3 rings, but only two are laid out here. The third is missing."

Lestrade nodded with satisfaction and made a further note on his pad, as did Dr. Watson.

"You mentioned witnesses?" inquired Holmes.

Abberline consulted his notes. "Several, as I stated, but none with any better information than the 5:30 time."

Holmes replied with another question while his hand felt the woman's dress. "Be that as it may," he stated, "the good doctor observed it had rained over night as we were driven here. What time was the rain?" He waited for an answer while he felt below the body.

The policemen looked among themselves before a constable stepped forward.

"It was raining at five when I came on my rounds, inspector," he offered.

Holmes nodded, then stood again and examined the court more thoroughly. At length, he announced his findings to the two inspectors.

"I probably have little to add over what you already know other than the woman was killed prior to the start of the rain. Her clothes are wet, but the pavement below is dry. The woman and her gentleman, though that term hardly applies, came back here to transact their business, but it was before the rain started.

"I suspect he pushed her into the fence. She slumped to the ground where he strangled her. With her throat in such a state, it is difficult to detect any signs of recent bruising, but have the coroner pay close attention. With her dead, or nearly so, he slashed her throat and performed the mutilations. As to the objects arranged at her feet, I have no thought as if yet. Some private ritual by the killer, but I cannot guess the purpose. His business finished, he left the way he entered."

"But he must have been covered with blood!" Lestrade protested.

"Not as much as you might think," Watson explained. He pointed again to her face. "The tongue and burst veins in her eyes indicate strangulation. If she were already dead, or even nearly so, then there was no pressure behind her veins and arteries to force the blood upon the killer."

"We have seen many men walking the streets in this area covered with blood. Who would pay notice to one more? A woman's blood looks the same as a cow's or sheep's!" concluded Holmes.

"And what about this?" asked Abberline. He gestured towards a tub of water. A folded leather apron lay on the edge, half in, half out of the water.

Holmes walked over and looked at the apron. He lifted a corner and glanced to Abberline. "I noticed it of course, but it has been here for some time. You can tell because it is completely soaked through. Is there some reason why this may be of importance?"

Abberline hesitated before advancing an answer. "Our prime suspect as of now is a man known as 'Leather Apron'. His actual name is John Pizer. He is both a shoe and hat maker. I need not remind you Polly Nichols had just gotten a new hat."

Holmes examined the apron closely. "I would estimate this apron has been in this water for several days, inspector. It is much too sodden to have just been placed here this morning. I am afraid it has nothing to do with this case."

Abberline quietly digested this information. "You see nothing else? Nothing that would indicate who the killer might be?"

Holmes looked sadly at the body, then spoke to his associate. "What do you think, Watson? As a medical man, I mean. Does the killer know his anatomy?"

Watson regarded the poor, wretched creature at their feet once again. It was apparent he found the whole business distasteful. Nonetheless, he forced a critical eye and applied what he could of Holmes' methods.

"Notice the viscera. He removed them without rupturing the intestines. That must imply some skill and experience at this sort of thing. Most medical students do worse even after much practice. You say this was done in less than half an hour?"

"If our witnesses are correct," returned Lestrade.

Watson was not pleased with the thought that someone of the medical profession could be involved with the killing. Still, he withheld his judgment and, in Holmes' fashion, dispassionately related his assessment. "If he performed this deed in poor light and less than thirty minutes, then some surgical skill is definitely implied."

"Excellent, Watson," commented Holmes. "Excellent."

"But where does that leave us, Holmes?" demanded Abberline.

"You have now had two such killings in barely a week," returned the detective. "If the news agencies are to be believed, this is the fourth murder since April." His voice took a tone of gravity which was rarely heard from his lips. "I would suggest that leaves us to be prepared for more murders!"

"That's of damned little use to us!" stated Abberline flatly, unhappy with the response..

"I am sorry I cannot do more at this juncture, inspector," returned the detective.

There was a moment of rising tension before Lestrade spoke to fill the gap. "Still, inspector," he interjected, his voice more animated than normal, "Mr. Holmes has always helped the police to the best of his ability. Just last week he helped clear up the robbery at Manor House. Adams would have escaped without Holmes' intervention."

"Unfortunately, Lestrade, this case is one of a capital nature and is much more before the eye of the public."

The dull roar of the mob beyond the wall seemed to grow to punctuate Abberline's statement. It illustrated how badly the inspector needed for a resolution. Holmes nodded his understanding. He was all too familiar with the pressures of the mob and the press.

"I am doing the best with the information I have, inspector," he said. "If anything else becomes apparent, I will let you know immediately."

The arrival of the coroner brought an end to the uncomfortable conversation. Though Holmes did not say, he was happy to have Abberline leave to speak to the police physician. Holmes led the way back up the stairs and Lestrade followed closely behind.

"You must forgive him, Holmes," said the detective. "This case weighs heavily upon him."

Holmes nodded gravely in his understanding. "But no more so than the rest of us. Still, I shall not be the one that bears the brunt if we fail to bring this killer to justice." He regarded the rabble before the residence. "I think Watson and I shall return to Baker Street for the moment, Inspector. If I can assist you further, please do not hesitate to send a summons."

The two regained the police carriage and, with only the delay required to navigate the crowds descending on Hanbury street, began a more leisurely return to their lodgings. Holmes was silent for a while, but turned his attention to his friend when they were still some distance from their destination.

"Well, Watson, what do you think of this commission?"

"It is beyond my experience, Holmes." For a man of words, he found it difficult to express the revulsion felt at the sight of the dead prostitute.

"And mine, Watson." He paused, looking out the carriage window for a moment. They left the utter slums of Whitechapel behind and were in the more pleasant surroundings of familiar London. "And mine," he repeated, the words so low Watson barely heard them. With a burst of energy, he straightened and directed his full attention upon his friend.

"Let us use this time wisely, Watson. I shall lay the case before you as best I know it. It shall help refresh my memories of the facts while preparing you for our future endeavors."

Watson nodded, obviously pleased Holmes was sharing his information. The detective knew his friend resented the details he often withheld, but for Holmes, it was as natural was drinking water or having a pipe after dinner. For the detective, data was his life blood and, though he was loath to admit it, parting with it was as precious as opening a vein to part with a quantity of blood.

"My involvement began last week, the day after the death of the last unfortunate woman, Polly Nichols. Lestrade appeared at our rooms the night you had dinner at your club. He started with the Manor House case, but that was a simple resolution. After I explained how he might trap Adams and his accomplices and learn the location of the bank notes, he brought up the recent murder. In truth, I believe it was his primary object in coming and that he already had the solution to the other.

"The press is making a very great deal of these killings, Watson. There shall, no doubt, be an extra on the street by the time we reach Baker Street. The police have no leads on which to proceed."

"Surely two killings in such a place as Whitechapel is not unusual," the doctor protested.

"True, Watson, true, but it is the nature of these killings that make them different. And it may not be two killings, Watson. It may be as many as four."

Watson showed a thrill of horror at the revelation. "Four?"

Holmes nodded gravely. "Four is the number, though I have my doubts and even Lestrade agrees. The story begins in the spring. In early April, a prostitute by the name of Emma Smith was brought into Whitechapel Hospital with internal injuries to her abdomen. The exact nature of the injuries cannot be repeated in polite company, but they caused internal bleeding and, eventually, peritonitis. As is so often the case, the inflammation proved fatal and she was dead within four days. The police were not notified until after her death, so they had little to go on other than the evidence given by the woman's companions. They explained she was attacked by a gang trying to extort money from her and the other prostitutes in the area. When she would not comply with their demands, she was assaulted and some foreign object was thrust into her in such a grievous fashion as to cause her injuries and eventual death. Given the time between the initial assault and the police notification, there was little that could be done to find her attackers and the crime remained unsolved."

Watson nodded gravely, quickly adding notes to the growing list for this case.

"All remained quiet until the night of the 7th of August. One street over from the site of Emma Smith's attack, another prostitute was found brutally murdered. This woman, Martha Tabram, was found stabbed to death with over 39 wounds on her body. The nature of the wounds showed they were inflicted by a military bayonet or some other long knife. Since she was last seen in the company of a soldier, the police turned their investigation in that direction, but were again unable to bring the killer to justice.

"Two unsolved crimes, particularly in Whitechapel, did not unduly concern the police. The facts are both women were prostitutes, the assaults occurred in fairly public places, and left no evidence as to the perpetrators. It indicates a pattern the officials do not want to see continued. Still, there was little or nothing to say the two crimes were connected other than they happened only a block apart and both women were of the same profession. The sexual nature of the assaults also served as a link, but with Emma Smith's confession of being attacked by a gang, the police were content to leave matters where they lay. Events, however, were not to permit this simple resolution."

"Might I add an observation, Holmes?" ventured the physician.

"Indeed, doctor. What might that be?"

"You say this Martha Tabram was assaulted by using a long knife of some sort."

Holmes looked to his friend. He was indeed in fine form this September morning.

"And your opinion?"

"No doubt such a weapon was used upon this latest victim. The wound to the neck and the removal of the viscera speak to such a tool."

Holmes nodded gravely, accepting his friend's professional opinion on such matters without question.

"But not something as heavy as a bayonet, I would think," concluded the doctor.

At this comment, Holmes sat up and took more notice of his friend's observations. "You think not?"

Watson shook his head. "I examined sufficient bayonet wounds, my dear Holmes. It is a crude weapon. It would have severed this woman's head easily with sufficient force, not skirted around the backbone as we saw."

"Indeed, doctor, indeed!" said Holmes. This was first hand information of the sort he could use. "And something further?"

"No bayonet could be used to remove the viscera

without damaging it. Something of a more medical nature is required."

"Watson, you are invaluable this morning! If you ever have doubts, remember this moment. I know nothing of bayonet wounds."

Watson smiled widely, pleased that he had contributed something useful to his friend's endeavors. Holmes touched his companion's knee in reassurance, and continued his narrative.

"On August 30th, a third prostitute was found murdered, though this was a few blocks from the previous sites. This victim, Polly Nichols, was assaulted and killed on a public street and her body mutilated in a more gruesome fashion. Her throat was cut and she was disemboweled similarly to this poor creature we just saw. But this time, the press caught wind of the crime and the latest murder was catapulted to the front pages, as you well know."

While Watson was aware of them from the newspapers, it was the first he was told of Holmes' involvement in the investigation.

"Why did you not say something earlier about this?" he asked.

Holmes shrugged. "I do not think the case of much interest, Watson. I have stated before that crimes of passion are extremely difficult to solve and these, most certainly, fall into that category."

Watson was shocked at the prospect. "Passion? You call such horrible mutilations passion?"

"Calm yourself, old friend," he said, leaning across to grab his shoulder. He leaned back in his seat and closed his eyes. "Consider the facts, Watson. At least three women of the most common sort are brutally killed. All are stabbed and mutilated in locations where they are found by the public within minutes of their deaths. Yet, despite the public nature of the scenes of these atrocities, not the slightest glimmer or clue exists as to who would wish to commit them."

"Is there something that links these women together?" ventured Watson.

Holmes dismissed the idea with a wave of his hand. "It is possible, I suppose," he admitted. "We shall know more once this current victim is identified. The police have been unable to find a link other than their profession."

Holmes leaned forward in earnest. For a man that practiced the most in profession dispassion to the nature of his cases, his true emotional involvement escaped at the most inconvenient times.

"Four women, prostitutes, are brutally murdered," he stated, his open hand in front of the doctor so he could indicate his points. "They have no money or possessions that could provide robbery as a driving force. So what is the motive for destroying them in such a fashion? That is our only clue at the moment."

"You suggested a gang involvement on the first killing."

Holmes nodded his agreement but there was no look of pleasure. "You *are* in truly splendid form this morning, Watson. Truly splendid. There are many gangs operating in Whitechapel. Perhaps one is trying to coerce the prostitutes into buying their protection. What better way than a series of gruesome murders?"

"And the ritual display of these last two bodies?"

"An attempt to add to the terror they are trying to create. It is just a working hypothesis, of course."

"Of course," agreed Watson with some skepticism. "So what is your plan of action, Holmes?"

Holmes stared out the window the carriage, the familiar buildings around Baker Street clear in the early morning light as they approached their residence.

"First, we shall return to Baker Street and see what Mrs. Hudson has laid on for breakfast. Then I shall think on this, Watson. I shall think very hard."

Monday, September 10 *A Pattern Emerges*

Holmes disappeared late the afternoon of the eighth and did not return again until the morning of the tenth. For almost two days, he wandered Whitechapel in a variety of disguises, learning what he could of each of the identified victims. He returned, eyes sunken and face drawn, exhausted from his lack of sleep for the last forty-eight hours.

"Holmes! You will do no one any good in this state." The detective did not respond to the complaint, instead falling into his chair and retrieving the Persian slipper to fill his pipe. Watson handed him the morning Times. "We shall have a busy day as it is," he continued, trying to moderate his tone. "The inquest of this Annie Chapman woman opens this morning. Surely you will want to attend?"

Holmes glanced only quickly at the newspaper headline, and then tossed it unceremoniously into the corner with several other back issues. "Why do I care to hear the opinion of twelve untrained people?" he asked, lighting his pipe as he did so. "I know everything to be said at the inquest, perhaps a good deal more. The only thing they could produce of interest to me is the name of the murderer and that, I am sure, will not be given."

"How could you know more than the inquest? When you left on Saturday, you did not even know the woman's name!"

Holmes chuckled and took a long draw on the pipe. He was sinking into a contemplative state, his eyes focused on nothing in particular.

"I have been busy these past two days, Watson. Along with the police, I have talked to every witness they will produce at the hearing save one, and he has nothing material to add anyway.

"Annie Chapman was a nere-do-well, known to her intimates as 'Dark Annie'. She was married but has lived apart from her husband for four or more years. She lived with a sieve maker for a while, and so sometimes goes by the name Siffey or Sievey. She has children, but has shown little interest in them since leaving her husband. By all accounts, our Annie was a clever woman and often earned money by selling flowers or crochet work. Still, she was not particularly fussy where her income came from and would go on the game to make extra..."

"Holmes!" protested Watson, shocked at the crudity of the remark.

The detective raised an eyebrow at the outburst. They had never discussed intimate relations before and so their respective views were unknown to each other. Holmes' almost total disinterest in women had kept Watson away from the subject, even during the period the previous year when he married and his first wife died. Still, there was a proper way to approach the subject and, to take it so casually even given the part-time profession of the victim, was more than Watson cared continence. But to Holmes, it was simply one more fact to be discussed in connection to the case, no more nor less important than any other fact at this early point in the investigation.

"There is a growing mood of suppression of such talk in this country, Watson," he stated flatly. "I would suggest you look beyond the societal norms in this matter. We are dealing with a killer or killers of the basest kind and prostitutes..." He held off a protest with a raised hand. "..are the selected victims. If we cannot discuss the case openly and frankly, we shall have little ability to reach a successful conclusion."

Holmes stopped, fussing with his pipe until he again had a proper draught. As the cloud of smoke grew about him, he continued his recital of the facts.

"Annie had a few regular gentlemen, and one of these led to a fight with a Liz Cooper a week ago today. This accounts for the older bruises we observed when we examined her on Saturday. On Friday, she was seen several times in increasing states of inebriation. She showed up late at her lodging house but did not have the money for her bed. Announcing she would have it soon enough, she went back out on the street. This was about 2:00 am. She must have had a miserable night with the rain. About 5:30, she was seen on her way to the market talking to a man described as about forty years old and 'shabby, genteel' appearance. They were apparently discussing terms as the witness recalls hearing him say 'Will you?' and her replying 'Yes.' The body was found at six by a lodger in the building. The rest you know."

"And the police know all this?"

"Every bit, along with much less useful information."

"And so this is what you have been doing these past

two days?"

"That and more, Watson. I take it you have never been to Whitechapel during the hours of darkness?" He did not wait for a reply. "A more wretched place would be difficult to describe. I believe a person could cry 'Murder' on the streets and raise little more than a few shut doors and windows. I know your dislike for the profession in question, but the streets abound with women plying their trade. If our murderer is singling out these women, I fear it will be a fertile ground for his efforts."

"What else have you discovered these past two days?"

"I do not think the gang theory will hold water, Watson. I talked to a large number of these women, plus members of several of the gangs. The women have not been approached for protection. The gang members deny their involvement."

"And you believe them?" There was not if incredulity in Watson's tone.

"By and large, yes," returned the detective. "You cannot get blood out of a turnip. Perhaps if these were women making enough to afford permanent rooms, or associated with a house of ill repute, but they are not."

Holmes let out a sigh. It had been a decent working hypothesis, but he had managed to disprove it almost immediately.

"Finally, I am sure the gangs would have no compunction of the display of the bodies in this horrid fashion. I just seriously doubt they possess the skill shown or that they would run the risk involved. No, gangs as the solution just do not fit!"

"So if you eliminate the gangs as a possibility, what shall the inquest say?"

He chuckled drily. "Murder by person or persons unknown, Watson. As I stated, we already know that."

"But you mentioned a witness that had nothing to do with it?"

"John Pizer, Abberline's 'Leather Apron'. Apparently, they found him yesterday and he has a solid alibi for the morning of the murder. Abberline wants him to testify so the press will leave him alone."

"A sound idea," agreed the physician.

"Undoubtedly. Besides Annie Chapman, I also reviewed the inquests of Polly Nichols, Martha Tabram, and Elizabeth Smith. None have anything to add. Nichols' story in particular was similar to Chapman's. There is no description of her killer because she was alone when last seen." Without apparent cause, Holmes bolted upright in his chair. Despite his haggard appearance, he was seized by one of those fits of energy so unique to the man. "Come, Watson, there is work to be done."

Holmes retrieved his coat and hat. Watson was several steps behind him on the stairs and Holmes was already hailing a cab when Watson reached the street.

"Where are we going?"

"Whitechapel," the detective said to the driver.

With a crack of his whip, the driver sent the Hansom cab clattering across the cobblestones.

"What do you hope to find there?" Watson asked at length. The route was growing familiar, though this was only his second trip.

"I was asked questions about the Polly Nichols murder, but never examined the scene first hand. It is time I did that."

"But that murder was last week! What evidence can you hope to find?"

"We shall see, Watson. We shall see."

Holmes lapsed into silence for the remainder of the trip. They reached Brady Street and Bucks Row in short order. The driver was paid and he showed uncommon energy leaving them to their own devices. The street was lined with residences on either side. Holmes walked down one side, stopping to examine a spot on the road.

"I believe they found the body here, Watson. You can still see the blood stains between the paving stones to some degree." Holmes surveyed the street. He noted the buildings and windows facing towards the scene of the murder. "The body was found about 4:00 AM by two workers. A constable was here shortly thereafter. They took her to London hospital, which is only a street over from here, but she was already dead."

He looked at the spot on the pavement, then over to Watson. "What can you deduce from this?"

Watson looked about the street. "It had to be done in some silence," he noted. "If the woman were allowed to scream, any number of people would hear it."

"Very good, Watson. What is more, the constable walked this very street not 30 minutes before and did not find a body. Yet he saw her almost immediately when he returned on his rounds. We have to believe the killer was able to murder and mutilate this poor woman in less than one half hour." He used his cane, gesturing to the windows lining the street. "And they all heard nothing."

He brought the cane down and headed further into Whitechapel. Their dress was certainly out of place amid the common laborers who crowded the narrow streets. It drew stares from any number of them as they walked briskly along. Coming to the intersection of Commercial Street, Holmes stopped again.

"The other two women were murdered within a block of this location, only a few hundred feet from Polly Nichols." He pointed north along Commercial. "And Annie Chapman was found only three blocks in that direction."

"But what does it mean, Holmes?" Watson demanded.

He threw out his arms in despair. "Everything, Watson, and nothing. It is no clearer to me now than it was two days ago." He hailed a cab and they boarded it to return to Baker Street.

"Do you make nothing of it, then?" asked Watson as he settled in the cab.

Holmes frowned, contemplating his reply before answering my query. "It is a dark business, this." He spoke slowly, considering his words carefully. "If we must go back to suspecting a single person of these deeds then we have a killer who is able to walk crowded streets and kill his victims in the most public places." The detective paused, a new idea occurring from his last observation. "For whatever reason, he does not fear being caught. It must not matter to him."

"Getting caught does not matter?" The very concept seemed unbelievable. "In all our cases, I can not recall a single perpetrator who wanted his crime discovered."

"No doubt," stressed Holmes, warming to the idea. "Yet, he must not be concerned since he performs his crimes so publicly." Holmes rubbed his eyes, confused at such an idea. "Perhaps it is his way of flouting the law. He will do these things and laugh at the police as they try to apprehend him."

It made little sense to the doctor. "A murderer must have some reason to kill. Surely, there is some connecting link between these women, something that would drive someone to seek revenge against them."

"I have found none thus far." Watson's eyes opened in surprise at the comment. "You can rest assured, Watson, if a relationship was there to be found, I would have discovered it."

"Without a doubt."

The detective smiled, a slight wry grin from turning up one corner of his mouth. The trust his friend placed in his abilities was at once touching and at the same time intimidating. He felt no such assurance himself.

"Perhaps your faith in me is misplaced in this instance."

His friend did not accept that proposition, but clearly saw the impact if the detective was unable to resolve the crimes. "I have seen you solve greater puzzles. But if you are powerless, what chance do the police stand of finding the fiend?"

Holmes chuckled again, with barely more humor. "They have their own, internal obstacles to overcome, I am afraid. I went to the coroner Saturday to re-examine the body. Do you know his assistants had already stripped it and destroyed the clothing? The coroner was beside himself with anger. He did venture something about the weapon, however, that you may find it interesting."

"And what is that?"

The cab clattered along, slowing on its approach to Baker Street.

"It was a long knife, the blade being six to eight inches. In fact, Dr. Phillips thought it was probably longer. He did not think it was a sword or bayonet because of the shape of the incisions. He felt the most likely knife to be used, and one he is well familiar with, was a post-mortem knife. If the doctor who performed the autopsy on Martha Tabram was incorrect in his assessment then that might also be the tool used in her murder."

"It certainly fits with my experience," replied Watson. He was clearly unhappy at the association of his own profession to such a series of crimes. "I do not care for the implication that a doctor could commit such *atrocities*!"

Holmes feigned insult. "And why not?" He continued in a more moderate tone. "Doctors are human beings, sharing the same failings as the rest of us. I could relate far too many case histories where doctors were the perpetrators of murders as terrible as these."

Watson sat silent, flustered at the response from the detective. Before he uttered a protest, Holmes allowed a mischievous grin to pass quickly across his lips. It was there for just a fleeting moment before his normal stern countenance returned and he continued in a more somber tone.

"If not a physician, he was at least a man with some medical knowledge. Your own testimony supports that fact," Holmes pointed out, reminding Watson of his observation at the scene of Annie Chapman's murder. "Dr. Phillips believes it would take him close to an hour to inflict the injuries we saw, yet we know the killer had less than thirty minutes."

Watson was somber as he answered. "The idea that a medical man is responsible for such horrors fills me with dread." He almost displayed a visible shudder at the prospect. "To accuse a member of my own profession is almost more than I could bear."

"Steady," returned Holmes, his voice reassuring. "We know nothing yet."

The hansom stopped before their residence and the two men entered the building. Both were comfortably set before Watson replied to Holmes' statement. It would only be later that he realized he changed the subject on Holmes, bringing it closer to the detective's field of endeavor and away from the medical profession.

"What of the police? What of this Abberline?"

Holmes puffed steadily on his pipe. "Abberline and I are old acquaintances. I have shown him the errors of his conclusions on more than one occasion. Still, he is a competent detective. He is a melancholy man given to drink at times, but otherwise performs his duties as required. Will he find this killer? That I cannot answer. In point of fact, I cannot be sure of much of anything. I do have a concern, however."

"What might that be, Holmes?" Watson inquired innocently.

"If all four women are the victim of the same madman, a fact which is not proved at this point with any certainty, then a disturbing pattern is developing." He paused, pulling out a match to relight his pipe. When it glowed again to his satisfaction, he continued. “There is increasing violence to each of these crimes, as if the killer is losing more control with each one.”

“That is monstrous!”

The comment was wretched

“Yes,” he replied in his usual, calm manner. Holmes was sinking into a black mood. “As I’ve mentioned before Watson, these types of crimes are the hardest to solve. These killings, as black as they are, have left us with few clues as to how to proceed. Not only are they crimes of passion, but the killer is deliberately hiding his tracks while taking care to publicly display his handiwork.” He puffed on the pipe. “Monstrous indeed.”

“Then what is your next course of action, Holmes?”

The detective let out a deep sigh. “I am afraid there is little I can do. The police have cast a very wide net, and that is exactly what is required at the moment. I shall continue to investigate as best I can until something more interesting presents itself.”

Wednesday, September 12 *Mycroft Holmes*

Sherlock Holmes had rarely found himself at such a juncture as he was with the case of the Whitechapel murders. For an additional two days, neither he nor the Metropolitan Police had put forward any meaningful plan to prevent a recurrence of the ghastly crimes. The cloud of pipe smoke only fouled the air and even his violin playing offered no comfort.

"I tell you, Watson, I am almost driven to the needle again!" declared the detective, dropping the violin on the dishes on the table without thought of damage to either.

Holmes spoke of one of his less savory habits with practiced disregard for Watson's feelings on the matter. Still, the physician sympathized with the impasse the detective had reached.

"None of this in the Times has a bearing? There are three more murders in the east end and the discovery of a woman's severed arm in the Thames!"

"Perhaps," returned Holmes. His tone was quite serious but there was a devilish glint in his eye. "Which arm was it?"

Watson quickly found the page and reviewed the

article.

"The right arm, severed surgically at the shoulder..." he started before seeing the smile upon his friend's face. "I see." He folded the paper and set it down. "You make sport of me in your frustration!"

"Sorry, old boy," replied Holmes. "I noted the story earlier, but doubt it has any connection to Whitechapel." The detective stepped to his chair. He reached for his pipe, but pushed it away in distaste. "I have no direction to turn at the moment"

"If there were only some other authority to whom you could present the facts of this case," Watson ventured.

Holmes' eyes widened slightly at the suggestion.

"What do you mean?"

Watson's thoughts were not fully complete, but he tried to present them to Holmes in the least muddle fashion he could manage. "Think of yourself as Lestrade…" he began.

For the first time in days, Holmes broke out in genuine laughter. "I must indeed be in a sorry state if you are to make that comparison!"

Both chuckled at such a thought, but Watson persevered in his analogy.

"Hear me through, Holmes. When Lestrade is presented with a case beyond his powers, he has a court of higher appeal. He lays the facts before you in hopes your insights will surpass his own."

"Continue with your thoughts, Watson. You may have hit upon an idea."

"What idea?" he asked. "From all that you have told

me, it seems obvious your faculties of observation and deduction are due to your own systematic training. No other in the country demonstrates these skills to compare to your abilities."

"As a detective, that is true, but brother Mycroft has trained himself to be a processor of information."

The events from Friday were still fresh in Watson's mind.

"Mycroft did not display much ability in the case of Mr. Melas! You, yourself, were unhappy with his handling of the case!"

Holmes smiled, as he sat down at the writing desk and jotted a note to send ahead to the Diogenese Club.

"My brother lacks practice in dealing with criminals in a practical way," replied the detective. "I will provide the experience with criminals. He need only look for connections in the data! I will invite him over for brandy and tobacco. For a change, it shall be I consulting my older brother."

For a year marked by cold weather and rain, this evening was unexpectedly dry and warm. No doubt, this aided in Mycroft's decision and they were rewarded with a return note from the elder Holmes accepting the invitation. The brother arrived precisely on time, and his heavy steps sounded on the stairs as he slowly brought his weight up the single flight.

"Glad to meet you again, doctor," said Mycroft, taking Watson's hand in his. The older Holmes turned to his brother. "By the way, Sherlock, I expected to see you round last week to consult me over that Manor House case."

"No, I solved it," said the detective, smiling. "It was easy enough."

"Adams, of course."

"Of course. He had the support of the Besarabians for muscle, but it was to no avail. Dosenovitch lost two of his best men on that caper."

The Besarabian gang was the most feared, most violent gang in London. Holmes had crossed their path on numerous occasions. They had even been mentioned in connection to the Whitechapel killings, though the detective had eliminated them as suspects for the moment.

"I was sure of it," concluded Mycroft. And in another echo of his younger brother, the brilliant mind turned immediately to the reason for the visit. "But enough of that trivial matter what of the *other* case?"

Holmes smiled at his brother again, the action and words a dare to his brother's abilities. "What makes you think I am involved?"

Mycroft laughed heartily at the family joke. "You always were the brother with the sense of humor. When I see the Metropolitan Police and Scotland Yard floundering, I know where they must turn." He turned his sharp gaze upon his younger brother in a knowing satisfaction. "That is why you have invited me. You wish to present the facts for my consideration."

"Precisely, Mycroft," returned Holmes.

Holmes retold the facts of the case in his logical and cool fashion. Mycroft listened to the presentation intently, only interrupting occasionally for a clarification or more information. When Holmes was finished, his brother closed his eyes in quiet consideration. It was like watching some great steam powered machine in operation as Mycroft sat silently, his eyes closed, but clouds of tobacco smoke issuing from a cigar.

Watson prepared to ask a question but Holmes shook his head. The two men sat in silence until after a long while, Mycroft's eyes opened and he tossed the remainder of his cigar into the fire before pouring another brandy.

"A deep and dark situation, indeed," pronounced the older Holmes.

The corner of Holmes' lip tightened briefly in a wry grin but was lost just as quickly. The thin detective faced his corpulent counterpart, their gazes locked. Neither flinched, nor seemed aware of the third man in the room observing them.

"You have nothing to add, then?" concluded Holmes.

Mycroft was unimpressed by the comment. "I may have a conclusion that eluded you, if I might be permitted to elucidate." Holmes nodded and the brother continued.

"There is considerable daring in killing women in such public spaces, and then leaving them to be discovered. Any on the current list of suspects would, in keeping with their coarse roots, attempt to hide the body and the crime, and so disguise their involvement. This man's actions speak of a cold, even detached, nerve. He is hardly afraid of the hangman's rope."

"I have made a similar observation, but how does that further my investigation?"

Mycroft leaned backed and sniffed at his brandy. Sherlock, in return, did the same, though setting his snifter down and retrieving his pipe. He held the slipper out for his brother, who declined with a slight wave of the hand. Watson, always the better host, offered the elder Holmes the humidor. Mycroft allowed a slight smile to cross his lips in gratitude and withdrew a cigar to his liking. The room quickly filled with tobacco smoke and Mycroft continued his observations.

"The public display appears to be the as much a point of the killing as the actual murder itself." Mycroft took a brief sip of his brandy and Watson took the moment to interject.

"But what does that mean?" he ventured, unable to make sense of the explanation.

"It means," returned Mycroft with great deliberation, "he is seeking attention and notoriety." Watson stared blankly at the comment, and Mycroft straightened himself to explain further. "To that end, *any* woman is a potential victim, Doctor. These unfortunates apparently crossed his path at the wrong time. Their *occupation* makes them readily available targets for this creature. Wouldn't you agree, Sherlock?"

Holmes considered it for a moment before replying. "Yes, your point is well made, brother Mycroft."

Watson, for his part, was bedeviled by the observation. "It makes little sense to me."

"Consider," said Holmes. His tone was not reproachful, but rather that of a school master explaining a difficult lesson to a student. "Recall this case of the unfortunate interpreter we have encountered these past two evenings. While odd, the motive was never in doubt. The criminal was either after the Kratides money or Sophie Kratides herself. You yourself deduced as much."

Watson nodded in agreement, taking a puff on his cigar. "That is true."

"But these poor women in Whitechapel..." Holmes did not need to explain their condition further. "They are neither physically desirable nor do they possess material means."

Understanding dawned.

"So the object is the murder itself."

Watson's tone was hushed, perhaps awed, by the new knowledge. It hung as heavy in the air as the combined pipe and cigar smoke of the room.

"Have you ever heard of such a thing before?" asked Mycroft, his tone even more serious.

"It is rare but I have heard of such cases," responded the detective. "None where the murderer sought public revelation of the crimes, however. You have more?"

"Another abstract thought," offered Mycroft. "If our murderer is targeting prostitutes, I ask what type of person might find that profession particularly offensive."

Watson managed an answer before Holmes could interject.

"Someone of a religious nature?" he ventured.

"Precisely," concluded Mycroft. "Someone with a great concern for the moral depravities of Whitechapel and has taken it upon themselves to rectify the issue."

Holmes shook his head, unconvinced.

"There are no religious symbols attached to the murders, at least none that occur to me."

"Perhaps you need to reconsider?" prompted the

elder.

"Perhaps," conceded the younger.

"And if that is the case, how will you proceed?"

The detective shook his head and puffed on his pipe, thoughts arranging in his mind as clearly as if they could see them projected in the smoke filled air.

"There is an obvious conclusion," he stated.

"You can't mean..." gasped Mycroft

"What?" demanded Watson, unable to reach the automatic conclusion the two brothers sensed between them.

Holmes took the pipe from between his teeth. He wanted nothing to mask the meaning of his words.

"I make no secret that this Whitechapel case is not to my liking. If my methods are unsuited to find the killer, then I will simply not pursue the case."

Watson and Mycroft sat in silence. The physician could not remember an instance where the detective had given up on a case.

"But what of Lestrade and Abberline?" he asked. "Will you leave them to their own devices?"

"And why not?" snapped the detective. "This seems an instance when the man power of the regular forces can be much more effective than my services. Am I to spend my talents in a fruitless attempt to resolve a hopeless case?"

"You might save the lives of innocent women!" returned Watson with some ire.

Holmes looked to his brother for support. "What is you conclusion, Mycroft?"

The big man shrugged, then slowly levered his bulk from the chair. "You must follow your own instincts, Sherlock." He took a deep breath before starting slowly towards the door, speaking as he moved. "I can tell you this case has caught the attention of the highest levels of our government." He paused at the door before opening it. "The Home Secretary has expressed his desire to see it resolved as quickly as possible. I assured him I would urge you to do so."

Mycroft opened the door, looking with distaste at the flight of stairs before him. He looked back to his brother. "Good evening, Sherlock...Dr. Watson."

The door closed slowly behind him and they could hear his foot falls as he made his way slowly down the stairs. As the sound of the outside door closing reached them, Watson fairly exploded upon his friend.

"You cannot be serious, Holmes! This is precisely the sort of crime that demands your attention."

"It may demand it," returned the detective, holding his hands apart in apparent helplessness. "But what am I to do?"

"Help Lestrade! Help the denizens of Whitechapel!" chided Watson.

Holmes reached for the Persian slipper and began to pack his pipe.

"Very well, Watson," he relented with a sigh. "I shall devote my time to this case for the moment." He lit the pipe and drew in a lung full of smoke, expelling it with deliberate slowness. "But I make no promises."

Tuesday, September 18 *Miss Mary Morstan*

Holmes kept the most irregular hours, though he thought little of it. As darkness fell, he would depart Baker Street and remove himself to one of his other small apartments. He would change clothes and don a disguise before proceeding to Whitechapel. Some nights, he was a tradesman, others an old sailor, but he was always something different and always a persona that would blend into the swell of humanity that constantly moved on the streets. He spent each night searching for some clue of the unknown assassin. And when the search proved unsuccessful, he returned in the early hours to Baker Street. There, he would sleep for part of the day, then smoke and think.

It took no great act of deduction to conclude Holmes was making no progress. Watson might leave for several hours and return only to find his friend in the same position as when he left, the floor about him covered with tobacco ash and spent matches. It was a sign of his own deep thought that he was barely aware of Watson's departure and return on those occasions. But a note from a Miss Mary Morstan seeking his advice arrived that morning and roused Holmes from the stupor that had descended upon him.

Holmes shaved and changed clothes. He even aided the doctor in straightening their bachelor apartment before the arrival of the prospective client. He was waiting in keen anticipation of the unknown issue which had brought her to him. When the bell rang, he was ready to position himself by the mantel and greet the young woman when Mrs. Hudson brought her to the rooms.

Miss Morstan was a young, blonde lady with pleasant features. She entered with a firm step and outward composure, but these failed to hide the uneasiness of her visit. Her clothes, though neat and trim, bore the message that she possessed limited means. Holmes noted Watson was immediately taken with her, but pushed the thought from his mind. All that concerned him was her case. He needed something, anything, to remove his mind from the morass of the Whitechapel affair. As she took the seat which Sherlock Holmes indicated for her, her trembling lip and hand showed every sign of agitation.

"I have come to you, Mr. Holmes," she said, "on the advice of my employer, Mrs. Cecil Forrester. She states you aided her greatly and was much impressed by your kindness and skill."

"Mrs. Cecil Forrester." He recalled the case but remained as attentive as ever. "I am glad she regards me so highly. The case, as I remember it, was simple."

"She did not think so, and feels my situation is inexplicable and strange. It has been such a distraction she urged me to seek you out."

Holmes rubbed his hands, and leaned forward in his chair with an expression of concentration upon his hawk-like features. There could be no doubt this was the break he needed from the standstill of the Whitechapel murders. But when he spoke, he was brisk and direct.

"State your case."

She began a clear, concise narrative. It was a long story about her father, an officer in India. He had disappeared without a trace on the very day of his arrival in London many years before. Then four years later, she started receiving fabulous pearls from an unknown benefactor, a person that wrote to her as a "wronged woman." And for every year since, she had received one of these pearls.

She handed Holmes a small box that contained the gems. He examined them quickly, confirming that their value was unquestioned.

"Most interesting," said Sherlock Holmes. "And what has occurred to change this situation?"

"I received this letter."

She handed it to him and he snatched it and opened the envelope quickly.

"Post mark, London, S. W. Date, September 17. Man's thumb-mark on corner, probably postman. Best quality paper. Envelopes at sixpence a packet. Particular man in his stationery. No address." His eyes scanned the words in an instant. "An invitation from your unknown friend. What do you intend, Miss Morstan?"

"That is exactly what I want to ask you."

For the detective, there was no doubt as to the course of action. Any mystery demanded a resolution.

"Then we must certainly go!" His voice barely contained his anticipation. He looked to his friend "And Dr. Watson, of course: he is the very man. Your correspondent says two friends."

"You are both very kind," she answered. "I can be here at six."

"No later," cautioned Holmes. "One last point: Is this handwriting the same as that upon the pearl box addresses?"

"I wouldn't know, but I have them here," she answered. She produced the several wrapping sheets from her purse.

"You are a model client!" said the detective in true praise. He spread the papers upon the table and glanced from one to the other. "They are disguised hands, except the letter," he said presently, "but there can be no question they are the same."

"Then it appears I shall get to meet my benefactor," concluded the young woman.

"Precisely!" agreed the detective with enthusiasm. "We shall see you at six!"

The visitor left and Watson stood at the window and watched her walk briskly down the street until he lost her in the somber crowd.

"What a very attractive woman!" he exclaimed, turning to his companion.

"With a very attractive case!" returned Holmes, rubbing his hands in anticipation. He was already on his feet to retrieve his coat. "I am going out now. I have a few inquiries to make, but I shall be back in an hour."

And he was gone before Watson could comment. This was indeed the elixir the detective needed to forget about Whitechapel.

It was half-past five when Holmes returned, bright, eager, and in excellent spirits. Still, Watson greeted him in a huff.

"That was hardly an hour!" he chided. "I was afraid you would be late for our six o'clock engagement!"

Holmes' mood was too good to be dampened by Watson's surly greeting.

"A quick trip to Scotland Yard to confirm some of the facts for this case became extended when Abberline and

Lestrade discovered I was working on the matter. They want my time dedicated to Whitechapel."

"No doubt," the physician agreed. "What did you discover about Miss Morstan's matter?"

"There is no great mystery," Holmes explained, taking the cup of tea which Watson poured out for him. "The facts admit of only one explanation."

"You have solved it already?"

Watson showed a good deal of distress at the announcement. Holmes suppressed a smile: a quick resolution meant there would be less time to associate with Miss Morstan. He chuckled at the idea, and tossed his stricken friend a small lifeline.

"Well, that would be too much to say, but compared to the tangle in Whitechapel, this case is positively lucid!"

Watson smiled, heartened at additional explanation. "Then what have you found?"

"By consulting the back files of the Times, I discovered that Captain Morstan's friend Major Sholto, of Upper Norwood, died upon the twenty-eighth of April, 1882."

"And within the month, Miss Morstan receives the first pearl."

"Exactly." Holmes stood, rapidly changing clothes for their evening adventure while continuing to explain. "Captain Morstan disappears and the only person in London whom he would visit is Major Sholto who denies seeing him. Four years later, Sholto dies and within a week Captain Morstan's daughter receives a valuable present. This is repeated year to year, culminating in a letter describing her as a 'wronged woman'. The only possible wrong she could have received was the deprivation of her father. No doubt, one of Sholto's heirs knows something and is compelled to right the wrong."

Holmes had completed dressing. Like Watson, he had not prepared for a night at the theater. Instead, they wore more comfortable clothes, the sort of apparel worn when on a case.

"But what a strange compensation!" observed Watson. "And why now rather than six years ago?"

"I trust our expedition of tonight will explain that," said Holmes pensively. "But here is a four-wheeler, and Miss Morstan inside. The young lady is indeed punctual."

Watson picked up his hat and heaviest stick, but Holmes slipped his revolver into a pocket. It was clear the detective thought the night's work held the potential to be serious.

Miss Morstan was muffled in a dark cloak, though the evening was warm and humid. Her face was composed but pale, her self control perfect as they set out upon the quest. She answered the additional questions which Sherlock Holmes put forward, as well as producing a few documents relating to her father's time in India. Holmes unfolded the paper upon his knee and methodically reviewed it with his lens.

"It is paper of native Indian manufacture," he remarked. He snatched the paper up, examining one part much more closely in the dim light of the coach. "This is interesting. The "sign of the four": Jonathan Small, Mahomet Singh, Abdullah Khan, Dost Akbar."

"What can that mean?" asked Watson

"I confess I am not sure." Of itself, that was an unusual admission for Holmes as he rarely admitted ignorance in the presence of a client. It was another sign of the pressure of the East End murders that he did so now. "It is evidently of some importance since it has been kept carefully in a pocketbook."

Holmes neatly refolded the paper and handed it back to their client.

"Preserve it carefully, Miss Morstan. It may yet prove important." He frowned, his thoughts obviously occupied by the strange note. "This matter may be deeper than I first supposed." He leaned back against the cushion, thinking intently.

It was not yet seven o'clock, and a dense, drizzly fog moved across the city. Down the Strand the lamps were barely visible, misty splotches of diffused light which threw a feeble glimmer upon the slimy pavement. It continued their long year of wet and depressing weather.

At the Lyceum Theatre, they were met by a tall Indian man and ushered into another carriage. The situation was curious as they drove to an unknown place, on an unknown errand and yet they had good reason to think important issues depended upon the expedition. Holmes remembered Mr. Melas had embarked upon such a journey the week before, and that led to a series of dire circumstances. He noted Watson was about make a comment and no doubt mention the similarity. But Holmes shook his head and touched a finger to his lips, silencing his friends with the motions. There was no need to induce fear in their client.

In the growing fog, it was not clear where they were heading. But Holmes' knowledge of London meant he was never at a loss for their location and continually updated his companions. It was not long before they reached the home and were introduced to the curious personage of Thaddeus Sholto.

He was a small man with a bristle of red hair around the fringe of a bald and shining scalp. He wrung his hands together nervously and his features were in a perpetual smile. Nature had given him a visible line of yellow and irregular teeth and he strove unsuccessfully to conceal by passing his hand over the lower part of his face.

"Your servant, Miss Morstan," he kept repeating in his thin, high voice. "Your servant, gentlemen. Pray step into my little sanctum. A small place, miss, but furnished to my own liking."

After the brief introductions, Sholto explained their situation at length. He regularly sucked on a hookah to relieve his nervous nature as he related the story of Captain Morstan's death and the treasure that contributed to his heart failure. And it was the discovery of that treasure by Sholto's brother Bartholomew which precipitated the letter that brought Miss Morstan and her friends to this house.

"If your father had the treasure, why has it taken these six years to produce it?" queried Holmes.

Thaddeus shook his head sadly. "Father was beset by greed, a trait that also plagues brother Bartholomew. He hid the treasure and never revealed the location. Two days ago, Bartholomew finally divined its location. So now we must go off to Norwood to confront him and demand our equal shares."

"Another carriage trip?" asked Watson, displaying some exhaustion.

Sholto's head bobbed mechanically. "A trip well worth Miss Morstan's effort," he explained. "The total treasure may well run into several millions and she is entitled to her share."

At the mention of this gigantic sum, they all stared at one another open eyed. If the amount proved true, Miss Morstan would change from a needy governess to the richest heiress in England.

They returned to Sholto's carriage and continued their journey. Thaddeus explained the story of the treasure further on their way, including how it contributed to the death of his father. And when his father died, he found a note referring to the "Sign of Four". Holmes prevented Miss Morstan from revealing they had a similar note, and their arrival at their destination allowed the subject to be changed.

"This, Miss Morstan, is Pondicherry Lodge," announced Sholto.

The lodge stood on its own grounds, surrounded with a high stone wall topped with broken glass. A single narrow iron door provided the only means of entrance. Sholto took a lamp from the carriage, and knocked on the gate with a peculiar rap.

"Who is there?" cried a gruff voice.

"It is I, McMurdo. You surely know my knock by this time." There was a grumbling sound and the door swung slowly back. A stocky, deep-chested man blocked the way, the yellow light of the lantern revealing his protruded face and distrustful eyes.

"Mr. Thaddeus? But who are the others? You may enter but these must just stop where they are."

This was an unexpected obstacle. Thaddeus Sholto looked about him in a perplexed and helpless manner.

"I guarantee them!" he protested, his voice cracking with strain.

"Very sorry, Mr. Thaddeus," said the porter inexorably. "Folk may be friends o' yours, and yet no friend o' the master's. I know nothing of none of 'em!"

"Yes you do, McMurdo," announced Holmes genially. "You must remember the amateur who fought three rounds with you at Alison's?"

"Not Mr. Sherlock Holmes!" exclaimed the prize fighter. "You shoulda' stepped up and given me your right cross! I'd ha' known you straight away."

With that resolution, the gatekeeper stepped aside and allowed them to pass. They had barely started up the path when a cry rose before them. From the great, black house sounded the shrill, broken whimpering of a frightened woman. Sholto held up the lantern in an attempt to illuminate the source, his hand shaking until the circles of light flickered and wavered all round them. Miss Morstan seized Watson's wrist, and they all stood, with thumping hearts and straining ears.

"It is Mrs. Bernstone, the housekeeper!" said Sholto. "She is the only woman here."

He hurried to the door and knocked in his peculiar way. A tall, old woman opened it and her shaking voice greeted Thaddeus, though the words were hard to follow. She allowed only Sholto to enter and the door closed behind him, the sound of their conversation into a muffled monotone. Their guide had left the lantern and Holmes swung it slowly round. Great rubbish heaps stood everywhere about the grounds, casting odd shadows in the shifting light of the lamp.

"It is as though all the moles in England had been let loose," observed Watson.

"Accompanied by a good many badgers," concurred Mary Morstan with a weak smile at the thin humor.

"The treasure seekers were six years in their search," explained Holmes.

The door of the house burst open, and Thaddeus Sholto ran out, fear and terror in his eyes.

"There is something amiss with Bartholomew!" he cried.

"Come into the house," said Holmes in his crisp, firm way to take command of the situation.

They all followed him into the housekeeper's room. The old woman was pacing up and down, scared and restless. The sudden appearance of the group, even with the familiar Thaddeus among them, stretched her nerve even further.

"The master has locked himself in his rooms and will not answer!" she cried with a hysterical moan. "I went up and peeped through the keyhole. I...I..."

Words failed the distraught woman and she broke into uncontrolled sobbing. Miss Morstan took charge of the housekeeper while Holmes grabbed the lamp and led the way towards the interior of the house.

Watson had to aid Sholto as they climbed the three flights to the brother's room. Thaddeus indicated the door with a shaking hand. Sherlock Holmes bent down to the keyhole, but instantly recoiled with a sharp breath.

"Watson!" said he. "What do you make of it?"

Watson looked through the keyhole and recoiled in horror. Straight ahead hung a face identical to their companion Thaddeus, but the features were twisted into a horribly fixed and unnatural grin.

"This is terrible! We must get inside!"

Holmes quickly looked at the lock.

“Just a moment!”

He withdrew his picks and was quickly rewarded with a click as the lock released. They stood in the doorway, the eyes of the unfortunate Bartholomew focused on that spot as if the dead man was watching them. Behind, Thaddeus stood, a picture of terror and distress. With the full view of the interior open, he let out a sharp cry.

"The treasure is gone!" he said. "They have robbed him of the treasure!”

“Get hold of yourself, man!” snapped Watson.

The physician tried to calm the nervous little man who, understandably, was shaken to his core by the sight of his dead brother.

Sholto stammered, wracked in his own agitation. “It was on the floor by the desk! As I left, I heard the door lock behind me."

“What time was that?" asked Holmes

"Ten o'clock!” His voice rose in panic. “He is dead, and the police will be called! I shall go mad!" He jerked in a convulsive frenzy.

Holmes put his hand upon Sholto’s shoulder to help steady him.

"Have no fear, you have my assistance in the matter. Drive to the police station and report the matter.” Holmes’ voice was calm and reassuring, having a visible affect on Sholto’s nerve. “We shall wait for your return."

The little man obeyed in a half-stupefied fashion. He stumbled down the stairs, and spoke to the women on the lowest floor. There was a wail from the housekeeper at the news while Thaddeus Sholto shouted for McMurdo. After the door slammed, silence reclaimed the house and Holmes, ever the detective, turned his attention to the room.

Thursday, September 19 *Pondicherry Lodge*

Holmes threw himself to the floor, his magnifying glass out and studying the carpet minutely. Watson, for his part, stepped carefully past to examine the body.

“How long do you think we have?” he asked

“A half hour at least.”

Bartholomew Sholto's chamber was fitted up as a chemical laboratory. Rows of bottles, Bunsen burners, test-tubes, and flasks littered the work table. In the corner, a carboy of acid leaked a stream of dark colored liquid and filled the air with a pungent, tar-like odor. A ladder led to a large opening in the ceiling. At the base lay litter of lath and plaster and a long coil of rope sat carelessly nearby.

By the table, Sholto was seated with his head sunk upon his left shoulder and that ghastly, inscrutable smile upon his face. Watson felt his limbs. He was stiff and cold and had clearly been dead many hours. By his hand lay a heavy brown stick, a stone head rudely lashed on with coarse twine. Beside it was a torn sheet of paper with a few words scrawled upon it. Holmes tapped it meaningfully.

"You see how things can take on new significance."

Watson read the words written upon the paper.

"*The sign of four*. But what does it mean?"

"It means murder," said Holmes, stooping over the dead man. "What of Mr. Sholto?"

"Dead many hours, though the body is rigid beyond expectation."

"A poison?"

"Most likely it was a powerful vegetable alkaloid. A strychnine-like substance would produce the extreme rigor." Watson touched the man's head, and then continued. "Look here!" A long, dark spine was stuck in the skin above the ear.

"A thorn," concluded Holmes "Be careful! It is most likely the source of the poison."

Watson had reached for it, but thought better and left it alone. Holmes followed the line of its direction.

"Look, Watson! It came from the direction of the hole in the ceiling!"

"This matter grows darker with every turn."

"On the contrary," Holmes answered, "it clears every instant."

"Clears?" protested the doctor

"Without a doubt!" Holmes expounded, with something of the air of a professor to his class. "The door has not been opened since last night, but what of the window?" He checked it quickly. "Locked on the inner side; frame solid. No water pipe near and the roof is quite out of reach. Yet here is a print upon the sill. What do you make of this, Watson?"

The doctor examined the round, well-defined muddy print.

"Not a foot mark, surely." He snapped his fingers in realization. "The wooden- legged man! And the odd club on the desk shows he has forgotten his walking stick!"

"Quite so, but he was not alone. Could you scale that wall?"

The room was a good sixty feet from the ground, and there were no obvious footholds or crevices in the brickwork.

"Absolutely impossible," Watson answered.

Holmes agreed. "Without aid, it is so, but what if I lowered you that rope? Then an active man could climb up, wooden leg and all." Holmes nodded, pleased with his conclusion. “Yes, yes indeed. When finished here, he uses the rope to lower the treasure and departs in the same fashion while, as you observed, forgetting his cane. The assistant draws up the rope, shuts and locks the window, and leaves the way he originally came.” Holmes fingered the rope, and then held a glass on a part for Watson’s benefit. "Our wooden-legged friend was not a sailor. There is more than one blood mark, especially towards the end."

"How came the accomplice?" Watson asked. "The door is locked; the window is inaccessible." He looked to the ladder. “You said the thorn came from that direction.”

"Exactly. We must now extend our researches to the secret room which held the treasure."

He climbed the ladder and swung himself up into the garret. His friend followed quickly. The chamber was about ten feet by six feet. The floor was formed by the rafters, so one had to step from beam to beam. The roof ran up to an apex above and the accumulated dust of years lay thick upon the floor.

"There," directed Sherlock Holmes, putting his hand against the sloping wall. "A trapdoor leads to the roof. This is how he entered. Let us see if we can find some other traces."

He held down the lamp and, in that dust, the prints of a naked foot were clear: well-defined, perfectly formed, but scarce half the size of those of an ordinary man.

Watson said in a whisper, "A child?"

The detective denied the conclusion with a shake of his head. "There is nothing more to be learned here. Let us go down."

"What is your theory, then, as to those footmarks?" Watson asked eagerly when they regained the lower room.

"'My dear Watson," said he with a touch of impatience. "Where was Major Sholto posted?"

"The Andaman Islands." Realization dawned. "An Islander? Here?"

"So it appears." Holmes turned his attention back to the floor, muttering to himself. At length, he broke out into a loud crow of delight. "We are in luck. One of our perpetrators had the misfortune to tread in the creosote. You can see the outline of his foot at the edge of this evil smelling mess."

"What then?"

"Why, we have got him," Holmes concluded. "I know a dog that would follow that scent to the world's end."

"What if they took a cab?" asked Watson.

Holmes let out a sigh of disappointment. "Consider: you are a one legged man carrying a heavy treasure chest and accompanied by a four foot tall Aborigine. To top it, you are leaving the scene of a crime In the early morning hours that will surely push even the Whitechapel murders from the headlines once the news is broken. Are you going to hail a cab?"

The doctor smiled at the simplicity of the answer. "They are on foot, of course."

"Without a doubt!"

Their attention was drawn by heavy steps and the clamor of loud voices from below. The hall door shut with a loud crash and the sound of many steps upon the stairs drifted up.

“Here are the accredited representatives of the law,” announced the detective

As he spoke, a portly man in a gray suit strode heavily into the room. He was red-faced, with a pair of small eyes. He was closely followed by constable and the still distressed Thaddeus Sholto.

"This is a pretty business!" he cried in a muffled, husky voice. "But who are all these? The house is as full as a rabbit warren!"

"I believe you recollect me, Mr. Athelney Jones,” said Holmes quietly.

"Why of course!" wheezed the inspector. "Mr. Sherlock Holmes, the theorist. I'll not forget how you lectured me in the Bishopgate jewel case. True, you set me on the right track; but it was more by good luck than good guidance."

“It was a piece of simple reasoning."

Jones made no further comment, his eyes instead going to the ill fated Bartholomew. "But this is a bad business! Lucky I happened to be at Norwood over another case when the message arrived.”

“Yes,” observed Holmes dryly. “Lucky.”

The policeman examined the Sholto brother quickly, noting the thorn sticking from the skin. He plucked it, holding it carelessly. The index finger of his opposite hand approached the point in inquiry.

“What d'you think the man died of?" he asked casually.

“We suspect the thorn is tipped in a deadly toxin,” stated Watson flatly.

Jones’ finger stopped with hardly any space visible between his skin and the tip of the thorn. He withdrew his hand sheepishly.

“My colleague, Dr. Watson,” said Holmes in a quick introduction.

Jones gave Watson a curt acknowledgement, setting the thorn carefully onto the table.

"Door locked, I understand. Jewels worth half a million missing. The window?"

"Fastened; but there are steps on the sill."

"Well, if it is fastened, the steps could have nothing to do with the matter. That's just common sense." Jones paced aimlessly about for a moment, and then looked at Bartholomew. "He might have died in a fit; but then the jewels are missing."

"And there is the poisoned thorn in his neck," emphasized the detective.

"Ha! I have a theory!" Holmes words seemed to have made no impression on the portly policeman. "Sergeant, and you, Mr. Sholto, step outside for a moment." Once the two men had departed, he explained to Holmes..

"What do you think of this? Sholto was with his brother last night, the brother dies in a sudden fit, and Sholto walks off with the treasure? How is that?"

"And the dead man very considerately gets up and locks the door from the inside," replied Holmes, his patience thin.

"And sticks a poisoned thorn in his own neck," added Watson.

"Yes, there is a flaw there." Jones considered the matter in silence for several more seconds. "How is this: Thaddeus Sholto quarrels with his brother. The brother is dead and the jewels are gone. No one saw the brother from the time Thaddeus left and his bed had not been slept in. Thaddeus is in a most disturbed state of mind." Jones nodded, pleased with this piece of reasoning. "You see how the net closes upon him."

"There are more facts," pointed out Holmes. "This card, inscribed as you see it, was on the table. Beside it lays this rather curious stone headed instrument. How does all that fit into your theory?"

"Confirms it in every respect," said the fat detective pompously. "The house is full of Indian curiosities. Thaddeus brought this club up, but thought better and employed the splinter. The card is a blind, like as not." He stopped, the slow motions of his thought process were literally etched on his face. "Then how did he depart? Ah, of course, here is a hole in the roof!"

Considering his bulk, he moved quickly up the ladder and squeezed through into the garret. In a moment, he returned.

"You see!" said Athelney Jones. "There is a trapdoor communicating with the roof, and it is partly open."

"It was I who opened it," admitted Holmes

He was a little crestfallen Holmes had made the discovery. "Whoever noticed it first, it still shows how our gentleman got away. Constable! Ask Mr. Sholto to come back in." When the two men re-entered the room, Jones stepped before the quivering Thaddeus. "Mr. Sholto, it is my duty to inform you that anything you say may be used against you. I arrest you in the Queen's name as being concerned in the death of your brother."

"There, now! Didn't I tell you!" cried the poor little man, his hands on either side of his head and looking from Holmes to Watson.

"Do not trouble yourself, Mr. Sholto," returned Holmes. "I shall clear you of the charge before lunch time."

"Don't promise too much, Mr. Theorist!" snapped the policeman.

"I will clear him, Mr. Jones," replied Holmes with obvious confidence. "And I will make you a present of the name and description of one of the two people who were here last night. His name is Jonathan Small: a poorly educated man, medium height, active, with his right leg off, and wearing a wooden stump. He is middle-aged, sunburned, and has been a convict. The other man--"

"Ah! The other man?" mocked Jones in a sneering voice.

"Is a rather curious person," said Sherlock Holmes, turning his back upon the inspector while touching the doctor on the shoulder. "And you will not believe my description on any account. A word with you, Watson."

He led his friend out to the head of the stair and spoke in a low voice. “Do you see how we get the second tier because Scotland Yard has concentrated all detectives with a hint of intelligence in Whitechapel?”

Before Watson could reply, Jones called from the other room. “What was that, Mr. Holmes?”

“Nothing concerning this matter, Inspector,” he called back. Still, he lowered his voice further before continuing. “Who would have thought his hearing that sharp?” Watson smiled broadly at the comment, but Holmes continued before the doctor could reply. “This unexpected occurrence has caused us to lose sight of the original purpose."

"Yes," the doctor answered. "It is not right that Miss Morstan should remain in this stricken house."

"Escort her home. She lives in Lower Camberwell, so it is not very far. When you have dropped Miss Morstan, go knock old Sherman up and tell him, with my compliments, that I need Toby at once."

"That miserable hound again?"

Holmes smiled remembering the last time Watson had called for the dog. "I would rather have Toby's help than the whole detective force of London."

"If I must," said Watson with a sigh of resignation. A chime from a clock on the lower floor announced the hour. "It is one now. Do you require anything else?"

Holmes withdrew his pad and scratched a quick note and handed it to Watson.

Lestrade:

Jones has arrested an innocent man in Norwood. Please see to his immediate release. Facts to follow.

Holmes

"Get that off to Lestrade."

"Will he accept your word?"

Holmes smiled, but did not reply directly.

"Off with you! I shall study the great Jones's methods while I await your return."

"Mind your temper, Holmes," chided Watson.

Holmes stepped back, feigning insult. "Have you ever known me to be anything but even tempered with the regular police?"

Watson pulled on his gloves in preparation to leave. He was unimpressed by the detective's mock protest of innocence. "I shall be pleasantly surprised if Inspector Jones has not accidentally pricked himself on the dart before my return."

"Be quick if you desire to avert another tragedy!"

A fleeting smile appeared on Holmes' lips and was as quickly replaced by a more somber countenance. He returned to the room and Inspector Jones while Watson headed down the stairs to rejoin Miss Morstan.

Holmes spent his time carefully while Watson was away. For over an hour, he followed the befuddled Jones about the house. The policeman expanded his theory at every turn until he had included all the members of the household in the conspiracy. It was with some relief when the inspector loaded his catch into a wagon and left for the station, leaving the detective with only a disinterested constable to guard the house.

Holmes returned to the scene of the murder. He went back up the ladder and onto the roof. He determined the direction the Islander had taken and followed it to where a drain spout was hooked in a corner. It confirmed his deduction, but the sixty plus feet to the ground dissuaded him from trying to duplicate the aborigine's feat. On his way back, he found an odd looking packet and retrieved it.

He returned to the ground level, nodding to the constable. Dawn was breaking as a coach came up the drive. Watson stepped from the cab with Toby. As all dogs, he was excited about this new adventure and became even more so as Sherlock Holmes approached.

"Ah, you have him there! Good dog!" The normally aloof detective showed great animation as he played briefly with the ungainly looking animal. He explained what happened in Watson's absence. "Athelney Jones displayed immense energy after you left. He has arrested not only Thaddeus but the gatekeeper, the housekeeper, and the Indian servant. I was lucky I was not taken as well."

"But no accident with poisoned thorns, I trust?" asked thc doctor.

Holmes laughed. "I strongly considered it, but managed to contain the urge." "Did you discover anything else?"

"I followed the path our friend took across the roof," explained the detective. "He dropped this in his departure." He held up a small pocket pouch woven out of colored grasses with a tawdry beads strung round it. Inside were another half dozen thorns like the one removed from Bartholomew Sholto.

"They are hellish things," said Holmes. "I'm delighted to have them, for most likely they are all he has. There will be less fear of us finding one in our skin."

"So we will proceed with this case?"

"You think I should not?" It took Holmes a moment to catch Watson's deeper meaning. "Ah, you believe I am forsaking the Whitechapel murders for Miss Morstan's mystery."

"Aren't you?"

Holmes shrugged. "I suppose, after a manner. But consider the Whitechapel affair has been stagnant for the past week while this case offers every opportunity for quick resolution!" His eyes glowed as he relished the prospect of tracking the case to its conclusion. "Are you game for a six-mile trudge, Watson?"

Watson relented and held up his walking stick to show his willingness and off they went.

In the early morning hours, the citizens of London were treated to the incredible site of two grown men following a barking dog. Their pace was brisk, set by the tugging of the dog on his leash. Except where Toby was fooled by a leaking barrel of creosote, he brought the two detectives to a dock on the bank of the Thames.

"They have departed," observed Holmes as the dog search fruitlessly up and down the dock for the continuation of the track. "Watson, mind Toby for a few minutes."

Holmes found some men near the dock and spoke with them for several minutes. It did not take him long to return with the information he sought.

"I have determined the name of the boat. It is the *Aurora*. Her master is Mordicai Smith."

"And do they know where the boat has gone?"

"They did not know that or anything about the passengers. Still, it is impossible to hide a whole steam launch." Holmes considered the river, looking both up and down stream. "We will need assistance to locate the *Aurora.* I believe it is time to return to Baker Street and make that the headquarters of our search."

They arrived at Baker Street late in the morning. Watson was relieved to return to their lodgings. It had been a long night, and his stomach growled uncomfortably. He wanted little more than to get to 221B, shave and eat a credible breakfast. But they found one more hurdle to cross before gaining that goal. Homes had barely set foot upon the cobblestones when a shout drew their attention.

"Mr. Holmes!" A man was loitering near the entrance to their rooms. He immediately approached them, speaking rapidly.

"Whatley Talman," he proclaimed, introducing himself. He took Holmes' hand and shook it enthusiastically. "I have been trying to gain an audience for the past week!"

"Yes," returned Holmes with no enthusiasm. "I remember your card. You are a reporter from the Central News Agency as I recall."

"Indeed, sir, indeed," he admitted readily. He took Watson's hand as well. "And you must be Dr. Watson." He did not give the doctor a chance to reply. "Mr. Holmes, I would like to ask you some questions on your involvement in the East End murders."

Holmes showed no interest in the reporter. "I have no comments at this time," he said.

"You deny you are aiding the police on the case?"

"I make no comment one way or the other," returned Holmes. He tried to push past but Talman was not so easily denied.

"Please, Mr. Holmes! I am only recently returned to England and need your interview to seal my position at the news agency!"

"I detected your American accent, Mr. Talman, though I must say you mask it well. Your manners, however, need to rise to English standards." He tried to move around the reporter again.

"Right you are, sir. I have spent most of my life in California and, most recently, worked for William Randolph Hearst at the *San Francisco Examiner.*"

"I have heard of neither and could care less," returned Holmes, finally making his way to the door.

Talman reached for Holmes shoulder, but Watson grabbed the man's wrist.

"Mr. Talman," said the doctor firmly, allowing his colleague to reach the safety of their rooms, "Mr. Holmes, has provided all the information he cares to release at this time. Now be off before I set my hound upon you."

They both looked down at the unlikely Toby. The dog, in return, looked back at both with a face clearly happy at the attention.

"But . . ." protested the reporter while Toby sniffed incessantly at his pant cuff.

Watson moved the other man about and managed to place himself in the doorway. It was a difficult dance to open the door, coax Toby inside, and prevent the news man from following them.

"*When* Mr. Holmes decides he needs to release information to the press, we have your card. Good day!"

He entered the building and shut the door in the reporter's face. Mrs. Hudson was waiting for them and regarded Toby with disfavor.

"Mr. Holmes! That man has been hounding me all morning. And now you return home with this … this …this mongrel!"

"Yes, Mrs. Hudson, and I apologize for both. Toby will be with us for only a few days."

"Unfortunately, the same may also be true of Whatley Talman!" pronounced Watson.

Holmes smiled at the thin jest, but Mrs. Hudson was not amused by either proposition.

"I do not want animals in my home, Mr. Holmes!"

Holmes took a more mollifying tone with their landlord.

"I assure you, he is both well behaved and indispensable to my current case." He placed a foot on the bottom stair, but paused. "Would you have the boy bring him up a bowl of water and perhaps some table scraps?"

He did not wait for a reply. Mrs. Hudson looked to Watson, her eyes pleading.

"We really do need the dog for a few days, Mrs. Hudson," he said. "I will guarantee his behavior."

Mrs. Hudson relented, calling to the house boy. Watson walked up the stairs slowly. He found Holmes watching him from the top of the stairs.

"Watson! I have used you badly. Your wound is bothering you."

"Thank you for your concern, Holmes," he said. "It is nothing that a couple hours rest and a proper meal will not resolve."

"A grand idea!" agreed Holmes. "Mrs. Hudson!" he called out to the hard pressed housekeeper.

Watson found a bath and a complete change of clothes refreshed him wonderfully. He was even more pleased to find the breakfast laid and Holmes pouring out the coffee.

"Here it is," said he, laughing and pointing to an open newspaper. "The energetic Jones and the ubiquitous reporter have fixed it between them."

Watson took the paper from him and read the short notice headed “Mysterious Business at Upper Norwood." It related the events and heaped undue praise on Athelney Jones. Watson was so amused, he was forced to read whole sections aloud. Both men were laughing so loudly, their eyes streamed and it was several minutes before they could compose themselves sufficiently to address their breakfast.

"Isn't it gorgeous!" said Holmes, grinning over his coffee cup. "What do you think of it?"

“Jones must pay the reporter to write such drivel!"

"I shall not comment!” laughed Holmes. “I believe we could make the same arrangement with our American friend on the street."

At that moment there was a loud ring at the bell, and they could hear Mrs. Hudson raising her voice in dismay, her cry followed by the clatter of several pairs of feet upon the stairs.

"By heavens, Holmes," Watson said, half rising, "I believe that they are really after us."

"No, that will be the Baker Street irregulars."

As he spoke, a dozen dirty and ragged street Arabs entered and quickly drew up in line, facing Holmes expectantly. Wiggins, taller and older than the others, stood forward. He was an occasional visitor to Baker street.

"Got your message, sir," said he, "and brought 'em on sharp. Three bob and a tanner for tickets."

"Here you are, Wiggins," said Holmes, producing some silver. "In future, they can report to you and you to me. Your instructions are simple. I want to find a steam launch called the *Aurora*: owner Mordecai Smith, black with two red streaks, black funnel with a white band. I want one boy at Smith's landing stage opposite Millbank to see if the boat returns. You must do both banks thoroughly. Is that all clear?"

The street urchins agreed quickly enough. Distributing coins among them, they departed as rapidly and as noisily as they arrived, trying the sorely pressed landlady as badly on their exit as they did with their entrance.

"You see, Watson. I have additional forces to call upon. You may rest your leg while they search for the *Aurora*." He stretched his hand up and took down a bulky volume from the shelf. "Let us see what has the gazetteer about our small friend from Pondicherry Lodge."

His eyes scanned the information quickly and he recited the more critical bits as he read.

"Andaman Islands…the Bay of Bengal…the aborigines claim the distinction as the smallest race upon this earth….average height is rather below four feet…fierce, morose, and intractable, though capable of forming devoted friendships…naturally hideous, with large, misshapen heads, small fierce eyes, and distorted features." Holmes looked up from the volume and smiled. "Unlikely to be found in a London cab, I am sure." He returned to the book and his summary. "Feet and hands are remarkably small…intractable and fierce...all the efforts of the British officials have failed to win them over... Not a friend of Major Sholto from that… A terror to shipwrecked crews, braining the survivors with stone clubs or shooting them with poisoned arrows." Holmes picked up the small grass pouch and waved it. He shut the book and returned it to the shelf

"An amiable people, Watson! I fancy Jonathan Small wishes he had not employed him."

"But how came he to have so singular a companion?"

"We had already determined Small came from the Andamans, so it is not so impossible this islander should be with him. No doubt we shall learn the details in time."

Watson fought to suppress a yawn and his friend regarded him with sympathy.

"Watson, you look done in. Lie down on the sofa and see if I can put you to sleep." He took up his violin from the corner and played a low, dreamy, melodious air. It was not long before the physician floated away.

It was late in the afternoon before Watson woke, strengthened and refreshed. Sherlock Holmes sat exactly as he had left him, save that his face was dark and troubled.

"You slept soundly," he said. "Wiggins has just reported and I feared our talk would wake you."

"You have fresh news, then?"

"Unfortunately, no. I confess that I am surprised and disappointed. I expected something definite by this time. Wiggins says that no trace can be found of the launch." He tossed a paper across to Watson "There was this in the afternoon edition."

Watson took the paper and noted the column over Talman's byline. It speculated at great length on Holmes involvement in the Whitechapel case while relating few facts

"A worthless collection of conjectures," Holmes noted. "None are grounded in fact. It has had another unpleasant effect. Take a look from our window."

Watson did as instructed. There were now several men gathered below.

"Reporters?"

"Without a doubt!" A tone of bitterness crept into Holmes' voice. "This Whatley Talman has placed us under blockade, hampering *all* of my ongoing investigations."

Watson noted his appearance at the window had created a stir. The reporters stared up at him and exchanged comments. Others began writing notes. He backed out of view.

"Oh dear. It would be best if Miss Morstan did not call again, lest she be swarmed by the press."

"Something that can be said of all my clients and informants," agreed Holmes.

Watson stretched and noted there was tea on the table. He prepared a cup.

"I am ready for another outing," he announced

"I can do nothing," Holmes explained. "If I go, a message might come in my absence and cause a delay. You can do what you will, but I must remain on guard."

Watson came to a decision. "Then I shall run over to Camberwell and call upon Mrs. Cecil Forrester. She asked me to this morning."

"Only Mrs. Forrester?" asked Holmes with the twinkle in his eyes.

"Miss Morstan, too," allowed the physician. "They are anxious to hear what has occurred. I shall return in an hour or two."

"Good luck! And you may as well return Toby while you are gone, for it is unlikely we will have any further use for him." The dog looked wistfully at Holmes while Watson slipped the leash around his neck. "That, at least, will make Mrs. Hudson happy."

Watson took the dog and left, making his rounds and spending a pleasant hour at Mrs. Forrester's. Their rooms were dark, though he encountered his landlady on his return.

"I suppose Holmes has gone out," he said to Mrs. Hudson.

"No, sir. He retired to his room, sir." Her voice sank to a worried whisper. "I am afraid for his health. After you left, he walked, up and down until I was weary of the sound. Then he was talking to himself and muttering, and every time the bell rang out he came on the stair head to inquire who it was."

"There's no cause to be uneasy, Mrs. Hudson," Watson answered. "We have seen him like this before when he has matters upon his mind."

Watson tried to speak lightly, but he shared Mrs. Hudson's concerns. Through the long night, he heard the dull sound of the detective's tread. There was no doubt Holmes' keen spirit chafed against the involuntary inaction. He was tied to Baker Street by the needs of two cases when he would much prefer to be in the field chasing the clues presented by the cryptic "sign of four".

Friday, September 21 *The Aurora*

That morning, Holmes appeared clad in a rude sailor dress with a pea-jacket and a coarse red scarf. A white wig and facial putty completed the disguise.

"I heard you up all night," Watson remarked, "and I see you decided to take action."

"These infernal problems are consuming me," said Holmes, working on his disguise slightly. "I hoped the issue presented by Miss Morstan would take my mind from the greater issue in the East End, or at least offer a temporary respite. Instead, I am balked by petty deficiencies and now can bring neither case to a conclusion. Worse, there is this."

He had tossed the morning paper at Watson where another front page article was filled with speculation on Holmes and the East End murders. If Talman's previous article was speculative, the new version loosed his imagination completely. Conjectures from the previous story were now facts. New, even more fantastic suppositions followed.

"This is libelous!" protested Watson

"Unfortunately, it is not. He does not quote me or the police in a single instance! What is worse, have you examined Baker Street this morning?" Watson admitted he had not. He glanced out the window and observed the street.

Where five reporters had watched their rooms the previous day, there were now a dozen. Everyone who walked past 221B was accosted by the newsmen. Anyone who looked as if 221B might be their destination was hounded by all of the reporters.

“That will make this more difficult,” Watson commented blandly.

“Difficult!” roared Holmes in an uncharacteristic fashion. “It will be impossible! My profession thrives on anonymity. If every potential client is faced by this hoard of reporters, I shall never have another case again.”

“Then we shall find a way around them,” announced Watson. “And no word on Small, Smith, or the *Aurora*?”

“Not one. I am off down the river, Watson," said Holmes, adding a battered cap to complete his transformation. "I see only one way worth trying, at all events."

"Surely I can come with you, then?" asked Watson.

"No; you must remain here. I am loath to go, for no doubt some word will come the moment I’m gone. Open all notes and telegrams. Act on your own judgment."

"I understand."

"I am afraid you will not be able to contact me, but I shall have news of some sort before I return."

With that, the detective was gone, passing Mrs. Hudson as she was bringing up their breakfast.

It was a long day for the doctor. At every knock on the door or sharp step passing in the street, he imagined it was either Holmes returning or an answer to the advertisement. Instead, it always proved to be yet another reporter looking to follow the false leads put forth by Talman. Only a routine telegram from Lestrade broke the monotony.

The Standard revealed Sholto and his housekeeper had been released, no doubt due to the telegram from Holmes. Further down was an advertisement searching for the location of the lost *Aurora* or Mordicai Smith and his son. The Baker Street address showed Holmes' involvement.

Close to three o'clock, Inspector Jones arrived unexpectedly and produced a telegram from Holmes. A glass of whiskey kept the policeman occupied until Holmes arrived, still dressed wearing his sailor disguise. Jones was at first surprised by the strange character, and even more so as bits of hair and face were pulled free. At last he recognized the detective under the remnants of the disguise.

"Oh, it is just you, Mr. Holmes," he said, a dismissive tone belying the skill of the disguise.

"You got my wire, I perceive?"

"Yes."

The detective looked to his friend.

"Anything else of interest in my absence, Watson?"

The doctor held up the telegram. "A note from Lestrade. He has some additional information and wishes your opinion."

Holmes continued to remove small bits of his disguise that clung to his face.

"That will have to wait until we conclude this affair," he said. "I will contact him in the morning."

Jones chuckled, taking another sip of his whiskey. "So they have you involved in the East End as well."

"I have provided my assistance when requested," replied Holmes. He disappeared into his room and returned in a moment wearing a dressing gown.

"I see your *theories* have not brought that case to a close," observed Jones when he returned.

"True, Jones, true," confirmed Holmes, "but it is an entirely different matter than this case."

"No doubt, no doubt," agreed Jones. "I have my thoughts on how to resolve that case!"

The pompous Jones hinted he held a solution that escaped his comrades. Holmes smiled and was not completely successfully in suppressing the sarcasm in his reply.

"I am quite sure, inspector. But how is your line of investigation proceeding in *this* matter?"

Jones was dejected, the depression increased by the nearly empty whiskey glass. "I had to release two prisoners, and there is no evidence against the other two:"

"Not to worry, for I shall give you two to replace them. You are welcome to the official credit as usual, but you must act as I direct. Is that agreed?"

"Entirely." Jones was resigned, knowing it was his only option to resolve the present case.

"I require a fast steam launch to meet us at the Westminster Stairs at seven o'clock, and at least two staunch men in case of resistance."

"There will be two or three in the boat. What else?"

Holmes spoke with great confidence while revealing nothing of his discoveries. Watson was used to such treatment, though Jones chafed at the omissions.

"When we secure the men, we shall get the treasure," explained the detective cryptically. Jones tried to interrupt with a question, but Holmes ignored him. "I want to return here after the capture and I will ask Miss Morstan and Mr. Sholto to join us. I think it only fair the rightful owners be present. Perhaps we may let the lady be the first to open the treasure, eh, Watson?"

"It would be a great pleasure to me." Watson was unable to suppress the wide smile on his face. Holmes spared him a conspirator's wink before turning his attention back to the policeman.

"The whole thing is most irregular," said Jones, shaking his head, "but I suppose I must accept it. The treasure will be handed over to the authorities until after the official investigation, of course. "

"Certainly. One other point. I should like a few details from the lips of Jonathan Small. There is no objection to my having an unofficial interview with him, as long as he is guarded?"

"If you can catch him, I don't see how I can refuse you an interview."

"Then we are set!" concluded Holmes. "I insist you dine with us, inspector, while we wait for the appointed hour."

It was a little past seven when the trio reached the Westminster wharf and stepped onto the waiting launch. Holmes tapped a green lamp on the starboard side with his stick.

"Extinguish that. We don't want our quarry to know the police are afloat tonight."

"Where to?" asked Jones.

"To the Tower, opposite to Jacobson's Yard."

The inspector gave the order and the little launch moved off smartly, quickly passing any other craft on the river. Holmes nodded with satisfaction as he surveyed their small boat. As promised, two burly constables sat forward. A third was at the rudder with a fourth stoking the fire.

"Excellent, Jones. Everything to order," said the detective.

"Jacobson's yard?" asked Watson

Holmes nodded, the action difficult to see in the growing darkness.

"I reasoned if the boat was not on the water, and it was not of any use below the water, then it must be out of the water." The boat slowed noticeably and Holmes gestured to a group of lights on the far shore. "Jacobson's yard lies there. The *Aurora* was pulled ashore on the pretext of fixing a fully functional rudder. I arrived in time to hear Mordicai Smith himself give the order to have her ready by 8:00 this evening."

"If you had mentioned that," observed Jones, with disgust in his voice, "we could have nabbed them when they reached the yard."

Holmes chuckled.

"And that is why I did not tell you!" He did not look to the detective, but kept his eyes focused on the boatyard. "Jonathon Small is a patient man, inspector. He has waited six years to lay his hands on this treasure. He is clever. If he perceived your trap and escaped, we would never find him." Holmes seated himself on a bench, but his eyes did not waiver. "No, we will wait for him to get to his boat, and then trap him on the river where he cannot escape."

Jones peered across at the yard, at the movement of boats around it.

"Which one is ours?" he asked

"I have an agent who will let us know."

Watson smiled. "Wiggins?"

"None other."

They sat in silence for a bit, and then Holmes straightened.

"There! There is the signal!"

A bit of white fluttered on the shore as a rakish launch left the yard and pointed its bow down stream. The policeman at the rudder immediately opened his throttle and steered after the boat.

“Excellent,” observed Holmes. He withdrew his revolver and checked again that it was loaded. He did not return it to his pocket but held it ready in his right hand.

“Gentlemen, this is not without some danger,” cautioned the detective.

Jones chuckled to dismiss the warning.

“My lads can handle a one legged man and a three foot aborigine!” he boasted.

Holmes let out a deep breath, his tone deadly serious. “Can they handle being struck by a poisonous dart like that which killed Bartholomew Sholto?” he asked. Jones fell silent and the detective continued. “Be ready. If the islander makes a hostile move, do not hesitate to shoot!”

They closed quickly on the *Aurora*. Four forms were visible in the glow of her boiler. The short, slim shape at the stern was doubtless Smith’s son, while the larger figure at the boiler was Smith shoveling the coal. A small, furtive outline stood beside another imposing silhouette.

“There is Small,” discerned Holmes. “I do not believe he will resort to violence, but we must not count on it.”

The contour of Small turned in their direction, and then suddenly raised a hand and pointed. Smith looked back for only a second before burst of white foam appeared at the *Aurora’s* stern and the launch leapt ahead.

“They’ve seen us!” snapped Jones. Jones looked gravely at her and shook his head. "She is very fast. I doubt if we shall catch her."

"We must!" cried Holmes between clenched teeth. "Heap it on, stokers! We must have them!"

The police launch was fairly flying, quickly passing the slower traffic. But even so, their prey was as fast. The churning foam at the *Aurora*’s stern clearly showed the exertions of her owner, but it was only after a quarter hour's chase that Watson would hazard an opinion.

"I believe we are closing on her."

"Yes, but not fast enough." Holmes glanced down to their dwindling supply of coal. "If we do not overhaul her soon, we shall be forced to burn the boat!"

"There must be some way to close the gap."

Holmes smiled grimly, his features dark in the dim light of the boiler.

"I regret the request for two additional policemen," he said, his voice hardly above the heavy throb of the engine. "Their extra weight puts the chase in peril."

Watson returned the grim smile.

"We could ask them to jump overboard," he prompted.

Holmes chuckled, but shook his head.

"Too much to ask even of our most dedicated officers," the detective returned, fixing his gaze on their quarry.

Watson glanced about the boat, looking for anything that might give them an advantage. He noticed the light on the side that had been extinguished, the one marking them as a police boat.

"There is another option," suggested Watson tentatively.

Holmes' head jerked in the physician's direction and Watson nodded towards the darkened lantern. Holmes smacked his forehead with the palm of his hand.

"You are right, Watson. I am a fool!" He yelled to the inspector. "Jones! Light the side lamp. Let them know who is chasing them!"

It took a moment for the request to penetrate the policeman, so intent was he on the chase. It took a few more seconds to keep a match lit in the breeze across their small deck. But, quickly enough, the green lantern glared.

"That should get their attention," remarked Jones.

Holmes moved forward, his two companions on either side. He strained, trying to make out the forms on the other launch. Though still out of earshot, it was obvious the display of the green light was having some effect.

They were a hundred yards behind now and there was a commotion on the deck. Smith recognized the launch following them and stood up in protest. Small pushed him aside and jumped to the boiler.

"We reach the crisis!" shouted Holmes. He brought his pistol to the ready and Watson did the same without hesitation.

At that instant, the small figure appeared on the gunwale, the misshapen silhouette of the islander stark against the boiler behind. There was a dim shout, reduced to a whisper by the sound of the police launch.

"Tonga! No!"

The movements of the aborigine were not in doubt. Holmes and Watson both fired, the shots so nearly simultaneous they sounded as one large crash. A third shot, from Jones, followed a second later. But the figure on the railing was already gone, knocked over the side by the first two shots.

"Holmes!" shouted Watson, though barely a foot away.

The detective reached to his shoulder and plucked a long thorn imbedded in his coat.

"I am uninjured, doctor," he replied calmly. He held the poisoned dart in his gloved hand. "I believe this is as close as I even want to be to one of these." He dropped it over the side.

The firing was enough for Smith's son. He turned the tiller hard and the launch ran up onto the bank. After a chase of over forty-five minutes, it was concluded in a moment. The police launch ran up next to the Aurora, the constables and Jones leaping quickly to the deck. Small leapt over the side, but his wooden leg betrayed him and stuck in the river mud. The two constables pulled him back onto the deck.

The object of their search lay on the deck, wetted to the waist and breathing hard. Holmes and Watson stepped across and looked down on the man that had thwarted the detective for the past few days. His features, starkly delineated in the flicker of the boiler, were composed at this moment of failure. The investigator stood over him in triumph, but Holmes rarely gloated. This was no exception.

"Jonathon Small, I presume," he stated calmly. "I am Sherlock Holmes."

Saturday, September 22 *The Sign of Four*

Their captive was reticent, answering few of the questions put to him. It was only after Jones yielded to Holmes' request to transport the prisoner to Baker Street that he showed any sign beyond complete submission.

"Whatcha' doin' that fer?" he asked.

Holmes smiled. "I want your story, Mr. Small. I cannot offer much, other than a few moments of kindness, before turning you over to the complete mercies of the authorities."

Small grunted, and let the constables place him and the iron box in the police coach. Though the detective had asked Jones to let them transport the prisoner and box, the police inspector was adamant on that fact. The suspect would not leave his sight on the trip to the Baker Street rooms.

"What do you hope to gain by this interview?" asked Watson as they clattered across the cobblestones.

Holmes smiled, his features sharply etched by the gas light coming through the front of the cab. "You know my curiosity. I must have answers!" Holmes chuckled slightly, tapping Watson on his knee. "Besides, there are still a few surprises left this night."

Watson looked to his friend. "And what does that mean?" he asked.

The detective's wry smile held firm. "That will be apparent soon enough."

The group arrived at Baker Street in due course. Mary Morstan waited in their rooms and Watson's faced brightened visibly when he saw her there.

"How…" he stammered.

"Mr. Holmes invited me, though the hour is quite late."

Holmes nodded solemnly at her comment. "Indeed. I felt you needed to hear Mr. Small's story." The detective glanced about quickly before returning his attention to the young woman. "No sign of Mr. Sholto, I perceive."

"Mrs. Hudson received this earlier," she replied, handing Holmes a telegraph.

The detective's eyes scanned it quickly. "He sends his apologies. He states his nerves are in too shattered a condition to face further trials of this evening."

"And just what are the trials of this evening, Mr. Holmes?" The police inspector was clearly unhappy with the arrangements. "I have a prisoner to get to the dock!"

Holmes waved Small into one of the chairs and poured him a whiskey. It was not until Small was settled that he looked to the policeman. "And one for you inspector?"

Jones agreed, sullenly sitting on the divan, and accepted the offered refreshment eagerly enough.

"We are gathered to hear the tale of Mr. Small, the Sign of Four, and the Great Agra Treasure," explained Holmes. "As I said, inspector, that is the price for my services in this affair. And, Mr. Small," he continued, "that is my price for these last few hours of freedom for you."

Small drained his glass and held it out. Watson refilled the glass and the man began his story.

"It began many years ago, shortly before the great mutiny...."

It was a long and interesting tale, with twists and turns to fill a penny dreadful. Small had been a corporal in the infantry and sent to India with his regiment. An unfortunate encounter with a tiger cost him his leg and his position. Stranded in India, he made a living as best he could by engaging in odd jobs around the barracks.

Barely had he recovered from his injury when the Great Mutiny began. Being English, he was entrusted to guard one of the side gates with three Hindis. Without warning, they had placed a knife to his throat and offered him a simple choice: join them in their plan to steal the treasure from a rich merchant or die. It was a simple choice, though it led to his downfall.

The merchant was killed, the treasure hidden and the four men swore their fealty to each other: the Sign of Four. But in equally quick turns, the body of the merchant was uncovered and their plot discovered. Convicted of theft and murder, all four were sent to the Andaman Islands. At that prison, Small's path crossed that of Major Sholto and Captain Morstan. The captain was kind to Small, because of his handicap and because he was a fellow Englishman. Sholto eventually convinced Small to reveal the location of the treasure for the price of an equal share and the freedom of Small and his friends.

But Sholto crossed Small, Morstan and the other three conspirators. He took the treasure and left the prisoners there. It was during this time Small found Tonga, his islander friend, and nursed him back to health. With the assistance of the islander, Small made his escape and returned to England.

"And I may guess the remainder of your story, Jonathon Small," said Holmes.

The prisoner, warmed by the whiskey and fire, looked at the detective with drowsy eyes.

"And what may that be, Mr. Holmes?"

"Morstan confronted Sholto, but was laid low by a sudden heart attack. Sholto discovered your return and hid in fear. When he died, you were no wiser to the location of your treasure. You had a confederate in the house – Lal Roa the houseboy, no doubt. Am I correct so far?"

Small smiled. "So close as to make no difference, sir."

"You got word of discovery and had your friend Tonga scale the wall. Tonga murdered the unfortunate Bartholomew…"

Small leaned forward with some energy. "Aye, but it was of his own accord. I had no intention of adding more blood to me hands!"

"Yes, I saw the footprints on how you chased him about the room. But you two made your escape by the same way you entered, returned to the *Aurora*, and hid until you were apprehended this evening. Is that correct?"

"Right as rain, sir," agreed their captive.

"Which brings us to this." Holmes tapped the heavy box. "I do not suppose you will provide a key?"

"In the river, sir."

Holmes smiled. "With the jewels, I presume?"

"What?"

The word was torn from Watson and Jones at the same instance. Jones laughed loudly at their discomfort, and held up his glass. Holmes smiled and refilled the glass, then returned it to Small.

"You figured that out, did you?" he said.

"It is a heavy box," said Holmes, "but not nearly heavy enough to be filled with precious stones and metal."

"It was my treasure, me and my mates," Small explained. "If we cannot share it, no one else will."

"You devil!" said Jones, rising to his feet in anger.

The prisoner laughed again. "And what will you do for this crime, policeman? Put me in prison for two lifetimes?"

The police inspector was beside himself. This final revelation was more than his patience would bear. He called to the constable waiting outside the room. "It is time to leave, Small!"

He grabbed the captive's arm and pulled him to his feet, but Small refused to move.

"I have but one more request. May I speak to Miss Morstan in private before you take me away?"

"Whatever for?" demanded Jones.

Small drew himself up.

"That is between me and the lady!"

Jones opened his mouth in protest, but Holmes stepped forward.

"I am sure Mr. Small will allow us to guarantee his good conduct for five minutes. Of course, anything he chooses to relay to Miss Morstan will remain in the strictest confidence."

Jones prepared to continue his protest, but Mary Morstan spoke up on behalf of the sympathetic Small.

"Please, inspector," she implored. Watson even thought she batted her eyes at the policeman. "A few more minutes cannot hurt."

Jones was obviously not prepared to resist such pleas for the captive.

"Five minutes," he warned, pulling out his watch. It was clear the limit would be strictly enforced.

The door closed behind the inspector and Small turned to face the young woman. Though she had spoken in his favor only moments before, her face now revealed more than a little trepidation. She drew up her courage to face him.

"What do you wish to say, Mr. Small?"

Holmes smiled, directing the two away from the door.

"No doubt," he said, lowering his voice, "something to do with the bulge in the lower lining of his coat."

Small looked at Holmes, first in surprise, then understanding. The detective had bested him earlier this evening, and this was no different.

"Miss Morstan, your father was the one person to show me human kindness. He did not do that because he had to. He could have treated me like any of another hundred prisoners. That is why I trusted him with the location of the treasure."

Mary Morstan nodded, truly touched by the emotion in Small's voice. The prisoner held up his manacled hands towards Holmes.

"If you will provide a hand, Mr. Holmes."

The detective reached to a pocket on the inside of Small's coat, and further into the lining. When he withdrew his hand, it was filled with emeralds, rubies, and pearls. Watson and Miss Morstan fairly gasped at the sight.

"Aye," explained Small, "the entire treasure did not go over the side. I hoped to save enough that if I got away, I might retrieve me mates from the prison in the Andamans." He paused, shaking his head sadly. "That isn't going to happen, and I hate the thought of Sholto and his kin being the only ones to benefit from my sad story.

"Thaddeus will be rich, but has lost a father and a brother. That is a payment he did not deserve. You have lost a father."

Mary Morstan held a clenched hand at her throat.

"This treasure is cursed!" she said.

Small chuckled. "No, milady, it is I who am cursed."

Watson spoke, but could not remove his eyes from the gems as Holmes handed him the first handful and retrieved the remainder.

"But the police must have searched you!" he protested.

"Inspector Jones is not the most capable of adversaries," smiled Small. He looked to the detective. "And you, Mr. Holmes. You are the other man to show me consideration, even in the pursuit of a rightful justice. No doubt, Miss Morstan may hand over a bauble or two as a fee for your services."

Holmes was about to speak, but suddenly thrust his hand into his own pocket as their door opened and Jones re-entered.

"The five minutes is up, Small."

The prisoner nodded sadly, and stepped towards the door.

"Mr. Small," said Mary, touching his arm to stop him. "Thank you indeed for those kind words about my father. I am happy he was able to relieve your suffering in such a terrible place, even if only to a small degree."

"Thankee, miss," said Small, his head hung low. "Thankee."

And before Jones could remove him, Holmes added to the sympathy of the moment.

"I shall make sure you have my address, Small. I shall testify on your involvement at the trial and clarify which were the actions of your associate."

"Thankee, Mr. Holmes." These last words seemed saddest of all.

"And you shall write me from your prison," continued Holmes firmly. "I have the funds to provide whatever luxuries the authorities may permit."

Small brightened at this addition to the detective's words. He smiled, nodding quickly in gratitude as the police inspector removed him.

All three stood in silence, staring at the closed door as if some new revelation might come back through it. It was Watson that presently broke the silence.

"You have lost a fortune, Miss Morstan," he stated flatly.

Mary Morstan shook her head. "It is a treasure that has cost everyone that touched it. Me, Thaddeus, Mr. Small and his companions."

"Too true, Miss Morstan," agreed Holmes. "But now the hour is late and your mistress will wonder at the delay." He turned to his friend. "Watson, I am sure you will accompany Miss Morstan to her home."

Watson smiled. "I am only too happy to do so."

Monday, September 24 *The Diogenes Club*

The mob of reporters was now a permanent fixture on Baker Street. While the number varied through the course of the day, some were always about. They took up vigil before dawn and many stayed until long after the street lamps had been lit.

For Holmes, it was all a terrible bother. They demanded information he did not have, and would not give them even if it was in his possession. For all of his notoriety, he actually led a reclusive life and this constant prying into his personal affairs was distracting. He had barely averted an "extra" being published the day before when his route took him in the direction of Whitechapel. At best, he felt reporters to be a contemptible lot. The group on the street below had long passed that lowly level. At worst, they threatened to drive away legitimate clients.

He turned to Watson, but his attention was drawn by shouts in the street. When he looked back to his friend, the physician had lowered his paper with a questioning look on his face.

"Messenger boy," commented Holmes. "Most likely from Mycroft." Before the doctor could ask, the detective explained. "The boys from the Diogenese wear a distinctive green uniform."

The shouts and inquiries of the reporters followed the boy from the street and could now be heard in the stairwell. It was a commanding order from Mrs. Hudson that silenced the men and forced the intruding newsmen back into the street.

The messenger entered their room and presented Holmes with the sealed envelope. The detective took it, but the boy remained fixed.

"I was told to wait for a reply," he said.

Holmes nodded, tearing the enveloping open. It took only a moment to scan the brief message.

"Mycroft requests our presence at dinner tonight. 9:00 – rather an odd hour for him." Holmes waved the paper at Watson. "You see. Even he appreciates how the vultures lurk outside our door."

Holmes found a pen and scribbled a one word reply on the note: *Delighted*. He refolded the sheet and replaced it in the remains of the envelope. He handed the note back to the boy with a coin.

"There you go, lad. Mind the jackals as you leave."

The young man was confused by the reference, but happy at the silver in his hand. He dashed off with a smile. The noise in the street grew again when he left the house.

"9:00 for dinner?" sniffed Watson. "What shall we do in the meantime? It is barely two."

"I have an experiment I need to conclude," offered Holmes.

"Creating a foul stench, no doubt."

"Or I could have a pipe and work on this Whitechapel problem…"

"Which will create an even fouler stench," replied the doctor.

"Or I might take a nap so I am fresh for my brother's questions this evening," the detective concluded.

Watson smiled and returned his attention to the *Times*.

"An admirable notion," he observed.

Holmes did take a nap, but it was not long. Instead, he was soon up and plotting his escape from the closely watched residence.

At 8:15, Holmes and Watson left Baker Street for a waiting carriage. Harassed by the newsmen on the few steps from their door to the coach, Holmes met them all with steely silence. Their cab started off at a brisk pace, quickly followed by a convoy of reporters in whatever conveyances they could locate on short notice.

But this was a game Holmes planned for. Their course was set away from the Diogenese club. In fact, the path was set towards Whitechapel. But it was not a direct route, and this was all part of the plan. The cabbie turned corners often and gave all indication of trying to lose the trailing newsmen. What the newsmen missed in their rush to follow the detective was a series of close turns, a quick stop, and the two occupants stepping out and into a coach passing in the opposite direction.

Holmes' ruse had worked as planned and they lost the reporters. They arrived at the Diogenes Club without any additional interruptions. Holmes placed his hand on Watson's shoulder before they entered the building.

“Remember, Watson. No speaking. They will show us to the dining room, we will indicate our selections on the menus, and we will eat in silence.”

“It all seems rather silly, Holmes,” protested the physician.

“It may be, but it is their rule and they are quite serious about it. You will be escorted from the room if you break it more than twice.”

Watson nodded. “Dinner in silence. I shall do my best.”

Holmes led the way and they offered their coats and hats to the checker in silence. From the moment they stepped in the door, no word was spoken. The maitre d’ took them to Mycroft’s table without as much as a whisper. The two brothers greeted each other with but a nod. Even the menus and dinner requests were communicated by pointing and gestures.

Holmes watched his friend, aware of the doctor’s discomfort in such a strange atmosphere. The room was three quarters full, yet there was not the sound of a single voice. Only the clicking of cutlery on china, or the occasional clink of glass betrayed the presence of the other patrons.

On more than one occasion, Watson came close to speaking. The first time, he managed to cover the indiscretion with the cough. The second time, he chopped the word off in the first syllable. There was visible relief on the doctor’s face when the meal was concluded and they were conducted to the Stranger’s Room for brandy and cigars.

“Thank goodness!” The words burst forth from

Watson as if he could hold them in no longer. "I never would have thought it was so difficult to remain quiet for an hour and a half."

Mycroft chuckled, settling himself in his chair and lighting his cigar carefully.

"We are men who spend our entire day speaking, doctor. We make suggestions, relay recommendations, give orders. Many of those men are so hoarse by the end of the day, the solitude of the club is the only thing that can reconstitute their voices for the following day."

Holmes took an obligatory sip of brandy, then produced and lit his pipe.

"So, brother Mycroft," he said between puffs. "What is it that has caused you to invite us this evening?"

Mycroft chuckled. "I told you this Whitechapel business has attracted the attention of the Prime Minister. There is great concern about how these atrocities can be used to support the Red Republicans. It is a menace we cannot afford to overlook." He finished his brandy and poured himself another. "We do not want a repeat of the Jewish riots from last spring."

"Do you think it can reach that level of discord?" asked Watson.

"Undoubtedly, sir," returned Mycroft. "We have seen it before. The government is prepared to use troops, if needed."

"Horrifying!" exclaimed Watson

Holmes nodded and smiled. "Horrifying indeed." He took another sip of brandy.

"Is this intended to force me into taking the case?" he

asked. "Or do you have some other purpose in broaching the subject?"

Mycroft laughed. "There is, of course, no fooling you, brother Sherlock. I saw your hand in this Sholto business a few days ago yet there was no mention of your name."

Holmes leaned forward. "You know my methods. I often work with the regular police on such terms."

"And in this case? Would the regular police have resolved it without your help?"

Holmes puffed the pipe, considering the proposition for a moment.

"I'm afraid Jones was quite lost in the matter. Lestrade or Gregson, I believe, would have gotten to the heart of the matter eventually."

"In time to prevent the escape of the guilty parties?"

It was the detective's turn to chuckle. "*I* was barely in time to prevent that. But you are correct. They would have been hard pressed to succeed in the time given them." He drew on his pipe and discovered it had gone out. He set the pipe down to continue the conversation without it.

"So that is your question?"

"Indeed. An answer is needed at the highest level."

Watson was lost. "What *is* the question?"

"My brother, and presumably the government, need to know if the London police can handle the Whitechapel case."

Watson was leaning forward, awaiting an answer.

"My dear Mycroft, I can think of no better force in the world to be on the trail of this killer then Scotland Yard and the Metropolitan Police."

"You mock me!" retuned Mycroft.

"No, I do not," replied Holmes. He retrieved his pipe and filled it. "I am aiding them as best I can, but this is not a subtle mystery where clues direct us to the guilty party. No, brother, these are violent and random acts. When an entire quarter of the city are potential suspects, it is beyond my powers to investigate all of them. No, it is with the official authorities and their manpower where our best hopes lie at the moment."

"*Hope* is not a reassuring term, Sherlock," observed the elder brother. "I may hope to find a five pound note in the street, but that does not replace the certainty of earning such an amount."

"You are correct," agreed the detective, "but we are at the mercy of hope at the moment."

"So I am to tell the Prime Minister and the Home Secretary that Sherlock Holmes *hopes* the police stumble upon a solution?"

"You may tell your august friends that I am aiding them as best I can in a very difficult situation."

"I see."

Mycroft considered the comment at length, sipping his brandy and taking irregular puffs on his cigar. Watson opened his mouth to break the silence, but Holmes held up his hand and gave a sharp shake of his head. He was familiar with his brother's way and he knew there was one more issue to be addressed. Mycroft set his cigar and snifter on the side table.

"So you will continue to take additional cases, I see."

"If I can make no progress on Whitechapel, I will consider cases of interest."

"No plea or retainer will dissuade you," conclude Mycroft, retrieving the brandy. "The government may bring more pressure upon you to focus all your attentions on this matter."

"The attentions I have focused are sufficient for the information we have available." Holmes lifted his own snifter towards Mycroft in a slight toast. "You can see that as clearly as I."

Mycroft nodded in agreement. "So be it then. Another brandy before you leave?"

Holmes looked at his still mostly full glass.

"As plain a dismissal as I have ever heard." He stood and stepped to the door. "Thank you for a pleasant dinner, Mycroft. The next time it will be at a club of my choosing, if only for the doctor's sake."

"Good evening, Sherlock."

"Good evening, Mycroft."

The trip back to Baker Street was made in a cab rather than walking as they had done on previous occasions. The night had turned damp, and the weather was sufficient to drive any remaining newsmen away. For the first time in several days, they were able to enter their residence without being pestered by the press. In their rooms, Watson poured them each a small amount of whiskey as they sat down on either side of the fireplace to dry out before going to bed.

"Is it wise to continue to work other cases?"

Holmes shrugged, a very uncharacteristic action on his part.

"I have no answer, Watson. I rarely work upon multiple cases at the same time. You know that. Indeed, the Whitechapel and Sholto cases interfered with one another while were awaiting developments."

"So what is your plan for tomorrow?"

"I shall be up early to await our new client."

Watson was perplexed. "New client? What new client?"

Holmes pointed the stem of his pipe at the bookcase. A walking stick leaned against it.

"We have had a visitor in our absence, doctor. If nothing else, I expect he will appear to reclaim his property."

Tuesday, September 25 *Doctor Mortimer*

Both men were up early the next morning in anticipation of their visitor returning. A discussion of the walking stick, a singular calling card by all accounts, told Holmes the visitor was Dr. James Mortimer, formerly of Charing Cross Hospital and currently a country resident that did much walking. Holmes could also see that the man had a small dog that was in the habit of chewing, but all the deductions did nothing to reveal the reason why the prospective client had called upon them. A commotion in the street drew Holmes to the window where he could see a man approaching their door and being accosted by the reporters.

"The vultures are even pursuing our live clients," noted Holmes.

"Is there any chance Lestrade might detail a constable to keep the street clear?" ventured Watson.

"An excellent suggestion, doctor! I shall inquire at the next opportunity."

Dr. Mortimer successfully ran the gauntlet of newsmen, but was visibly upset by the encounter as he was shown into the rooms by Mrs. Hudson. There was a quick round of introductions while Holmes guided the physician to a chair.

"I must apologize for our London press corps, Dr. Mortimer," said Holmes as he handed the physician his walking stick. "They are quite out of control over this Whitechapel business." Holmes looked to his landlady. "Perhaps some tea will help calm our nerves, Mrs. Hudson."

Holmes sat down across from Mortimer while Watson pulled out a notebook in preparation for the interview.

"Now, Dr. Mortimer, what has brought you to London to seek my services?"

Mortimer hesitated as if reconsidering his actions. But he drew up, his resolution firm, and told his story.

"Are you familiar with the death of Sir Charles Baskerville some six weeks past?" Holmes shook his head. "It was in Dartmoor, Devon, some 6 weeks past. His body was discovered early one morning. The coroner determined the death was due to heart failure."

"And you believe there was some other cause?"

Mortimer shifted uncomfortably under the piercing stare of the detective.

"I have reason to wonder what precipitated the heart failure."

Holmes smiled in anticipation.

"Now we come to the heart of the matter!"

"Exactly, Mr. Holmes. Sir Charles was out late at night, waiting by the gate. I determined he was there for fifteen to twenty minutes."

"How did you determine that."

"His cigar ash. It had fallen three times."

The detective chuckled. "You have read my monograph?"

"More than once, sir," acknowledged Mortimer. "From there, he ran – ran, mind you – back towards the house. His toe prints were clearly visible in the grass."

"Aha! You see, Watson? A model client! And Sir Charles was not a young man, I venture?"

"Indeed, Mr. Holmes. He was in poor health and would have no reason to run."

Again Holmes sensed the hesitancy on the part of Dr. Mortimer.

"There is more to this story."

Mortimer let out a long breath. "Yes, Mr. Holmes. Bear with me, for I must relay something of the folklore surrounding the Baskervilles for you to understand."

Mrs. Hudson arrived with the tea, and it was laid out and the cups poured. As they sipped it, Dr. Mortimer told the story of Hugo Baskerville, the founder of the lineage. It was a shocking tale of how Sir Hugo had kidnapped a girl from the village, chased her onto the moor, and fell prey to a demon hound. He explained how the hound had plagued the Baskervilles for the last 200 years of their history.

"A lurid tale indeed," agreed the detective. "But you expect me to believe this spectral beast is involved in the death of Sir Charles?" Holmes paused, noting the expression on the visitor's face. "You are a practical man, Dr. Mortimer, therefore you have some real reason to see a connection here."

"Indeed," said Mortimer, his pallor ashen as he continued. "I searched the grounds around Sir Charles, as I told you. What I did not tell the inquest was I found another footprint. It was the footprint of a gigantic hound!"

The announcement hung in the air for a moment. Watson felt a chill at the revelation, but for Holmes it was another piece of the puzzle.

"You have brought me an interesting case indeed, Dr. Mortimer!" he exclaimed. "No doubt an heir is due?"

"The last known heir, Sir Henry, arrives from Canada later today."

"And you seek my help in protecting him from this spawn of the devil?"

"Exactly."

Holmes paused, considering how much to reveal to the visitor.

"Your timing is not good, doctor, but I shall find a way to make room for this inquiry. It has elements I find fascinating!"

"I'm sure Sir Henry will be most appreciative."

"You say he arrives today? Then we can arrange for an interview tomorrow."

Mortimer stood, relieved his request was being honored. He held out his hand to shake Holmes'.

"Precisely what I required, Mr. Holmes."

"Send me a post on when and where. I will clear my schedule."

The doctor was shown out and Holmes rubbed his hands in anticipation of this new challenge. Watson was not pleased at this turn of events.

"Do you mean to abandon the East End case in favor of this one?" he asked.

Holmes returned to his chair with some energy and prepared his pipe.

"The East End investigation is not a case, Watson." He lit a match and drew the flame into the pipe's bowl. "It is a series of dead ends with little hope of resolution!"

Watson stepped to the window and watched their visitor run the gauntlet of reporters on the street.

"And this is a case?"

Holmes exhaled a fresh cloud of smoke. "Without a doubt!" This new problem had seized upon his imagination. "Consider this.

"In the case of Baskerville, there are clear motives for some human agency. The Baskerville estate represents a tidy sum and might be worth murder to obtain. Sir Charles was a man of some obtainments, and such men have enemies. In either case, it is a person and not some supernatural canine behind the course of events. This assassin is using the legend of the hound as a distraction or cover for his actions."

"And how do you know that?" sniffed Watson.

"The footprint, Watson! The footprint!"

Watson nodded, yielding to the evidence.

"So we have a clear motive and there are limited numbers of people who will benefit financially from Sir Charles' death or would want him dead. Immediately, the list of suspects is narrowed."

"And Whitechapel?"

"We are unable to determine a motive. And, until we discover the evidence that makes a connection between these pitiful women, the entire population of Whitechapel is suspect." Holmes let out a heavy sigh of resignation.

"Nothing came of Mycroft's suggestion of a religious motive?"

"I see nothing in the killings to suggest it. There are no religious motifs in evidence. None of the women I interviewed have seen any upsurge in preaching in the warren. I find it impossible to believe someone would wreak vengeance on these poor souls without first trying to save them."

Holmes shook his head in frustration, unable to deal

with the complete lack of progress on the matter.

"Even if I am imbued with the near mystical powers your stories attribute to me, how can I be expected to sort through millions of people to discover the guilty party? And that is assuming it is only one person and not some evil cabal responsible for the deeds."

Watson sat down in resignation. "So these dreadful crimes will continue without end?"

Holmes' pipe had gone out during the discussion. He relit it and tossed the spent match into the fireplace.

"At the moment, the police and their manpower are a more powerful tool for resolving it. I will continue to review whatever evidence they discover. But for now, I am going to think on how I might exit my residence to research information on Sir Charles and the Baskervilles."

He stood and went to the window, looking down at the milling crowd of reporters gathered below.

"And that problem, Watson, will take some little effort to resolve this morning!"

Wednesday, September 26 The Vigilance Committee

Meeting Sir Henry the following morning proved to be more interesting than Holmes had determined. The new tenant of Baskerville was loudly berating a servant when they reached his rooms. He dismissed the woman in annoyance and turned his attention to his visitors.

"I must beg your pardon," said Baskerville after the introductions. "It is not my usual habit to complain to the hired help, particularly in front of strangers."

"What is the problem?" asked Holmes.

"Of all things, it is a missing boot," explained Sir Henry. "I set them out to be polished and one turned up missing."

"I would have thought an establishment of this reputation would not make such a mistake," observed Watson.

"As would I," agreed Baskerville dryly. "And if it had only been once, I would have let it go, but twice in the same day was just too much!"

Holmes leaned forward in interest. "Twice you say?"

Henry Baskerville chuckled. "I set out my new pair and one disappeared. Then that one reappeared when I set out the old pair." He shook his head. "So now I must start breaking in the new pair more quickly."

The new baronet laughed lightly at the petty mystery, but returned his attention to the matter at hand.

"Whatever that might mean, I do not want to waste your time with trivialities, Mr. Holmes. Dr. Mortimer has explained to me the curse and what he knows of the death of Sir Charles." Henry Baskerville appeared the image of the sturdy frontiersman and dismissed the story of the hound with a casual wave of his hand. "I have no intention of such talk preventing me from returning to the family hall."

Holmes smiled. "Nor should it, Sir Henry," he said. "I just want you to be aware that there are some *concerns* with the events surround your uncle's death."

"Can you explain that further?" asked the Canadian.

"Let's just say I am making inquiries and when I find anything definitive, I will let you know immediately."

Sir Henry seemed content to let the matter stop there.

"Then let us get some breakfast," he said. "All this boot business has delayed my morning meal!"

It was agreed to proceed to a nearby restaurant and the group went to the street for the short walk. Baskerville and Mortimer led the way with Holmes and Watson a few paces behind. They had gone little more than a block when Holmes touched Watson's shoulder.

"Over there on the left, Watson. Do you see that cab?"

"The one moving so slowly?"

"Precisely!" hissed Holmes. "Quick! We must see who is in it!"

Holmes, as always, trotted off without waiting for his friend. But the detective was too slow, and a shout from the passenger caused the cab to speed away before he could reach it. Holmes returned to his waiting companion.

"What do you think?" asked Watson

"I think Sir Henry is being followed. Did you see the face of the passenger?"

Watson shook his head. "Not clearly. It was a man with a full beard."

"That was all I managed also," replied the sleuth. "I did manage to see the cab number clearly, though."

"So there may be some hope of tracking this unknown person down?"

"Perhaps. I will send a telegraph when we reach the restaurant."

They had a quiet and pleasant breakfast. Neither Holmes nor Watson made mention of the cab they felt was following the Baskerville heir. While they continued their chat over coffee, Sir Henry asked about the Whitechapel murders.

"They are quite well known in Canada," he explained. "Even the American papers were repeating the stories before I left."

Holmes dismissed the case with only a few words. "It is only the gruesome matter of the deaths that draws the press to take notice. Sadly, murders are far too common in that section of London, Sir Henry."

It took a moment for Baskerville to react to the comment. "I'm sorry, Mr. Holmes. I am still adjusting to being addressed as Sir Henry. In Canada, it was either Henry or even Hank to my friends."

"You shall have to adjust if you plan to reside at Baskerville Hall. When do you plan to leave?"

Baskerville looked to Mortimer. "Saturday. Is that correct?"

Mortimer nodded. “We plan to tour London for a few days since Sir Henry has not been here before.”

“My inquiries will not yield results by then,” explained Holmes. “I would ask you do not go about alone, Sir Henry. Dr. Mortimer, you can accompany him at all times?”

“Of course,” agreed the country doctor.

“Do you feel that is necessary?” asked Baskerville.

“Let’s just call it a prudent precaution. I doubt old family myths will track you down in London, but it pays to be careful. What staff is there at Baskerville Hall?”

The new lord looked to Mortimer for the answer.

“Just the butler Barrymore and his wife at this time. Sir Charles was content with a small staff.”

Holmes nodded. “And will you be staying at Baskerville Hall until Sir Henry settles in?”

Mortimer shook his head. “I must see to my own business and my family, Mr. Holmes. I will visit regularly, of course.”

Holmes considered the proposition. “I think a full-time companion would be best until this is all sorted out.” He turned to Watson. “Of course! Dr. Watson is just the man!”

Sir Henry was skeptical. “Don’t you think you are taking caution too far, Mr. Holmes?”

Holmes smiled. “I prefer to err on the side of caution.” He looked back to Watson. “And what about you, old fellow? Does your practice allow for a brief holiday in Devonshire?”

“If it is necessary, Holmes, I will be glad to accompany Sir Henry.”

“Then it is settled,” concluded the detective without waiting for more discussion. He glanced at his watch and stood. “I must beg your leave, Sir Henry. I must stop at Scotland Yard to consult on another matter this afternoon.”

"Of course, Mr. Holmes." Baskerville stood and shook his hand.

Holmes started to leave, but turned back with one final comment.

"And, Sir Henry! Might I caution you on crossing the streets in London? Many visitors are not used to the volume of traffic in the city."

"Thank you for the warning, Mr. Holmes."

With Watson attending to the needs of his practice, Sherlock Holmes arrived at Scotland Yard alone. The consulting detective did not visit the official force on a regular basis. Too many of the inspectors and officials considered him an amateur and disregarded his efforts, in spite of his continual success. But Holmes had promised Lestrade he would visit for a consultation, and the prospect of facing the horde of reporters at Baker Street was more daunting than a possible run-in with a police official.

"Holmes!" declared the police inspector. Lestrade appeared truly pleased to see the detective. He stood and quickly guided Holmes to a chair by his desk. "I am glad you could make it today."

"Do you have anything new?" he asked, getting straight to the work at hand.

Lestrade shuffled some paper and passed an official document across the desk.

"Here is the official result of Annie Chapman's inquest." The inspector's voice lowered to a whisper. "You were aware of the missing rings, but did you also know her uterus was removed?"

Holmes was repulsed by the revelation. His profession

allowed for savagery but he was still a product of the Victorian world.

"That is shocking!"

Lestrade rarely possessed a revelation that surprised the detective, but there was no pleasure in succeeding in this case.

"Indeed," he agreed sadly. "We must find this monster!"

Holmes returned the report. "Sadly, I have nothing new for you either. This additional information does nothing to help with my investigation."

Lestrade's shoulders slumped slightly. That, as much as anything, told Holmes how poorly the police had advanced on the case. He sympathized with their frustration, but truly had nothing to offer.

"Then we are adrift," concluded Lestrade.

Holmes changed the subject and handed Lestrade a note.

"Might I prevail on you to locate a cab for me?"

Lestrade took the note. "Does this concern Whitechapel?"

"No," said Holmes. "An unrelated manner. A client was being followed this morning."

Lestrade waved to a bobby. He handed the note off with a quick set of instructions.

"Just have the cabbie call at Baker Street," added Holmes. "I will reimburse him for his time."

Lestrade started to comment further, but his eyes fixed beyond Holmes' shoulder. "Oh no, not again…" said the inspector in a low tone.

"Inspector Lestrade!"

The voice was strong, if rough. Lestrade stood to greet the newcomer and Holmes also rose to face him.

"Mr. Holmes, this is Mr. George Lusk." Lestrade's introduction was brief. "Mr. Lusk and a number of merchants' in Whitechapel have formed a Vigilance Committee."

Lusk grabbed Holmes' hand and shook it furiously.

"Mr. Sherlock Holmes? I am more than pleased to meet you!" expounded Lusk. "I have sent you two letters and you have not responded to either of them."

The detective managed to withdraw his hand and regard the newcomer coolly. Lusk was a dark-haired, middle-aged man. His clothes were neat enough, but there were signs he was not terribly successful. A cuff on one sleeve was repaired, and not very well. The knees of his trousers were shiny, indicating their age. His shoes were obviously resoled.

"As you might understand, I am a bit behind in my mail these days," replied the detective.

"Our committee is interested in hiring your services to investigate these murders, Mr. Holmes. We are prepared to meet your salary requirements."

Holmes gestured to Lestrade. "I am already consulting with the official force on the matter."

Lusk was not to be put off and pressed further. "But are they providing all their information? I suspect they have made connections to the upper class…"

Holmes raised his hand to stop Lusk's rant.

"They are providing every cooperation and we are exchanging all the information that is available. Unfortunately, the lack of progress shows there is a lack of clues to afford any of us a direction."

The detective succeeded in quieting the businessman, so he took the opportunity to ask a question of his own.

"I trust your 'vigilance committee' is not in fact a vigilante committee? You can only increase public unrest by trying to take the matter into your own hands."

Lestrade spoke up to answer the question and provide Lusk support. "I can assure you, Mr. Lusk and his committee have cooperated fully with us, Holmes. They are providing additional men for our nightly patrols in Whitechapel."

Holmes nodded. "Very good, Mr. Lusk. Perhaps with all our efforts we can bring this horrible episode to an end."

The detective hoped to make a quick exit, but Lusk continually drew him into the lengthy conversation with Lestrade over the case. It was over an hour before he seized an opportunity to excuse himself and return to Baker Street.

An empty cab outside Baker Street announced the success of Lestrade's inquiry. Holmes managed to get past the reporters to find Watson and the cabbie having tea.

"Ah, welcome back," greeted the doctor. "I have been questioning the cabbie while we waited for your return."

"Have you?" said Holmes.

"Indeed." Watson smiled, a secret barely suppressed by his mirth.

"And what have you discovered?"

"A description of the man, how long he was following Baskerville, what pretense he gave." Watson paused again, announcing his last bit of information with a flourish. "I have even ascertained the name of the man who hired the cab!"

Holmes was tiring of the game. "Well?" he demanded.

Watson chuckled. "Tell my friend the name of your fare, Mr. Jones."

The cabbie was a bit confused by the back and forth between his hosts, but offered an answer quickly.

"He said his name was Sherlock Holmes, sir!"

The detective was stunned to silence for a moment, but then burst out laughing. Watson, too, could no longer contain himself. It was a moment before Holmes calmed himself to answer the questioning look of the cabbie.

"My apologies, Mr. Jones," said the detective, still trying to contain himself. "You see, I am Sherlock Holmes," he explained, identifying himself.

The revelation was met with a blank stare from the visitor.

"What does it mean?" asked the cabbie.

"It means I am following someone clever enough to recognize me," returned Holmes. "And bold enough to challenge me directly!"

"I see," replied Jones. His tone made it clear he did not.

"Never mind." Holmes had better ways to spend his time that clarifying the situation. He withdrew a one pound note and handed it to the cabbie. "Thank you for your time, Mr. Jones."

Jones brightened at the fee and nodded his gratitude as he left the room. Holmes turned back to his friend and fixed himself a cup of tea as he spoke.

"So we end where we began," said he. "The cunning rascal! He saw I would lay my hands on the driver, and so sent back this audacious message."

"And what does that tell you, Holmes?"

"It tells me this time we have a foe worthy of our metal. I can only wish you better luck in Devonshire. I am not easy in my mind about it."

"About what?"

"About sending you. This is an ugly and dangerous business, Watson. Mortimer may fear a demon hound, but there can be little doubt now that there is a human agent behind these actions. Yes, my dear fellow, I shall be very glad to have you back safe and sound in Baker Street when this is concluded!"

Saturday, September 29 *Separate Ways*

Inspectors Abberline and Lestrade were at 221B Baker Street early in the morning. Watson was packing for his trip to Baskerville Hall while Holmes finished his breakfast and glanced quickly through "The Times". As Mrs. Hudson showed the two policemen in, Holmes cast the paper to the side and gestured for the men to take seats.

"And what brings you by this morning?" he asked.

Abberline reached into his pocket and withdrew a postcard. He carefully handed it to Holmes.

"We received this from the Central News Agency this morning, They have had it for two days!"

Holmes reached for the card carefully, pulling out his magnifying glass to examine it in detail. The words in red ink covered most of both faces.

Dear Boss,

I keep on hearing the police have caught me but they won't fix me just yet. I have laughed when they look so clever and talk about being on the right track. That joke about Leather Apron gave me real fits. I am down on whores and

I shan't quit ripping them till I do get buckled. Grand work the last job was. I gave the lady no time to squeal. How can they catch me now. I love my work and I want to start again. You will soon hear of me with my funny little games. I saved some of the proper red stuff in a ginger beer bottle over the last job to write with but it went thick like glue and I can't use it. Red ink is fit enough I hope ha ha. The next job I do I shall clip the lady's ears off and send to the police officers just for jolly wouldn't you. Keep this letter back till I do a bit more work then give it out straight. My knife is nice and sharp I want to get to work right away if I get a chance. Good luck.

Yours truly

JACK THE RIPPER

Don't mind me giving the trade name

Wasn't good enough to post this before I got all the red ink off my hands curse it.

No luck yet they say I am a doctor now ha ha.

"Extraordinary!" said Holmes. "Notice the handwriting. Neat and regular, regardless of the ink drops and splatter. Hardly the sign of a monstrous killer. Not too much else to be had from it, I suppose?'

"It was passed through a dozen hands before we received it," noted Lestrade.

He passed the card to Watson.

"*Jack the Ripper.* A horrid nom de plume," commented the doctor.

"Interesting that," noted Abberline. "The locals started using that a week or so ago to describe the killer. Now here it is on the postcard."

"But *Dear Boss?"* protested Holmes. "Surely that is more in line with the language used by our American cousins than an Englishman."

"Perhaps," agreed Abberline, taking the postcard back from Watson. "There is nothing to prove it is actually from the killer."

"And nothing to disprove it, either," punctuated Lestrade.

Holmes sat in silence, his eyes focused on the ceiling while his fingers beat a quick tattoo on the table. He looked up at Watson.

"Paper and pen, Watson," he demanded. While the doctor fetched the materials from the desk, Holmes looked to the detectives. "I must see the doctor off on matters concerning another case," he explained. "Are either of you familiar with the Diogenese Club?"

Abberline nodded. "I know where it is."

The pen scraped across the paper in Holmes' normal quick scrawl. "This is a letter of introduction to my brother. I have consulted him on this matter, so he is aware of the facts."

"You have brought in another…" started Abberline.

Holmes raised his hand to cut short the protest. "My brother Mycroft has the trust of the Home Secretary, inspector." Abberline accepted the explanation. "Take my letter and the postcard to Mycroft. He may be able to make more of it than I at first blush." Lestrade took the offered letter and folded it neatly.

"I plan to be on the streets of Whitechapel tonight,

gentlemen. We will see if we can find some clue of who this *Jack the Ripper* might be." He checked the clock on the mantel. "Come Watson, we must hurry to meet Sir Henry and Dr. Mortimer!"

The exit from their residence was complicated by the press. Even with Lestrade and Abberline forcing the reporters away, it took several minutes to obtain a cab and, all the while he was being hounded with questions on his meeting with the police inspectors. When they finally were in the cab, and the driver had negotiated his way past the mob, Holmes slumped as if all energy had been drained from him.

"Are you all right, Holmes?" asked Watson.

"I do not know if I will return to Baker Street for a few days, Watson. It requires more strength than I possess to subject myself to it again." Holmes straightened and looked behind them.

"Do you think we are being followed?" asked the physician, also turning around to look.

"I do not know. I thought I recognized our bearded spy from this past Wednesday across the street, but there was no way to get a closer view because of the newspapermen. I was hoping he might follow us and give us another chance to intercept him."

"I see no one."

"Nor do I," agreed the detective in resignation. "We shall have to pursue this unknown stalker in another venue."

The ordered confusion of Victoria Station was a welcome respite from the disorder of Baker Street. It was easy enough to locate Baskerville and Mortimer near the train for Devonshire. After brief greetings, the two men boarded while Holmes touched Watson's shoulder for one more consultation.

"This may seem strange, but post your observations using this stationery."

Holmes held out a set of matched pink stationery, envelopes and paper neatly tied in an equally pink ribbon.

"As you wish," said Watson, taking the stationery from the detective. "Is there a favorite scent you would like me to use as well?"

Holmes smiled, the act both wry and rueful. "I have my reasons for the request."

Watson thought for a moment before the purpose dawned upon him.

"Our flood of mail at Baker Street!"

"Bravo, Watson!" confirmed the detective. "The paper is, naturally, unimportant. But the envelopes will stand out in even a bag of mail. But I will keep the idea of using a scent in reserve. That has merits of its own!"

Watson was confused at the suggestion and Holmes had to explain quickly.

"If we start receiving too many bags of mail, I can have you scent your letters, allow Toby to inspect the bags, and then I will know in where to search."

But the sleuth did not allow the momentary levity with his friend distract him from the seriousness of their quest. He changed subjects, driving home the reality of the matter.

"Above all, caution, Watson. Keep your revolver near you night and day, and never relax your precautions."

"You think it that dangerous?"

"I do. The death of Sir Charles points to that."

Watson nodded while he considered his friend carefully. "And what of the other matter?"

Holmes shrugged, an unusual reaction from the normally assured investigator. "I will do what I can. I will patrol the streets of Whitechapel in search of a lead, if I can brush off the press that continues to surround Baker Street."

"A veritable siege," concluded the doctor.

Holmes smiled quickly at the brief wit. "A not inaccurate description." He sighed, another unusual action "In truth, I would prefer to drop the whole Whitechapel business and accompany you to the moor. This case of Sir Henry's is more in keeping with my experience and tastes."

"I shall look after things at Baskerville Hall in your absence."

"I have no doubt on that point," reassured Holmes. "And have faith I will join you at the earliest convenience." At that moment, he spied Mortimer waving at them from the rail car. "Come, our friends have already secured a first-class carriage and are waiting for you."

Holmes saw his friend off, watching the train receding in the distance. A gust of wind wrapped around him, carrying with it a cool blast of mist. The detective considered the low clouds hanging above the city while planning his actions for the night.

Sunday, September 30 *Double Event*

After watching Watson depart, Holmes returned to Baker Street only after donning a disguise. For him, the day had not yet begun. First, he had to bypass the growing crowd of reporters that watched his residence at all hours of the day and night. After succeeding at that, he ate a light meal and took a brief nap.

Rather than cleaning up after the nap, he added dirt and grime to his face. Bushy eyebrows and stained teeth contributed to the disguise. He donned well-worn workers clothes, ill-fitting and slightly baggy. He added padding to his stomach to fill out his thin frame. At length, he regarded the resulting unshaven, dirty workman in the mirror with satisfaction.

He left by the front door, moving through the squad of reporters with only a few questions shouted in his direction. He found getting to Whitechapel more difficult as no cabbie wanted to take on a fare of such an obviously disreputable nature as presented by his disguise. He finally convinced a cabman to take him by providing payment up front. He had himself let out several blocks from Whitechapel and shuffled in on foot.

The evening was typical for late September in London.

There was rain in the air, pushed by a heavy wind. The streets of Whitechapel were filled with humanity going their various ways. People worked at all hours in that part of the city, taking what work they could get at any hours they could get it.

The investigator wandered from pub to pub, observing the women plying their trade and the low manner of men who accompanied them. He adopted a drunken stagger for his walk though, in reality, he had barely sipped any of the drinks he had purchased. The detective briefly considered hiring the services of one of the many available prostitutes. The thought of engaging her to ply her trade never entered his mind, but he did consider that walking about with one of the women might aid his disguise. The number of undercover policemen dissuaded him from the notion.

The streets appeared full of police dressed in civilian clothes. The trained investigator picked them out easily, standing on corners in unnatural groups, or wearing suits that were in much too good a shape for the denizens of Whitechapel. Above all, they all wore their standard police issue shoes, making each one as plain to Holmes as if they were in proper uniform.

Holmes' disciplined eyes moved from the policemen to the other people wandering the streets. Like himself, there were many men moving about in the gaslight. One could never be certain, but he felt he could discern the difference between those going to their jobs and the slower, more tired looking individuals who were returning from their employment. None of this aided in his quest and he felt that his normal methods of investigation were failing entirely in this matter. None of the men matched any of the witness descriptions except in the most general terms. He would have to follow half the population of Whitechapel if he used that as his only criterion.

"Watch where you're goin'!"

Holmes had let his attention fix on a couple across the street and did not notice a man moving out of a side doorway. He turned, quickly realizing the man he had bumped into was one of the undercover officers.

"Sorry govn'r," he said in a low voice, touching his battered cap as he tried to move around the policeman.

"Maybe sorry tain't enough!" growled the officer, clapping a firm grasp on his shoulder to keep him from continuing.

Holmes backed away a half step, trying to sound meek and contrite. "I says I was sorry. I'm just tryin' to get to the lodgin' house befores all the beds fills up."

The officer was having none of it. Apparently, the man had used the plain clothes duty as an excuse to frequent some of the pubs in the area. The smell of whiskey was heavy on his breath.

"I can get you a place for the night," the officer snapped. He held a clenched fist in Holmes' face. "In fact, I can fix you permanent right now, if you like."

The policeman had a companion, another undercover officer who grabbed his arm.

"Belkin!" he hissed in a hoarse whisper. "We're 'ere to keep on eye on things, not cause trouble! This man weren't doin' nothin'."

Belkin jerked his arm free of the man holding it. Doing so, his fist snapped towards Holmes, who blocked it away. The detective's actions were far too quick for someone that was at least partially inebriated.

"What's this?" demanded the drunken officer. "Are you takin' a swipe at me?"

The policeman swung at Holmes again, this time deliberately trying to strike him. The detective grabbed the officer's wrist firmly, preventing the blow from falling.

"I just stopped you from hitting me." The affected accent was gone and Holmes drew himself up to his correct height. His voice fell to a low growl as he finished. "I'm with you, you fool! Now let me pass!"

Belkin's arm dropped at the sudden change in tone from the man before him. His companion was none too happy with the change, either.

"Now you've done it, you sot!" he snapped. "This one's probably a bleedin' inspector!"

"Lucky for you," returned the detective, slumping back to his previous posture, "I'm just another investigator…"

Holmes started to walk past the men as he spoke, but his comment was cut short by the shrill blast of a police whistle from somewhere ahead. Again and again it sliced through the damp September air. As always, the private detective was immediately alert.

"Well, what are you waiting for?" he snapped at the two policemen. Without waiting for a reply, he took off at a dead run in the direction of the whistle.

Holmes ran as fast as he could, shedding some of the excess parts of his disguise as he did so. Through the twisting lanes of Whitechapel, he followed the frantic sounds of the police whistle. He forced his way through a crowd growing at Berner Street, confronted by a uniformed officer as he peeled the fake eyebrows from his forehead.

"No further," commanded the cop, his billy stick tapping firmly.

Holmes pushed past him with disdain. "I'm Sherlock Holmes!" He looked back to find his two companions had managed to keep close, though they were both panting, bent over with their hands on their knees as they breathed deeply. "Benkins! Help keep the crowd back!" he ordered as he walked into the darker reaches of the court.

Inside the gate, Holmes glanced quickly about. Lights were on in the upper floors of the boarding houses that lined one side. On the far end, a club of some sort was more brightly lit, with male figures silhouetted against the lights, vying to get a better view into the court. The side opposite the boarding houses was a group of commercial buildings which lay in darkness. He knew his cigarette makers occupied one of those building and marveled for a brief instant on how matters in the city always seemed to connect with one another.

The street lamps were out and most of the court was cloaked in darkness. A pool of light was framed on one side, furnished by a group of officers holding their lanterns. Holmes made his way directly to the group.

"Who is in charge here?" he demanded.

"Sgt. James, sir. And you are?"

"Sherlock Holmes," returned the detective. He did not wait, but pushed past the officers to the body. He knelt down and began his examination without asking for permission. "What information have you?"

The officer was sufficiently cowed by the detective's reputation and presence that he quickly recited what he knew.

"A Mr. Deimshutz from the club there found the body at 1:00 AM. The men lifted her…"

"They moved the body?" demanded Holmes curtly.

"Yes, sir. They thought she was just drunk."

"Damn!" cursed the detective in an unusual profanity. He forced himself to calm. "Continue, sergeant," he prompted.

"When they realized she was dead, they went out and found a group of officers."

Holmes pulled out his watch and checked it by the light of one of the lanterns. It was barely 1:20. He felt her face and reached under the rain sodden clothes to touch the body. It was still warm.

"Bring a lantern closer!" he ordered.

The bruising on the woman's throat was obvious, though the mutilations were much less severe than the previous case. Holmes stood and glanced around. A growing crowd was held outside the court and the men in the club were being contained.

"She is still warm, sergeant. Her clothes close to her body are dry. On a night like this, she could not have been here long. Certainly less than an hour; maybe a good deal less. What was this Deimshutz doing?"

"He was bringing his cart in with more supplies for the club, Mr. Holmes. His horse shied away and stopped and he didn't know it was a woman in the road until he got out and looked."

"Did he see anyone?"

“No, sir. As I said, he just thought she was drunk.”

“Curse it!” snapped Holmes, slamming a fist into his palm. “He probably interrupted the killer at his work!”

Holmes looked around the court again, his eyes more adjusted to the dim light. There were only two entrances. The one he had used was thoroughly blocked by the police.

“What of the other gate?”

“Still locked and secured,” assured the sergeant. “I have two men there, and a squad on the group in the club.”

Holmes nodded a grudging approval. “Good work, man,” he said. “Check everyone in the club for bloodstains on their hands or clothes. Question them to see if any of them know anything. Start talking to the residents of the boarding houses,” he said, pointing to the dilapidated buildings. “Perhaps one of them saw or heard something.”

“Yes, sir.”

He stopped the sergeant as he turned away.

“And have a man check the locks on the merchant buildings! I doubt he would break through there to get away, but you can never be sure.”

“As you say, sir!” The sergeant touched his helmet. Without hesitation, he then issued orders to the growing crowd of officers in the court.

Holmes looked about. There were only three easy access points to the court. Everything pointed to the gate he had used. The other was locked, so it would be difficult to use unless he climbed over it. The killer may have exited through the club, but would have been noticed unless he was a member or an associate. So with the horse cart partially blocking the gate, he had somehow slipped past Deimshutz and back into the main flow of Whitechapel. Such an act called for a cool head and steady nerve. For all his murderous rage, this killer always managed to keep his wits about him when engaged in his grisly work.

And as the master detective considered this and watched the policemen proceed about their duties, he heard the shrill call of more police whistles in the distance.

Holmes did not hesitate, walking quickly from Berner Street back to Commercial Road. All eyes looked to the west, where Commercial joined Whitechapel Road to become Aldgate. The detective ran in that direction.

The volume of the whistle grew. The officer could not be far away. In less than six blocks, he reached Mitre Square and found several constables standing over a still form. A woman lay in the light cast by their combined lamps, her abdomen opened as if she were on an autopsy table.

"How long?" demanded Holmes, not even bothering to introduce himself to the constables.

One stiffened at the firm question and answered automatically. "I patrol this square every fifteen minutes. She was not here at 1:30!"

Holmes snapped open his watch. It was barely fifty minutes past. He stepped away, shouting orders to the constables converging on the scene.

"Spread out! He's twenty minutes or less from this spot!"

On his command, most darted off in pairs and threes, each group taking a different route away from the ghastly scene. A few remained to secure the scene as a hansom pulled up. Lestrade and Abberline descended.

"Another one?" asked Abberline incredulously.

"I am afraid so," snapped Holmes. "I have dispatched your men. We may have him yet if the trail has not gone cold."

The words were hardly from his lips when the night air was again split by the sound of a police whistle. The whistle was close and they found the officer two blocks away on Goulston Street.

"This way, sir!" said the constable, holding a piece of cloth. The man elbowed his way past a number of gawkers, a few men and women still about despite the lateness of the hour.

Lestrade took the scrap from his hand. "What is it?"

"It appears it has been used to clean a thin blade," returned the policeman.

"If I'm not mistaken, the cloth is from this latest victim's petty coat!" concluded Holmes.

They were interrupted by shouting from further down the street. Holmes did not hesitate, but bumped into one of the bystanders as he turned in that direction. The detective had a brief impression of a younger man with chiseled features, but pushed past him without comment. A number of constables were shouting loudly, drawing the more officers. Holmes led his small contingent in their direction, where they were gathered around a fountain at the side of the street.

"The water is bloody!" announced a policeman.

Holmes was well pleased. They were hard on the trail of their quarry. The bloody cloth spoke to cleaning the knife; the bloody water to cleaning the hands. The unknown assailant was not far from this spot.

The detective's eyes darted about, looking for a clue as to which way the murder escaped. From further up Goulston, a group of five officers approached, covering the street from side to side. From both directions on Wentworth, the same was true. Had they encountered a man running in their direction, they would have apprehended him. There was only one way out, and that was the way they had come.

"Behind us!" shouted Holmes, reversing directions. Abberline and Lestrade struggled to catch up at the sudden change. "The criminal has double backed!"

They ran back down the street. The group near the constable was smaller; a few of the men who had been there earlier had departed. Holmes reached Aldgate and stopped, looking back and forth for any sign of someone leaving in haste. But everyone was standing about, waiting for more information from the police or for a glimpse of the corpse. His shoulders slumped: they had lost track of their quarry.

Lestrade did not need Holmes to explain. "Bloody hell!"

"Precisely," said Holmes. "We are close on the man's heels, and he still escapes us."

Abberline stepped closer. "Have you examined the bodies?"

Holmes shook his head. "I had a few minutes at the

first murder, but I have not done so here. The calls came too quickly."

There was a new flurry of shouts from Goulston Street. The constable who found the cloth was waving for them to return.

"Over here, sir! We found something else!"

They were led to a dead end alley, where a constable held a lamp on one of the walls. Words were written in chalk on the wall.

The Juwes are not the
men that will be blamed
for nothing

"What the devil does that mean?" asked Abberline.

"Scribbles," concluded Lestrade. "Nothing to do with our business."

"Constable?" asked Holmes.

"White, sir."

"Constable White, you found the cloth at the opening to this alley?"

"Yes, sir."

Holmes withdrew his notebook and jotted down the words from the wall. "I do not see this as a coincidence, though I cannot decipher the message. I will look at it when the light is better. For now, I need to examine the body."

Holmes returned to the site of the second murder accompanied by Lestrade. Abberline remained at the site of the wall markings to aid the constables working there.

On reaching Mitre Square, Holmes took a lantern from one of the constables and moved carefully around the disemboweled corpse, searching for any detail which would aid his investigation. The body lay under a street lamp, the woman's heavy clothing bunched beneath her. The abdomen was torn open in a horrid fashion and her entrails laid out on her shoulders. Besides the grievous wound at her throat, her face showed numerous cuts and nicks.

"That is new," pointed out Holmes to Lestrade.

"I see," said the inspector, trying to sound impressed by the observation.

The consulting detective moved off, working a circle around the body and checking the hard pavement. He bent down and picked a twig from the ground.

"You have found something?" asked Lestrade.

"A point of interest." He focused the beam of the lantern on what first appeared to be a twig. A closer examination proved it was something quite different.

"A grape branch."

Lestrade's tone was one of both disdain and wonder. Holmes carefully handed it to the policeman.

"A singular thing to find in such a location, is it not?" he observed, then continued his search.

For another half hour, he was engaged in moving carefully in a larger and larger radius from the corpse. At length, he returned to the body where the coroner was already at work preparing to remove it to the morgue. Holmes watched them in silence, unsure how to interpret the night's events.

"Sir?"

The detective found a constable near him, the man hesitant.

"Sorry to bother you, Mr. Holmes, but I know this woman."

"Yes?"

"Her name is Catherine, or Kate, Eddowes. We had her at Bishop's Gate Station early tonight."

Holmes' head snapped up, his interest piqued. "You had her in custody?"

"Yes, sir. A constable found her drunk and insensible around 7:30 and brought her into the station to sleep it off. She was awake and had her wits about her by 12:30, so she was released. I.." he paused, choked for a moment by the emotion of his own story. "I released her myself, sir. If...if.." His words faded away.

Holmes reached over and touched the man's arm. For one who prided himself on his cold detachment, he could be surprisingly sympathetic.

"You could not know, constable. There was no way to foresee such a horrible tragedy would befall her."

The man nodded, and walked silently away. Holmes shook his head in wonder. These murders affected them all in the most unpredictable ways. Lestrade strolled over as the doors were closed on the coroner's ambulance.

"Is there anything else, Mr. Holmes?"

Holmes shook his head, dejected at the lack of success. "The cobblestones yield nothing! I will return during the day when there is more light." He glanced past the policeman in the direction of Berner Street. "I suppose the other body is removed as well?"

"Yes."

"Then any evidence to be had there is probably trampled. I will inspect there in daylight as well."

"It has been a long night, Mr. Holmes," observed Lestrade, his voice heavy with emotion.

"Both long and unproductive," snapped Holmes in sudden irritation. He remembered the words on the wall of Goulston Street, and a bit of animation returned. "Come, Lestrade, let us inspect this cryptic message. Perhaps the night is not a total loss."

But as they turned to head off in this new direction, they were confronted by Abberline approaching them.

"Do not bother, Mr. Holmes!" he said, his voice bitter and angry. "That message no longer exists!"

"How can that be?" demanded the detective.

"It was the most singular and unbelievable experience of my professional life!"

The portly inspector spoke in anger, his voice rising. Several constables turned at the near shout and Abberline forced his tone to a hoarse whisper. Even so, he was barely able to relate the story through his ire.

"Sir Charles Warren himself appeared to follow the investigation."

Lestrade was impressed by the name. "The head of the city police?"

"The same," snapped Abberline. "We showed him the

words on the wall and he flew into a proper rage."

"Whatever for?"

"Juwes." Abberline spat the single word in disgust. "He feared the word would be seen and cause a fearful reprisal against the Jewish population of the city. He demanded the message be erased!"

"Erased!" Holmes spoke in horror at the very thought that valuable evidence would be destroyed. "You did not let him?"

"Mr. Holmes, I pleaded with him. I begged as I never have before in my life. Cover the words! Erase the single word! Anything that would leave the message intact until there was sufficient light for the police photographer to record it!" Abberline kicked the ground in anger and disgust. "He ignored us all. He grabbed a sponge and erased the words himself!"

"Warren can think no further back than his handling of the Jewish riots in the spring," concluded Lestrade.

"He worries about his career and we have this wretched business to resolve!"

Abberline's voice rose again. For the second time that evening, Holmes reached out a hand in sympathy.

"It is not your fault, inspector." He tapped the small notebook in his chest pocket. "We have the words. It is unlikely we would learn more from the actual printing."

"Holmes, you most of all appreciate the need to maintain the original evidence!"

The detective nodded. "I do indeed, Abberline. And I appreciate the difficulty of this case, inspector. I appreciate it much more than government bureaucrats, it appears."

"So you can shed no light upon this mystery?" There was a sense of hopelessness in Lestrade's words that touched even the cold heart of the great detective.

"None at the moment. But I am in it with you, my friends," returned Holmes. He pulled out a battered watch and checked the time. "It is past 5:00 AM and as you observed, Lestrade, it has been a long and eventful night. For my part, I plan to return to Baker Street and shed this disguise. I will return when the sun casts more light upon the scene. Rest assured, I will forward any discoveries I might make as quickly as possible."

It was a well-dressed Sherlock Holmes who awaited his brother in the Stranger's Room of the Diogenes club. The grime and ill-kept clothes of his disguise were gone. The detective paced with nervous energy stopping short as his brother slowly entered the room.

"You have had a busy night," said Mycroft, not bothering with a greeting.

"As you are well aware," returned the detective. "It is a fine, crisp Sunday morning. I thought I might convince you to journey with me to Whitechapel."

Mycroft was in the process of lowering his bulk into a chair and was frozen by the request. A smile darted across Holmes' face at catching his brother unprepared for such a proposal. The elder Holmes, for his part, regained his composure and finished seating himself. He gestured to the chair across from him while calling for the porter to bring tea.

"What a remarkable thought!" he said as the tea service was laid out before them.

The detective sat across from his brother, leaning forward in his chair with hands clamped on the top of his walking stick and chin resting upon them. His eyes were bright with amusement.

"I knew I would surprise you with that proposal."

Mycroft methodically prepared his tea, then lifted the cup and settled himself comfortably in the chair.

"You know, Sherlock, a month ago I would have laughed at the mere suggestion."

"And now?"

Mycroft smiled. It transformed Mycroft's usual stern visage and Holmes was pleased his request would be granted.

"Sharing your adventure with my friend the interpreter has given me a glimpse into this life of yours. I believe I begin to understand your fascination for the criminal."

"Then we may leave!" announced Holmes, jumping to his feet. "I already have a comfortable carriage waiting below."

The decision to go was more easily made than the reality of moving Mycroft from his lodgings. He first finished his tea at a leisurely pace, and then called for his coat and scarf. When well bundled against the elements, he slowly walked from the club. It took several more minutes to settle him within the coach.

"I was hoping we might proceed with some haste!" reproached Holmes as he seated himself across from his brother.

"I do *nothing* in haste," said Mycroft. "Haste makes for mistakes."

Holmes tapped the roof of the coach with his cane, and they clattered towards the East End.

“In my work,” sniffed the detective, “haste is often of the essence.”

They arrived at Berner Street. Holmes helped his brother from the carriage while instructing the coachman to await their return. A guinea reinforced the request. A constable still guarded the gate, and he touched his helmet as he recognized Holmes. He stepped aside, holding the gate open for the two men.

In the light of day, the scene of the crime was less intimidating. All corners of the small court were visible. Holmes led his brother to the right where the body had lain.

“She was found here, virtually in the roadway.” He knelt down, examining the cobblestones. “Some blood is still visible between the stones.”

“Last night’s rain has probably washed much away,” observed Mycroft. “You believe he was interrupted?”

“There can be little doubt. She was dead and her throat slashed, but little in the way of mutilation. Her body was still warm to the touch.”

“I see.” Mycroft waved his walking stick. “Certainly no place to hide, at least at this time of day. Your man is about his work and the gate starts to open. Over there!” He pointed to the opposite corner. “He must have moved to that corner and hid in the shadows.”

“No doubt,” agreed Holmes. “It is the only place he might have evaded detection.”

Mycroft waited while Holmes examined the indicated

corner. Despite a minute inspection, the detective found nothing of interest.

"It is to be expected. He was here too briefly."

Holmes straightened, looking towards the building containing the club. Mycroft smiled at the motion.

"You've had a revelation?" he asked.

"The killer must go from here to the scene of the next murder. He must find, kill, and mutilate her in less than a half hour. How does he do it?"

Mycroft considered the scene, the workings of his brain inscrutable behind his stern features.

"He can't", concluded the older Holmes. "Therefore, it was longer than half an hour." His cane tapped the cobblestones where the body was discovered. "He murdered this poor creature and was preparing to mutilate her. There was a distraction, probably someone leaving the club. He stops and withdraws into the dark corner. He decides it is too dangerous to continue his work here, so he leaves the body and seeks his sport elsewhere."

Holmes nodded in agreement. "Excellent, brother! The cart driver did not interrupt the killer. The police believed so because she could not have lain here too long before she was discovered. It is the only way our killer has enough time to commit the second crime."

The detective was pleased with this bit of reasoning. He pointed towards the gate.

"Perhaps there is more to be gained at the other scene." Mycroft turned to the waiting carriage, but Sherlock stopped him. "No, from here, we must walk for a spell."

Mycroft let out a long sigh. "That is a distasteful word,

Sherlock."

The two men started the walk towards Mitre Square. Holmes signaled and the coach followed at a fair distance. They had taken just a few steps before Mycroft paused. Holmes looked on expectantly.

"There is a third possibility, Sherlock."

"I have missed something?"

"Perhaps. What if the second crime was committed by a different person?"

"Another killer? One attempting to imitate the first?"

"You must concede the possibility."

Holmes was perplexed by the notion. The concept that he might be pursuing more than a single murderer had not occurred to him. He nodded to allow the prospect.

"I will try to factor that into the overall picture, Mycroft. But come, we must continue. See if there is anything along the way that we might connect to the killings."

The two men walked in silence, their piercing gaze sweeping from side to side in the roadway, each searching for anything that might prove a clue in the baffling case. People along the road shouted questions and insults, but neither brother responded to taunts. Their focus was absolute and unwavering during their short hike. But the stroll was fruitless, and neither the thin detective nor his larger brother found anything they could connect to the case.

They passed the guards at the entrance to Mitre Square, who acknowledged Holmes with a brief nod. Once within the square, Holmes pointed at the street lamp to his right.

"There is where he posed the body," he explained, stepping to the lamp. Mycroft followed in his slower tread, but agreed with the other's observation.

"Yes, Sherlock, I see your point. Posed indeed. But why?"

"For the news agencies!" snapped Holmes, anger creeping into his voice. "All for the larger headlines in the morning *Times*!"

Mycroft nodded, turning to view the entire area of the square. "The only street lamp in the entire square." Mycroft moved his bulk to where the body had lain, examining the cobblestones closely. "Yes, I can see where some of the blood ran, but you described the state of the body to me. Surely such mutilations, even if performed post mortem, would have left far more blood upon the ground." He raised his eyes to the building that lined that edge of the square.

"These are lodging rooms I take it?"

Every window hosted a dozen faces, each craning to catch a glimpse of the murder scene. And as quickly as each came, they were pushed along by a crowd behind, all of whom had paid their penny for a look out one of those windows.

"Crowded lodgings, I gather," returned Holmes.

"Too public a place to perform his killing and mutilation, I should think." Mycroft turned to the opposite side of the square.

"My thoughts precisely, brother Mycroft." He started for the opposite side, where the buildings lay dark and deserted. He had taken only a few steps when he cried out. "Aha! I believe we are on the right trail."

Mycroft peered at the dark spot on the indicated cobblestone. “Blood, you think?”

“Without a doubt!” returned Holmes confidently. “If these stones had not been wet last evening, you would have no doubts either. This way!” He pointed with his walking stick and started off at a pace his brother could never match.

Holmes still scrutinized the door as Mycroft approached, his breath spent.

“You are too much for me, Sherlock.”

The younger brother smiled. “I do forget your infirmity, brother. I am often caught up in the spirit of the chase.” He tapped the door with his walking stick. “But the time waiting for your arrival was well spent. This must be a bloody hand print, though partially washed by the rain. There are further splatters on these steps.”

Mycroft nodded, slowly lowering his bulk to sit on the edge of the stoop. “Indeed, I believe you are correct,” he said between gulps for air. “Might I offer to check these more closely,” he continued slowly, patting the wooden steps with his hand, ”while you perform a thorough investigation of the interior?”

Holmes nodded, realizing the extent to which he had taxed his brother’s physical abilities. “Spend your time here. I shall return shortly.”

Holmes was forced to press his shoulder roundly against the door for it to open. Once inside, it was obvious the buildings had been abandoned for some time, though there were indications of frequent visitors. Many sets of footprints marked the dirty floor, but he followed the twin drag marks that issued from a further room. The two broken lines were further punctuated by the occasional dark smear of dried blood. And in the far room, he found his true murder scene.

On a near wall, there was a slight splatter of blood and a fleck of skin. On the floor, the dust was disturbed by a long oblong shape and several more drops of dried, brown blood.

Holmes moved quickly. He found a more complete hand print and pulled out his tape. After recording the measurement, he moved carefully and was rewarded with the outline of a boot toe clearly marked in the dust with the help of another few drops of dried blood. He was in his element at last, able to find tangible clues created by the author of these crimes.

Mycroft was still upon the stoop, his magnifying glass at work upon an edge of a tread, when Holmes emerged from the interior. The elder brother was breathing more easily, and smiled at the detective.

"Your search was successful, I perceive."

"Our surmise was correct," confirmed Holmes. "Finally, I can create a picture of the killer."

"Then our time here is well spent," concluded the other. He heaved himself slowly to his feet. "I see from the stairs he dragged her out. Both heels made fresh marks upon each tread."

"Indeed. He killed her and performed most of the mutilation here before moving her body across the square and placing it beneath the street lamp. While he may have spent fifteen to twenty minutes inside, he need spend only a minute or two under the light."

"Yes. It would reduce his chance of discovery if he commits the crime in private, and then moves the body to a position to be discovered."

"It would appear so." Holmes looked at his brother, who was still breathing heavily from his exertions.

"Come," said Holmes, stepping down to his brother and taking his arm. "You have done more than enough. I shall let you ride the remainder of our tour."

With an uncommon tenderness, Holmes aided Mycroft from the square and into the waiting carriage. The driver moved them slowly up Aldgate, then into the more crowded spaces of Goulston Street. Holmes tapped his shoulder to halt the carriage.

"It was here that the words were found?" asked Mycroft.

"A few steps down that alley."

"And a scrap of bloody cloth on the street. He wanted to be sure it was found."

"Undoubtedly."

"Juwes. That is an odd usage indeed. You are aware of the Masonic connection to it?" Mycroft knew it was unnecessary to await reply. "Another thought, if I may be so bold? You saw it only briefly, in questionable light. It may have been J-i-e-v-e-s, Jieves."

It was a subtle point. Even for Sherlock Holmes, so assured in his own powers, had to admit the validity of his brother's observation.

"French for Jews." Holmes nodded. "That is indeed a possibility. We shall not know for certain unless we lay our hands upon the killer."

"I believe our work is concluded," announced Mycroft. Holmes communicated briefly with their driver, then settled across from his brother. "You say Sir Warren removed the words with his own hand?"

"And over the objections of all of his subordinates, if I might drive a final nail."

"I shall provide us a fine luncheon at the Diogenese Club, Sherlock." Mycroft settled back and closed his eyes in contemplation. "As to Sir Warren, you have provided nails and lumber." He sank down in some satisfaction, comfortable at last. There was even a slight smile on his lips as he concluded his comment. "I shall work them into a coffin."

Monday, October 1 — *Saucy Jack*

Holmes stood at his window, ignoring the shouted questions from the reporters below. He drew on the pipe, while examining the mob below with some interest. He concluded the size of the group had stabilized, simply because there was a limit to the number of reporters in the city. Still, neither Lestrade nor Abberline had assigned a constable to drive them from his doorstep. He sighed, knocking the bowl of the pipe against the window sill to clear the ashes, and withdrew into the parlor.

The letter he dispatched to Abberline the previous afternoon had yet to entice a response from the inspector. In the meantime, he set himself back to writing telegrams. He had a number of ideas on the Baskerville case, all which stemmed from Sir Charles' brother going off to disappear in the Honduras. It was always a challenge to prepare a detailed query without being so wordy that telegraphers objected to the length. Even so, the detective had a few operators on retainer, as it were, paying them a few shillings extra for addressing his special needs.

He finished the task and dispatched the houseboy to the telegraph office with the inquiries. He was trying to determine what to do next when a carriage arrived with constables and a request to come to the Yard. Holmes grabbed his coat and hat and was escorted to the carriage by the officers. He was further pleased to see that two of the constables remained behind and started clearing the street of the loitering reporters.

At Scotland Yard, Holmes was escorted to a room apart from the normal commons used by the detectives. Set up for conferences, it had a large table with chairs and the walls were lined with blackboards, all covered with various information related to the killings. As he waited for the inspectors, Holmes reviewed them, stopping before one that contained the words written on the wall in Whitchapel:

The Juwes are the men
That Will not be
Blamed for nothing

Holmes examined the odd phrase again before pulling out his notebook and writing on the blackboard. At that moment, Abberline, closely followed by Lestrade, came into the room.

"What the devil are you doing?" demanded the chief inspector.

"I recorded a slightly different version of this text," explained the detective.

The Juwes are not
The men That Will be
Blamed for nothing.

After completing the phrase, Holmes concluded by writing "*Jieves?*" at the bottom of the board. Abberline reviewed the additions before taking his seat in a bit of a huff.

“It is jibberish!” He shook his head, a flush of anger rising to his cheeks. “Still, that pimple Warren erased them before we could be sure!” Abberline tapped his finger on the table for emphasis. “I am nearly driven to distraction by the Metropolitan police and their meddling in this. Add to it the involvement of the City Police and the pressure from the Home Secretary…” He let his words of frustration die, but the consulting detective was sympathetic.

“My brother is not without influence in the government,” he explained. “I have relayed these conflicts to him.” He recalled his brother’s reaction to Sir Charles’ actions. “I can say nothing definite, but I think Sir Charles will be otherwise occupied and too busy to take a personal hand in matters from this point forward.”

“That would be at least one weight off our necks,” said Lestrade.

The consulting detective smiled, taking a seat across from the two policemen.

“And I concur with your analysis of the words, Abberline. My brother made the other observation, that the word may have been ‘Jieves’ instead of ‘Juwes’. But that still sheds no light on the meaning of strange phrase.”

The chief inspector agreed.

“I am inclined to believe it is a false lead, that it was simply placed there to distract us. The press has tied the Emma Smith killings to the rest, including the possible gang involvement. Our man will know that if he is reading the papers.”

“Yes, I think we can be sure he is reading the newspapers,” agreed Holmes, somewhat reluctantly. His thirst for clues and puzzles had to be put aside in face of the facts. “Unless new details emerge to tie this into the killings, I believe you are correct. We were close on our killer’s heels Sunday morning. It is quite possible he did this just to draw our attention and aid his escape.”

Lestrade was intrigued by the possibility.

“If that is the case, this man has as cool a nerve as I have ever seen.”

Holmes rubbed the center of his forehead to dispel a slight headache.

“Indeed. It will not do to underestimate him.”

“Still, there is this.” Abberline held up Holmes letter. “We examined that room this morning, and it would seem you are correct. We desire to keep the information confidential for the moment.”

“Of course,” returned Holmes. “Only myself and my brother are aware of it at the moment, and you may trust our discretion.”

Lestrade leaned forward. “And you think your estimate of the killer’s height is accurate?”

Holmes smiled. “Have I ever been wrong by more than an inch either way?”

Lestrade sat back, a smile on his face.

“Something concrete at last!”

“There are a great many men in London that are that height and wear those types of shoes,” cautioned Abberline. “But you are right. It will let us eliminate a large number of suspects.”

“And what else?” asked Holmes.

"I am unsure of your conclusion that the killer may be of the middle or upper class, Holmes. The people in the area think the police are shielding a member of the upper class who is doing this for sport. The government is sure it is being done by Red Republicans intent on bringing down the government." He paused, the weight of the investigation heavy on his face and in his voice. "I wonder if they may not be far off. There was almost a riot this morning when some poor sot was being arrested and someone suggested he might be 'Jack the Ripper'. I have Lusk and his 'Vigilance Committee" stirring up trouble. And now you give me this implying a member of the upper classes?"

Holmes nodded gravely.

"My analysis is, of course, strictly confidential, Abberline, and I do not make the suggestion lightly.

"First, our man seems to possess medical knowledge. If that is the case, it is unlikely he is a member of the lower class, unless his fortunes have fallen from some height.

"Second, the prints of the shoes showed they were a common type, but not well worn. It implies the killer has these common shoes to wear while going about this business but has something different to wear at other times. A member of the lower class could not afford a second pair of shoes.

"Finally, there is the grape branch," continued the detective with a flourish.

"I was wondering when that might come in!" piped Lestrade.

The detective smiled. Lestrade was one of the better inspectors in the Yard. He might not see how a clue added to the complexion of a case, but he was always quick enough to accept it was important when Holmes deigned to mention it.

"Grapes are not a treat well known in the East End," explained Holmes. "For that clue to be found near the body implies the branch came from our killer and the killer has sufficient income to purchase them."

"I can agree with that," said Abberline, yielding the point. "But all together, your view of this killer is all supposition and few hard facts."

"Not *supposition*, Abberline," corrected Holmes. "Deductions."

"But a member of the upper class?" protested Lestrade. "I just do not see how it is possible!"

Holmes shook his head. "I do not engage in politics, Lestrade. In crime, all classes are treated equally. Would you expect a member of the upper class to appear in a fine carriage wearing tall hat, tails and white tie when visiting Whitechapel? No, our man is someone who has taken pains to blend into the surroundings. He is not caught because he is successful in his efforts.

"And do not take the conclusion of 'upper class' too literally, gentlemen," the detective continued. "I say 'upper class' as a general term, but I am using it to describe the killer's financial condition. He is a man with means and does not scrape by in the day to day manner common in the East End."

Lestrade accepted the explanation. Still there was a glint in his eye that alerted Holmes there was more to come.

"You are holding something back," he stated.

The two policemen exchanged glances. Lestrade reached into his pocket and withdrew a postcard, sliding it across the table to Holmes. The writing was the same style and red ink as the one they previously showed him.

I was not codding dear old Boss when I gave you the tip. You'll hear about Saucy Jack's work tomorrow. Double event this time. Number one squealed a bit. Couldn't finish straight off. Had not time to get ears for police. Thanks for keeping last letter back till I got to work again.

JACK THE RIPPER

"Ah…same scribble and ink. No doubt the handwriting matches. Early Sunday postmark." The detective considered that for a moment. "Maybe too early for the extra editions, but perhaps not." He re-read the words and handed the card back to Lestrade.

"A clever forgery," he announced. "However, it is a fake."

Both policemen were amazed at the announcement, but it was Abberline who was the first to question it.

"How can you say that? He said he would remove the ears and, in fact, Stride's ears were nicked as if he was going to remove them!"

"True," agreed Holmes. "But consider we have now identified the actual location of the second murder and know our man had sufficient time, in private, to mutilate the corpse. If he had wanted to send the ears as proof, he needs only spend a few extra seconds to remove them. He did not.

"Either these letters are fakes, or the killer is deliberately making statements to cast doubt on them. I do not think our man would go to that trouble. He is too intent over the public seeing his work. When he decides to taunt the police directly, there will be no doubt it is from him."

Abberline and Lestrade were forced to concede the logic of Holmes' argument. Even so, Lestrade was not willing to completely abandon the clue.

"But the postmark! Who could have known of both murders so quickly?"

"A very good point, Lestrade, and a vexing puzzle." The detective pondered it for a long minute before being able to make a reply. "Whoever has written these is someone who has followed the case closely. As we determined from the first postcard, he is a man of education who is trying to disguise that fact. The term "boss" implies an American or Canadian. And the follow-up card and taunt of 'keeping the last letter back' implies he wants to see them published."

Lestrade shook his head sadly. "A newspaper man. Someone with ties to America."

"Precisely."

Abberline was not pleased with that determination.

"Must we now determine the guilty party and prosecute them for interfering with the investigation?"

Holmes chuckled. "Abberline, you have done me a favor and removed the news hounds from my doorstep. I shall return it. I believe I know who wrote these, and I shall take it upon myself to put an end to them."

"Excellent," returned the inspector.

"But in turn, I must ask for another favor," replied Holmes.

"And what is that?"

"My mail!" said the detective in frustration. "I have bags of the stuff and get more every day! Watson has made the effort to sort it out, but I have sent him to Grimpen on another case."

"And you want us to review your mail?" Lestrade asked with some incredulity.

It was Holmes' turn to yield to the efficiency of the official force. It was a rare turn of events when he was forced to do so.

"Gentlemen, you have put together an efficient method of reviewing and sorting. The fact you can turn up that postcard in so short of time proves it. I have no doubts you will find a brother or two of that card within my mail. But I have reached a point where I can either investigate the case, or review my mail. There is insufficient time to do both!"

"And mail unrelated to Whitechapel?"

"I must trust your discretion," Holmes returned. "I am at such a crossroads, I am unable to find the unrelated missives. I will look through the mail bags for anything I immediately know does not concern Whitechapel. Everything else I shall rely on your review."

Lestrade, who had worked with Holmes so much more closely over the past several years, appreciated what an event it was to have the consulting detective request assistance from Scotland Yard.

"You may trust us, Holmes. I shall personally break

anyone who violates that trust!"

It was a relief to arrive at Baker Street. For the first time in two weeks, Holmes was able to enter his residence openly without be accosted by a mob of newspaper men. A constable strolled in front of the residence and touched his cap to the detective. Holmes returned the salute with a courteous nod.

A mail bag sat to one side of the room. Homes tossed his cloak, hat and stick to the side, and lifted the bag to the table. Mrs. Hudson would appreciate, no doubt, that he took a few moments to remove the tableware and tea service from the table before emptying the contents of the bag.

It took but a moment to spot the thick, pink envelope in Watson's handwriting. He took that out and was preparing to return the remainder to the mailbag, but suddenly had a thought. He sorted through the remainder, tossing them into the bag as he completed each group. At last, he found what he knew would be there: a postcard written in red ink.

With little ceremony, he scooped the remaining letters into the mailbag and set the bag to one side. Lestrade was sending a constable to collect them all in the morning. He took the other two pieces of mail, turned up the gas in the darkening room, and sat down.

The postcard was much like the one Lestrade presented earlier. The writing was sloppy, with dots of splashed and smeared ink. The postmark was the same as the one received by Scotland Yard. Whoever had sent them was not being careful in that regard. He read the words carefully:

I saw you Sunday after I finished number 2. Glad to see the police have called for help, but I think Saucy Jack is a step or two ahead of even the master detectv.

JACK THE RIPPER

Holmes tapped the corner of the card against his temple, as if he might absorb some vital bit of data from it through osmosis. There was nothing in the words to indicate it was written by the actual killer, and certainly nothing that would not be known to a reporter at the scene. He set it to the side and took Watson's envelope.

The report was written on white paper. Evidently, getting Watson to use the pink envelopes had strained his conservative nature to the limit. But as he read, he appreciated his friend's literary talents. His description of the trip, the scene, the people all helped Holmes visualize Grimpen and Baskerville, changing the plain map pinned to the wall into a three dimensional locale for the detective.

The cast of characters was fleshed out in the lengthy missive. Besides Mortimer and his wife, there were the Barrymores, the housekeeper and his wife. Nearby were the Stapletons, a brother and sister who had moved from the north country to pursue his dreams of being a naturalist. Mr. Frankland of Lafter Hall, an eccentric who spent a fortune in litigation as little more than a hobby. Most interesting of all was that Selden, the Notting Hill murderer, had escaped from prison and was loose somewhere on the moor.

Holmes nodded, recalling the case. Selden had been caught before he arrived on the scene, even though the local inspector had asked for his assistance. He had been loose for five days and was believed to have been claimed by the bog. *Five days.* Not nearly enough time for the madman to be involved in any of the Whitechapel killings.

The detective could not help but muse over the fact that two such beasts as Selden and this Jack the Ripper were loose at the same time.

The last page was on different paper and hastily scribbled in pencil. Obviously, Watson had added it at the last minute.

Holmes:
Just saw the post for London on the two murders Sunday morning. Trust all is well. Do not hesitate to ask for my return if assistance is required.

Your friend,
Watson

The detective smiled. Watson was ever ready to provide his support. He took Watson's letter and the postcard over to his writing table.

First, he wrote a quick note to Lestrade about the postcard that could be taken with the mailbags in the morning. He did not send the card along, since he believed it to be a fake. He had a glimmering of who the perpetrator was, but needed more confirmation.

He pulled down his reference book. His memory served him correctly, and he penned a telegram to the *San Francisco Examiner*. A quick response from that organization would confirm his suspicions on the origin of the postcard.

The letter from Watson had laid out a list of possible suspects in and around Baskerville Hall. There was always the possibility that the culprit was still unrevealed, but Holmes could investigate those that Watson had listed. There were another half-dozen telegrams generated as a result.

Finally, he spent a much longer time writing a return letter to his friend to assure him that Grimpen was the place where his services were needed at the moment. Thus far, he could not have asked for a better field agent than his trusted friend, and he tried carefully, in his own cold and calculating way, to reassure Watson how invaluable his assistance was.

When finished he set his pen down, kneading his right hand to relieve a cramp. It had been a full evening's work. He rang the bell and sent the house boy off to the telegraph office. The letters would be posted in the morning. He rubbed his eyes to relieve the strain, then took the letter from Watson and returned to his chair. He filled his pipe from the slipper, lit it, and sat immobile, letting his mind wander the Grimpen Mire and consider each of the various denizens in turn.

Tuesday, October 2 *Whitehall*

Holmes was awakened by a great pounding at the door and the sound of commotion coming from the lower level. Loud complaints from Mrs. Hudson followed the heavy footfalls up the stairs to his rooms. The detective barely had managed to close his dressing gown before Inspector Gregson, the young and promising protégé to Lestrade, burst in. His face was flustered, his voice unnerved.

"Holmes! We need you immediately!"

"Calm yourself, Gregson!" Holmes voice was a sharp bark, the rebuke like a slap to the panicked policeman.

Gregson calmed visibly, but his words still came in a rush.

"We must leave at once! There is another body!"

Holmes gestured at his attire. "I trust I may be allowed to get dressed first?"

The sarcasm had the desired effect and the inspector quieted further.

"Of course, sir!"

There was a tone of embarrassment in the reply. Holmes retired to his bedroom to quickly dress but could hear the policeman pacing nervously in the sitting room. Gregson had almost reached his original state of agitation by the time the detective returned.

The coach rushed through the London streets, but the course was not directed towards Whitechapel. Instead, they drove towards Westminster.

Gregson rocked in his seat across from Holmes, and not all of the motion was due to the carriage. The policeman wrung his hands in torment and the detective finally broke his own cardinal rule and asked for more information in hopes of relieving the man's distress.

"We are lost in this horror. Truly lost, Mr. Holmes!"

The detective tried to bring his young companion back to a world of rationality. For Holmes, it was the only way and the only manner he had available was to ask questions.

"Where is the body if not Whitechapel?"

"Whitehall, sir! On the very grounds where the new Scotland Yard building is being constructed!"

"Scotland Yard!" Holmes could not suppress his surprise, but tried to hide the irony he felt at the revelation. "Was it displayed like the others?"

Gregson shook his head, his voice touched with fear. "Worse, sir. Much worse!"

Holmes could not imagine how it could be worse than the display he witnessed two days before, but held back any comment. The sight had worked the policeman to a fever pitch, and he did not want to test the young man's nerves further. He fell silent, wondering what he would discover at Scotland Yard.

The scene at the construction site spoke to the panic Holmes saw in the young policeman. All manner of officials dashed about, from constables to full inspectors. The workmen, for their part, stood about in amused groups until the constables singled them out with questions. Adding to the general air of confusion, the inevitable hoards of reporters also moved through the crowd.

Holmes was recognized immediately as he stepped from the police coach, and the swarm of newsmen pressed in his direction. Gregson organized a cordon of constables to keep the reporters back and shield the detective as he was led to the foundation of the new building. Lestrade came forward, his hair awry and his manner panicked and disorganized.

"Holmes! I am glad you came so quickly!" " The detective felt a thrill that his name was shouted with such enthusiasm.

"Lead on, Lestrade." Holmes forced himself to be his normal brisk and business-like self. The fear in the air was palpable, and he needed those about him to focus on the work at hand. "Gregson says there is a body!"

The police inspector guided their way into the interior, the detective falling in step beside him. Holmes usually had no problem keeping up with the shorter Lestrade, but the policeman set a rapid pace that challenged his longer legs.

"It was discovered in a store room this morning. A workman states he placed some tools in the room on Saturday. No one else admits to being in it since."

They rounded a corner and a group of men at a door

on their left blocked their way.

"Let us through, please," barked Lestrade.

The men parted before them and Holmes entered the darkened room, lit only by a dozen constable's lanterns. The body, or what remained of it, lay in the center of the room. The detective felt his throat tighten as his eyes adjusted to the dim light and he saw what lay upon the floor.

The naked torso of a woman rested on some scraps of cloth. Arms, legs and head were missing. An older man, with a short beard and pince-nez spectacles looked up from the corpse. Holmes recognized him as Dr. Philip Bond, one of the Yard's surgeons.

"What do you make of it, Bond?" asked the detective as he pulled out his glass and knelt down to inspect the remains more closely.

The surgeon mopped his forehead with a handkerchief though the room was cool. As with everyone else, the unease was written upon his features.

"She was probably around 24, no outward sign of injuries. The amputations were all performed post mortem."

Holmes tried to move the stub of her left arm, but it was completely rigid.

"She has been dead quite some time based on the rigor."

The police surgeon nodded. "Definitely. At least a week. The surgical *work* is very neat and professional."

Holmes spent several minutes going over the grizzly discovery. Each wound was inspected, then the surface of the torso for any possible clues. There was little to be found, though he used tweezers to pick off a suspicious scrap of clothe. He rose, looking to the police surgeon.

"The cuts are all extremely clean. The right arm is removed much higher than the left."

"Yes, I noted that."

Holmes tried to remember something Watson had mentioned about a severed arm. His keen memory recalled the brief discussion.

"Several weeks back, you were mentioned in the Times regarding a woman's arm found in the Thames."

The comment broke upon the police surgeon as if a light were dawning.

"By God, Holmes, you have hit upon it!" Bond returned to the body, inspecting cuts on the body's right shoulder. "Yes, I will not be at all surprised if that is not this young woman's arm!"

"According to the Times, you thought the arm was placed in the river as some sort of medical student prank following the murder from the previous Saturday. Why did you think that?"

From the uncertain panic in his voice from minutes before, his tone took on one of professional discussion. The horror of the remains lying on the floor were forgotten as he talked with the detective, two colleagues engaged in a casual conversation.

"The neatness of the surgery," he explained. "This was not done by some butcher." He gestured down to where all the limbs and head were removed. "Each amputation shows the signs of a tourniquet being applied. The surgeries were done quickly and with the proper tools. That is why I thought I might be a medical student."

Holmes pointed to the body, his voice taking on the tone of a lecturer. His manner was having the desired affect on the policemen around him. All were now listening to him rather than looking at the gruesome remains on the floor.

"So, we have here a young woman, cause of death uncertain. She has been dead a minimum of 3 weeks. We know this because that's when her arm was discovered and it was removed post mortem. All of the appendages have been removed professionally." He turned back to the police surgeon, his pointed question punctuating the facts to draw a conclusion. "And where, Dr. Bond, might a body be kept for that period of time and show no insect infestations, as are obviously missing in this case?"

Bond nodded, agreeing with the conclusion suggested by the detective without hesitation.

"A morgue."

"A morgue," concluded Holmes, suppressing the normal condescension he felt when he arrived at an obvious conclusion the police had overlooked. "That fits with the professional removal of limbs and the delayed decay of the body."

Lestrade was still confused by the point being made. "But if she were held in a morgue, would not the body's disappearance be reported?"

Bond smiled, completing the thought suggested by the master detective.

"Mr. Holmes is suggesting my original conclusions on the arm are correct. This is not a body, but a medical cadaver."

Lestrade's confusion turned to anger at the announcement. He fairly stumbled over his own words as he spoke. "You are suggesting this poor woman's body was used in this fashion by medical students, then summarily dumped here as a *prank*?"

"I am virtually certain of it, Lestrade." Holmes paused, considering the unsightly remains and their location. "But prank is not the word I would use."

He paused for a longer time, considering possibilities. At length, Lestrade interrupted the reverie, his anger little abated by the delay.

"If you suspect something, you best let me know, Holmes!"

Holmes waved him off.

"Suspect, yes, but that is far from knowing in this case, Lestrade." He held up a hand to forestall the inspector protest. "I am sure this has nothing to do with Whitechapel. It may be someone trying to use the notoriety of the case for their own amusement or to create headlines."

"Your phantom newsman again?"

"This is no phantom," returned Holmes.

He knelt down, considering the body in the dim light. "Twenty-four you say, Bond? Thick build, dark hair. Probably childless."

"That appears accurate, Holmes," agreed the surgeon.

Holmes stood and looked around for Gregson. He waved to the young inspector but spoke to Lestrade.

"I will launch some inquiries. There cannot be too many cadavers received matching that description in early September. If Inspector Gregson can escort me past the reporters, I will begin at once."

Lestrade touched Holmes' shoulder to stop him before he could leave.

"This is going beyond the bounds of pranks, Holmes. Not only is it using some poor woman for a heartless hoax, it is interfering with active investigations!"

The detective nodded. He would not be pleased with someone disrupting one of his cases, but he saw a connection with other events at the periphery of the Whitechapel crimes.

"Trust me, Lestrade. If my suspicions are correct, I shall put an end to it as surely as if you had the perpetrator in the dock!"

Thursday, October 4 *The Modern Age*

Another thick letter arrived from Watson, but the detective had no time to review it. That morning, he had to attend the Eddowes inquest and give evidence, since he had investigated the scene.

It was his first appearance at one of the Whitechapel inquests. When called, he gave his evidence in a dry, direct manner. Whatever questions were asked, he answered without embellishment.

"Mr. Holmes," asked the coroner, "You are noted within the police fraternity for your ability to create theories about crimes."

"I prefer to call them deductions," replied the detective wryly.

There were a few chuckles in the room at the comment, but the coroner was not amused by the response.

"Deductions, then," he returned. "And do you have any *deductions* you can share with this inquest?"

"Doctor, I have no deductions at this point I have not already shared with the police. Anything else I might add would be idle speculation."

He made no mention of the discovery of the probable murder scene. In a discussion with Abberline and Lestrade, they had decided to keep the information private in the hope it would give them an edge over the killer. It would add nothing to the results of the inquest and still contributed little to the identity of the murderer. Without direct questions concerning the issue, he felt no need to offer the information.

"Indeed!"

"Yes, sir. We are plagued by a surplus of *conjecture* as it is, and I see no need to add to the volumes appearing in the press." He stopped and looked at the coroner in all candor. "If I develop the slightest theory that will help bring this monster to justice one day sooner, I will not hesitate to lay it before the police officials without a moment's hesitation."

"You appear to be playing your involvement in this affair rather close to the vest, Mr. Holmes. That is not your reputation."

"Reputations do not always reflect actual practice, sir. I never speculate about the nature of a case in public, regardless of written newspaper accounts to the contrary."

Lestrade stood up before the coroner could direct another question.

"Sir, may I be allowed to comment on Mr. Holmes involvement in this case?" The coroner nodded in his direct, and the inspector continued. "Mr. Holmes has always aided the department whenever we have requested his assistance. This case is no different. I would also add that Mr. Holmes is the soul of discretion and always limited his comments on cases, either one in the department or his own private consultation, to matters dealing with the resolution. I can assure the speculations attributed to him by the press are pure fabrication."

The coroner yielded the point, but there seemed a tone of sarcasm in his reply.

"Thank you for vouching for Mr. Holmes' character, inspector."

Lestrade straightened, obviously offended by the response.

"Sir, there are few men of whom I can truly say I would trust with my life without hesitation. Mr. Holmes is one of those men."

The coroner was taken aback by Lestrade's response. Holmes sensed that a rebuke might be forthcoming and stepped into the uncomfortable silence.

"Do you have any other questions that require my services, doctor?"

The coroner appeared to consider continuing his rebuke, but he did not. Instead, his reply was simple.

"No, Mr. Holmes, we have no further questions for you. Thank you for your time."

Holmes stood and bowed slightly to the panel

"Always at your service, gentlemen."

Holmes waited for the remainder of the inquest. As expected, the result of "murder by person or persons unknown" came quickly. He waited for Lestrade, and thanked the inspector for his kind endorsements. The two men were leaving the building together when they were confronted by Tallman, the reporter.

"Mr. Holmes, Mr. Holmes!" shouted Tallman, leading the pack of newsmen that pushed in their direction.

"Yes, Mr. Tallman?" returned the detective, his tone cool.

The reporter was unaffected by the icy response.

"Inspector Lestrade summarized your comments to the press…"

"Very succinctly, in my estimation!" interrupted Holmes.

Tallman chuckled, but was undaunted.

"As you say! You have nothing further to add than your statement in the inquest today?"

Holmes stopped, eye to eye with the American.

"Mr. Tallman, if I have anything additional for you, you may rest assured I shall contact you directly."

The reporter smiled. "You are promising me an exclusive in the presence of my peers?"

Holmes, smiled and made no reply. Two constables appeared and cleared a path for the detective and police inspector to a waiting cab.

"I do not like that American," observed Lestrade. "He is far too pushy, in my opinion."

"*Pushy*," repeated Holmes. "As good a word as any, I supposed."

The detective smiled, a devilish grin he usually reserved for sharing a confidence with Watson.

"I will share a speculation with you, Lestrade, if you must promise not to repeat it."

"Regarding that Tallman fellow?"

Holmes leaned closer and lowered his voice.

"I believe Tallman is responsible for the red ink postcards."

Lestrade sat back, shocked at the accusation.

"I shall have him arrested for interference!" the inspector sputtered, clearly angry at the implications.

Holmes chuckled. "We will not need criminal prosecution, Lestrade. I am awaiting confirmation and, when I have it, be assured we shall see no more of those postcards from *Jack the Ripper*."

There were a number of telegrams sitting on the table next to Watson's letter. Holmes took them and quickly sorted them. The first stack held the responses to his inquiries regarding Baskerville. Another group came from several sources unrelated to his inquiries, so he would need to read their contents and determine if they applied to the current investigations. The final two telegrams, however, held the responses to his most immediate questions. The first was from San Francisco, California, in the United States. The second came from St. Thomas Hospital.

Holmes quickly opened the first message and read the few lines. With eager anticipation, he quickly ripped open the second. With his customary cry of triumph when his deductions were confirmed, he took out a blank telegram sheet and scratched a hasty invitation.

"Mrs. Hudson!"

His call to the landlady was unanswered and in his usual impatience, he called her a second time before her tread was heard on the stairs.

"Mrs. Hudson," he said, when she came to his door. "Have Billy run this down to the telegraph office at once!"

"Yes, Mr. Holmes."

The landlady turned away, but Holmes as quickly called her back.

"And lunch, Mrs. Hudson! I am ready for some lunch!"

"Yes, Mr. Holmes. And anything else?"

"I am expecting a visitor at four o'clock. A pot of tea would be nice."

"As you wish, Mr. Holmes."

The long suffering landlady turned away and went back down the stairs. Holmes returned to his mail and telegrams while waiting for her to return with his luncheon.

A letter from Watson detailed the minutia of occurrences since his previous missive. The doctor spent a considerable effort discussing the criminal Selden and how his presence on the moor had the entire community in a state of fear.

Two of the telegrams dealt with that subject. Holmes tore open the first one and dropped it after a quick reading. The second provided the answer he expected. The wife of Barrymore, the butler, was the connection. Her maiden name was Selden and the dreaded murderer was her brother. It explained why the killer remained in the area. There was an odd point in Watson's narrative on how Stapleton refused the offer of assistance from Baskerville, confident he and his sister could defend themselves from the killer. Stapleton was a very confident man to believe he could defend himself from such a man as Selden.

Holmes considered whether or not to send the information on Mrs. Barrymore's connection to his friend and decided against it. Watson was a man of some action: if he were provided with that detail, he would undoubtedly confront Mrs. Barrymore with the fact. At the moment, Holmes felt it best to keep the information to himself. Beyond that was he could not be sure if all his communications to Watson were secure. It was always possible someone was aiding Baskerville's unknown stalker and the detective did not want too much information to fall into the wrong hands.

Another telegram was from Honduras, confirming something Holmes suspected as well as providing a name. There was a Rodger Baskerville, the child of the younger brother of Sir Charles. This Baskerville had fled the country under suspicion of embezzlement, heading for Texas. Holmes recalled meeting a Texas Ranger on a case that had spilled over from America two years before. It provided him with a contact to continue his investigation in the wilds of the American West.

The last telegram related to the Baskerville matter was from Devonshire but failed to collaborate some of the information Watson had relayed on the Stapletons. It raised more questions in the detective's mind about the couple, as well as providing a new direction for his inquiry.

The telegrams in the final stack proved to be people trying to provide helpful hints on catching the Whitechapel killer. Holmes stuck them into a handy empty envelope and set them near the morning mail bag delivery so they could be sent off to Scotland Yard with the rest.

By the time he finished reading, Mrs. Hudson arrived with his lunch. And while he ate, he had time to reflect on the wonderful modern age he inhabited. With the help of telegraphs, he was conducting investigations that took him to three different countries, and he was doing it all from Baker Street.

He smiled to himself at the thought. With another half-dozen Watsons, he might be able to run his consulting business like Mycroft and never leave the comfort of his sitting rooms. He could garner information and pronounce conclusions, all without the need to travel and look at the clues himself. He chuckled and set the thought aside as quickly as it had appeared. There would be no fun in conducting his business in such a manner. No fun at all.

Tallman was, if nothing else, punctual. The constables had been alerted and allowed him past their effective cordon of the residence. Mrs. Hudson showed the reporter to the rooms. Her distaste for their visitor was written plainly across her features.

"So this is the inner sanctum!" said Tallman, examining the sitting room carefully.

"Perhaps some tea?" offered Holmes, gesturing towards an open chair at the dining table.

Tallman sat and Holmes immediately poured them each a cup. The detective sat across from him and Tallman eyed him warily.

"So are you going to tell me everything you can deduce about me to impress me with you powers, Mr. Holmes?" asked the reporter.

Holmes smiled, adding a touch of cream to his tea.

"I do not engage in parlor tricks, Mr. Tallman. There are only two things about you on which I would care to comment."

"And what might those be?"

"That you are a man that owns few shirts and that you were dismissed from your last job for publishing complete fabrications."

Holmes lifted his cup to sip his tea and was gratified at the reaction on Tallman's face. But the reporter showed he was made of stern stuff, and his hand was steady as he drank his tea.

"Those are two interesting observations. Mr. Holmes. And how did you deduce them?"

Homes smiled and produced the postcard and slid it across the table. Tallman lifted it and read it quickly before setting it back down.

"Are you offering me an exclusive on publishing this material, Mr. Holmes?"

Holmes laughed out loud at the comment.

"Indeed you are a cool customer, Mr. Tallman." He reached across and tapped the card. "We both know who wrote this card, and the similar ones to the police. I am offering you an opportunity to stay out of jail!"

Again, Tallman took a sip of tea to maintain his composure before answering.

"And who might that be?" he asked.

"A man with few shirts," replied Holmes. "For when you write with a pen in the obvious haste and carelessness displayed on this card, you cannot help but have ink splatter." Holmes reached across and grabbed Tallman's wrist, turning it so the inside of the cuff was visible to both men. "And if the author has few shirts, then there is a good chance we will see the ink splatter on the cuffs and sleeves, as we do in several spots on the shirt you are wearing!"

The newsman looked blankly at the red spots on his cuff. When he spoke, there was resignation in his tone.

"And how did you deduce the other?"

Holmes snorted and pulled out the telegram.

"I had not heard of William Randolph Hearst until you mentioned his name. Since I needed his assistance, I looked into his background and found he has built a very interesting reputation in America." Holmes tossed the reply before Tallman with a dramatic flair. "When no less a personage than William Randolph Hearst confirms my suspicion about the circumstances for your leaving his employment, there is no deduction involved! To be dismissed from Mr. Hearst's service for fabrication is to carry that art to the most extreme level!"

Tallman looked at the telegram mutely for a long moment. His silence was as much confirmation of the detective's work as a complete confession.

"I have improved my methods since then," stated the reporter.

"Indeed!" Holmes slid the other telegram across to him. "When the police find a body in New Scotland Yard that matches a cadaver received at St. Thomas Hospital on September 6th?"

The remaining color drained from Tallman's face.

"And the chancellor confirms there is a Stephen

Tallman enrolled as a student? A cousin perhaps?"

"My half-brother," whispered Tallman, his hand at his throat.

Holmes grabbed the second telegram and clutched it, holding the fist with the yellow paper inches from Tallman's face.

"And I hold his future as surely as I hold this paper! A word from me and he is expelled!"

The reporter fell back in his chair, speechless. There could be no doubt his plan was revealed. At length, some of Tallman's composure reasserted itself and he was able to speak.

"Now what?"

"Inspector Lestrade wants to arrest you for obstructing the investigation and I have half a thought to allow him to do it! You and your brother should pay the price for such shameless exploitation." Holmes shook his fist before the reporter and let his words sink in for a few moments before continuing. He softened his tone slightly as he continued. "At the moment, I am a kinder heart than the police inspectors."

The detective reached across the table and picked up the postcard, displaying it clearly to the reporter.

"There will be no more postcards or bodies. If I see any actions I even suspect involve you, I will provide Abberline everything I know and allow him to handle the matter."

The reporter's face showed a momentary flash of relief at the statement. It was quickly replaced with concern.

"And my employer?" asked Tallman meekly.

"What of him?" asked Holmes with disdain. "He needs to come to his own terms as to the quality of material he decides to publish! But have no doubt that if you attribute one more false statement to me, I will present these facts to your publisher as well and I will break you."

Tallman nodded his acceptance.

"And this also applies to the police! Abberline and Lestrade have enough difficulty on this case without you contributing false clues! Do you have any questions?"

"No, sir," returned Tallman, his voice beaten.

"Then good day, Mr. Tallman," snapped Holmes in a tone that did not invite a reply.

Holmes watched the reporter leave, waiting until he heard the front door close behind him before rising. At his writing desk he pulled out a telegram sheet and wrote a quick note to Abberline, letting him know the red ink postcards were frauds and the situation was handled. Then he began a letter to Watson and the first comment was an apology for discrediting Tallman while his friend was still out of town.

Saturday, October 7 *Deathly Quiet*

The gray dawn filtered through the windows at Baker Street as Holmes returned from another patrol in the streets of Whitechapel. The previous night was uneventful, and Holmes secretly hoped Saturday night would be quiet as well. He had observed the killer's preference for Friday and Saturday nights, so Sunday morning should indicate they were again into a safe period.

He stripped off his disguise and donned his housecoat. A mailbag had been deposited in his absence. Watson's latest letter was near the top and he withdrew it, and then set the bag outside the door for collection. So far, his alliance with Scotland Yard in that regard had been outstanding. The large mailbags disappeared and the few pieces unrelated to Whitechapel were returned within a day.

The bulk of Watson's letter detailed the scene of Sir Charles's death. The letter, plus Mortimer's earlier description, provided the detective with the best view of the yew alley he could want without actually being there. Holmes also thought the letter was another example of how Watson always sold his own skills as a detective short. In focusing on the scene of the crime, Watson had precisely pinpointed a piece of the puzzle that worried Holmes to no end.

Why had Sir Charles been in such a place in the middle of the night? The man had been waiting for someone, for there was no reason to doubt Mortimer's excellent observation. Who was this unknown person and what was the purpose of the rendezvous?

The letter detailed more of the day-to-day activities of the residents in the area. It also revealed the dark spirit of the place affecting the normally down to earth physician. He wondered openly if there might, indeed, be some black art at work in the crime. He snorted in disgust that he would allow himself to entertain such a notion.

Holmes set the letter down, worried for his friend's physical and mental well being. He felt his eyelids droop and he let them. He had been on his feet for most of the last eighteen hours and needed some sleep before returning to Whitechapel in the evening. Still, his mind raced as he nodded off. He was no closer to resolving the London case, and there was devilry afoot on the Grimpen Mire. He would have to go down there. For all of Watson's outstanding qualities, the case demanded his hand to force it to a conclusion.

Holmes was refreshed late in the afternoon after bathing and shaving. He was completing the early supper Mrs. Hudson had brought up when a telegram arrived. Seeing the origin was Texas, he eagerly tore it open.

His acquaintance in America had found the information. The man and his wife came from Honduras and spent some weeks in Texas. They had left with a cloud suspicions surrounding them regarding several burglaries for with the police had no positive proof. The Texas authorities thought they were making their way to Canada, but could not be certain.

The connection to Canada made perfect sense to Holmes. Sir Henry had been in Canada at the time, though he did not have the Baskerville title. Might this relative from Honduras have intended to eliminate his competition even then? But Henry Baskerville had spent his time in the wilds of Canada, and conceivably had been too difficult to locate. Or, perhaps, Holmes was presuming too much.

In either case, the detective knew officials he could contact in Canada. He wrote a long telegram to the colony, then a shorter one thanking his friend in Texas. Bit by bit, pieces of the Baskerville case were presenting themselves. He merely had to continue his efforts to ferret them all out.

He had just dispatched Billy to the telegraph office when Lestrade arrived.

“Good evening, Lestrade!”

The policeman wore shabby clothes as a disguise. Holmes noted the worn pair of shoes on his feet. The Scotland Yard inspector did not like to admit it, but he did usually follow Holmes advice.

For his part, the detective had also donned workmen’s clothes. For a change, his makeup was rather sparse: bushy eyebrows and glasses, plus dirt smudge on his face to highlight certain features and obscure others.

“I think that should do it for this evening’s outing!” he announced, pleased with the results.

“Fair enough,” commented Lestrade. “I can see you in there, but I would have to give you a hard look to identify you!”

Holmes bowed in appreciation of the compliment.

"Oh, before we go!"

Lestrade pulled several typed sheets from his pocket and handed him to the detective. Holmes looked them over, reading absently as he did.

"Asquith…Cunningham…Druitt…Ferringer. What are these?"

"A list of suspects we have interviewed in the past three weeks."

Holmes shook his head and handed the sheets back.

"That's of little use to me unless there is something to indicate their connection to the crimes."

"Inspector Abberline wants you to have them. Maybe something will spark your attention, Holmes."

"As you wish." He set the list on the table. "Where is the good inspector? I thought he planned to join us."

Lestrade shuffle uncomfortably. "He is pursuing another avenue of investigation this evening."

"That is sufficiently cryptic!" chuckled Holmes. "What might that be?"

Lestrade hesitated, but his resolution gave way.

"What is the point in hiding anything from you!" he said in frustration. "Are you familiar with the psychic Robert Lees?"

"I have encountered the name before," conceded Holmes.

"We received a letter from him earlier in the week. He seems to have information relevant to the case and

Inspector Abberline is consulting with him this evening."

"A séance, no doubt!" snorted the detective.

"That is unfair, Holmes!"

Holmes checked his makeup one last time and led Lestrade from the rooms.

"You are right, Lestrade."

As apologies went, Holmes' words were rather weak, but Lestrade accepted them with a smile. Any apology at all from Holmes was an rare event.

"I argued against it, but Lees has powerful friends. Abberline finally relented."

They boarded their coach and settled in. The policeman seemed almost embarrassed by the admission.

"What sort of information does he claim to have?" asked the detective

Lestrade shrugged. "That he has seen the killer in a vision. His description in some respects matches yours."

"And how does Abberline plan to use Lees' *talents*?"

Lestrade tugged on his ear nervously, but explained in a matter-of-fact voice.

"I have to admit, Abberline is being rather clever. He is going to take Lees to the scenes of the killings and try to use him like a psychic bloodhound to follow the killer's path."

Holmes snorted. "Does he expect to get any results?"

The inspector chuckled, a slight nervousness to the sound.

"Who knows?" he shrugged. "But Abberline decided

that if Lees actually has an accurate intuition on the killings, he will be able to follow the movements of the killer as best we know them. If not, we can safely ignore his *insight*."

"I will grant you that," said Holmes, "though I expect nothing to come of it."

"As do we, but we will show our superiors that we followed their suggestion." Lestrade shook his head sadly. "In truth, Holmes, we lose nothing by this distraction."

The cab approached the outer reaches of Whitechapel. Holmes tapped to alert the driver to stop. He did not want to be seen riding. After paying the cabbie, the two men walked together, continuing the discussion in low tones.

"Another cold night," observed Lestrade, pulling his coat closer to him.

Holmes nodded.

"At least there is no feel of rain in the air."

"Yes," agreed the police inspector. "We have certainly seen more than our share of that this year!"

Holmes agreed and then changed the subject. It was time to inform the Scotland Yard detective of his plans for the week.

"If nothing occurs tonight, Lestrade, I intend to go to Grimpen on Tuesday."

Lestrade stopped, surprised by the announcement. He quickly started walking again, but there was a certain desperation in his voice as he spoke.

"You will abandon us to our own devices?"

"London will need to look after itself for a week or so," returned Holmes. "There is murder afoot, and I know I can prevent that killing. I will be back before the next crisis."

"Lees foresees a killing next Friday!"

"And I believe next Friday and Saturday are too soon," countered Holmes. "None the less, you will be able to contact me if my services are required. I can be back within a day."

"Holmes…"

The detective interrupted Lestrade's protest.

"My case in Devonshire has identifiable suspects and victims, Lestrade. I will bring it to a close as quickly as I can."

"Very well."

"And I may need the services of an inspector once I identify the suspect," continued Holmes.

"I can't leave London!" said Lestrade.

"I will not call you until I am ready to make the arrest," assured Holmes. "And, if at all possible, I will do it mid-week. We know this killer prefers Friday and Saturday."

"I will mention it to Abberline."

Holmes reached over and gave the policeman a reassuring pat on the shoulder. It was an uncharacteristic gesture from the normally aloof detective, but it was plain how the Whitechapel case was tearing at the resolve of his friend.

"When I return from Grimpen, I will devote all my energies to helping you and Abberline close this business, Lestrade. It has gone on far too long."

Tuesday, October 10 *Grimpen*

Holmes arrived in Grimpen well after dark. His plans and trip were as intricate a web of deception as he had ever created. He changed disguises on the trip to Victoria, then again upon the train. He started in one direction, the switched trains to eventually arrive in Cornwall while changing disguises and personas yet again. He brought one of the boys from London to act as his agent and runner. To top it off, he laid plans to hide out on the moor, where his presence would go unnoticed.

His arrangements for his mail were equally elaborate. He had a letter from Lestrade that would instruct the local postmaster to hold Watson's mail addressed to him while at the same time letters and telegrams from London would be forwarded to Grimpen under a variety of aliases. Whomever the unknown person that had stalked him in London proved to be, there would be no notification that Sherlock Holmes was now operating on the moors.

And yet, for all his planning, Holmes felt a sense of disquiet as he stepped off the train in Cornwall. The air was damp and heavy, and fog obscured what little he might have seen in the dark night. He had memorized the maps of the area and taken note of Watson's careful descriptions, but it all meant nothing in the night. He collected his meager baggage and set out to the north towards Grimpen, determined to leave no trace of his arrival and quick departure.

Watson's letters had described the Neolithic structures on the moor. He determined to make one of those ancient structures his base. But to be effective, he had to arrive before dawn to hide his presence. So he set a brisk pace to cover the miles and, while he walked, he thought.

First, his mind returned to London and the discomfort he felt in leaving Lestrade and Abberline without his assistance. For a man known for his decisiveness, he continually reviewed and questioned his decisions on the Whitechapel matter. Was he reading the pattern correctly? Would there be no killings over the next two weeks? Had he abandoned the police to their own resources at a critical time?

It was a feeling of guilt that plagued him as he trudged through the fog, though he would be loath to admit it. There was the guilt of leaving his friends. There was more guilt from the inability to stop the killer. There was guilt about sending Watson alone to such a place as Grimpen to fend for himself.

That thought would wrench his mind from Whitechapel and bring it to the moor. Had his plans been thorough? Had he missed any suspects? Were the inquiries he had made sufficient to reveal the guilty party? Would he prevent the tragedy of Sir Charles from being reenacted with Sir Henry?

But Holmes, as always, was resolute. His plans were set, there was nothing to do but follow them. He walked on into the night, never missing a turn. And as the first gray hints of dawn appeared, he was past Grimpen and at his destination.

So far, his plan had worked. He found a hut that was fairly weather tight and at the same time clean, cleared a spot to roll out his blanket, and prepared to take a nap. He needed to rest for a while so he could be on the moor in the afternoon.

His attention had to be focused like a searchlight on Baskerville Hall and he tried to set thoughts of London aside. But trying and succeeding are two different things, and he managed only a fitful nap on the hard ground.

Friday, October 13 *The Moor*

For Holmes, the adjustment to the moor was much the same as if he simply moved to a different city. In the first two days, he learned the lay of the land, where he could walk, were he could not. He learned how to move quickly and keep himself out of sight of the various structures.

One of his first discoveries was the location of Selden. It was obvious to the investigator that Selden must also inhabit one of the Neolithic structures, though the criminal was well removed from Holmes' residence. The detective considered revealing the criminal's location to the authorities, but that would also reveal his presence. After observing the criminal for a while, he quickly determined that he was a broken man and quite harmless to anyone as long as he stayed on the moor. In its way, the moor was as effective a prison as Dartmoor.

The day's routines were already set. Cartwright would arrive late morning with the day's food and mail in the morning. Holmes would review the mail, write any replies for the boy to take back to Grimpen and send him on his way. Then it was a bite to eat, and off to observe the different inhabitants. Hiding places abounded on the moor, and his binoculars allowed him to observe without getting too close. Watson had written about the busybody Franklin and how the man always observed the moor and Holmes had noticed the glint from Franklin's telescope on more than one occasion. It cautioned him to use his own binoculars only while in the shadows.

By late afternoon, he would return to his lodgings and eat another small meal before moving close to Baskerville Hall to keep watch overnight. He had observed the Barrymores' signaling from the house to meet Selden and provide food. While the Barrymores were engaged in an illegal activity, Holmes did not see how it cast any direct threat against Baskerville. His sole purpose was the protection of the lord of the manor, so he took no action against the servants or the criminal.

This particular Friday was a beautiful and sunny day compared to the normal wet and gloomy weather plaguing England through the summer. Holmes had followed Stapleton, but the naturalist headed deep into the Grimpen Mire. The detective found a place where he could wait and observe, believing Stapleton would return to his starting point. But as he waited, a new figure appeared from the Stapletons' house, a woman who could only be the sister, Beryl.

Holmes expected her to turns towards town, but she surprised him and headed across the moor. He could see her destination, a secluded outcropping where the view from the house around the moor was blocked. And since that was the case, the detective quickly looked back towards Baskerville Hall and saw the form of Sir Henry walking towards the same location. And before he could chide Watson for allowing Sir Henry on the moor alone, he spied his friend following a discrete distance behind.

The detective followed the woman, always aware of Franklin and his telescope. He saw the couple meet, but could not get close enough to hear their words. They spoke for a long time, and then embraced. At that same moment, there was a shout and sound of feet in the underbrush. Holmes had almost forgotten about the brother.

"Baskerville! How dare you take such liberties!"

Stapleton stormed past Holmes' hiding place barely a dozen feet away. If he were not so fixed on his sister and Sir Henry, Holmes knew he would surely have been noticed. The detective withdrew to a safer location, but it was even further away. The angry shouts between Stapleton and Baskerville could be heard, but the words were unclear. Beryl left the men, and Stapleton continued to shout. Holmes feared he might have to step in to prevent a physical assault when Watson appeared from behind Sir Henry. At the arrival of the second man, Stapleton made a final threatening gesture, and hurried after his sister.

The detective knew he could rely on Watson for a thorough report of the affair from Baskerville's perspective. He followed he brother as best he could, but the man was moving much faster than Holmes could manage if he wished to remain hidden. Stapleton caught up to Beryl, grabbing her rudely and shouting angrily again.

As before, they were just too far away from Holmes to make out all the words. He worked as close as he dared when Beryl tore herself from her brother's grasp and shouted.

"If I am to play the part of your sister…" she yelled furiously, but did not finish the tirade.

She turned away from the man and stomped back towards the house as quickly as she could manage. Stapleton watched her for a long time, and then followed at a slower pace. He no longer appeared the angry brother, but now seemed merely in deep thought.

Holmes turned away from observing the couple. He sat down in his hiding place, his back against a rock, his mind racing.

If I am to play the part…

That told him Beryl was not Stapleton's sister. And if she was not his sister, then who was she and why the charade? He had not found a brother and sister that ran a school in Scotland, but there was a husband and wife. They had left after a scandal. *If the Stapletons were that couple…*

There was a realization. He was not searching for a brother and sister, he was searching for a husband and wife. And that being the case, he had to correct his inquiries in Scotland. The change of relationship may speak to hiding from the scandal in Scotland or something more sinister. Holmes now knew this couple had secrets they were concealing, something more sinister than the Barrymores and their relationship with Selden. Yes, they definitely deserved more of his attention.

The growing shadows told him it was getting late and his watch confirmed it. The detective headed towards his hovel for his evening meal. He allowed himself a short nap before leaving to take up his position near Baskerville Hall. It had been a rewarding day.

Sunday, October 15 *Night Pursuit*

Holmes took up his nightly position where he could watch the approaches to Baskerville Hall. It was a beautiful, clear night with a brilliant full moon making its way up the eastern sky.

The detective shifted, trying to get more comfortable. It was at times like this he missed his pipe. Smoking a couple of bowls on such a bright, crisp evening would help him think and pass the time, but the tell-tale glow from the bowl or a whiff of smoke would give his carefully chosen position away. He could not take the risk of smoking when he did not know who else might be watching the hall.

With his suspicions turned towards the Stapletons', Holmes toyed with the idea of watching their house instead of Baskerville Hall. He dismissed it quickly. If his suspicions were correct, Stapleton would make any moves upon Sir Henry on the moor, and the position near Baskerville Hall would allow him to thwart them. If he were wrong and watching the Stapletons' house, Baskerville Hall would be unguarded.

He sighed. He had reviewed all these thoughts numerous times before. He pulled out his watch and checked the time. It was just a bit past ten. There was a still a long night ahead.

At Baskerville Hall, a single light appeared the upper window. Holmes nodded because the time was near for the Barrymores' nightly signal to Selden. He looked away from the building and, true to form, the answering signal was visible on the tor. Holmes looked back to the house and the light, which normally was shown for a minute or more, was now stationary and then was extinguished as he looked.

Holmes preferred routine. When an established routine was broken, it usually indicated a problem. To confirm his fears, a door opened at Baskerville Hall and two silhouettes appeared. He had no doubt that the forms were Baskerville and Watson. He should have guessed the two men would discover the Barrymores' secret and they were now heading into the moor to discover who was signaling back.

The detective left his hiding place and started shadowing the two men. Their position was clearly marked by the lanterns they carried. For his part, the bright moonlight provided enough light to make his way clearly. Still, he cursed himself for leaving the issue of Selden unresolved. Now here were Watson and Baskerville on the moor at night, the very situation he was trying to avoid. And Selden, while meek enough when left to himself, might react completely differently if confronted.

He moved quickly and quietly through the underbrush. Watson and Baskerville were, on the other hand, noisy and talking to each other as they moved. He hoped their actions would scare the fugitive away before they could arrive at his signaling location.

The lay of the land was forcing him away from the other two men. By the time they reached Selden, he would be on the far side of the tor, He decided that was acceptable, as he could gain the high ground to watch over his friends and perhaps be in a position to defend them if necessary. Still, he was unhappy with Watson's and Baskerville's actions. It was a foolhardy move on their part.

The signal light was still sitting on a rock when they arrived. Holmes crawled across the top of the tor, looking down at Watson and Sir Henry, who were searching the area and making a perfect mess of the grounds. He looked about, trying to spy Selden. There was the sound of a rock shifting on the other side of the clearing, and he spotted its shadow bouncing down the cliff face. There was another shadow, Selden no doubt, moving away from the location

Sir Henry shouted and the two men moved in that direction. The last thing Holmes needed was for them to confront the criminal in the dark. What was required was a distraction. The detective made a noise and stood up, revealing himself.

Watson turned in his direction, his face clearly visible in the moonlight. At the same time, Holmes knew his own features would be in shadow. He planned to lead them away from the criminal, but instead, the most unexpected thing happened. A long, low howl drifted across the moor. It was a chilling sound and he watched Watson's head snap in that new direction.

Holmes took advantage of the sound and dropped back out of sight. It was unexpected, but the combination of his appearance and the ghostly sound was enough to confuse the two men below. The chilling wail dissuaded them from searching any longer and they turned and started back to the manor. Holmes worked his way back off the tor so he could follow them and make sure they arrived safely.

Holmes wondered at the wail, a sound emanating from deep within the bog. He had felt its power, the chill on his spine and the hairs rising on the back of his neck. He could only guess at the impact it would have on Sir Henry, whose family fortunes were so closely tied to the legend of the hound. In one of his letters, Watson mentioned Stapleton had offered a bittern as the source of the sound. The detective dismissed the idea. He knew the sound of a hound and he knew the sound of a bittern.

There was, as Mortimer had suggested, a hound on the moor. And if the hound was in the middle of the bog and Stapleton spent time there, then a connection was made. If he could discover the hiding place, he would prove the case. In the morning, he would make the attempt to reach there again.

Wednesday, October 17 *L.L.*

The last two days had been a frustration for the great detective. As he moved into the bog on Monday, it began to rain. A risky proposition had quickly become exceedingly dangerous, and he was forced to withdraw. The rain continued heavily throughout Tuesday, so no further investigation was possible. He was forced to spend a miserable day of inactivity in his stone hut, unable to send or receive word on anything. Even the boy, Cartwright, was unable to reach him with the mail or supplies.

That morning, at least, showed a moderation of the weather. Cartwright appeared with fresh supplies and, more importantly, mail and telegrams.

No word was forthcoming from London and Holmes breathed a sigh of relief. At least his absence was not causing an issue there.

There were telegrams from Canada. One confirmed a couple now known as the Vandelours had departed from there, but that no information could be found on them prior to that. Another was a confirmation that no information could be found on the location or status of Baskerville after he entered Canada from the United States.

Holmes smiled with satisfaction. In this case, two negatives yielded a positive. One couple disappears upon entering Canada, but another couple appears upon leaving. He could not prove conclusively Stapleton was the missing Baskerville, but there was little room for any other conclusion.

The last bit of mail was another of Watson's thick letters. It confirmed the events of Sunday night, as well as a reasonably good description of how Holmes appeared on the tor. The detective smiled at reading the account of the "tall, slim man" who was seen.

Sir Henry and Watson confronted Barrymore with the aid they were giving Selden and Watson detailed the full confession of the circumstance. They intended to sneak the man out of the country, and Watson and Baskerville agreed to turn a blind eye to the deed. Holmes felt relief at that, as it removed a cause for the two men to venture onto the moor again.

Meanwhile, their good turn to Barrymore had resulted in an unexpected benefit. Barrymore explained a letter he had seen in the fireplace the morning of Sir Charles' death. The note asked him to meet a woman, or at least it was Barrymore's assumption based on the hand writing. The correspondence was burned as per her request, but the butler was able to read it clearly before the ash disintegrated. It was signed only with initials: L.L.

This was indeed the break in the case for which the detective was searching. It finally provided a reason for Sir Charles to be on the moor in the middle of the night. Holmes fairly rubbed his hands in glee at this piece of evidence. As the letter continued, Watson determined that LL was a Mrs. Laura Lyons who lived in nearby Coombe Tracey and the daughter of Frankland, the busybody.

Watson announced he would attempt to interview the woman.

Homes fretted again. He possessed information Watson would need for the interview, but he still possessed no way to relay it in a safe manner. Particularly, now that he had Stapleton singled out as the primary suspect, he could not risk the bird flying.

He determined to make a final attempt to penetrate the bog the next day, if the weather cleared. If it could not be done, he would take a more direct approach. Days were ticking off the calendar and he needed to be in London by the following weekend.

Thursday, October 18 *The Hut*

Holmes had rarely felt so frustrated. His latest effort to discover Stapleton's secret in the bog was stopped by failing light. He had gotten further than he had before, but the going was too slow. Stapleton was truly practiced for him to be able to enter and leave the treacherous mire in such a short period.

As he left the interior, he could make out a person walking from Frankland's. He pulled out his binoculars and focused them. The image was still indistinct at the distance, but he recognized Watson from his walking stick and limp. It was easy to see the direction the doctor was aimed. He smiled. No doubt he had been revealed and he was about to have company.

He approached his hut carefully. He did not know how nervous Watson would be, and Holmes had considerable respect for his skill with the service revolver. He noticed a cigarette on the ground outside the hut, as well as the fresh foot prints. He stopped short of the doorway and spoke clearly.

"It is a lovely evening, my dear Watson. I think that you will be more comfortable outside than in."

Watson walked outside laughing, carefully pocketing his revolver as he did so.

"So it was you I saw on the tor Sunday night!" he said, shaking Holmes' hand "When did you get here?"

"Last week."

"And you could not tell me?" There was a sense of hurt in the tone of Watson's words.

"In truth, I could determine no way to get you the information without knowing it would be compromised. There has been a lot I would have liked to relay you."

The two men leaned upon stones, their conversation as casual as if they had only been apart for a day instead of close to three weeks.

"Then you are the other man on the moor? Frankland saw your boy and Selden told Barrymore there was another man about."

"Ah, that's what I get with trusting criminals with my presence. I may as well have let Selden carry you a note!" He rose and peeped into the hut. "Ha, I see that Cartwright has brought up supplies and mail." Holmes immediately began to page through the mail, pausing at one envelope. "How odd. A letter from Lestrade."

Watson's heart skipped a beat. "Another murder?"

"That would have warranted a telegraph." Holmes tore the page from the envelope and scanned it quickly. "Another potential letter from the murderer. He will send details if I wish."

"Have you formed any new opinions on that culprit?"

Holmes smiled. He had plenty of time to think about the wretched Whitechapel case while he was alone on the moor. He felt he may have reached a dim view into the mind of the killer, but did not feel confident in sharing his thoughts yet.

"None," he answered, the single word belying his thoughts.

"And no murders since the twenty-ninth?"

"None," said Holmes, his voice reflective. "I find that odd. I expected him to strike around the eighth."

"Why the eighth?"

Holmes leaned closer, glad at last to share some of his conclusions. "Look at the pattern: If we accept Tabram as a victim, she was killed on the seventh, Chapman on the thirty-first of August. Nichols on the night of the eighth of September; Stride and Eddowes on the thirtieth. The next likely night was the eighth or ninth of October, but there were no killings. If I am correct, the last two days of the month are the next danger period." Holmes slammed a fist into his palm. "Watson, it is imperative to conclude this case and return to London by the twenty-ninth!"

"Our priority must be Sir Henry!" stressed Watson

"Of that I am too well aware!" snapped Holmes, his voice showing unusual anger. "We must draw these foul proceedings to a close!"

"Are you any closer?"

"Between your letters," he said, reaching into his pocket and producing the sheaf of pages, "and my research and observations, I think we can conclude here in the next day or two. Have you been to Mrs. Lyons yet?"

"I went to Frankland for a letter of introduction, but he wants nothing to do with her."

The conversation was interrupted by a cry from outside. And that shout was followed the by howl of a hound, the same frightful sound they had heard on Sunday. But this time, the sound was much louder and much closer.

They ran outside, and looked across the moor. They could see the shadow of a man running, tripping, climbing on the rocks. Behind him, but closing quickly was a dark shape, black but edged in a ghostly luminescence. It was a gigantic hound in full stride.

Watson pulled his revolver and Holmes did the same as they ran after the fleeing figures. Watson shouted as they ran.

"Look at the clothes! That must be Sir Henry! He promised he would stay at the manor!"

The man ran, scrambling on all fours to reach the top of the tor, but the hound was upon him. There was a momentary struggle and a terrible scream as the man fell backwards down the sheer face. Then there was another sound, something that might have been the call of some marsh bird. The ghostly shape of the hound froze for an instant before bounding into the bog at a pace the detective and his friend could never match.

For their part, they ignored the spectral shape as they struggled through the craggy rocks. The victim lay twisted, bloody and motionless. Watson stopped, his face drained colorless.

"Sir Henry!" he said in horror.

Holmes pushed past him. "His clothes maybe," said the detective, carefully twisting the face. "It is my neighbor, Selden, wearing some of Sir Henry's fine American suits by way of the Barrymores."

Watson sagged, visibly relieved at the revelation. "This is dreadful!"

"I'm afraid Sir Henry's largess sealed his doom."

"What was that animal? I have never seen a hound such a ghostly shade!"

Holmes took his friend back to where Selden's and the hound's footprints were still visible in the dying light.

"Regardless of color, the hound is all too real! The scratches and bite marks on Selden will attest to that as well."

"Why would the hound attack Selden?"

Holmes smiled. "Think about the events in London. It will come to you."

The detective returned to his normal, inpatient self. He did not wait for Watson to determine the answer nor did he explain it. Instead, he pointed back towards his hut.

"Enough of this cloister in the Neolithic village! Help me gather my belongings and I will return to Baskerville Hall with you."

"No more need to go skulking about?"

"Our case approaches an end, Watson. It is time to arrive here openly, and I would prefer the comfort of the manor to one more night on the moor."

It took only a few moments to gather Holmes' meager camping gear. As they left the hut for the last time, Watson glanced back towards the scene of the evening's tragedy.

"What of that poor man?"

"We shall have to send someone to fetch him I the morning. We cannot extricate him from the rocks in the dark."

"It does not seem Christian to leave him there."

"There is nothing more to be done tonight." The lights of Baskerville Hall beckoned from across the moor. "What news do you have of events at the hall?"

Sir Henry was pleased and surprised at the arrival of the detective. He immediately wanted to discover what had been learned, but first there was the unpleasant task of informing the Barrymores of Selden's death. While the butler saw to his wife, Baskerville played the host and found the makings of a cold dinner in the kitchen that he could lay out before his friends.

"So what have you learned?" he demanded as Holmes ate.

"I think you have an American cousin, the son of Rodger Baskerville, Sir Charles' brother."

Sir Henry nodded. "The one who died in Honduras. You believe this cousin is operating against me?"

"Exactly," confirmed the detective. "Watson says you are engaged to dine with our friends the Stapletons tomorrow?"

Sir Henry chuckled. "The last time I saw Stapleton, I thought I would never hear from him or his sister again. Then he appeared this morning to apologize for his behavior and to tell me he would welcome me as her suitor!" He chuckled at the thought. "Between his irrational behavior and your admonishment to never go on the moor at night, I seriously considered turning him down."

Holmes took a sip of wine, then dabbed at the corner of his mouth with his napkin.

"I would like you to go, Sir Henry. I think it will help bring this matter to a conclusion." He leaned forward, very serious. "There will be some danger in this. Watson and I will make a show of leaving, but then return by the late train. You must appear to be on the moor alone and unprotected."

"And you think it will bring this matter to resolution?" asked Sir Henry. Holmes nodded. "I am no coward, Holmes. I would rather run this risk and end this dreadful curse than have it hanging above my head another day!"

"Good show, old man!" said Watson.

"Then our plan is set. With luck, this will all be behind you by this time tomorrow," announced Holmes.

The men cleared the table, and Sir Henry led them up to their rooms. As they climbed the stairs, they passed portraits of the previous holders of the Baskerville title.

"This cavalier!" said Holmes, stopping at one of the older paintings. "This is Sir Hugo?"

"Indeed, he is the cause of all the mischief. That is the wicked Hugo who first encountered the Hound of the Baskervilles."

They all contemplated the portrait.

"He seems a quiet, meek-mannered man," observed the detective, "but I dare say there was a lurking devil in his eyes."

"At the moment, I have to agree with that!" smiled the Baronet.

Sir Henry brought them to their rooms and left for his own. Holmes led Watson back to the stairway in silence and he held a candle up against the time-stained portrait of Sir Hugo.

"Do you see anything there?" he asked quietly.

"There is something of Sir Henry about the jaw." Watson struggled to voice his observation. "There is a familiarity about the eyes, but I cannot place it."

Holmes handed his candle to Watson and held his hands up across the portrait so only the eyes were visible.

"How about now?"

"Good heavens!" cried Watson in amazement. "Stapleton!"

"I suspected as much. I lost track of Sir Henry's cousin when he disappeared into Canada. Stapleton and his sister came from Canada, but I could find no information on them from before that. It was not a big leap to connect the two together."

"I had my suspicions, too," explained Watson. "But this is the first positive evidence I have had to support them."

"What caused your suspicions?" asked the detective.

Watson chuckled. "Nothing so concrete as one of your deductions, Holmes. It was a matter of elimination. There was simply no one else to consider!"

Holmes smiled at his friend's admission, but his tone was deadly serious when he spoke.

"We will play a dangerous game tomorrow night, Watson. Sir Henry shall be the bait to draw out our quarry." He tapped the painting. "Sir Hugo had the reputation for viciousness that earned him the curse of the hound. If Stapleton is our man, he has inherited that and is clever and cunning. We must be on our best guard for Sir Henry's sake."

Friday, October 19 *The Hound of the Baskervilles*

Holmes and Watson arrived in Coombe Tracey the next morning. The detective first went to the post office, which also served as the telegraph office for the small town. The detective quickly consulted the train schedule, and then jotted a telegram to Lestrade in London.

"We shall have the official police here by 7:00 PM," he told Watson.

"And what of us?"

"There is a 1:00 PM train to London and we will be on it. We will see Cartwright safely on his way, but we will exit at Salisbury and return. We should be back no later than five."

"You are having Sir Henry run a terrible risk, Holmes."

The detective agreed, his mood somber.

"I am too well aware, Watson, but I must bring this affair to a conclusion, both for Sir Henry's sake and so we can return to the case in London!"

Mrs. Laura Lyons was in her office, and Sherlock Holmes opened the interview with a directness which took her off her guard.

"I am investigating the death of the late Sir Charles Baskerville," he said. "We know that you had arranged a meeting with him on the night of his death and did not keep it."

"How can you know that?" she asked defiantly.

Holmes was very direct and unyielding when the situation required it. He did have the luxury of obtaining the woman's story in a leisurely fashion.

"Your letter was seen before it was destroyed. Though Sir Charles complied with your wishes and burned it, the ash was still readable."

"There is no crime in failing to keep an appointment." Her tone was defiant.

The woman replied as the detective expected. It allowed him to respond in the manner he had planned.

"I will be perfectly frank with you, Mrs. Lyons. This case is a murder, and the evidence implicates not only you, but your friend Mr. Stapleton and his wife as well."

Holmes' revelation had the desired effect. The lady sprang from her chair in horror.

"His wife!" she cried.

"What was your connection to Sir Charles?" demanded Holmes.

With that demand, the woman's reserve broke. Mrs. Lyons dabbed at the tears in her eyes as she sat back down and explained.

"Because of my failed marriage, father abandoned me. Sir Charles, the dear, became my benefactor. He established this typing business for me and helped with money from time to time." She cried for a moment, and then collected herself.

"Sir Charles was nothing but a gentleman to me!" she stressed. "He asked nothing in return and did whatever he could to help sort out my problems. His lawyers are working to secure my divorce."

Holmes answered with a statement. He had deduced her involvement with Stapleton, and he only needed her confirmation.

"You were befriended by Mr. Stapleton and he knew of your connection to Sir Charles."

"Yes, sir." She cried again. "He offered me marriage once my divorce was secured! I did not know that woman was his wife!"

"And the purpose of the letter?"

She sobbed, but managed to continue speaking.

"Mr. Stapleton convinced me that my connection to Sir Charles might damage the man's reputation. I was to have Sir Charles use Mr. Stapleton as our go-between."

"And the meeting so late was to assure privacy," said Watson, jotting a note. "For Sir Charles' sake."

"Yes, yes..."

"And then, after Sir Charles agreed to the meeting, Stapleton convinced you not to go as it was another unseemly meeting that might harm the old gentleman."

"Yes," she confirmed. She took a deep breath before asking her next question. "Was I the cause of Sir Charles' death?"

"No!" said Watson firmly, placing a reassuring hand on the woman's shoulder.

Holmes regarded the woman with little pity. He made no secret of his contempt for her gender. To him, the whole affair simply illustrated how easily woman could be manipulated and used. He opened his mouth to speak, but caught the stern glance from his friend. He reframed his words and tone before he spoke.

"You have been cruelly used, Mrs. Lyons, by an evil and despicable man. All blame rests with him."

There was little sympathy in his manner, but neither was there accusation.

"What will I do?" she moaned.

"Have no more connection to Stapleton!" cautioned Holmes. "If he tries to contact you today, make any excuse, but do not see him!"

"And tomorrow?" she asked.

"And tomorrow," replied Holmes, in words as cold as death, "he will no longer be able to haunt your life."

The two men collected Cartwright and had an early lunch before going to the train station. As they walked out to the waiting train, they were met by Stapleton.

"Mr. Sherlock Holmes?" the man asked.

Holmes was aloof as always, showing no hint of surprise at the encounter.

"You must be Mr. Stapleton," he returned.

"To be sure, sir! To be sure!" Stapleton replied, a smile on his features. "I heard from Sir Henry you had spent the night at the manor but were heading back to London already. I simply had to take this opportunity to meet you."

"Indeed?" Holmes could not fathom why Stapleton would actually want to meet him. "Whatever for?"

Stapleton took his hand and shook it.

"To meet a man of your notoriety, sir! I have followed Dr. Watson's writings so avidly, I simply had to make your acquaintance." Holmes withdrew his hand, but Stapleton continued speaking. "You are leaving so soon?"

"I do not investigate the supernatural," replied Holmes. "I have found no evidence to indicate the death of Sir Charles falls within my expertise."

Stapleton regarded the detective, his features puzzled.

"You consider the death of Sir Charles to be the work of the supernatural?"

"I consider the death of Sir Charles to be the result of a weak heart," replied Holmes. "Attempting to ascribe supernatural causes because of an old family legend is a waste of my time."

The conductor called, announcing it was time to board their train.

"It is time to go," said Stapleton. "It was a pleasure meeting you, Mr. Holmes, if only briefly." Stapleton took Watson's hand. "Dr. Watson, safe journey home!"

"Thank you," replied Watson, his tone clipped.

They boarded the train and settled themselves into a private compartment. Stapleton waited on the boardwalk until the train moved from the station.

"He wants to be sure we are leaving," said Watson.

"No doubt. The man has a cool head to confront me so openly," said Holmes.

"And you say you discovered him because of the butterfly?"

Holmes chuckled.

"I found no evidence of the Stapletons in Devonshire until they appeared in Grimpen. Stapleton claimed discovery of the butterfly and there can only be one discoverer of a species. That was a man named Vandelour. So either Vandelour was Stapleton, or Stapleton was lying. And what was the point of lying on such a thing?" Holmes leaned closer to his friend. "It was Vandelour and his wife who ran the failed school. They had come from Canada. Baskerville and his wife disappeared into Canada; Vandelour and his wife emerged."

"Was he planning to eliminate Sir Henry even then?"

Holmes was uncertain.

“I cannot be sure. If that was the case, he was unable to locate the future baronet in the wilds. In any case, he came to England and, we know for certain, created his plans once he reached Grimpen.”

“What a devious mind to concoct such as plan as you describe!”

Holmes leaned back and closed his eyes.

“Yes, and now I have given him what he wants. He believes I am fooled and found no evidence to reveal his plan. He will feel free to act tonight.” He shuffled to a more comfortable position. “I am going to take a nap, Watson. I suggest you do the same. It promises to be a long evening!”

Holmes’ timetable proved accurate. They returned to Coombe Trace, carefully inspecting the station before revealing themselves. The detective expected Stapleton would be at his house preparing for his guest, but he could not be sure if he had agents. It was also unclear how involved the wife was in the entire plan.

Lestrade’s train arrived on time. The two men met the police inspector as he stepped from the car.

"You are mighty close about this affair, Mr. Holmes. What's the game important enough to draw me from the East End?"

“Murder, Lestrade. The solution of one and the prevention of another.”

“I recall no unsolved murders in Devonshire.” Watson smiled widely at the comment. The policeman saw the grin and shook his head sadly. “Another of your bizarre mysteries, Holmes?”

Holmes chuckled as his friend’s discomfort.

"Bizarre is the very word, Lestrade!" replied the detective. "Come, we have time for dinner before making our appointment tonight. I shall regale you with a tale that will enthrall the most hardheaded man on the force! Are you armed?"

The little detective smiled and patted his hip pocket.

"Good! Watson and I are also ready for emergencies!"

Holmes directed his friends towards a pub and Lestrade spoke while they walked.

"I do have some news for you, Holmes."

The detective was instantly alert. "Regarding Whitechapel?"

"I do have some more information on that, but it will wait for the moment. No, this deals with that Greek affair you and Gregson resolved last month."

"Pray continue."

Lestrade smiled. He rarely had the opportunity to present information to Holmes that the detective did not already know or surmise.

"That man Latimer who was behind the whole affair. A perfect villain by all accounts."

"What of him?"

"One of our informants said that he has been spotted in London. I thought you might want to know, since he vowed vengeance and all."

"He shall have to wait his turn," said Holmes with a darting smile. With his walking stick, he gestured into the darkness beyond the town, encompassing the emptiness of the mire. "In the meantime, he is more than welcome to seek me out here!"

"It does not seem a very cheerful place," commented Lestrade with a shiver, as he regarded the lake of fog which covered the Grimpen Mire.

The dog cart creaked under the weight of the three men plus the driver as they made their way towards Merripit House.

"I thought this turn in the country would be a relief from the horror of Whitechapel." Lestrade sniffed at the cool, damp air, heavy with the scent of the mire. "Instead it seems I have just replaced the disquiet of the city with the disquiet of the swamp."

"I trust we shall bring this case to a more immediate and satisfactory conclusion," responded Holmes.

"Bizarre is hardly the word, Mr. Holmes, if it plays out as you have said." Lestrade stopped, pointing at their way ahead. "I see the lights of a house."

"That is end of our journey." Holmes tapped the driver on his shoulder. "We will walk from here." He lowered his voice. "And do not talk above a whisper! We cannot be sure how far our words will travel in this heavy air."

They moved along the track towards the house, but Holmes halted them about two hundred yards away. Watson and Lestrade looked to the brightly lit house, but Holmes' attention was elsewhere

Over the great Grimpen Mire hung a dense fog. The moon shone on it, and it looked like a great white lake, with the distant tors the only forms breaking its surface. Holmes's watched it, and he muttered impatiently as he considered its sluggish drift.

"It is moving towards us, Watson."

"Is that serious?"

"Very!" Holmes consulted his watch. "Baskerville cannot be very long now. It is already ten o'clock. His life may depend upon his coming out before the fog is over the path."

“They appear to be finishing cigars,” said Watson. “I see Sir Henry, Stapleton and a servant. There is no sign of Miss Stapleton.”

Wisps of the fog moved about them and their view of the house diminished. Holmes struck his hand passionately upon a rock and stamped his feet in his impatience.

"The path will be covered in a quarter hour. In half an hour, we won't be able to see our hands in front of us.”

"Shall we move back upon higher ground?" suggested Lestrade

"Yes," agreed the detective. He pointed down the path leading back to the manor. “Sir Henry will come this way. Stapleton will wait until he is farther from the house before making his move.”

Holmes led them onward as the fog thickened about them. At last, he held up his hand.

"This is far enough. We are almost a half mile from the house," he explained. "We dare not take the chance of his being overtaken before reaching us." There was the snap of a twig behind them. The dim sound of firm footsteps drifted through the fog. "That must be Sir Henry!"

The three men found hiding places among the stones. The steps grew louder, and through the fog, as through a curtain, appeared the shape of Sir Henry. He came swiftly along the path, passing close to where they lay, and went on up the long slope behind. But as he walked, he glanced continually over either shoulder, clearly a man who was ill at ease.

"Be ready!" cried Holmes. There was the sharp click of his pistol cocking. "It is coming!"

The sound of panting and paws against the soft ground swept across them from the mist. At that instant, Lestrade gave a yell of terror and threw himself upon the ground. Watson was on his feet, but appeared paralyzed by the dreadful shape which had sprung from the shadows. Even Holmes, with all his expectations, was shocked by the apparition.

It was an enormous coal-black hound, but not such a hound as mortal eyes had ever seen. Fire breathed from its open mouth; eyes glowed with a smoldering glare. Its muzzle, sides and legs were outlined in flickering flame.

With long bounds, the creature followed hard upon Sir Henry's footsteps. Holmes and Watson fired together as they recovered from their amazement, followed a second later by Lestrade. The hound emitted a hideous howl, showing at least one shot had hit him, but it did not slow the beast.

Sir Henry was looking back, his face white in the moonlight, hands raised in horror, and glaring helplessly at the frightful thing. The cry of pain from the hound dispelled all the fears held by Holmes, Watson and Lestrade. If the beast was vulnerable, he was mortal and if they could wound him, they could kill him. Holmes ran hard, followed by Watson, then Lestrade. They heard scream after scream from Sir Henry and the deep roar of the hound as it fell upon its victim.

Holmes emptied five rounds from his revolver into the creature's flank as it stood upon Sir Henry. Watson and Lestrade followed suit and, with a last howl of agony, it fell. All four feet pawed furiously, and at last it slumped limp upon its side. Watson stooped, panting, and pressed his pistol to the dreadful, shimmering head, but there was no point in pulling the trigger. The giant hound was dead.

Sir Henry lay insensible where he had fallen. Watson moved to his side, checking quickly while Lestrade thrust a brandy flask between the baronet's teeth. Two frightened eyes looked up at them.

"My God!" he whispered. "What was it?"

"We laid the family ghost to rest once and forever," announced Holmes. “A ghost made real by an evil man.”

“Only some scratches and a few bruises,” announced Watson, helping Sir Henry to a sitting position. From there, they raised him to his feet and let him find support on a nearby rock.

Holmes stood over the dead creature, unsure of its exact breed. It mattered little, for in size it approached that of a lioness. Watson knelt down to inspect it, for even in the death, the jaws dripped a bluish flame and the small, cruel eyes were ringed with fire. Watson placed his hand upon the glowing muzzle, and as he held it up, the fingers smoldered and gleamed in the darkness.

"Phosphorus."

"A cunning preparation," agreed Holmes. He turned to their client, a man still uncertain of his feet and who was fixated on the dead beast. "I owe you a deep apology, Sir Henry, for not preparing you for this fright. I knew there was a hound, but not such a monster as this.”

Saturday, October 20 *Return to London*

In the morning, the fog had lifted and they were guided by an eager Mrs. Stapleton to the point where they had found a pathway through the bog. She explained she had been beaten and bound in the house during the dinner the night before because she announced her intention to reveal the plan to Sir Henry. With great glee, the battered woman showed them how Stapleton had marked his path, and Holmes led them into the heart of the mire.

Rank reeds and lush, slimy water plants sent a heavy odor of decay into the air. The occasional false step sent them waist deep into the bog, and all three would have to work to extricate the person from the bog's fiendish hold. At one point, Holmes stopped and reached into the slimy water for a dimly visible object.

"It is Sir Henry's missing boot," he said, holding up his muddy prize.

"Thrown there by Stapleton in his flight?" asked Watson. A realization dawned. "That is how Stapleton gave the hound the scent! And Sir Henry's clothes confused the hound in Selden's case."

"Correct," confirmed Holmes. "Stapleton kept it after using it to set the hound upon Sir Henry. He fled when he knew the game was up, still clutching it, so he came at least this far in safety."

"But why risk your life on such a trifle?" asked Watson.

"It proves my deduction was correct," returned Holmes. To the detective, the need for conclusive proof was obvious.

At length, they found Stapleton's secret: a kennel for his massive dog. Holmes explained how Stapleton kept it, moving the beast to an outhouse at Merripit when its services were needed. But of Stapleton, there was no sign. Holmes looked out upon the mire that surrounded them.

"I see no sign of him on the ground. I fear Stapleton never made it here last night. He must have lost his way in the fog."

"Then where is he?" asked Lestrade.

"The bog has claimed him," concluded Holmes.

Watson nodded solemnly. "Then I would say that is justice!"

Lestrade clapped a hand on the doctor's back.

"I can certainly agree with that, Dr. Watson!"

"One last thing, Holmes," said Watson. "How would Stapleton claim the inheritance? He certainly could not step forward and reveal himself."

"Oh, there are ways," explained the detective. "Most likely, he would return to Honduras and reestablish his identify as the son of Roger Baskerville and resolve his legal difficulties. Knowing you are about to inherit millions makes it a simple matter to use bribery to overcome the law in such a place. He could then arrange to have the holdings sold here and the proceeds sent to him there."

Holmes looked to his two friends. "I believe that concludes our case. We have dispatched the monster here, gentlemen. We must return to London with haste and repeat our performance there."

It was not long before the trio ensconced themselves in a comfortable railroad car. Uncharacteristically, Holmes constantly checked his watch to confirm the train remained on time. The actions did not cease until, with a loud whistle and a blast of steam, the locomotive started on its way east. Holmes leaned his head back and closed his eyes.

"Exactly right," he announced, snapping the watch close and returning it to his pocket.

"You still plan to be on the streets of Whitechapel tonight?" asked Lestrade.

"Barring a derailment," returned the detective. He sat up and prepared his pipe. As a precaution, Watson stood and cracked the window slightly, allowing a stream of cool, morning air to enter the close space.

"And is there news from London?" Watson nodded at the stack of newspapers Holmes had gathered beside him.

"I have news that is not in the papers," replied Lestrade, his voice in a conspiratorial tone.

Holmes smiled, lighting his pipe and leaning back. To Watson, it seemed they may as well have been at Baker Street, with Holmes holding court amid a cloud of his fierce, Turkish tobacco smoke.

"Illuminate us!" instructed Holmes.

"Another postcard was received on Tuesday."

"It never fails," observed Holmes. In response to Watson's questioning glance, he continued. "I left for Grimpen that morning." He turned back to the police inspector. "You know I find these letters to be highly dubious. Most, no doubt, are hoaxes of the worst sort."

"And we agree, Mr. Holmes. I have seen the amount of mail you are receiving!" Lestrade laughed, the action a bit forced. It was the need to find some humor in the horrid situation.

A darting smile swept across Holmes lips.

"Yes, Lestrade," he admitted. "I am quite impressed with your handling of it. You have taken a task requiring hundreds of hours of labor, and successfully broken it down so clerical workers sort the wheat from the chaff." Holmes leaned forward in anticipation. "Now, perhaps you can tell us about this new missive."

Lestrade leaned forward. For once, he was able to provide Sherlock Holmes information he did not already posses.

"It was addressed to Mr. Lusk of the vigilance committee."

"I have met him. What was there in the text that convinced you that it was genuine?

"The text...well, the text was as lurid as the previous missives, probably more so. What set this apart was it included a piece of evidence as a bona fide."

"Conclusive?"

Lestrade shrugged. "That would be more in Dr. Watson's field," he added wryly. "The debate continues, but most of the surgeons agree the package contained half a kidney from Catherine Eddowes!"

Lestrade's announcement was dramatic and he was rewarded by near silence from the great detective. Holmes managed but a single word in reply.

"Indeed."

Lestrade reached into his pocket and pulled out a folder sheet. "Would you like to read it?"

Holmes waved his hand to Watson, who took the sheet. The detective preferred to hear the words first, rather than be distracted by any clues in the print. To that end, Watson unfolded the page.

From Hell

Mr. Lusk
Sir I send you half the Kidne I took from one woman prasarved it for you tother piece I fried and ate it was very nice I may send you the bloody knif that took it out if you only wate a whil longer

Signed Catch me when you can Mishter Lusk

Watson stumbled over the misspelled words and odd phrasing. When he finished, he handed the page to Holmes.

"A copy, of course," apologized Lestrade. "You may inspect the original at the yard."

Holmes' sharp eyes scanned the few lines quickly. "You have maintained the spelling and punctuation?" Lestrade nodded. "To an untrained eye, you might suppose it is the work of barely literate person." He handed the sheet back to the police inspector.

"We have our doubts about that, too, Mr. Holmes. It may very well be a man of letters attempting to appear more common."

"I would confirm that idea, Lestrade. Some of the poorly spelled words are done too badly. Even someone making an attempt at a little known word can usually manage a more phonetic spelling." He leaned back, puffing his pipe. "You said there is discussion on the validity of the artifact?"

“Catherine Eddowes was missing a kidney and we kept that information from the inquest. A few of the surgeons believe too much time has passed from the murder to account for the preserved condition of the organ. Others believe it was preserved in a bottle of spirits.”

“Anything else to indicate it is valid?”

“It is the kidney of an alcoholic and matches the observed condition of her remaining organ. There is also a portion of the renal artery attached that matches the remnant in her body.”

Holmes looked to Watson, who nodded in confirmation. “Alcohol leaves it marks on the internal organs. I should think the artery would be conclusive.”

"That is the conclusion of the majority,” replied Lestrade.

“And I will find no mention of the letter in these?” Holmes tapped the stack of newspapers with the stem of his pipe.

“Mr. Lusk has agreed to withhold it for a time.”

“Admirable,” said Holmes.

He leaned back, his pipe filling the small compartment with dense smoke. The stream of air from the cracked window stirred strong currents and eddies. Watson was confused by the letter.

“But why these letters? And why to Lusk?”

Lestrade tried to explain.

“We have been receiving thousands of pieces of mail, doctor. And many more go to the newspapers and, as you know, Mr. Holmes. They fall into four groups: ideas to catch the perpetrator, complaints he isn’t caught yet, and some claim to be from the killer."

"You said four groups."

"Confessions," said Lestrade. "Unfortunately, they never prove true."

"But why claim to be the killer?"

The concept was as hard for the physician to grasp as it was for the inspector to explain.

"You can imagine how excited we were when we received the first one. Then more and more came in from all parts of the country. We try to check them all out, but most are obvious fakes. The motive is unclear."

Holmes chuckled, blowing out another cloud of smoke.

"It is perfectly clear, Lestrade. It is the notoriety. These murders are being talked about around the planet. These misguided people hope to attain some form of fame from association with them."

"Then why send this letter to Lusk?" asked Watson. "Why not send it to the newspapers or the police?"

"Because Lusk is not receiving hundreds of letters." Holmes continued speaking, though his eyes were focused elsewhere, his mind concentrating on the ideas he was relating. "We have noted before the public displays the murderer makes of his victims. This letter is in the same vein, an attempt to stir headlines in the press. To do that, it must be recognized for what it is: an actual letter from the killer himself!"

"Whatever for?" asked Watson.

"On that, I can merely speculate." His gaze returned to his companions and he pointed at Watson with his pipe. "Consider. Watson, if you decided to dispatch Lestrade," he explained, pointing at the inspector, "you would not advertise the fact."

Watson agreed readily. "I would try to hide my involvement with all my ability. I would even try to hide the body, if I could." He eyed Lestrade slyly. "I can think of some rather exotic poisons that might hide the fact of the murder completely."

"Very sweet, Watson," replied Lestrade. "But what is your point, Holmes?"

Holmes grabbed one of the papers and tossed it across to the inspector.

"This killer doesn't want to hide the killings. He wants them displayed on page one of every newspaper in the empire!"

"But why?" asked Watson.

"He is a small man, hidden amongst millions in one of the largest cities of the world. And now, through happenstance, he has found a means to be noticed, to be talked about in every home within range of our telegraphs."

"But no one knows who it is!" protested Lestrade. "What you are saying is sheer contradiction."

Holmes tapped his index finger against his temple. "We are working within the constraints of a troubled mind," he explained. "While our Mister 'X' strives to hide his identity, as does any killer, he needs it to be known the deed was performed by his alter ego, Jack the Ripper."

"So the motive for the killings is to appear in the newspapers?" asked Watson in disbelief.

"Not entirely," explained the detective. "This is more a byproduct of his killings, which he would do anyway. I believe he kills because he likes to kill."

Lestrade looked at the detective in open mouth wonder.

"Committing these horrid crimes only because he *likes* it?"

"Yes." Holmes lit a pipe, looking out the window as the landscape slid past. "He probably loathes women, but has no individual in mind."

Watson also had difficulty understanding the concept.

"But why prostitutes? Surely he was at least wronged by that class of women to make them his particular target!"

"When you hunt rabbits," asked Holmes, "do you look for a particular rabbit or simply accept whichever poor creature crosses your path?"

"It is not the same thing!" protested the doctor.

"It is exactly the same thing!" The detective was warming to his subject now, and the muddled thoughts from the past weeks were falling into place. "And when you hunt rabbits, do you go into the field where they are plentiful or do you break into someone's residence to shoot their pet in its cage?"

"The field, of course," Watson returned.

"There you have it. He needs a certain amount of time to perform his deed. Why work at luring a respectable woman into such a situation when he can entice these lost souls with the promise of a few pennies?"

Holmes watched the faces of his two companions as they digested his theory. Both men were befuddled by the prospects of what he had lain before them. It was a long time before the police inspector was able to voice his opinion.

"You are making no sense, Holmes."

Holmes leaned back, drawing slowly on his pipe. He closed his eyes again and his voice grew softer. He expected such a reception to the concept.

"You are correct, Lestrade. It makes no sense. No sense at all."

Sunday, October 21 *Baker Street*

Sunday at Baker Street was an oddly relaxing day given the events of the past several weeks. The lack of any new murders since the end of September had calmed the public to a degree, though the newspapers continually fanned the flames of hysteria.

Watson, after sleeping in his own bed for the first time in three weeks, spent the afternoon with Mary Morstan, entertaining her with the case in Dovenshire. Holmes was gone before Watson awoke, making good his promise to visit Scotland Yard. So it was not until later, after a quite supper, that the two men relaxed with tobacco and brandy and Holmes took the opportunity to inform Watson fully on what had occurred in his absence, in particular the Juwes message.

"But surely Juwes is a misspelled word," said Watson. "You believe this maniac has tried to hide his education before by misspelling words."

"That is certainly one possibility," agreed Holmes. He was in his element at Baker Street. In comfortable surroundings and approaching this worrisome case as an intellectual pursuit, the frayed nerves so obvious at Baskerville Hall were nowhere to be seen. "There are several others."

"Such as?"

"As my brother pointed out, there is a Masonic meaning to Juwes, referencing the three men who killed the great architect. But it is an obscure reference and not even widely used by the Masons themselves.

"Another possibility is we transcribed the word incorrectly in the poor light of the lantern. It may have been Jieves, the French spelling for Jews."

Watson nodded, puffing his cigar. "An attempt to blame the Jewish community."

"Possibly. It may also point to the most dangerous gang in Whitechapel, the Bessarabians."

"I don't believe I have heard of them."

"And pray you do not," returned Holmes. "They are a group of transplanted Russian Jews, though they owe allegiance to neither their previous nation nor their religion. They are fierce and violent. Remember Emma Smith was thought to be killed by a gang. It is not outside the realm of possibility to have the Bessarabians commit such a crime."

"So that is at least five possibilities."

"Six, if you include it has nothing to do with the crime and was just someone's mindless scribbling. Or seven, as a simple distraction: he drops the cloth, scribbles some words on a wall, then gets away before they are discovered." Holmes explained the final point. "Our man has shown more than average cleverness in his actions. Such a move, particularly when so closely pressed by the police, shows he keeps his wits about him. In any case, not your average murdered by any means."

Their discussion continued, back and forth, on into the evening. Watson broached the subject of the Baskerville case.

"You always say that there is something to be learned from every case and that it can be applied to the next. What of Stapleton and the hound? How might it apply here?"

Holmes clapped his hands in enjoyment at the question.

"Watson, you are positively marvelous. You have a knack for asking seemingly unrelated questions that drive back into the heart of the matter!" Watson lifted his brandy glass in acknowledgement of the compliment, but let Holmes continue without interruption. "Yes, indeed, Watson, what is to be learned from this recent nemesis?

"One lesson to be brought from Grimpen to London, dear fellow, is attempting to get into the mind of the killer. If you learn his thoughts, learn his behavior and motivation, then you have the chance to catch him. That is what I was doing when I was on the moor."

Watson was incredulous. "You believe you can do that with this Whitechapel creature?"

Holmes shrugged, puffing on his pipe for a moment. "He is clever enough in his own fashion. He has eluded the police." He drew again on the pipe and was unsatisfied with the result. He struck a match. "He was quick enough to double back on the chase and escape me." A cloud of smoke grew about him as he brought the pipe back to life. "Even with modesty, I must concede that was no mean feat." The embers died out, and Holmes proceeded to clean the ash before commencing the ritual of refilling the bowl. "By all agreements, this killer may be mad but it has not caused his mind to cease functioning. He is far more intelligent than the police, or I, have credited."

Watson considered the glowing tip of his cigar before granting a grudging concession on the point. "But you imply there is more than one lesson to be learned from Grimpen," he observed.

"So there is," responded Holmes. His pipe refilled, a satisfying gloom of tobacco smoke grew about the detective. "A second lesson is to peel back the case, removing layers as on an onion."

"How so?"

"There are the killings, of course, but they have become obscured by this uproar created by the press. Our first goal must be to clear away some of the excess clutter, much as we did with Mrs. Lyons and the Dartmoor murderer in Devonshire." Holmes nodded in his self created fog, satisfied with this new method of approaching the case. "Yes," he continued as he puffed, "we must get rid of the extraneous factors caused by all the attention in the press. Then, perhaps, we might be able to proceed more rationally."

Watson drew one last, long draw from his cigar and tossed the stub into the fireplace. It was unusual for him, but he reached for the humidor and withdrew a second cigar. Before lighting it, he also poured himself a bit more brandy. He offered the bottle to Holmes, who waved it away. He lit the cigar, drawing in the fragrant smoke for a moment before continuing.

"What other lessons have you brought from the mire?"

"Yes," agreed Holmes, staring off into space for a moment. "Lessons work best by trilogy, do they not?" He sipped his remaining brandy, giving himself some time to compose his thoughts.

"The third lesson...the third lesson..." The voice whispered, concentrating on the idea. Then the face snapped in the doctor's direction, the cool, calculating eyes locking with Watson's. "Simple enough, dear friend. With Sir Henry, we made a mistake. We were both surprised by the hound when it appeared. That mistake nearly cost Sir Henry his life."

Watson sniffed at his brandy before taking a drink. "And the lesson?"

"Plain enough, Watson." The determination in Holmes' voice was uncompromising. "We can make no more mistakes. Every mistake we allow will be counted by another dead body."

The doctor nodded, yielding yet another point to his friend. He downed the remainder of his drink in a gulp. "Then we shall make no more mistakes."

"Let us hope," agreed Holmes in a soft, somber tone. "No more mistakes."

Monday, October 22 *A Brother's Tale*

Mrs. Hudson laid a splendid breakfast for the two men. Watson ate with some relish while Holmes ignored the food on the table before him. He concentrated on the morning *Times*, hoping to spy some clue that would further his investigation. The doctor, recognizing his friend's mood, ate in silence.

Watson, for his part, had taken up the task of reviewing the lists provided by Lestrade. His cross referencing had produced a few names, but the detective had little interest in such a mechanical method of investigation.

Holmes, uncharacteristically, was undecided on a course of action for the day. That fact, as much as any, displayed the disarray of the case. But a sharp ring of the doorbell drew them from their respective thoughts and both stared intently at the doorway.

"Visitor?" queried Watson.

"A telegraph, I suspect," returned Holmes. Before Watson could ask another question, Holmes answered it in a quick snap. "Hardly another murder," he observed. "Lestrade or Abberline would have sent an officer at the first notice." There was a tap at their door. "Come in, Mrs. Hudson," invited Holmes.

Mrs. Hudson entered, a small silver plate in her hand. "A pair of telegraphs, sir."

Holmes was on his feet and took the missives, dismissing their landlord with a callous wave of his hand. He stepped quickly to the window, ripping open the first of the yellow envelopes. He read it eagerly, then tossed the paper angrily to Watson.

"That is the problem when you ask people to do favors! The demand the same in return!" he snapped. "I needed the Yard's assistance with our mail, so Lestrade uses it assign my services as if I work for him!"

Watson quickly read through the telegram.

"He has an issue with this gentleman, a successful barrister with friends in high places. Surely you can take an hour to put the man's fears at ease and allow Lestrade to concentrate on the case?"

"And what of my concentration on the case?" protested the detective. "Does he show any consideration for that?"

Watson suppressed a smile at his friend's anger. "You are getting nowhere, Holmes. Perhaps this will provide a short break and some needed information."

"Bah!" Holmes grabbed the other telegram. "And this other is from the man, himself." Holmes returned to the table and poured a cup of coffee. "William Druitt claims to have important information on Whitechapel." Holmes tossed the paper to the floor. "Spare me from one more person with *important information*!"

"Druitt, you say?" asked Watson, a thought dawning. "Surely, that name is familiar!"

The doctor stepped over to his stack of notes. Sorting through them, he quickly found what he was seeking.

"Ah," he concluded, turning back to Holmes.

"Something of interest?"

"You be the judge." He handed several sheets to the detective. "These are the lists of suspects provided by Scotland Yard. The first is a list of medical students whose *stability* has been called into question. There is a Montague Druitt about halfway down the list."

"A coincidence," scoffed Holmes. "The name is not unheard of."

"No doubt," agreed his friend. "But the other is a list of men encountered in Whitechapel over the past few weeks. It is quite lengthy and of little use, as you continually point out."

"And Montague Druitt is on this other list?"

Watson smiled. "It is alphabetical. Third page, towards the bottom."

Holmes flipped the pages, confirming the information. He took the indicated page and tossed the remainder to the floor and retrieved the telegraph from the accumulating rubble.

"Druitt indeed," he replied. He set the papers on the table and took a drink of his coffee. "There is nothing to indicate they are related," he concluded, still put out at the request from Lestrade.

Watson tilted his head, conceding the point. "Still, it may be worth listening to this Druitt."

There was a new animation in Homes' eyes as he reached for a dish of eggs and moved some to his own plate. "It may, Watson. It may indeed."

Holmes went towards the back room. If he was to have an unknown visitor, he would need to change from his dressing gown.

By two, the lodgings of Baker Street had undergone a miraculous transformation. The dining table and chairs were gone. The floor, strewn with papers from one end to the other, was clear of debris. The mail bags were dispatched to Scotland Yard. The two men were now properly dressed and posed to greet their visitor. Holmes was framed in the window, his gaze fixed at the bustling street below.

"Aha!" he exclaimed. "Unless I miss my guess greatly, this is our visitor now."

He turned to face the entrance as the bell rang at the front door. It was only a moment before the houseboy brought William Druitt to their door. He was middle- aged and slim with graying hair at his temples. He displayed a nervousness that Holmes found reminiscent of Thaddeus Sholto. His face, however, carried worries indicating greater troubles.

Introductions proceeded quickly. Holmes gesture towards a chair for the visitor and took the seat opposite him. Watson took his accustomed position by the fireplace, his notebook ready to record the interview.

"I do appreciate your taking the time to see me," started Druitt hesitantly. "I realize how valuable your time must be."

A quick grin of acknowledgement flitted across Holmes' face. "Then you well understand I must immediately drive to the point, sir. What brings you to our lodgings?"

Druitt fidgeted in his chair, appearing both befuddled and perplexed.

"Come, sir!" demanded the detective. "You ask for my time, and I have been good enough to grant it. I get a dozen requests such as yours a day, so please do not squander the opportunity."

Druitt took a deep breath, straightening as he did. He started again, his voice firmer.

"You understand this is difficult, sir. I informed the authorities, but they dismissed me. I could think of no one else, other than yourself."

"And what information did you give the authorities?"

Druitt swallowed hard, and his voice quavered as he spoke. "It is hard, Mr. Holmes. The unfortunate truth is I believe my brother to be the villain known as Jack the Ripper."

Watson scribbled a quick note. Holmes leaned forward, eyes bright at the admission.

"Many have made that claim in the past several weeks, Mr. Druitt. Why should I consider yours valid?"

Druitt, with the accusation before them, was more at ease as he continued. "Do you have a brother, Mr. Holmes?"

Again, the little, darting grin passed his lips. "As a matter of fact, I do indeed have a brother."

"Then you will know the complexity of my visit." Druitt

smiled sadly. “I love Montague, despite his flaws. But I cannot stand to the side and allow this monstrosity to continue.”

Watson was always the one to provide gentle prodding when it was needed in their interviews.

“Why should you believe your brother is guilty of these crimes?”

Druitt looked down to the floor, his voice sad but firm. “It is no one thing, Dr. Watson. There are a number of events in my brother’s life which have inexorably led me to that conclusion.”

“Illuminate us!” demanded the detective.

William Druitt related a story that seemed not at all unusual. Montague was born in 1857, the second child in a family of seven. The son of a successful surgeon, he attended public school until the age of thirteen, when he won a scholarship Winchester College. His departure was a loss to his mother, who doted on him. He excelled in sports and polemics and was successful in both, being known both for his cricket play and his skill in debate. A scholarship to New College, Oxford, followed in 1876. He had his Bachelor of Arts 1880, and his Masters by 1883. He applied to the Inns of Court in 1882 to become a barrister.

“And what of the years between New College and applying to the Bar. What of those?”

“He studied Medicine for a while,” explained Druitt. “As I said, father was a surgeon and built the family fortune on it. My younger brother Robert has also taken medicine as a profession.”

“And Montague?” asked Watson. “He, too, was to be a

surgeon?"

"He *considered* the possibility," said Druitt slowly.

"Ah," noted Holmes. "A significant pause. But pray continue." He waved his hand. "We shall return to this period in due course."

The younger Druitt began teaching at Valentine's in the same year, a position he still retained. He was finally called to the bar in 1885, but his practice did not flourish. He spent his time teaching and waiting in his chambers for clients who never came. Their mother, meanwhile, had declined mentally and was institutionalized earlier that year.

"When?" demanded the detective.

"July the seventh," returned Druitt. "Montague has not born it well."

"In what way?"

"He has grown nervous and disturbed over the last three months." Druitt paused, and then corrected himself. "No, Mr. Holmes, I dare say that is not quite accurate. He has grown *more* nervous and disturbed since mother was placed in hospital. He has mentioned to me more than once that he fears he shares mother's ailment."

Holmes was becoming impatient with the pace of the man's story.

"Nervousness is not a cause for murder, Mr. Druitt. You believe something else his preying upon him?"

Druitt pulled out his handkerchief and dabbed the sweat that had formed on his upper lip.

"You can tell from his educational history that there was all expectation that Montague would become quite successful. He has driven himself hard to achieve that success, but it continually eludes him."

"He is just thirty-one," pointed out Watson.

"That is true, doctor," acknowledged Druitt, "but he has himself to a strict timetable and he has failed to meet it."

Holmes considered the man before them. "And what of you? You seem well dressed for a solicitor, Mr. Druitt."

"How do you know..."

"Your card, sir, when you presented yourself!" Holmes let out a deep sigh. He tried not to display signs of irritation when clients missed such basic observations. The detective's continued words were a quick, impatient staccato. "Come, sir. There is more to you than success as a solicitor."

"Our father died in 1885, a short while after Montague was admitted to the bar. Being the elder bother, I inherited the bulk of the estate."

"And the balance?"

"6,000 each to the three daughters; a sum set aside for care of our mother. 500 each to the three younger sons."

Watson was amazed at the amounts. "Five hundred for the sons when each of the daughters gets six thousand?"

"A man is expected to make his own way in the world. That was my father's creed."

"And yet you are given the estate," observed Holmes.

Druitt shuffled uncomfortably. "My father's terms were his own."

"No doubt." Holmes, as was his wont, shifted subjects completely. "Let us return to 1880. You say Montague studied medicine?"

"Yes, briefly."

"Why did he not continue?"

Again, the elder Druitt fidgeted. Watson noted even a touch of color rising in his cheeks.

"There was a scandal at the school. Father kept it quiet, but the school would have him no longer. It was then Montague decided to apply to the bar."

"What was the nature of the scandal?" inquired Watson.

Druitt's cheeks flushed a deeper red, but he did not speak.

"Come, man!" demanded Holmes. "You come here to accuse your own brother of the most heinous crimes! Doubtless this scandal has a bearing. What is it?"

Druitt took a deep breath, as if to steel his nerve and stiffen his resolve. "He was found performing a foul vivisection on a female cadaver."

"Not unlike the crimes we are seeing," stated Holmes.

Druitt nodded, his eyes on the floor. He could not meet the gaze from either of the other men in his shame.

"But that is not all," continued Holmes. "You have more than the single incident to give you cause to make this accusation, do you not?"

The elder Druitt continued to speak in a low tone. There was no hesitation now that the perversion of his brother was revealed.

"Montague liked to follow father as a child. Though he was mother's favorite, he always sought father's approval. Showing interest in surgery was one way he did so. In medical school, his teachers noted his skill with the knife. Had there been no scandal, he would certainly have excelled as a surgeon. Father was greatly disappointed at his dismissal."

"No doubt, no doubt."

Holmes leaned back and lit his pipe. Druitt opened his mouth to speak, but Watson held up a hand to counsel silence. The investigator was silent for several minutes before bringing his attention back to the conversation.

"When did you say he was called to the bar? Specifically?"

Druitt thought for just a moment. "April, late April, 1885. The twenty-ninth, I believe."

"The twenty-ninth," whispered Holmes, the words barely audible. "Three and a half years ago." He tone returned to normal level. "And your mother admitted in July on the seventh?"

"Yes, sir."

Holmes smiled. "And does your brother have a fondness for grapes?"

The brother was perplexed by the question, and answered slowly. "When he has the opportunity..."

The detective smiled again, pleased his suspicion was confirmed.

"What are there other reasons you believe him guilty of these crimes?"

Druitt swallowed hard. If he was embarrassed by the

thought of the scandal, these new thoughts were positively mortifying to the older brother.

"I believe..." He paused, stuttered before finished. "I believe my brother to be sexually insane."

Watson was flabbergasted by such a bold observation. To Holmes, it was a phrase that seized his attention. His eyes burned bright with interest as he bent forward slightly to hear the explanation more clearly.

"What leads you to draw such a conclusion?"

The solicitor coughed nervously. "For a man of thirty-one, he has shown little interest in women. I wonder that he is not deviant or perverse."

"You do not mean he has an interest in other men?" asked Watson, the disgust in his voice barely suppressed.

"No!" protested Druitt vehemently. "Nothing of the sort. I have seen nothing to indicate he would engage in such activity!"

"Then we can dismiss the homosexual references," concluded Holmes, his tone intended to provide relief to the two offended men in the room. "But if not in that way, in what manner do believe his insanity manifests itself?"

"I watched him kill a rabbit once, Mr. Holmes."

"Many men kill rabbits, Mr. Druitt. I have eaten several of them, myself."

"I know, sir, but he took such *pleasure* in the killing."

Holmes smiled. He puffed on the pipe and Watson recognized the signs. The detective was drawing a conclusion.

"And not just the killing, was it, Mr. Druitt?"

"No, Mr. Holmes. It was as much the skinning and preparation of the animal that appeared to excite him. In full fact, I was deeply disturbed by his actions."

"And when was this?"

"In late July, sir."

"Nor would one expect you to take much note," agreed Holmes. "Anything else?

"My brother plays cricket in London. I know without a doubt he was in London when at least two of the murders were committed."

Watson wrote some notes, apparently bypassing many of the sexual references made in Druitt's descriptions. A definite reference to the younger brother's presence in London at the same time as the murders was a hard fact he could note without embarrassment.

"Do you, by chance, have a photograph or drawing of your brother?" asked Holmes.

The elder Druitt nodded, searching his vest pockets before withdrawing a small print. He handed the picture to Holmes. The detective stared at it intently.

Druitt, who did not know Holmes, saw no change in Holmes' appearance. Watson, on the other hand, noted the quick flash of recognition followed by a tightening of his friend's jaw. There was more to this picture than the detective was willing to explain at this moment.

"Might I keep this?" he asked, gesturing with the photograph.

"Aye, sir, you may. It is an extra copy I brought for just that purpose."

Holmes slipped it into his vest pocket. He stood

suddenly, an action Watson recognized as signaling the end of the interview. The detective walked to the window. He finished his comments to Druitt, but his attention was elsewhere as he was already focused on the facts laid before him.

"Thank you, Mr. Druitt. At the moment, I cannot offer you an opinion, but I shall take your information under advisement."

"Thank you, sir."

"Watson, get the details on Montague's residence and movements. We may need to investigate more deeply if my conclusions warrant it."

"Of course, Holmes. In truth, sir, I will please me greatly if you prove my brother has no connection at all to these horrid events."

The detective turned back to the solicitor, his voice cautionary. "Mr. Druitt, there is little to indicate your brother is directly connected to these crimes. Still, there is something of interest in what you present." He paused, deep in thought, before concluding his comments.

"Rest assured, everything you have related will be held in the strictest confidence. If something should comc of it, we shall do our utmost to minimize your family's involvement in the matter."

A relief, as if a great weight were lifted from him, washed across William Druitt. "Thank you, Mr. Holmes."

Watson escorted Druitt to the door and obtained information on Montague's lodging and employers. When he returned to the rooms, he found Holmes showing the most animation he had done since becoming involved in the case. He was fairly rubbing his hands together in anticipation of following this new lead.

"I think you make too much of this, Holmes," cautioned the physician. "There is nothing to indicate any connection between this Montague Druitt and the killings."

"You do not see it, Watson? We have every reason to suspect this man. You find him on two of the police lists. Now his brother comes to us because he suspects him of involvement in the murders. These are leads well worth pursuing!"

Watson sat down across from his friend and withdrew a cigar from the humidor. For over seven weeks, the detective had pursued the Whitechapel case with nothing to show for it. The physician feared his friend was reduced to grasping at straws and said as much. Holmes, for his part, was not so easy to dissuade.

"I believe we have just been given the background of the type of man we have been seeking," explained the investigator.

"Frankly, Holmes, I cannot see it. The police have shown little interest in Montague Druitt. Why do you think otherwise?"

Holmes leaned forward. "To help you understand, I must first change your perspective on our killer."

Watson filled his pipe and relaxed, allowing the detective to explain.

"The police are searching for a monster," explained Holmes. "They believe they will find a man like the killer Selden, a man so obviously out of control that he is easily spotted and collected."

Watson nodded, his agreement with the proposition clear. Holmes smiled. Sometimes, it was too easy to bait a trap for his friend.

"Does a man such as Selden seem capable of committing highly intricate murders, displaying the bodies as we have seen, and escaping the police even when they are close upon his heals?"

Watson chuckled. "I will allow you that point, Holmes. A man such as Selden could not commit these crimes. Now you must explain what type of man does commit these crimes."

Holmes smiled. "Fair enough, but we are not searching for a man. We are searching for a predator in human form. He is a man who blends into the surroundings. Our killer is so…" The detective struggled to find a word. "*…mundane.*"

"Mundane?" protested Watson. "This person is a madman, Holmes!"

"No doubt, but not in the way you imagine. If he were, he would have been caught already. No, Watson, I think we are dealing with something very different than what we have encountered before. He appears so normal, no one would believe that he is capable of these murders."

"Like a school teacher."

It was the detective's turn to chuckle. "Precisely."

"So why would think a teacher and barrister is capable of these crimes?"

Holmes arranged his thoughts, assembling the picture he had constructed from the brother's testimony.

"Consider that his mother was confined to asylum on

July the seventh and the first murder took place exactly one month later in August."

Watson remained skeptical. "That is exceedingly thin, Holmes."

"True," agreed the detective as he packed his pipe. "But the next murder occurs on August thirty-first."

"Which is not the anniversary of his mother's confinement," emphasized the doctor.

Holmes lit his pipe. "But it is close to the anniversary of his admission to the bar." Before Watson could protest, the detective explained further. "The next murder occurs on September eighth, and this latest is on the thirtieth. Do you see anything in common with those three dates?"

Watson thought for several long seconds, but finally was forced to shrug and indicate his ignorance.

"The first is a Friday; the next are Saturday and Sunday." There was a twinkle in Holmes' eyes that told Watson this was significant. The doctor considered the facts again, and a light slowly dawned.

"It suggests the murder is a professional man with little or no duties on Saturday and Sunday."

Holmes laughed aloud in pleasure at his friend's success in seeing the connection.

"Bravo, Watson! Bravo!" The detective felt a keen animation from William Druitt's revelations that he had not encountered previously on this miserable case. "I have noted how often you play the fool in your stories of our adventures, Watson," noted Holmes. "You truly do yourself a grave injustice, even though it is obviously done to help the telling of the story."

He took a long draw from the pipe, exhaling the smoke slowly and with some satisfaction. "But you are exactly right, my friend. The timing speaks to a professional man, not the day laborers that inhabit the East End."

"And Druitt is both a barrister and a school master."

"Precisely!"

"But the first murder! Surely, that was a Tuesday morning."

"Yes, Watson, but the Monday was a bank holiday. Offices and schools were closed."

Watson considered the timing for a moment. "He must still get back to Blackheath and make himself presentable before classes. The same is true of Friday the seventh. And someone covered in blood would be noticed on the trains, even at that early hour."

Holmes, as usual, had already considered the possibilities.

"We must first ascertain what time his classes commence. He may only teach afternoon classes, which would provide sufficient time for him to return to Valentine's, clean up, and even rest before appearing at the school. And as I have said before, he may not have been so bloody as the conditions of the victims might imply. Further, he might have a location near Whitechapel that he could wash himself and possibly even change attire before returning to Blackheath. On the twenty-ninth, he used a convenient fountain for the task!"

Watson nodded, accepting the plausibility of the premise. "And what else?"

"He has had medical training, as well as watching his

father practice. His skill with the surgeon's knife was recognized by other professionals."

"The same skills displayed by the murderer." The doctor thought for a moment, then issued an objection. "But I thought the weapon used on the first murder was a bayonet?"

Holmes was not prepared to concede the point and offered additional observations. "While that is true, the first murder was committed by stabbing the victim repeatedly. Would not a post-mortem knife produce the same type of wounds? As you pointed out, a bayonet is a far too clumsy a tool to perform the mutilations we have encountered!"

"No doubt," Watson acknowledged, while remaining unconvinced. "Still you are no closer to connecting this barrister to any of the crimes."

The detective leaned forward. "There are three conditions that must be met to link a criminal to a crime. The criminal must have the motive, the means, and the opportunity to commit the crimes.

"Montague Druitt lives in Blackheath, which is less than twenty miles from the heart of Whitechapel. He lives alone, with few friends, so he is not missed on forays into Whitechapel and the police lists prove that he does make such trips.

"He is barely an hour away if the trains are running on time. He is a professional man with light duties on Saturday and Sunday, giving himself time to recover from the exertions of the killings. His brother has testified he was in London proper for two of the killings. I submit that proves he has the opportunity to commit these crimes."

He held up his right index finger to indicate one of the

three conditions was met.

"There is the exception of the August seventh killing. That is early morning on a working day for the man."

"Remember the day before was a bank holiday. He arrives in Whitechapel late that evening and conducts his business. I would offer that he could not know what effort or time would be involved in the endeavor, since this was his first killing though not his first excursion to the East End. And after the Tuesday killing, he changed to a timing more convenient to his life's schedule."

Holmes saw his friend did not accept the rationale provide. He continued with his next point in an effort to convert him.

"He is the son of a surgeon, with a lifetime to watch his father practice surgery. He studied medicine briefly and was noted for his skill with the surgeon's knife. I submit that proves he has the means to perform the mutilations we have seen."

He lifted his right hand showing two fingers, confident the second condition was fulfilled.

"Based on our current knowledge of the man, I can concede this point," replied Watson in a doubtful tone. "But there are many men besides this Druitt that have the requisite skill to perform the mutilations we have seen. And that still leaves the issue of *motive*. Do you believe this monster kills solely for the joy of killing? How does that connect to this barrister?"

Holmes nodded, somber. As always, Watson had laid his finger on the crux of the matter, the one piece that did not fit the puzzle.

"Indeed, that is the rub in all this," he admitted. "His

motive remains deucedly unclear, but let me put forward a string of observations:

"He was very close to his mother, and she was committed on 7 July. The murders begin one month to the day later;

"His brother considers him sexually insane, whatever he might mean by that, and these crimes have an undeniably sexual component;

"The man himself has stated the fear that he shares his mother's weakness of the mind; he was removed from medical school for committing a vivisection of a sexual nature; and his brother has noticed he takes pleasure in killing."

Holmes' pipe was out. He knocked the dead ash onto the carpet and began to refill the bowl. He looked at Watson to see if the series of points had swayed his opinion.

"None of those observations says much, Holmes." Watson tapped the police lists. "Certainly little of it causes him to rise as a suspect much beyond any of these other names."

"Each one individually is nothing," said Holmes, "Together, they paint a picture of a disturbed man, possibly sufficiently disturbed to create a motive for committing these crimes within the tortured paths of his own brain."

Holmes held up his hand, three fingers visible, to conclude his trilogy.

The doctor wavered, but was not convinced by the technical arguments of his friend. "This may all be true, Holmes, but your premise remains slim."

The detective smiled, his eyes aglow in pleasure. “Ah, but there are two bits of hard evidence you have ignored.”

Watson was perplexed by the statement. He glanced quickly through the rough notes of the meeting, but stopped one page before the end. He smiled at last, knowing part of the answer.

“The grape branch,” he concluded. “You found a grape branch at the Eddowes murder, and Druitt’s brother confirmed his fondness for grapes.”

“And the light dawns,” said Holmes in feigned reverence.

“Piddle!” retorted Watson. “Thousands of people eat grapes. That is no more a connection than an apple core.”

“It is one more fact that aligns on Druitt’s side of the register.”

“A very small one. Wait! You said two bits of hard evidence.” Watson paged through his notes again, searching for the additional fact alluded to by his friend. “I see no other point in William Druitt’s testimony…”

Realization struck, causing the doctor’s words to falter.

“The picture!” he said in amazement. “You recognized him from the picture!”

Holmes withdrew the print from his pocket and handed it to Watson. It showed a young face with well chiseled features. The dark hair was neatly parted in the middle and reflected the equally well-kept appearance of the clothing. The sharpness of the jaw line and nose was slightly suggestive of Holmes. Watson handed the picture back.

“I did not just recognize this man,” explained Holmes, carefully returning the picture to his pocket. “I saw him on

Goulston Street the morning of September 30th. I not only saw him, Watson. I actually spoke with him!"

He held up his hand in triumph, four fingers spread wide. Holmes finally felt he could set a firm course for the case.

"What is your next step? I am not convinced, but I will, as always, provide my assistance. Perhaps your efforts will result prove him innocent."

Holmes laid his pipe aside and stood, looking for his walking stick and gloves. "I shall go to Blackheath and make preliminary inquiries into Montague Druitt."

"Then I shall go with you," said Watson, placing his notebook in his pocket.

"No," replied the investigator. "I will go alone and in disguise. If this is a clue to our quarry, I want nothing to alert him. "

Watson was unhappy at the rejection of his offer. Holmes continued on a lighter note.

"You have been neglecting Miss Morstan these past weeks. This will give you another opportunity to make up for it!"

And with that, the detective was gone, his attention turned north and focused on Blackheath and Valentine's school.

Wednesday, October 24 *New Rooms*

Holmes did not return to Baker Street for an entire day. When he did, he was nearly ecstatic with his discoveries. He moved about the rooms purposefully, packing a bag as he did. The movement woke Watson, who came from his own room bleary-eyed with sleep.

"Aha, Watson!" he cried.

Watson shook his head wearily.

"I suppose the game is afoot," he said with a yawn.

"Indeed! Our Mr. Druitt is a cricketer. He has been in London for at least four of the murders!"

Watson rang for their morning tea and sat down at the table.

"But if he is playing cricket, is he also not in town on some weekends when *no* murders occur?"

Holmes dismissed the proposition with a wave of his hand.

"A negative has no meaning in this case, Watson. I have proven opportunity for all of the crimes since August 7th."

Mrs. Hudson appeared to lay out the tea and Holmes sat at the table with some relish.

"Something more substantial is called for this morning, Mrs. Hudson!" cried Holmes. When the detective was on the trail, his enthusiasm carried him along with little outside effort. Unfortunately, he failed to see that those surrounding him were not similarly infected with his fervor. "A proper breakfast please, while I tell Watson about the rooms I have secured for us in Blackheath!"

"Mr. Holmes!" protested the hard pressed landlady angrily. "You have not provided proper notice!"

The master detective stopped, wondering how he had offended her. He reviewed the conversation and laughed.

"No, you misunderstand!" he said. "I cannot possibly leave your wonderful accommodations, Mrs. Hudson. It has taken me far too long to get you accustomed to my peculiar needs! I shall maintain these rooms until I retire."

Mrs. Hudson shook her head in sad resignation. She seemed almost disappointed at that prospect.

Holmes explained further. "These are temporary in connection to the current investigation."

"Thank you for the explanation, Mr. Holmes," replied the landlady. "I just had a momentary hope my house would be returned to a more *sedate* nature." She stopped at the door. "I shall have your breakfast in twenty minutes."

If Holmes detected the sarcasm in her comment, he ignored it in his keenness to explain further to Watson.

"New rooms?" interrupted the physician before he could continue.

"Temporary, Watson," stressed Holmes. "Temporary!

We shall be salesmen currently engaged in canvassing Blackheath."

"And what shall we be selling? In case I am asked?"

The detective dismissed the implied objection with another wave of his hand. His zeal in pursuing the current lead could not deflect him from his course.

"I shall determine that before we take up residence."

Holmes moved his chair closer to the table and poured tea for both of them. Watson prepared his cup in silence and sipped it to assure it was satisfactory before speaking.

"Might I be permitted an observation?"

"By all means!" Holmes conceded, leaned back in his chair to await the comments.

"You have just completed a grueling case upon Grimpen Mire. As a physician, I might point out that you are not accustomed to a camping life, yet you spent almost two weeks in the elements upon the moor."

"A fair statement," allowed Holmes.

"After a day of little rest, you are presented with one man out of hundreds as a possible suspect in these horrid murders." Watson pointed to the police list. "And now, at your whim, I am to move to Blackheath to track this suspect?"

The detective had no doubts of his decision.

"Yes," he stated bluntly.

Watson sighed, taking a long drink of his tea.

"Balderdash!" he responded.

Holmes laughed out loud at the reply.

"You do not trust me on this?"

Watson was at his honest best.

"In truth? No!"

Again, the detective laughed. The action appeared to unsettle his friend, so he let it die, and sipped his tea before continuing.

"You know that I am not rash..."

Watson snorted to interrupt.

"Except for staying two weeks upon a dangerous bog; or chasing dangerous criminals upon the Thames in police steamboats at night; or running into a room filled with .."

Holmes held up a hand to halt his companion.

"Those occurrences have nothing to do with this! I have thought this through."

"Indeed!" Watson let the sarcasm ring in the single word.

"Yes." Holmes was earnest as he continued. "Do you not think I have found more in Blackheath to confirm my suspicions? His schoolmaster states he has become erratic since August. I have proved he has had opportunity in all the killings. His barrister practice does not exist. He simply sits in his offices and broods the entire time."

"Brooding does not entail murder, Holmes! We all brood. There are many times with you and your damnable needle I can use as examples!"

The last comment was like a slap in the face to the detective. He paused, reconsidering his arguments. When he continued, he changed his attitude to convince his friend of the necessity of the actions he was proposing.

"Watson, you have seen me at my best and at my worst. It is a statement few men can make."

"Too true," returned the doctor. "The issue is that I am not sure which I am observing here."

"I have engaged the rooms for only a month at this point," Holmes relented. "We shall be in London on the weekends, either following Druitt or on our own."

The lack of response from his friend brought another change in tone, to one the great detective rarely used.

"Please, Watson." His voice almost pleaded with his most trusted companion. "I require your assistance on this case or I shall go mad!"

Watson rubbed his eyes, clearing more of the sleep from them. He, too, had experienced a trying time upon the moor. But, as always, he yielded to Holmes' judgment. In this case, however, he added his own caveat.

"Very well. Holmes. A month." His tone showed that he would accept no compromise in the matter. "If you have found nothing to convince me within a month, we will return to London!"

Holmes clapped his hands in triumph.

"Undeniably, Watson, that is the very word! *Convince.*"

There was a knock and Mrs. Hudson entered with a tray of sausages and flat cakes. As she laid them on the table, Holmes concluded the discussion.

"If you are not convinced within the month, I shall trust your verdict and seek another path."

They arrived at the new rooms in Blackheath, carpet

bags in hand. Extra bags were included so they might present the pretense of having "wares" to display. The rooms were plain and well worn and much smaller than Baker Street. They consisted of only a sitting room flanked by two bedrooms.

Watson sniffed the air like a cautious dog and Holmes admitted to himself there was an air of mustiness to the location. The doctor put his bags into one of the bedrooms, then came out and looked at his friend directly.

"One month," he reiterated.

Holmes chuckled, placing his bags in the remaining bedroom.

"So where is this Druitt located?"

The detective pointed to the ceiling.

"In the rooms immediately overhead," he explained.

Watson slapped at one of the chairs, raising a small cloud of dust. He hit it a few more times, waved the dust away and sat down.

"So what is your plan?"

"Quite simple, Watson. He teaches at Blackheath in the afternoons. Mornings will find him at his barrister's office, though it seems he has little or no business. We will follow him and confirm that is all he is doing."

"But we know he does go to Whitechapel on occasion."

"True," Holmes admitted. "Those will be the difficult times, to follow him into London without being seen."

"You said we are to masquerade as salesmen?"

"Suppliers of medical equipment, since you are well

versed in that arena. In truth, I do not expect our identities to remain secret for long."

"Really?" asked an incredulous Watson. "Then why bother with the deception?"

"We bother because it will give us a few days of freedom of action."

"You believe our identities will be revealed?"

"Druitt has already seen me," explained Holmes. "Unless I am to appear in disguise at all times, he is bound to recognize me."

Watson chuckled. "But you so enjoy your disguises, Holmes!"

The detective missed the gentle mockery in his friend's comment.

"Unfortunately, the longer you wear a disguise, the more likely some part of it will fail and reveal the deception. No, it is best to keep things simple." Holmes paused, framing his words before continuing. "We have one other function to complete before he discovers our true identities."

"What would that be?" asked the doctor.

"I wish to inspect his rooms tomorrow while he is at Valentine's school."

"Holmes!" protested Watson.

Holmes dismissed the complaint without consideration.

"Watson, we must determine if this is our man before he can strike again! Searching his rooms may reveal a decisive clue. It is less likely, but it may also prove he is not the criminal we seek. In either case, it is worth the risk to make the examination."

"And if it does neither?"

"Then we will continue to observe him for your stipulated month," replied the detective.

Holmes was usually loath to explain his thoughts to anyone. This case demanded a greater flexibility in that regard.

"I know you have your doubts, my friend," he said. He was unable to suppress all of his own uncertainty. "I must confess I have my own as well. But at this juncture, Montague Druitt is the only identified suspect I have to investigate."

"And if we disprove his involvement?" asked Watson.

"Then we disprove it," answered the detective flatly. "And if that is the case, I am back to the beginning of this cheerless investigation."

Thursday, October 25 *Montague Druitt*

The rooms were dim in the afternoon light. Watson stood, waiting for his eyes to adjust to the interior before closing the door quietly and following Holmes carefully into the center of the room.

He looked around slowly as his eyes grew accustomed to the shaded light of Druitt's room, and he felt his heart beating faster. If his friend was correct, they were at the heart of the Whitechapel crimes. And if they were caught, only ruin and shame could follow.

"Amazing," whispered Holmes. "You must be careful to move *nothing."*

"Why?"

"Look around you."

The room before him was a model of perfection and neatness, with every item carefully laid out. Watson had long ago grown used to the clutter of Baker Street. If Druitt were Holmes opposite, the room before him was further proof. Watson felt he was at a furniture dealer, where samples rooms were set up with care and precision to display their wares. Indeed, Druitt's apartment was of such neat arrangement as to appear unoccupied.

"The man is meticulous," commented Watson.

"Do you understand how this might connect to these staged murders? Everything about them is arranged precisely as the killer desires them – just as is everything in this room." He moved towards the bedroom, careful to touch nothing,

"How can we possibly search such a place?" asked Watson. "We can never hope to return everything to exactly the same position."

Holmes held a finger to his lips and Watson fell silent. The keen eyes of the detective moved across the bedroom with precision, then paused and returned to the dresser.

"There," he said.

On the top of the dresser lay an odd collection of items. A broken necklace, and old comb, a single glove, a ring, and several other assorted items lay there. The arrangement seemed random and at odds with the precision of the remainder of the room.

"What can you make of these?" asked Holmes, looking at them carefully.

Watson snorted. "Bits of junk," he replied. "A woman's glove; a piece of broken mirror; an old hair brush; a broken candle. What can they possibly mean?"

"All items which might belong to a woman," prompted Holmes. He reached over, carefully removing the copper ring from the collection. "Annie Chapman was missing a ring, if you remember."

"You don't think..." Watson's heart beat faster as he let the comment die on his lips.

"I do think," replied Holmes. "These may represent

trophies of a sort, one from each victim. But only he knows for sure what they mean. None of these can be linked back to a specific woman."

"There are a dozen items there!"

"Fifteen," corrected Holmes.

"He has only killed five!" protested Watson.

"We are only aware of five. Perhaps he has not always felt the need to display them so publicly." The detective let out a sign of frustration. "Or they may represent something completely different!"

Watson felt a shudder of disgust run down his spine. "This is too much, Holmes."

A firm hand gripped his shoulder.

"Steady! Nothing is proved by this."

He looked around the room, his indexing finger tapping his chin.

"What else?" he asked to himself as much as anything. "Aha!"

He pointed to a storage trunk. He quickly stepped over to it and just as quickly picked the lock.

"Is that wise?" asked Watson, clearly remembering the detective's admonition from a few minutes before.

"I will be as careful as I can be." His arm was deep in the trunk, feeling about carefully. "Lo!" he said in quiet triumph. "What is this?"

He produced a small bundle, laid it on the floor and unrolled it. It contained tools and a number of lock picks.

"Burglary tools?" questioned a surprised Watson.

“So it appears. It would seem our Mr. Druitt has other interests besides the law and teaching.”

Holmes rolled the bundle and replaced it in the trunk. He locked it and made sure everything was as it was before. He stood and looked around the room, a puzzled expression on his face.

“Is there something else?” asked Watson

“Definitely,” said Holmes. “Wait here.”

The detective moved quickly around the room checking behind and under all the furniture. He found nothing else worth noting.

“What are you looking for?”

“A knife,” returned Holmes. “But I cannot find it.”

“If there is no knife, then perhaps he is the wrong man.”

Holmes did not accept that solution.

“Or it means he has not hidden it here,” he replied. “Come. We have learned all we can today.”

“There is something here that can be linked to a victim?”

Holmes shook his head sadly. “No, but it is sufficient for me.”

They retraced their steps. Holmes went to the table in the main room and laid the single ring on it, clearly visible and out of place among the few carefully arranged items.

“What are you doing?”

“We cannot visit without leaving a calling card.” It was such a simple thing, a single copper ring on a table.

Anywhere else, it would go unnoticed. In this room, it was the same as writing on the walls in broad strokes.

"From today, he will know someone is watching him."

"Is that safe?"

"Not entirely," returned the detective. "But safety is not my concern. If he is our man, we must start to bring some pressure to bear upon him. If he is not, it will make no difference."

They left the rooms and quietly returned to their lair on the floor below. For Watson, it was as trying as anything they had attempted.

Later that afternoon, there was a tread on the stairs. The person walked past and continued to the rooms above. Watson looked up from his newspaper, but Holmes held a cautionary finger to his lips.

They heard the footsteps above them. The sound stopped for a moment, but suddenly moved quickly about the room. It was not long before they sounded on the stairs again. Holmes cracked the door slightly to listen. Watson walked quietly over so he, too, could hear the muffled words drifting up the stairwell.

A man's voice was very loud. Undoubtedly, the lodger had discovered where Holmes had moved the ring.

"Someone has been in my rooms!" Druitt said, his voice at a nearly hysterical pitch.

"But there ain't been no one up there," replied a woman, no doubt the landlady.

"Some of my possessions were moved about!"

Druitt was clearly unhappy. Even such a minor change had upset the neat arrangement of his life.

"You have new tenants below me!" he exclaimed. "It must be them!"

"I haven't 'eard a sound from them all day!" replied the landlady. "Good, proper gentlemen they appear! Was anythin' taken?"

"That's not the point!"

The landlady laughed.

"Mr. Druitt!" she chided. "Why would someone bother to sneak into your rooms and not take nuthin'? Does that make any sense?"

"Mrs. Patrick..." protested the boarder, but she would have none of it.

"I keep a nice house here, Mr. Druitt. Maybe you was just mistaken about something being moved?" she offered.

"That is not possible!" he replied in a huff.

"I will keep an eye open, Mr. Druitt, but right now I got to be lookin' to fixin' dinner."

The conversation was over. It was but a moment before there were heavy steps upon the stair again.

Holmes quickly closed the door. He was not surprised when they heard their quarry stop outside. He cautioned Watson for complete silence. Druitt loitered for several seconds, obviously trying to decide if he needed to confront his new neighbors. He apparently settled against the notion and continued up to his rooms.

Watson whispered, "He suspects us."

"As well he should!" Holmes said, a slight grin darting

across his lips. He continued on a more cautious note. "Be careful to never leave anything about that will reveal our true identities. I think we may expect a return call from Mr. Druitt at some time when we are not present! We know he has the tools; we shall find out if he has the skills."

Watson nodded. "And for now?"

"We wait."

Holmes walked over to the chair opposite the one Watson was using and considered the newspaper. "Are you through with the personal columns? There is always something of interest in there."

Watson sat down and handed his friend the requested section.

"We are stalking a mad killer," he snorted, "and you are reading the personals!"

Saturday, October 27 *A Cricket Match*

Early Saturday, Holmes woke Watson cautiously.

"Come! I want to be ready to follow Druitt when he leaves."

The detective was a little surprised that the suspect had not gone to London on Friday night. But his research showed he was playing a cricket game in London that afternoon, so there was no doubt he would be leaving in the morning.

The two men dressed in slightly shabby clothes and took up inconspicuous positions in the street. It was a chilly day and Watson stamped his feet in impatience until the barrister appeared. With Holmes directing their moves, they followed Druitt to the Blackheath train station and onto the crowded train. Holmes managed to find them seats where they could keep an eye on their target without him directly spotting them. Watson shifted uncomfortably on the hard wood.

"What next?" asked the doctor as the train lurched into motion.

"We will need to be careful in Victoria station so we do not lose him," replied Holmes, his voice low. "If he does give us the slip there, we shall endeavor to catch him at the cricket field."

But Holmes, as always, was Holmes. He maneuvered through the crowds in Victoria station with practiced ease, the doctor close behind and sometimes struggling to keep up. On the street, Druitt took a cab, so Holmes hailed one as well. They followed him to his chambers and the pair took a position to watch both entrances.

"It makes sense," explained Holmes. "The chambers will be mostly empty today, so he can use them to change and store his clothes before heading to the match."

Sure enough, the barrister appeared within a few minutes, now wearing a cricket uniform. They followed him to the field and settled down to a long afternoon of cricket.

Holmes had no interest in the game, though he watched Druitt avidly, trying to pick out clues to his personality from his mannerisms and interactions with the other players. Watson, who had developed an interest in the game while in Afghanistan, watched avidly. But even as a fan, by mid afternoon the doctor dozed off while the detective maintained his vigilance.

Watson woke in time to watch the last wicket. When the game was concluded, most of Druitt's team went off to celebrate together. Druitt left alone, headed back towards his chambers.

"That is interesting, don't you think?" asked Watson.

"What is that?"

"That he leaves by himself. One of the drawing points of games is to gather with friends after it is concluded to have food and a pint."

The solitary Holmes was surprised at the assertion.

"Really? I thought his leaving was normal."

Watson let out a sigh. "You need to be around people more often, Holmes!"

The twilight closed about them as Druitt returned to his chambers. The lamplighters were making their way down the street when he reemerged. He was wearing his clothes from that morning and carrying the same satchel. He engaged a cab, but it headed towards the East End instead of Victoria Station.

"Now we shall see how he does this!" said Holmes as their hansom followed the barrister.

Druitt led them to a boarding house on the outskirts of Whitechapel. It was the sort that let rooms by the night. The barrister entered and Holmes applied a disguise as they watched the residence: bushy eyebrows, a fake mustache, dirt to his face. Watson also applied the dirt, though not without displeasure.

Druitt reappeared wearing a shabbier set of clothes. He walked away from the boarding house and into white chapel.

"Is he trying to blend into the East End?" asked.

"Unquestionably," concluded Holmes. The detective looked to his friend. "This is where we must be the most cautious. We will need to stay closer in the crowded streets and must never lose sight of him."

The cabbie showed some surprise at the changed appearance of his two fares but did not question them as Holmes handed him two bob for a one bob trip. Watson slapped his hands against his upper arms to warm up a bit and sniffed the air.

"Cool and damp, but I think no rain."

"That will be fortunate if we are to be walking about all night," returned the detective with some relief.

They started lazily down the street, maintaining their view of Druitt on the opposite side. The streets were not overly crowded, but certainly more than would be encountered in a respectable neighborhood by this time of night.

Druitt, as well as Holmes and Watson, were approached by women. But the object of their observations seemed uninterested in any of them. He merely walked on, jostling between the people and moving deeper into the East End.

"I see what you mean about the police, Holmes," said Watson, his voice low. He shifted his eyes towards a group of three men standing together outside a pub. "If those are not constables, I have learned nothing from you these past several years."

Holmes looked in that direction.

"They are not constables, Watson," he said in his normal monotone. "One works at a slaughter house, one is a cobbler and the other undoubtedly a furrier."

He looked at the crestfallen expression on his friend's face and could not bear the thought of causing him more discomfort. He laughed and slapped Watson on the back.

"I'm sorry, old boy," he apologized, still chuckling. "Just a little joke. You are correct. Without question, they are policemen, as are the other two groups further up the block."

Watson sniffed with contempt.

"I try to apply your methods, and then you have fun at my expense when I am correct!"

Watson tried to hold the look of anger on his face, but could not do so any better than Holmes had hidden his own joke. The two men laughed aloud as they continued on, to all appearances two close comrades out for a night's entertainment.

"So, Watson," asked Holmes, as they watched Druitt pass two more women who were obviously vying for his attention, "you have much more experience with men on the prowl than have I. Is this normal? Is a man who admits to the police he only comes to the place to consort with casual women this selective?"

"Naturally, I have never used the services of such women," Watson explained with some indignation. "Yet I have watched many enlisted men in such areas of India. And you are correct: I have never seen one so discriminating."

Druitt walked but continued to exhibit this behavior. He did stop and talk to two or three women for a few brief moments before moving on, but the majority he pushed past and did not give them a second look. After an hour of this, he reversed his course and, maintaining the attitude towards the prostitutes, eventually gained the edge of Whitechapel and returned to the boarding house.

Holmes and Watson followed and watched the suspect enter the building. Holmes pulled out his watch as he found a shadowy doorway.

"Barely midnight!" he announced. "Unusual for a man who must routinely stay out until two or three to commit these atrocities."

"Unless your suspicions are incorrect," pointed out his friend.

Holmes looked at his colleague's weary features.

"Why don't you head back to Baker Street and get a good night's rest?" he suggested.

"And what will you do?"

"I will keep watch, though it seems our quarry has gone to bed early this evening. I will try to get word to you if he makes a move, otherwise you can meet me back here by eight."

"And you will simply stay here?" asked Watson, incredulous.

Holmes snorted. "I have maintained surveillance far longer than overnight under conditions much worse than this, Watson. Go to our rooms and get some well-deserved rest. I shall sleep on the train back to Blackheath tomorrow."

Watson opened his mouth to protest again, unwilling to let his friend maintain the vigil alone. But then he yawned, and accepted the truth of Holmes' observation.

"It *would* be nice to sleep in my own bed!"

"Eight o'clock," repeated Holmes, smiling. "Much later, and you may find our bird has flown, and me with him!"

Watson returned, refreshed, at the appointed hour. Holmes still stood watch and Druitt had not budged. It was not until ten that the barrister appeared, and he displayed only the most straight-forward actions by boarding a cab and heading towards Victoria station. Holmes flagged their own cab and Watson handed Holmes a telegram as they settled in.

"From Lestrade." Holmes read it quickly. "Abberline requests my presence at a meeting with Sir Charles Warren tomorrow at ten."

Watson smiled. "As your physician, I would recommend a good night's sleep tonight."

"As you say if I must confront an official gathering. I will need to get more information on what is required before entering that lion's den." He checked his watch looked at their target's cab. "I will head to Scotland Yard if you believe you can follow Druitt back to Blackheath."

"I believe I can do that," the doctor replied.

"We are past the crisis this time, Watson. There should be no problems."

"But what of next week?" asked the doctor. "Are we to repeat this performance?"

"Next week, and the week after, and the week after!" snapped Holmes in irritation.

His mood was more indicative of his frustration with the case than anger at his friend's question. Still, he did take the time to answer Watson directly.

"We will do this every week, Watson, until I have proven Druitt innocent or have him arrested for these crimes."

The cabs arrived at Victoria Station. Watson waited for Druitt to move into the crowd before leaving to follow him. The detective watched his friend walk off and had the cabbie head towards Scotland Yard.

He was disappointed with the results of his scrutiny. Not for the first time, he questioned if he was on the correct track. Perhaps his friend was correct, and his effort in Druitt's direction was wasted. He tried to push the doubts from his thoughts, but they still plagued him when he arrived at Scotland Yard.

Monday, October 29 *A Meeting of Bureaucrats*

Holmes arrived at the conference room near Sir Charles Warren's offices at ten as requested. He joined Abberline and Lestrade to one side, trying to sort out the notables from the servants as he did. As he was doing so, one young man came over and shook his hand enthusiastically.

"Pardon my interruption, Mr. Holmes." He was a clean shaven young man in his mid-twenties and smiled brightly. He was sharply out of place with the middle-aged and older men in the room.

"Constable Walter Drews, sir," the man continued. "I've been a great admirer of your work and have been trying to follow your methods."

"Pleased to meet you," replied Holmes mechanically. "I hope those methods serve you better than they have for me in this matter thus far."

Drews showed surprise at the comment, but quickly responded in the cheerful voice. "I'm sure that's not true, Mr. Holmes! Not true at all."

There was no chance for a further exchange as Sir Warren tapped on a glass, bringing the assembled investigators to the table.

Holmes had planned to sit with Abberline and Lestrade, but found instead all places had carefully printed name plates. He was at the end of the table, sitting across from a graying man not much older than himself. He read the name plate and saw it was Robert Lees, the psychic. He sat down, nodding to the spiritualist. He now had no doubts where Warren placed his opinion in this matter.

"Mr. Holmes, sir," introduced the man beside him. "Dr. Forbes Winslow. I am a great admirer...."

Holmes was not given a chance to respond as Sir Charles again tapped the glass to bring silence. The Commissioner of the Metropolitan Police was in full uniform, befitting the moment. There was so much gold piping among the commissioners and assistants at the table, the detective began to think he should have worn his tails and white tie.

"Gentlemen," he began, the crispness in his voice slicing the air like a knife, "we are here to discuss the series of murders in Whitechapel. The notoriety gained in the press has caused the Metropolitan Police..."

"And the City of London Police!" The protest came from Lt. Col Henry Smith, the Assistant Commissioner of the City of London Police. He, too, was resplendent in a military uniform.

"And the City of London Police," continued Warren, the irritation clear in his voice, "much disruption with little opportunity to capture this killer."

"It seems the Metropolitan police is wasting their effort trying to interview every man in the Whitechapel," commented another man Holmes recognized as James

Monro, head of Special Branch. The detective recalled that when Warren received the Commissioner's post, Monro had also been in close running for the position.

"Special branch is here by request of the Home Secretary, Mr. Monro. As you are not directly involved in the investigation, please do not abuse the privilege!"

"I take exception with that tone, sir!" protested the man seated next to Monro.

Sir Melville MacNaughten was an assistant in Special Branch. In the political world of the London police, he had been passed over for appointment as the Chief Constable. His clashes with Sir Charles Warren were well known.

"Sir Melville," returned the Commissioner, "you are here only because Mr. Munro asked for your presence…"

"And the Home Secretary approved."

"I am well aware of your friends, Sir Melville."

"Sir Melville," sniffed Monro contemptuously, "has made an exhaustive, independent study of these murders."

Holmes watched the bickering continue. Smith, from the City of London police, was the commissioner responsible for the Eddowes murder since it fell under his jurisdiction, but the other three men merely bounced his requests back and forth as if it were a tennis match. Abberline and Lestrade, with their medical expert Dr. Swanson and the young constable Drews, shifted uncomfortably as their superiors continued the squabble. Holmes, Lees and Winslow, as the civilians in the group, may as well have not been present.

Holmes looked around the room. One wall had a large mirror that seemed oddly fixed to the wall. He smiled, understanding part of the purpose of the meeting. The most obvious person that should have been present in the room but was not was Sir Henry Matthews, 1st Viscount Llandaff, the Home Secretary. He was the one man to whom all these bureaucrats reported. Holmes deduced the Viscount was watching the proceedings from behind a two way mirror.

Warren finally brought the administrative dispute to an end by standing up and raising his voice.

"Gentlemen! We are here to discuss a matter of great importance to this city and the empire! May I be allowed to continue?"

The other men ceased their complaints and allowed Warren to make his point.

"I, too, have been studying these crimes with much interest and I think, with all due respect, Inspector Abberline and his men have overlooked an obvious connection."

Abberline, to his credit, looked to his superior in all innocence.

"And what might that be, sir?" he asked, his voice nonplussed.

Warren sat down slowly, allowing the anger he had towards Monro and McNaughten to subside and refraining from redirecting it at his subordinate.

"Inspector, you eliminated the gang issue very quickly. Reports continue to surface of the Bessarabians and their extortion of the local businesses in Whitechapel. Is it not possible these murders are just an extension of that extortion applied to the prostitutes working the streets?"

Abberline looked to Lestrade to answer the suggestions.

"Sir, we can find no connections between the gangs and these killings. There may be a connection on Emma Smith, but that would place her killing outside..."

"Have you investigated the gangs?" interrupted Warren

"As best we can, sir," replied Lestrade.

"And how is that? Have you actually talked to their leaders, brought the force of the law to bear upon them?"

"If I may interject, Sir Charles?" asked Holmes.

Warren was obviously not pleased by the detective's intrusion. But Holmes knew his presence in this room could only have been dictated by persons above Sir Charles. That knowledge gave him a certain feeling of immunity in rising to his friends' defense.

"I have reviewed both the cases and the police procedures in use. The assessment that the Bessarabians, or another Whitechapel gang, is involved seems most unlikely. I can assure the commissioner that any attempt by the official police to present the matter to the gang leaders directly would result in a great deal of bloodshed."

Warren made a note on a sheet, then folded his hands and looked to the consulting detective.

"Perhaps, Mr. Holmes, as an *unofficial* policeman, you might turn your skills towards disproving a gang connection?"

The rapid response from Warren startled Holmes as he had not expected the police commissioner to have such a quick reply. But, as always, he did not betray that emotion on his features. Instead, he made a note of his own on the sheet before him before answering the request.

"I believe I can accomplish that, Sir Charles." He looked at the commissioner in all innocence. "Would tomorrow be sufficient?"

The frank response flustered Warren.

"Yes, I think that will do," he answered.

Though Warren accepted the detective's comment with studied blandness, Abberline and Lestrade looked towards Holmes in expressions of horror.

"Holmes!" protested Abberline. "You will be taking your life into your hands!"

Holmes waved off the protest as casually as he could manage.

"Dosenovtich and I are old friends," he said lightly. "I am sure he can fit me into his schedule in the morning."

The policemen were unconvinced, but Sir Charles moved the meeting along.

"Good! Here is the next issue I want to address with the entire group." He nodded towards Abberline, who stood and began handing out sheets to all those present.

"This our best list of known suspects, contributed by the efforts of Inspector Abberline's unit as well as others in this room. I must stress that the existence of this list *cannot* leave this room!" He looked to each of them in turn with a deadly earnest that doubtlessly had served him well in battle. "If any of these names reach the press, the man's life will be forfeit!" He finished, but his attention was fixed on Monro and MacNaughten. "Do I have everyone's solemn word they will not reveal this list to anyone?"

Everyone around the table murmured their acceptance of the terms.

"Thank you." Warren looked to the end of the table. "Dr. Winslow, Mr. Lees, Mr. Holmes. I believe we have some organizational issues to address. Thank you for attending."

That was as frank a dismissal as Holmes had received in a long time. It also confirmed that he ranked even lower than the psychic in the eyes of the police commissioner. He stood, made a plain farewell, and accompanied Lees and Winslow into the corridor.

"Mr. Holmes," said Forbes as the doors closed behind them. "I am pleased we were able to meet, though I wish we had more time to talk. I must be off to my rounds."

"No doubt, doctor," Holmes returned, returning the handshake.

"Please investigate the last name on the list. Inspectors Abberline and Lestrade have no interest in this man, but I believe there may be reason to suspect him."

With that, Winslow collected his hat and stick and was gone. Holmes took his hat and gloves from the steward, but found Lees was at his elbow. The man was slight and quiet and had waited during the exchange with Winslow without comment.

"Mr. Lees, sir," said Holmes, with a touch to his brim. "Good day, sir."

"A moment of your time, if I may," said Lees. Holmes stopped and the psychic continued. "I know you have no belief in my methods, Mr. Holmes, but please accept that my intentions are the same as yours – the resolution of these terrible killings."

"It is not your intention that I question, Mr. Lees. It is simply the effectiveness of your methods."

"That is common to all unbelievers, Mr. Holmes. I am not offended by your honesty."

Lees held out his hand and Holmes took it. They had barely touched when Lees pulled his hand away with some force. Holmes could not contain his surprise at the action. Lees, for his part, was most apologetic.

"Forgive me, Mr. Holmes! Occasionally, when I touch someone, I am overcome with a vision."

"Ahh." The detective had a difficult time restraining the derision in his tone. He summoned up the courage to continue without sarcasm. "And what, pray tell, did you foresee?"

"Most odd, Mr. Holmes. Most odd indeed." Lees looked at him, his watery blue eyes intense. "*Where Marylebone, Blackheath, Camberwell, and Whitechapel intersect.*" His voice was soft, almost otherworldly, though Holmes hated the thought of that description. "Does that mean anything to you?"

Holmes did not see any connection between Druitt and Camberwell. For all his love of puzzles, he did not see how four widely separated sections of London could *intersect*.

"I am afraid it does not," he replied coolly.

Lees nodded. "It will soon," he said with assurance. "It will soon!"

That evening, Holmes and Watson arrived at the Diogenese for the usual silent dinner with Mycroft. It was only after retiring to the Stranger's Room that their first words were spoken.

"You were with Viscount Llandaff behind the mirror of course," observed Sherlock.

"Well, of course!" returned the elder brother. "It took a considerable amount of my influence to have you in attendance."

Holmes did not answer as he took his chair, waiting for his brother to make his point in his own time. Mycroft, for his part, was settling in, lighting a cigar and arranging his brandy. As he did, he continued what, for him, amounted to small talk.

"Did you like our display of governmental efficiency this morning, Sherlock?"

Holmes snorted. "I had already deduced as much from Abberline and Lestrade's frustration."

"Monro and MacNaughten have the ear of the Home Secretary. Warren cannot remain for much longer without catching this fiend." Mycroft withdrew a sheet of paper from within his coat. "Which brings us to their list. They have so few names after two months?"

"It is either that or a list of hundreds," returned Holmes. "There are only three potential candidates, and I believe one is guilty."

"I see." Mycroft surveyed the list. "Surely not the Duke of Clarence?"

"He was in Scotland."

"And who is this Aaron Kosminki?"

"He is a mental incompetent. I think the police felt the need to add a Jew to their list because of the Juwes message."

Mycroft chuckled. "No doubt. They will always fall back on the obvious. Michael Ostrog?"

"A Russian with gang associations," explained the detective. "He is currently in a French jail."

"Humph," grunted Mycroft. "I suppose even Warren will figure out he's not guilty at some point. G. Wentworth Smith?"

"A Canadian, but there is nothing to connect him other than he lives in the area. He was Dr. Winslow's suggestion because of some erratic behavior. Even Winslow has withdrawn his support."

"Dr. Stanley?"

"A madman of some sort, but he left for America before the last murders." Holmes lit his pipe. "I certainly think him capable of these atrocious crimes, but he can hardly commit them if he is no longer in the country."

"A Jill the Ripper? Are they serious?"

"A woman could get close enough to another woman, but I believe a woman would be too weak for the strangulations."

"And Sir William Gull!" Mycroft was positively offended at the inclusion of the name. "The man is half paralyzed from a stroke and 70 years old!"

"He is also a skilled physician and has a fondness for grapes."

Mycroft nodded. "I am aware that a grape branch found at the last murder."

"And don't forget the psychic!" chimed in Watson.

Mycroft looked at the doctor in disbelief, but Holmes explained further for his brother's benefit.

"Thank you for reminding me," said the detective. "The psychic Robert Lees led Abberline to Gull's residence, so his guilt is obvious."

"Piddle!" scoffed Mycroft. "I was against allowing him in the conference, but even I get overruled on occasion."

"Doubtless," agreed the younger brother.

Mycroft eyed the list carefully through his thick reading glasses. "George Chapman."

"A vile creature who, in the course of time, shall come to an evil end. He is not guilty of these crimes."

"There is but one name left," said Mycroft. "Montague Druitt?"

"Guilty." The single word was spoken in the coldest tone that Watson ever heard issue from Holmes' lips.

"I see," said Mycroft suspiciously. "You have evidence to present."

"You know me too well, brother."

"But these other names!" protested the elder Holmes. "How do they come onto this list? Are they even to be taken seriously?"

"Each for their own reason," explained Holmes. "Chapman is certainly a villain capable of murder, but he would not bother with crimes of this nature. The request to investigate the Duke came from the palace itself. Dr. Stanley has a reputation for dangerous hobbies; a 'Jill the Ripper' would certainly be able to approach the victims without suspicion but could never strangle them with her hands."

"And Druitt?"

"I shall lay the case before you and let you decide," explained Holmes.

For the next thirty minutes, the detective detailed the evidence they possessed, including that garnered by entering the man's rooms. When he finished, he sat back, poured a touch of brandy and relit his pipe.

"And that is all?" Mycroft was incredulous his brother had so few facts to support his assertion.

"He fits the description; I saw him at the scene of one of the killings."

Mycroft looked over to the physician.

"What do you think, Watson?"

"I believe your brother is jumping at conclusions, but he also has the uncanny ability of being right."

Mycroft folded the list and returned it to his pocket.

"Then it is simple. Tell Abberline to have the man arrested or committed."

Holmes shook his head. "If I am wrong, his life will be forever ruined."

"I agree with Dr. Watson that he is an unlikely candidate. But if you are right," Mycroft pointed out, "no one else will die."

The detective made no reply, so the elder Holmes continued.

"Since you will not follow my advice, what action will you take?"

"Druitt is all we have. I will continue to watch him,

particularly on Friday and Saturday nights. This case is like an onion, brother. We must peel off layer after layer to reach the truth."

Mycroft snorted. "And the Bessarabian gang is a layer?"

"It will answer the question of Emma Smith." The detective finished his brandy and knocked the ash from his pipe into the fireplace. "Dosenovitch has agreed to an audience. We shall know in the morning."

"You rose to Sir Charles' bait quickly enough on that point!" chided Mycroft.

"I believe he intended to use it as a point to discredit me. I shall be safe enough seeing Dosenovitch."

"How can you be so sure?"

"I will have my bodyguard with me."

Both men looked to Watson. The doctor was surprised by the sudden attention.

"I see. Now that you feel a need to resort to brawn over brain, I am suddenly useful to you!"

Tuesday, October 30 *Bessarabians*

"Do you really believe this is necessary, Holmes?" asked the doctor in a hoarse whisper. "I have come to loathe Whitechapel. When I feel there are no further dangers to be found on these cruel streets, you produce another!"

"I can see no other way, Watson."

They left the hustle of the main streets further behind. Like Watson, he was all too aware of their solitude among the rough looking characters lining the streets.

"I think you are risking both our lives to no good purpose!"

There was a tinge of anger in the doctor's voice. Obviously, he was not pleased with their current mission.

"We shall be safe enough," said the detective. "Dosenovitch has guaranteed it."

"That means so nothing to me!" snapped Watson.

He withdrew his service revolver, opened the chamber and closed it again with a snap. He reached into his other pocket and pulled out a handful of cartridges. He nodded in satisfaction and returned gun and bullets to their respective pockets.

"I see you are prepared."

"As always. I don't suppose..." he ventured.

The corner of Holmes' lip turned up in something approaching a wry grin. "In this case, my friend, I am carrying my revolver as well." The detective paused, pointing to a dilapidated warehouse before them. "There lies the gang's headquarters."

The hansom stopped, the cabbie grateful to collect his fee and leave the place more rapidly than they had arrived. The two men stepped down and Holmes pulled out his watch.

"We are a touch early. Abberline and the constables will not arrive for another twenty minutes." He snapped the watch closed, his eyes darting about. "I fear we must proceed. We can be in no greater danger on the inside than we are on this street."

Watson drew himself up, stiffening his resolve. "I trust your judgment, Holmes."

The detective straightened, gesturing at the building with the tip of his walking stick. " 'Once more unto the breach'," he quoted, then stepped off smartly.

They were greeted at the entrance by as rough a pair of hoodlums as Holmes ever recalled. The larger of the two blocked their path and spoke in a thick Russian accent.

"What you want here?"

"You will find," returned Holmes in as casual a manner as can be imagined, "that we are expected. Let Dosenovitch know Sherlock Holmes is here."

The brute stepped aside while the other man opened the door and led them into the dim interior. Around disorganized stacks and crates and through piles of refuse, they were conducted to an inner room. Dosenovitch, the leader of the Bessarabian gang, sat at a table in the center of the room, a full dozen of his henchmen gathered with him. A lone empty chair waited.

Holmes stepped to the chair, regarding its dirty surface with some distaste before seating himself. He and the leader regarded each in silence for a long moment before the Russian spoke.

"You are not welcome here, detective. You have caused our organization too many troubles over the last years."

"And, no doubt, I shall do so in the future," replied Holmes cheerfully. "However, it is to save you troubles that I am here today."

The Russian's eyes narrowed suspiciously. "Save us troubles? Ha!" The coarse laughter was echoed by the henchmen, who moved slowly to either side.

"Indeed." Holmes raised a hand and the movement of the men stopped. "Pray, move no further."

"And why not, Mr. Sherlock Holmes? We have you on our ground now. We will take advantage of that!"

"I think not." Watson punctuated his comment by the audible cocking of his service revolver. He held it in a steady hand, unwavering as he aimed it towards the gang's chief.

"You dare draw a pistol..." started the enraged Dosenovitch.

"The good doctor has had considerable practice with that revolver on the Afghan frontier, Dosenovitch. I dare say he cannot miss at this distance."

"We are many. You cannot kill all of us!"

"That may be true, but I shall kill you," stated the doctor flatly.

"Tut, tut," interrupted Holmes. "I say, Dosenovitch, do you ever read any of Watson's rather gaudy treatises on my exploits?"

There was sweat on Dosenovitch's brow. It was with effort the large man turned his attention from the gun pointed at him.

"I have heard of some of them."

"In one, Watson relates how I shot a perfect VR in the opposite wall of our chambers. Truth be told, that was actually Watson's doing."

"It helped relieve a case of writer's block," said Watson with a slight shrug. Even in that movement, the aim of the weapon did not vary.

"In any case, I dare say he will drop you and another five of your men before you reach him." The words had the desired affect upon the henchmen. They shuffled uncomfortably at the threat. One or two even inched backwards slightly. Holmes concluded amiably. "It seems a high price to pay when I merely came to talk."

Dosenovitch considered the unflinching hand of Watson and then noted the weakening resolve of his own men. With a quick motion, he had them withdraw to their original positions. As they gathered behind their leader, Watson eased the hammer down on the revolver and pointed it to the ceiling. His gaze remained fixed on Dosenovitch.

"What do you offer us?" asked the Russian.

"You will provide me with information. If it is what I expect, I shall inform the authorities you are innocent of the Ripper killings."

Dosenovitch regarded the two men through narrow eyes. At length, he nodded slowly in agreement.

"Will you confirm that your gang is not responsible for the killings that have occurred since August?"

"Of course," replied Dosenovitch. The tone of his response left much to be desired.

"And why should I trust that?" snapped Holmes. "What proof do you offer of your innocence?"

The color rose in Dosenovitch's cheeks, visible even where the heavy beard covered his features. "You doubt my word?"

"Unfortunately, I must," returned the detective.

Dosenovitch spread his hands in innocence. "We provide a service of protection. To get that service, you must pay. These women cannot even feed themselves. How can they afford our services?"

Holmes smiled, a quick, darting action that disappeared as quickly as it appeared. "To be fair, I deduced as much. There is, however, the case last spring of Emma Smith." The name caused the gang leader's eyes to narrow. He could not hide the fact he was familiar with the woman. "By her own words, she was attacked by a gang, and there is only one predominant gang in Whitechapel."

"So we are revealed by our own success." Dosenovitch leaned forward. "A new member was too enthusiastic."

"He must be revealed to satisfy the police," directed Holmes.

There were chuckles at the request. Dosenovitch smiled as he replied.

"He has been disciplined, Mr. Holmes. He will not bother anyone."

"How can I be sure?"

Dosenovitch laughed outright.

"It was a *permanent* solution," he said in his heavily accented voice.

Holmes nodded. When necessary, the gang was more effective than traditional law enforcement.

"So you will tell the police as you promised?"

"I will keep my word." Holmes looked down into the eyes of the other man. "If I find any evidence to the contrary, trust there is no place on this earth where you shall be safe from my reach."

He turned and left at a sharp pace, not waiting for their guide to lead them. Watson withdrew more slowly, walking backwards and keeping his pistol at ready until he had closed the door behind him. He followed Holmes as they quickly left the building.

Emerging into the wintry daylight, Holmes withdrew his watch. "Twenty minutes precisely, Watson."

As if on cue, a police wagon rounded the corner, a dozen or more stout constables hanging onto the sides. Abberline rode in coach immediately behind them.

"Mr. Holmes," greeted the policeman as the coach drew to a stop.

"Inspector," returned the detective. "They have confirmed they are innocent of the current string of killings. The man responsible for Emma Smith has been dealt with. It was clear from the gang boss that the guilty party was executed."

"I see. Then we are not needed?"

Holmes and Watson exchanged glances. The doctor did not wait for confirmation from his friend.

"I, for one, need your company on our way out of this cesspool!" He stepped over and climbed into the coach across from the police inspector. "Are you coming, Holmes?"

"I can agree discretion is the better part of valor this morning," returned the detective. He climbed into the coach and settled into the seat beside Watson.

"Then what is your next step?" asked Abberline as the coach moved forward, picking its way from the depths of Whitechapel.

"I will return to Blackheath and monitor Druitt."

Abberline shook his head. "The man is a respectable barrister and teacher. You are wasting your time there!"

"I have eliminated every other suspect on your list!" The patience in Holmes' voice was paper thin. "Stanley has fled to America; Chapman needs only to provide an alibi; I just removed Sir Charles' Bessarabian connection!"

He leaned forward until he was eye to eye with the police inspector.

"There *is* no one else!"

Wednesday, October 31 *Neighbors*

Watson was late returning to Blackheath. A patient had kept him in his surgery longer than anticipated. So it was in the early evening that he climbed the flight of stairs to their temporary quarters. And as he was preparing to insert the key in the lock, a voice spoke from behind him.

"Ahh, doctor! You must be one of my two neighbors!"

Watson turned and found himself face to face with Montague Druitt. The young man was smiling pleasantly and held out his hand.

"I live upstairs. Druitt."

Watson took his hand and tried to remember his alias.

"Avery. John Amery. And I am not a doctor, merely a purveyor of surgery tools."

"I would have thought a doctor. Oh well," the young teacher said, "my guesses have been wrong before." He gestured towards the doctor's cane. "Military man?"

"Assisted in a surgery in Afghanistan," returned Watson. He tapped his leg. "Stopped a Jezail bullet I'm afraid."

"I thought I detected a limp. Then your friend must be

the doctor."

"He's really more of a chemist. Complain to him if he stinks the place up."

Druitt chuckled.

"I will do that! I am off to dinner," announced Druitt, turning back towards the doctor. "It was a pleasure meeting you Mr…Avery. We must all do dinner sometime."

"We are only here for a short while," replied Watson.

Druitt continued down the stairs without a response. Watson watched him for a moment, then opened the door and entered the darkened apartment. Holmes stood at the edge of a window, carefully looking out through a slight break in the curtains.

"I heard your encounter with our Mr. Druitt."

"Sorry, Holmes," Waston apologized. "I was late because I was delayed in London and I met him on the stairs."

"No harm, old fellow," returned the detective cheerily. "It was bound to happen. You relayed our cover story admirably, by the way." Holmes stepped back from the curtain and turned up a lamp. "I do not think he believes it, though."

"Neither do I." Watson tossed his cane and hat aside and sat in one of the chairs. He rubbed his wounded leg to ease the pain. "What are we doing here, Holmes?"

"We are watching our main suspect. You know that." The detective took his chair across from Watson and filled his pipe. "You still have doubts about Druitt?"

Watson snorted. "He seems a pleasant enough chap. He works in two honest professions. Other than seeking his sordid pleasures in Whitechapel, there is nothing to connect him to these murders. And he is certainly not the first respectable man to find diversion on those streets!"

Holmes blew out a cloud of smoke. "What else would you have me do?"

"In truth, I do not know," confessed the physician in resignation. "If the police would provide a more likely suspect, I would have you pursue him!"

He got back to his feet and walked over to the brandy decanter. Pouring himself a drink, he downed it in one gulp.

"The leg is bothering you," said Holmes.

"It is this damnable wet weather!" cursed Watson. "If it would at least rain, I would get some bit of relief."

Holmes walked over to the fireplace to knock the remains of his tobacco from his pipe.

"Come on, old man. I will find us some place decent to eat."

Watson smiled and looked for where he had thrown his cane.

"That is the first thing you have said that makes sense since I walked in here," he said, managing a pained smile. "I cannot face another of Mrs. Patrick's meals."

The detective returned the smile.

"We can agree on that, at least!"

Thursday, November 1 *A Quiet Dinner*

Holmes sat alone at dinner, waiting a meager meal as was his wont during a case. He became aware of a man standing by his table. He did not bother to look up.

"Mr. Druitt, have a seat."

Montague Druitt sat down across from the detective. His clothes were immaculate, along with the arrangement of his hair. Though it was late in the day, he appeared clean shaven, as though he had shaved quite recently.

"Mr. Sherlock Holmes, I presume."

"As you well know, I am sure." Holmes tapped his wine glass with his fork. "Would you care for a glass of Claret? It is quite adequate. And I might recommend the kidney pie as well. Mrs. Patrick is not much of a cook."

Druitt looked down his nose at the offer. He ignored the invitation and continued.

"No doubt, it was you who left my rooms in a shambles on the 25th."

"No doubt."

"And your meaning?"

Holmes took a final bite of his dinner, then pushed the plate way.

"I am investigating events in Whitechapel." A sip of wine provided a dramatic pause. "You are implicated."

Druitt laughed at the accusation.

"And for this you hound me?"

"Hound?" questioned the detective. "I have hired a room that, by coincidence, lies below yours. As to your residence, I suspect they were not nearly as disarrayed as you imply." He smiled again. "Perhaps I would have heard someone in the rooms above had they caused any great damage."

"Still, it is breaking and entering. I am, after all, a barrister."

"And you have nothing to connect me to something that you cannot even prove occurred." He picked up his glass of claret. "Good evening, Mr. Druitt."

Druitt leaned across the table, more earnest than before.

"I am not finished, Mr. Holmes."

Holmes locked eyes with Druitt, his gaze unblinking.

"Then speak to me of something to hold my interest."

"Do you intend I admit guilt to crimes of which I am innocent?"

"I intend you speak the truth."

Druitt was earnest as he continued. "But I do speak the truth!"

Holmes smiled, a patronizing gesture. "I do not believe you."

"Do you have proof?" asked the school master.

"Insufficient for a jury, which is why you remain free."

Druitt stood. There was more than a hint of anger in his deep-set eyes.

"I suggest you leave me in peace!" he snapped, his voice filled with ire.

Holmes did not stand, but met his stare with calm assurance.

"Believe me, Mr. Druitt, when I say that I would like nothing more than to prove you have no connection to the events in Whitechapel." He took another drink of wine. "However, at every turn I find more and more connections between you and those crimes."

"I have never been to Whitechapel!" Druitt insisted.

"The police say different. You were detained there less than three weeks ago and made to explain your presence!"

Druitt was flustered at having the facts thrown in his face. He sat down again, more contrite as he replied to the accusation.

"Surely, I am not the only bachelor that has sought some temporary companionship in the East End?"

"I catch you in a lie and you hide behind the hordes of men who take their pleasure in such a fashion?"

Druitt lowered his voice. "You must understand my position, Holmes!" he hissed. "If that were discovered at Valentine's, I would be ruined!"

"So it would seem," agreed the detective.

"Then you will maintain your silence?"

"I will remain silent on the lesser crime until I can prove the greater," explained Holmes.

Druitt pulled back as if he had been slapped.

"Then you seek my destruction on one cause or the other!"

Holmes shook his head. "I do not seek your destruction. I seek justice for those you have harmed!"

Druitt stood again. This time, he was finished with the interview.

"If I find you are following me, I shall seek legal action to prevent you."

Holmes smiled. "Then I will make sure you do not see me following you!"

Druitt leaned close. The innocent demeanor was gone, replaced by a face filled with hatred. The calm, refined voice was now a growl.

"Then we shall see, Mr. Sherlock Holmes. I shall find the secrets of your life and use them to *my* advantage."

"You may try, Mr. Druitt," replied the unruffled detective. "Men more clever and dangerous than you have made the attempt and failed."

Druitt slammed a hand loudly on the table and left. Holmes used his napkin to clean some wine that was spilled on the table by the action and calmly finished the glass. His nemesis was clear and the gauntlet thrown. It only remained to be seen if the confrontation would lead to a conclusion of the case.

Later that night, Holmes had drifted off to sleep in his chair. In an unusual turn, Watson had to wake him.

"What is it?" he asked quietly.

Watson held a finger to his lips for silent and then pointed to the ceiling.

It took the detective a few moments to awaken completely. As he did, he could hear the rhythmic sound above them. It was the sound of Montague Druitt as he paced back and forth in his small rooms.

Holmes settled back to listen while Watson headed towards his bedroom. The detective sat in the darkness listening as the pacing continued, back and forth, back and forth. The barrister paced until dawn lit the edges of the windows.

Sunday, November 4 *Frustration*

Watson limped painfully into Baker Street, relieved to be in his normal quarters. Holmes followed, wiping away some of the grim on his face. For two days, they had trailed Druitt around London without results. Two long nights in Whitechapel had resulted in nothing more than an embarrassing encounter with a constable who wanted to question them.

"I do not know how much longer I can go on with this, Holmes," announced the physician in frustration. "You maintain your belief in Druitt's guilt, but we have found nothing to confirm it!"

Holmes would not relent. "It is him! I am sure of it!"

"Then why no killings?" asked Watson sharply. "No attempts this week; none last week!"

"Because we are close on his heels," offered the detective

The doctor was unconvinced. "Abberline and Lestrade disagree!" His words were heated, the anger barely suppressed. "I have a surgery to maintain. I cannot continue to divide my time between London and Blackheath."

"If we continue to dog him, we deny him the ability to carry out these dastardly deeds," explained Holmes. "We must stay on him, Watson, and none too gently. He must know he is being pursued."

"He already knows!" Watson's voice rose. "He has confronted both of us. He knows and he protests his innocence."

"And yet I know he is guilty!" Holmes slammed a fist down on the table in frustration, loose items sliding to the floor at the impact.

"Then prove it so we will remove this beast from the streets!" yelled Watson in response. He rose and went to the side table. He lifted the brandy decanter and set the empty vessel down in annoyance. "This cannot continue! Either bring it to a conclusion or find another method."

"There is only one other method!" returned Holmes darkly. "And if I am forced to remove him, then I will be as guilty as he is!"

The men stood in silence, the ugly truth hanging between them like a foul odor. At length, Holmes walked to a cabinet and withdrew a brandy bottle. He handed it to his friend, who slowly refilled the decanter.

"As you say, Watson, I cannot prove my belief. That method must be held until there are no doubts."

Watson poured a brandy and returned to his chair.

"What is next?"

Holmes walked to his chair and sat heavily. "Will you give me one more week?"

Watson sipped the brandy. "Very well, Holmes. One more week."

Tuesday, November 6 *Erratic*

On Monday, Holmes received another telegram from William Druitt. They followed Montague to his barrister chambers that morning, then went on to Baker Street to keep the appointment with his brother.

"Mr. Druitt," said Holmes, welcoming him into the sitting room. He brought the man to the sofa and sat across from him. "How may we assist you?"

William Druitt was nervous and sweating. He pulled out a kerchief and mopped his forehead before he spoke.

"It is Montague. He is very agitated! What is happening?"

"In what way?"

"I am not even completely sure. I visited him at his chambers last week, and he spent the entire time pacing the room. Last Friday...last Friday I was contacted by his head master." Druitt wiped his forehead again. Watson poured him a cup of tea in hopes it might calm his nerves. "His behavior in his class is equally erratic. He spends large amounts of time speaking to himself. The head master feels he will need to dismiss him."

"We have been keeping him under observation, but he has done nothing to show he is guilty of any crime," explained Holmes. "He has discovered we are watching him, however."

"Is that all?"

"I have seen nothing that would cause him to be this upset," said Holmes.

"Nor I," added Watson.

Druitt's hand shook as he sipped the tea. The drink did have some calming effect for the man and he was able to continue on a more composed note.

"If he loses his teaching position under these conditions, he will never get another. And as a barrister, he has no clients. He will be ruined!"

"No clients?" Holmes asked. "None at all?"

"None. The effort has proven a complete failure."

"Perhaps that is what weighs so heavily upon him," suggested Watson.

"I do not know!" The elder Druitt was returning to his own state of agitation.

"Might I give you some advice, Mr. Druitt?" offered the detective.

"Please!"

"Have you considered having him committed?"

Druitt shuddered at the suggestion.

"I did, but it is our mother, you see. He lives in such fear of having her affliction, he refuses to discuss the matter. He flew into a complete rage the last time I suggested it!"

"I do not know what else I can do, Mr. Druitt." Holmes tried to keep his voice from sounding as helpless as he felt. "I could find an asylum that would restrain him, but he is a barrister. He would get his day in court."

"And he is perfectly cogent when he wants to be," agreed Druitt. "A judge would release him."

"Then our hands are tied," said the detective. "I can only continue to watch him. I have assured the doctor we will only continue this for another week."

"I live in such horror that my fears are true and now, even if they are not, I must believe my brother is insane."

It appeared he was about to break down. Watson placed a firm hand upon his shoulder.

"Steady, man. Steady! We are doing what we can."

Druitt nodded sadly, handing the empty tea cup back to the doctor.

"Very well, Mr. Holmes," he said. He stood and looked to the detective. "Another week. Please keep me informed of any developments."

The brother left and Watson looked to his friend.

"Is there nothing we can do? What about this Dr. Winslow you met the other day? Might he commit Druitt once you explain the situation?"

"For what?" demanded the investigator. "We have found nothing to connect him to these crimes in any way. Without proof, we are legally blocked from any action."

Holmes walked to the table and poured himself a cup of tea. He looked out the window and sipped it slowly.

Watson had seen him like this before.

"You suspect something."

"Perhaps, but what is a suspicion into the mind of a madman worth?"

Watson let out a huff of frustration. "And that is all you care to say?"

"As you know too well at this juncture, suspicion is not proof, Watson."

Watson escaped the confines of Baker Street to have dinner with Mary Morstan that evening. Mrs. Forrester accompanied the couple, acting as chaperone as was befitting the courting of a single, young woman. It was a leisurely meal and he was more than happy to put thoughts of the horrors of Whitechapel from his mind.

They returned to the residence after a long and pleasant evening. Watson escorted the women to the house, was allowed a few minutes alone with Miss Morstan, then walked back to his waiting cab with a mind full of pleasant thoughts.

His coach pulled into the road and he heard the driver muttering. He looked up and was surprised to see a hansom sitting to one side ahead of them. The houses in the district were well separated, so traffic was invariably light. It was strange to see a cab on the road, and Watson looked at it in detail as he passed it.

The interior was dark, with only a single occupant. The person had a checked scarf pulled up across their face, hardly an unusual sight in the cool, damp air of early November. As his cab passed the Hansom, that driver reigned his horse, and, with careful maneuvering, reversed direction and drove off in the opposite way.

The doctor watched it for a moment, but lost interest and turned forward. He pulled out a cigar and lit it. It was the pleasant end to a pleasant evening and he turned his thoughts back to the young woman he just left.

Wednesday, November 7 *Hunter and Prey*

Holmes and Watson returned to Blackheath. Druitt maintained his usual routine, leaving for Valentine's school, staying for his appointed hours, then returning to his rooms late in the day. His evening routine was equally set. Most nights, he would eat a dinner prepared by the landlady, Mrs. Patrick. The remaining nights, he would seek a meal elsewhere.

So it was no surprise when they heard him returning down the stairs. The detective and his companion were prepared to follow, waiting until they heard the front door close before walking down to the street. However, Holmes was surprised when he saw their target pass beneath a street lamp down the block as they began their practiced method of following him.

"Look at how he is dressed!"

Watson watched as Druitt passed by the next light.

"Rather disheveled for seeking a meal in Blackheath," he concluded.

"Without a doubt!"

Not only was his appearance at odds with his normal

practice, but his path was clearly aimed at the train station.

"He means to return to London tonight!"

Holmes and Watson continued to track their quarry, doing whatever the detective dictated to hide their pursuit. But when they boarded the train, they were forced to ride in the same rail car as Druitt. Holmes found seats as far back as possible, attempting to remain out of his sight.

"No doubt, he is heading for Whitechapel!" announced Holmes, his voice a tense whisper.

"On a Wednesday night?"

"Yes," hissed the detective, "and we are not dressed the part!"

Holmes saw the man seated across from him was wearing a well worn scarf. He took off his own neat scarf and held it out to trade. The man, startled at the offer, nonetheless quickly accepted. Watson needed no urging. He soon had changed coats and hats with passengers around him. By the time they stepped off the train in Victoria Station, they had managed to make their appearance much less genteel and considerably more shabby.

"There he goes!" said Watson, pointing to a hansom parked a hundred feet ahead of them.

"Then let's be off!" said Holmes, selecting another and handing the driver a fiver as they entered.

They settled in, their cabby pressing through the traffic to follow the cab Holmes indicated. As they stared after their target, he felt Watson's cane tap his foot.

"Foot gear, Holmes! The constables may spot you!"

They enjoyed a chuckle at the slight joke as they

worked their way from Westminster towards the east end.

"I meant to ask how Mrs. Forrester and Miss Morstan were," said Holmes, his focused trained on the other cab.

"Fine," replied Watson. "Mrs. Forrester is heading to Cornwall today with the children."

"I trust she will find better weather there."

"Undoubtedly."

The doctor smiled at the joke, for whatever weather was in Cornwall would find London within the day. Holmes was not in a mood to continue the small talk. He tapped his walking stick in nervous energy as he spoke.

"I am not happy with this change of routine! If he is not following custom, he has become unpredictable."

The doctor needed no great explanation to clarify the point.

"Why the change do you suppose?"

"He may be on the hunt!" Holmes returned, his tone severe. "I don't suppose you brought the service revolver?"

Watson tapped the pistol in his pocket. "I was ready for a quiet dinner or any eventuality!"

"Admirable." The detective cursed himself under his breath. "I, on the other hand, am woefully ill-prepared."

"Unarmed?"

"I was expecting dinner, not a ride to Whitechapel! That is what complacency gets you, Watson." He tapped the walking stick, twisting the handle and sliding it out slightly to reveal the blade within. "But I am not totally unprepared!"

*　　*　　*　　*　　*　　*　　*

In Whitechapel, Druitt left his cab, but walked towards the river. Again, it was a different route than he normally followed, and Holmes was concerned about the change. The object of his search was quickly revealed.

"Street vendor," Watson announced. "Fish and chips!" He glanced towards his friend. "A splendid idea, since we have not had any dinner." He stomach grumbled in agreement.

Holmes nodded in approval, but still had to make a suggestion.

"Use a different vendor!"

Watson purchased the food and caught up with his friend, handing him the newspaper cone with the fried fish and potato slices. Holmes maintained his watch on Druitt, periodically changing sides of the street.

At first, they juggled their food and walking sticks. At last they disposed of the newspaper cones by handing the remains of their meals off in trade for changes in hats and scarves.

"I am a fool!" snapped Holmes as they finished their new purchase. "If he is on the hunt, he must have the knife upon him! All these times we have followed him, and that would be the proof we need!"

"Of course!" agreed Watson.

"Look for a constable!" ordered Holmes. Before Watson could reply, he spied one himself. "Over there! In fact, I believe that is Gregson!" Holmes was already in the street heading towards the policeman, but he looked back to Watson. "Keep after Druitt! I will keep my eye on you."

He did not wait for an answer from the physician, but moved as rapidly as he dared toward the inspector.

"Gregson!"

"Mr. Holmes?" The policeman regarded his colleague's dress with some amusement. "Not up to your normal standards, sir!"

"No time!" Holmes was slightly out of breath, but pointed down the street. "Watson is following our suspect. We believe he is looking for another victim, but he needs to be checked for the knife!"

"Where?" demanded the officer, immediately alert.

"Come! I will point him out to you!"

They moved quickly down a block, coming abreast of Watson on the far side of the street. Holmes picked out Druitt and identified him to the police inspector. Gregson, with two constables, left in a brisk trot to confront Druitt while Holmes moved back across the street to rejoin his companion.

"Will he run?" asked Watson as he approached.

"We shall see!" replied the detective.

The policemen cornered the suspect, but he yielded quickly to their authority. The detective and his friend watched the tableau from a distance, observing how the officers talked to Druitt and how the barrister allowed them to search him. It was almost fifteen minutes before the policemen walked away, allowed Druitt to continue on.

Gregson came back to the waiting detective, shaking his head.

"Sorry, Mr. Holmes, you got it wrong this time. The man is not carrying a weapon of any kind, much less a long knife!"

"I watched you search him, Gregson. It appeared a very thorough job of it!"

"The lads are used to people hiding weapons, Mr. Holmes. It can mean their lives if they miss anything."

Holmes let out a sigh of exasperation.

"Sorry to bother you, Gregson. Thanks for your help."

"No problem at all, sir," returned the policeman. "Much rather safe than sorry in this case! Besides, I needed to speak with you. We received another tip that Latimer is about."

"My sources say nothing on the matter," Holmes replied. "They say he is still on the continent."

"Just a friendly warning, sir," said Gregson.

With a touch to his cap, the inspector strolled off while Watson and Holmes walked forward to continue their surveillance of Druitt.

"If there is no knife, then there is no danger," said Watson.

"So it would seem," replied the detective. "We will keep an eye on him nonetheless."

Druitt wandered the streets of Whitechapel. He crisscrossed the warrens where the murders had occurred. He stopped and talked to prostitutes. He even bought drinks for two of them, but he did not engage their services. By one in the morning, Druitt worked his way from Whitechapel and was in a cab returning to Victoria Station.

"Excellent time," observed Holmes as he checked his

watch. “He shall just make the last train to Blackheath. He will have time for five or six hours sleep before preparing for his day at school and in chambers.”

“In chambers, Holmes,” pointed out Watson. “It is Thursday and he does not need to return to Valentine’s tomorrow.”

Holmes nodded.

“Well taken, Watson! We shall need to follow him the entire day and keep his chambers in view all day.”

“Yes,” the doctor replied. It was an unhappy retort. “I thought we might finally have him when you thought of the knife.”

“So did I, old boy,” replied Holmes. “I wish I had thought of it before.”

Watson shuddered, feeling a cold chill. Holmes was immediately concerned.

“Is the night getting to you?”

“Not the cold,” explained the doctor. “Just a feeling of disquiet.” He looked to the investigator earnestly. “You have never hunted, Holmes?”

“Tromp through the underbrush in the attempt to slaughter a small animal with a firearm? No.”

“I have,” explained the doctor. “Real hunting. In India, I was on a tiger hunt.”

“Real indeed,” agreed Holmes. “At least that is a quarry capable of defending itself. Was it similar to this?”

The surgeon nodded. “In many ways, it was.” He leaned forward, trying to catch a glimpse of the cab a couple blocks ahead of them He continued, his voice reflective. "I always remember the Punjabi becoming very scared at one point."

"And why was that?"

"We had been following the tiger for three hours, but had never gotten a shot. Then the Punjabi read the track on the ground, and his eyes widened in fear."

Holmes smiled. "You are letting your literary skill guide your dialogue, Watson!"

The physician chuckled. "Perhaps, but it is worth it to make the point."

"What was the point?"

"The tiger had left the path and was now hunting *us*."

The conversation ceased for a long while as Holmes digested the information. The analogy seemed too fitting a way to explain Druitt's change in habits. The detective could not recall that he had been hunted before. Perhaps this is how it felt.

Thursday, November 8 *The Pattern Breaks*

"My compliments on your attire, Watson." For once, Holmes seemed genuinely pleased with his companion's attempts. The detective nudged Watson's foot with his own. "I note you took my suggestion on the shoes!"

Watson regarded the worn and scuffed footwear before turning to his friend. A rattle of rain swept past them and was gone. He pulled the coat tighter about him.

"They are an old pair of mine. They were too badly worn to repair, and I rubbed them on the cobblestones to add to the appearance of wear."

"Admirable," returned the detective.

After completing his teaching duties, Druitt left directly for London and his chambers at the Inner Temple. The two men spelled each other observing the location, taking advantage to change into clothes more suited for the inevitable trip into Whitechapel that evening. Holmes pulled out a battered watch and checked the time.

"The offices are closing. We will see how long he remains afterwards."

"Are you still sure this is the best method of trailing

him?" asked Watson.

"It is the best I can come up with at the moment," answered Holmes.

Watson touched his friend's shoulder and glance towards the Inner Temple.

"He seems well dressed tonight," commented the physician.

Holmes turned, immediately singling out the lone figure that emerged from the building.

Watson smiled. "He is wearing his normal suit, and I hazard he is considerably better dressed than either of us."

Holmes pushed away from the doorway and started down the street. Watson walked beside him, their pace matched to the man on the opposite side of the street.

"His coat seems bulky," observed Holmes. "And he is not carrying his satchel. Perhaps he does not plan a trip to Whitechapel this evening."

"Where else would he go?" asked Watson as another shower swept over them. "He must be wearing something beneath the overcoat. It is a cold and damp night."

Holmes pulled his meager coat around his thin frame.

"I envy him that, if nothing else." Holmes touched Watson's arm to stop him. "Wait! He is engaging a cab."

Watson pulled up a corner of his jacket. "We will be able to hire a cab dressed like this?"

Holmes smiled, producing a sheaf of one pound notes from beneath his battered coat.

"I imagine I can manage it."

Watson smiled. Holmes success over the years had accumulated more than sufficient funds to pay for such a slight venture. The cabbie first eyed them with suspicion, but the note from Holmes quickly removed any reservations he maintained.

"Tell me, Holmes," asked Watson as he settled in his seat. "Why are we following him so closely? Why not let him go and track him less openly?"

"To what end?" returned Holmes, trying to maintain a glimpse of their quarry without revealing his face too clearly.

"As we did with Stapleton on the moor," explained the doctor. "Why not give him the illusion of freedom of action, but then catch him in the act and stop him?"

Holmes sighed. "Because London is not Grimpen. There, we had only one victim to protect and we knew where he would be. Here, we have thousands, and they can be anywhere." He looked up at the ruddy face that peered at him through the cab's trap door. "Follow that hansom two blocks down."

The cabbie glanced up, then quickly down.

"Yes, sir."

Holmes' arm snapped up, two one pound notes grasped in his hand.

"Do not lose it, and there is another pair of notes for you."

The cabbie snatched the money eagerly, thrusting it into his coat pocket.

"Yes, sir!" he readily agreed.

The trap door of the cab closed above them, and the

chase was on.

The cabs rattled through the streets of London, though Holmes had to occasionally caution their driver about approaching their prey too closely. They were clearly heading towards the East End, but the cab before them was taking an indirect route.

Watson leaned against a turn as they came onto another street, watching the other cab turn a corner before them. At the same moment, a spurt of rain struck them, further decreasing their view.

"Dirty weather tonight, Holmes."

The detective had a door open and was wiping the glass before them as clean as he could.

"Too true, doctor." The detective looked into the night. "He's getting closer to Whitechapel than he usually does."

"What does that mean?" asked Watson

"I am not sure. This is all so odd. No stop at a boarding house; no satchel and change of clothes. He will draw the attention of the police if he is stalking the streets so well dressed."

Druitt's cab stopped and he got out. Holmes and Watson followed suit, trailing the man into the first block of the Whitechapel area.

"He's walking faster," said Holmes, picking up his own pace as their target disappeared around a corner in front of them.

They rounded the same corner mere seconds later, but Druitt could not be seen.

"There!" shouted Holmes. "The alley on the left. It is the only place he can be!"

The detective ran, Watson close behind him. Further up, the alley split in two and Druitt's coat and hat on the ground lay at the intersection. To the right, a scarf lay in the empty alley. Holmes picked up the coat and threw it back upon the ground, stamping his foot in frustration. Watson, as always, was pragmatic. He looked at the scarf.

"I see checks are coming back in fashion," he observed, picking the scarf from the street. "He must have come this way!"

"Why do you say that?" snapped an angry Holmes as he started towards the alley into Whitechapel. "About the scarf, that is."

"The man I saw outside Mrs. Forrester's two nights back was wearing a checked scarf just like this one," replied Watson innocently. "But we must hurry!"

The doctor was close behind Holmes when the detective snatched the scarf from his hand.

"Are you sure?" demanded the detective.

Watson shrugged. "I only saw it for a moment, but it was very similar."

"He has doubled back again! Bloody hell!" cursed Homes, the words ripped from his throat. "Lees told me two weeks ago! *Where Marylebone, Blackheath, Camberwell, and Whitechapel intersect!* There's not a moment to lose!"

Holmes grabbed Watson's arm and pushed him into the other branch heading the opposite direction. They ran until they emerged onto the main street. A cab moved quickly away from them before turning a corner and disappearing from view.. Watson's arm stabbed into the night where a hansom sat a block away.

"Over there, Holmes!"

The men ran to the other cab, getting there out of breath. Holmes was shouting to the driver as Watson pulled himself in from the opposite side.

"Cabbie!" He did not wait for the trap door to open. "A fiver if we are in Camberwell in less than twenty minutes!"

There was no reply but the crack of the whip. Watson looked at his friend in horror.

"Camberwell?" He knew too well that Mrs. Forrester and her governess lived in Camberwell.

"Druitt said he would discover my secrets and make me pay! I have no secrets," replied Holmes, grabbing the sides of the lurching coach as they rounded another corner at breakneck speed. "I have less to protect." He eyed Watson across the short space between them. "The same is not true of my friends."

Watson choked on the words. "You can't mean…?"

"I can." Holmes forced the words out. "He has bested me again!" The cab steadied as they entered a straight stretch of road. "Who will be at the estate this evening?"

Watson's mind raced. There was no doubt to the meaning of Mary's comments from two nights before.

"Mrs. Forrester has taken the children to a relative in Cornwall for the week," he answered. "The staff has been given the time off until Monday! Mary is there, alone."

Holmes said nothing, but clenched his fist in frustration at the information.

"But Druitt cannot know that!" protested Watson.

Holmes let out a deep breath. "You know it, old fellow. You know it." He grasped Watson's hand to reassure him. "We can be no more than five minutes behind him now, and we are catching up!"

Watson did not hear the words of reassurance.

They tore through the London streets at an unbelievable pace. Watson was later amazed that no one had been run down by their cabbie in his insistence to win the promised reward. At this point, their pace slackened and Holmes rapped hard on the trap door above their heads.

"What is the problem?" he demanded.

"Me horse, sir. To keep driving her at this pace could kill her!"

The detective's voice betrayed no sympathy at the plea.

"Then I shall buy you another!" He handed the driver another five pound note. "And there is still the fiver to be paid on our arrival!"

They arrived at Forrester estate, the cabby's horse covered in white foam and breathing heavily, but still standing after its admirable assertions. The mansion before them lay dark, only a single room on the back side showing a light. Holmes withdrew his revolver. Watson's was already in evidence. The detective's hand kept him from leaping from the coach.

"Think man!" Holmes cautioned. "Think! It will do no good to accidentally shoot your lady in an effort to protect her!"

Watson paused, breathing heavily.

"What do you propose?"

Holmes held a finger over his mouth, and handed a five pound note to the driver with an admonishment to remain. He led the doctor from the cab in silence, approaching the front of the darkened building. The door was open, a gaping black hole upon dark grey face of the structure. Again, Holmes had to restrain his friend.

"I shall take the back," he whispered quietly, letting go of Watson's arm. "Count to thirty, then go in by the front."

Watson nodded, but Holmes tapped him sharply on the arm.

"Thirty, I say!" he hissed. "And remember there is an armed man in the house that will take nothing but pleasure in your demise!"

Holmes was melted into the darkness. Watson stared at the open door, trying to catch his breath and slow his racing heart. He tried to count to thirty, but kept stopping and starting over. Finally, he relented. He cocked his pistol and raised it to the ready. As cautiously as he could manager, he entered the house.

Each step rang in his ears, though his mind told him they could not be so loud. He paused as he entered the interior, letting his eyes adjust to the darkness of the rooms. Even so, his concern for Mary Morstan drove him forward faster than the limits of his caution.

Beyond the open door, there was nothing to indicate the presence of an intruder. He looked carefully around every corner, making his way slowly towards the back of the house. As he did, his eyes became more accustomed to his surroundings.

Then, in a flash, a dark shape lunged from a black corner. He twirled to face it, but held his fire at Holmes' caution and the thought of his beloved Mary. Too late, he saw the metallic glint. He tried to twist away, but felt the burning bite of the long, thin blade as it slashed across his right shoulder. Watson, stout and firm as he was, let out a cry of pain at the impact. Despite his steadfast reserves, he fell to the floor, his revolver dropping from his hand in the process.

The pain screamed from his injured arm, but the military doctor regained his wits. This was not the first time he had been injured in the cause of duty. The dark shape of the revolver lay before him. He stretched out his left hand as the black shadow of the attacker returned, the thin sliver of metal held high above him, piercing eyes glaring from above the dark scarf that covered the attacker's face. Watson grasped the cold, reassuring weight of the pistol and rolled, his finger instinctively squeezing the trigger.

The shot exploded in the confines of the room. The flash of the cartridge blinded Watson for a split second, but he did not hesitate. The threat to his life motivated him as little else could as he continued to roll over and fire a second round into the space occupied by his attacker.

"Watson!"

The desperate cry of Holmes' voice did not mask the sound of his assailant's footsteps.

"Dear fellow!"

The shadow of Holmes' form blotted out what little

light was in the room as Watson dropped his revolver and grasped his wounded shoulder with his left hand.

"After him, Holmes!"

"You are wounded..."

The doctor cut off Holmes' reply.

"I will be fine! After him!" he urged.

Watson could see enough to discern the sharp nod of his friend's head as he disappeared in a run. As he did, light grew from the back of the house and the silhouette of a woman carrying a lamp appeared.

"Mary!" said Watson, wincing at the pain from his wound.

"John!" she screamed.

She set the lamp down and was at his side in a moment. It was a wonderful gesture, Watson later recalled. He only wished the terrible pain from his wound would have let him appreciate it.

Holmes ran into the night, trying to hear the footfalls of his quarry. Nothing but silence reached his ears. Fog thickened about him, but still there was naught to indicate which direction his prey had taken. Then, in the distance, he heard another sound. The growing rush of rain swept over him.

The detective stopped. The solution of his pursuit for the past two months pressed upon him with the suddenness of lightning. He stopped, for once unsure what to do as the rain struck him. He looked up and all became clear.

Holmes stood in the rain, the drops washing across his face like tears. It seemed as if he were paralyzed for the longest time. At length, he returned to the house, seeing no point in continuing the pursuit.

"Holmes!" shouted Watson as he re-entered the room. "Did you catch him?"

Mary Morstan was busy tending to Watson's wound. If she were concerned that a man was seeing her in her night clothes, she either did not notice or did not care.

"He got away," replied Holmes dully. "Your wound?" he asked, showing more animation.

"It is long, but not fatal," replied the doctor. "Mary has stemmed the bleeding for the moment." He grasped her free hand in gratitude. Then, in concern, he looked back to his friend.

"What is the matter, Holmes?" he demanded. "Why are you not in pursuit?"

Holmes leaned against the wall opposite his companion. In exhaustion, he allowed himself to sink to the floor.

"I may have done what you suggested, Watson. I have turned the beast loose on London and there is no hope of finding him."

His voice was dull and lifeless. Watson, still impelled by the wound in his shoulder, would hear none of it.

"Then go!" he urged. "Track him down and end this madness!"

Holmes twisted his head from side to side.

"I have failed miserably, Watson," he admitted, his tone in deep despair. "I have been wrong from the start!"

"What the devil are you talking about?" said Watson.

Holmes ran a hand across his face and flicked it towards the wounded doctor.

"It is the rain, don't you see?" he said. His head hung low in shame. "He kills only in the rain. Every assumption I made was wrong!"

Watson struggled into a sitting position though Mary Morstan tried to hold him back.

"Leave me alone, woman!" he snapped. He looked across the short distance to his friend and spoke in short, harsh sentences.

"What the bloody hell is wrong with you, Holmes?" he demanded. The detective looked up in response to the language, but did not move. "Scotland Yard did not find this fiend, you did! Now go to Whitechapel and catch him!"

"Watson…" started the detective.

"Damn your eyes, Holmes!" cursed the doctor. "You have dragged me through hell itself to find this monster!" He struggled, rising to his feet, holding his revolver with his left hand. "If you will not go after him, I shall. I will kill the bastard with my own pistol if that is what it takes to stop this horror!"

Watson was using the wall as a support. Mary attempted to hold him back without success. Even so, the wash cloth she held to his wound deepened in color at his exertions.

"John!" she cried. "You must calm yourself."

But Watson was determined. He stepped forward, but

found himself pressed back against the wall. His eyes focused, and the face of Sherlock Holmes was close before his.

"Old friend." The words were soothing and sympathetic. "You have done your part for this night." Holmes showed Watson his own pistol. "I will find Druitt tonight and, if this is what it takes to stop him, I will do so!"

Holmes turned away, as if to exit. Watson suddenly found it difficult to form words, and had to speak slowly. The effort of rising was too much, and he slid against the wall to the floor.

"And when you have a chance," he asked, his voice weakening. "Send a cab so that I might find a surgeon."

Holmes traded cabs at the first opportunity, sending the cabbie who had served them so well back to collect Watson. His new driver pushed his animal with the same enthusiasm towards the East End.

The detective's mind raced. There was no way to trace Druitt once he reached Whitechapel. He could find endless policemen to assist in the search but how did you find one unknown man in the entire city? Holmes needed to find either Abberline or Lestrade, but where would they be?

He pulled out his watch. It was still before midnight, but the steady drum of rain on his cab did not speak well. If only he had pursued Druitt directly instead of pausing to help Watson. But he dismissed that thought as quickly as it occurred.

Holmes reached Whitechapel and did not care to protect his identity. He had the cabbie stop at the first group of constables he identified.

"You men!" he shouted. "Does anyone know where I can find Lestrade or Abberline?"

"Bugger off!" replied a constable and turned his attention back to his mates.

"Damn you!" said Holmes, grabbing the man's shoulder and swinging him about. "I am Sherlock Holmes and you will do what I say! Do you know where to find Abberline or Lestrade?" he demanded

"Back towards Mitre Square, I think..." replied the cowed policeman.

"Very well, I will search in that direction." To head in one random direction was as good as another in the present situation, Holmes decided quickly. "Now listen carefully. Spread the word quickly and *quietly*, man. Do you understand?"

"Quietly, sir," he stammered in reply.

"Quietly," stressed the detective again. "If you do not do this quietly you will cause a panic and there is no telling who may get hurt or killed in the process. Is that clear?"

"Yes, sir. Abberline has been beatin' that into us!"

"Good. Let all your men know I fear the Ripper is on the street tonight. Medium height, slight build, dark hair, clean shaven,"

"Medium, slight, dark, clean," the constable repeated.

"Now go! All you! And pass the word to Abberline and Lestrade that I am looking for them!"

Holmes walked into the night. The dirty weather had driven many of the Whitechapel's inhabitants from the streets. The detective was thankful for that, though he realized all it did was reduce the number of potential targets for the killer.

It was ten minutes later when a police coach pulled up next to him. Abberline called from within.

"What is all this bother, Holmes?"

The detective climbed into the coach, relieved to be out of the rain for short while.

"Druitt. He is loose in Whitechapel. He tried to attack Miss Morstan, Watson's friend."

"Do you have proof?"

Holmes shook his head. "We tracked him, but lost him. Watson did not see his face. Watson is wounded…"

"Is it serious?"

"I do not know. I was forced back on the trail."

"So you believe it is Druitt but you have still provided no proof?" Abberline let out a long, exasperated breath.

"And if not the man I was following, who else would be responsible?" countered Holmes.

Abberline snorted. "We have been warning you of Latimer for the past three weeks. And if not him, Dosenovitch has any number of reasons to seek revenge against you!"

The detective was not swayed by the arguments.

"You say I have no proof, but neither do you for Latimer or Dosenovitch." Holmes stubbornly held to what he knew to be true. "I tell you it is Druitt!"

"We shall keep an eye out for him," replied Abberline,

his anger with the detective barely suppressed. “It is unlikely he will remain on the street for long on a night such as this!”

“I will find him, with or without your help!” Holmes stepped out of the coach and back into the rain. “Whether you accept it or not, Druitt is the man we seek!”

Abberline had no reply and the carriage drove off. Holmes watched until it turned a corner, then he started walking. Perhaps the policeman was right about Druitt, but he could not accept it. The incident in Camberwell spoke to more than chance. The presence of Mary Morstan alone in the deserted house fit too well with his conception of the Whitechapel murderer.

The thought of the woman brought Watson back to the forefront of his mind. He was tortured by the idea that it was his failure which led to his friend being wounded. And so he walked on, tracing and retracing the streets and the alleys, looking for some sign of Druitt.

And for all his efforts that long, rainy night, he found nothing.

Friday, November 9 *Miller's Court*

Holmes returned to Baker Street in the dim morning, haggard and worn. Watson and Miss Morstan were there.

The physician sat on the couch, his upper body wrapped tightly in bandages. There was a broken line of red splotches across the back of the bandages that indicated the length of the wound.

"How is it?" asked the detective.

"Painful," replied Watson, shifting uncomfortably.

"The surgeon left laudanum," said Miss Morstan. She held the bottle and opened it. She started to measure it in a small glass.

"Only half," instructed Watson. "I have experience with both morphine and laudanum. I need only half of what he prescribed."

"John…"

"Mary, I know of what I speak. Only half will hold the pain at manageable levels."

She smiled, and returned some of the liquid carefully to the bottle.

"You're the doctor," she said, her smile helping ease the pain as much as the drugs.

"A dozen stitches," Watson explained, "but I will be as good as new in a few days."

"I'm glad to hear it." Holmes sat down and spoke to his friend directly, paying no attention to the woman in the room. ""We have been lucky. There was no killing last night."

"What happened?"

Holmes told his tale quickly, for after the events in Camberwell, nothing else had occurred.

"I tracked down Abberline. He was not happy with me when I related the story but he will take no action with the information we have available."

The doctor paled at the comment. Miss Morstan had her hand to her throat, clearly shocked at the revelation.

"How can he deny the events of last night?" protested Watson.

The doctor needed no further convincing of the detective's conclusions. In his true bull dog fashion, Watson was ready to go back on the hunt for the mysterious killer, and he needed no prodding to believe it was Druitt.

"We did not see him get in the cab. We cannot even be sure the cab went to Camberwell. Abberline believes it was Latimer or Dosenovitch seeking revenge. Lestrade thinks we broke up a burglary since the house was supposed to be unoccupied. Neither one will believe it was Druitt."

Watson blustered at the prospect. It was enough when

Abberline cast doubts on the detective's conclusions, but in this instance Watson felt they finally had conclusive proof of Druitt's crimes.

"And so they believe it is mere coincidence?"

Holmes had to concede to the official police stance. "We still have no direct evidence pointing to Druitt. Did you see his face?"

"Sorry, Holmes. He wore a dark scarf up over his face and his cap was pulled low. I only saw his eyes."

The great detective sat in silence for a long while, considering the possibilities. Then he spoke quickly, as if trying to make up for the lost time.

"We must get Miss Morstan out of here, of course." His eyes darted to the young woman. "Can you join Mrs. Forrester in Cornwall?"

"Undoubtedly," she answered.

The doctor was less sure. "Will that be sufficient?"

"I trust it will for the moment. It is well outside Druitt's sphere." He looked at his friend with concern. "Watson, are you able to travel?"

Watson glanced at the clothes draped over a chair in the corner. The shirt and coat, with the dark blood stains down the left side, lay on top.

"I shall need a change of clothes, and shave, but yes, I can travel." His voice was resolute, though his face showed he felt less sure than he would admit.

"Excellent! I will send a telegraph to Mrs. Forrester explaining the situation. From what you have said, she will be more than accommodating. Miss Morstan, please prepare to leave as soon as you can. Watson..."

"Of course, Holmes…"

There was a pounding on the door below, followed by the rush of feet on the stairs.

Lestrade burst into the room without knocking. He was not wearing his hat and his hair was wildly unkempt. His eyes betrayed an emotion near panic and it was so unusual to the small inspector that Holmes was on his feet and immediately at his side.

"Good lord man, what has happened?" he demanded

Lestrade was completely out of breath. He gulped for air, trying to find the words.

"We found a body, Holmes, in a room at Miller's court…" he gasped, breathing heavily.

Holmes' face grew pale at the revelation.

"The Ripper?"

Lestrade shook his head, confused. "You shall have to judge for yourself, Holmes. The body…" Words failed the detective. He took a final gulp and forced out a conclusion. "You shall have to judge for yourself."

"You have a cab waiting?" Lestrade nodded, still struggling to catch his breath. The detective looked to his friend. "Watson?"

"Go! I shall see Mary back to Camberwell, and I'll send the telegraph to Cornwall."

Holmes responded with a sharp nod. "I shall try to catch up to you at the station!"

Holmes was gone, following the inspector down the stairs at a run.

Any ride in a hansom cab was considered a risky business. Holmes had had more than his share of treacherous journeys made in haste on one mission of importance or another. But late in life, he would still recall this trip as the most terrifying.

Lestrade urged the driver on, ignoring all rules of the road and any obstacles before them. Holmes finally broke his cardinal rule of not asking for information before examining the scene to prevent Lestrade from exhorting the cabbie further.

"Lestrade, what of the crime?" he asked, his voice rising above the rattle of the cab.

Lestrade could not focus his eyes. His mind seemed fixed on a vision of what he had seen earlier.

"It is ghastly, Holmes, ghastly. I saw the remains through the window, but no one has gone into the room yet."

"You have not inspected the scene?"

"No," he insisted. "Abberline is standing guard, waiting for a photographer and you to arrive." He grabbed Holmes' shoulder in a fit of emotion. "We are lost, truly lost, Holmes! If you can find no definitive clue from this murder, all hope is gone!"

The note of hysteria in the policeman's voice was unmistakable. Holmes grabbed his wrist and held it firmly, removing the hand from his shoulder.

"Get hold of yourself, Lestrade!"

His words were sharp and loud, and he gripped the detective's wrist for emphasis. Holmes was near the point of slapping the other man to quiet him. Lestrade, his eyes wild, winced at the strength of Holmes' grip. The pressure had the desired effect, and the inspector calmed visibly before he continued.

"The body was discovered around ten o'clock this morning by the landlord. The door was locked from within."

"Good, Lestrade, good." Holmes gripped the side of the cab as they careened around another corner. "But you can see through a window into the room?"

"Yes." Lestrade shuddered visibly. The slight policeman had difficulty in continuing, he words choked. "It is a ghastly sight, Holmes. Nothing like the other killings."

The cab slowed, as they encountered a huge crowd of people in Whitechapel. The driver had to urge his horse on, the mob reluctant to fall aside and let them pass. The angry shouts were continuous as they finally reached the security of a police line.

Lestrade led Holmes towards the small court. The ashen faces of the constables were evident, every one of them grim. The usually stoic Holmes felt a twist in his stomach. If so many of the police were upset by the sight, what awaited him in the small room off the court?

Abberline met the two, holding up his hand to halt their progress.

"We knocked the door open," he said. He looked at Holmes, his features hard. "The photographer is engaged at the moment. When he is finished, I would like you to go in first, Holmes."

"Me, inspector?"

"You!" Abberline was angry, his temper restrained by only a thin veil of civility. "You had us running about all night looking for this man Druitt. Meanwhile, the Ripper was safe and sound in a warm room doing…that."

"Inspector Abberline…"

"Enough, Holmes! You shall have your opportunity to be the first to inspect the body, or what is left of it!" Abberline shouted the words, his emotions erupting, uncontrolled. With effort, he calmed himself before he continued. "We need to know who this ghoul is before another day passes!" he hissed.

There was the sound of a man retching. The photographer stood outside the door, doubled over and vomiting. He wiped his mouth with a handkerchief before returning inside. He was out again in a moment, carrying his equipment rapidly. He seemed to be running from the terror within.

Holmes took a deep breath. Obviously, the interior was worse than he imagined. He removed his coat, hat, and vest, and handed them to Lestrade. He rolled up the sleeves of his shirt and approached the door. Without waiting for his eyes to adjust, he stepped into the dim interior.

The smell struck him first. In the previous killings, the Ripper had not as much as nicked the viscera of the victim. Here, the bowels were slashed and the contents spread about the room. His eyes focused. There was blood and scraps of flesh in every direction. On the bed lay the corpse, the body so badly mutilated it was hardly recognizable as human.

The abdomen lay open, the contents removed. They lay about the room in odd piles. Arms and legs were torn so savagely, the white bones showed through the red blood. The skin was missing, leaving a grinning skull perched on the body, two baleful eyes fixed on the entry. They were the only remnant of the victim that still possessed an air of humanity.

Holmes felt the bile rise from his stomach, but he forced it down. He liked to think of himself as a calculator, nothing more than a Babbage machine to take in the facts of a crime and produce a result. With effort, he compelled himself to be nothing more than an impersonal processor and to ignore the fact that the wreckage of flesh and blood strewn about the small room had once been a living human being.

His practiced eye examined the bed, floor, walls, and furniture. The signs were all present: a bloody hand print on the wall; a boot mark on the floor. He found, measured, and recorded them all. After thirty minutes, he withdrew to the welcome, cool, fresh air outside the room where the police inspectors awaited his analysis.

"It was a long, thin blade; very sharp. It is consistent with the other murders."

"What of the killer?"

"A frenzied mutilation." Holmes took a deep breath, trying to clear the stench of the room from his nostrils. "He had a long time to work on the body, two hours or longer. She was alive when he slashed her throat: you can see the spray from her jugular on the wall. Fortunately, she was already dead when he began the mutilations.

"Your killer is average height – five seven, or at most five eight. You can tell from where he placed his hands on the wall. It is the same square toed boot I observed back in September. There was the print of his forearm on the bed – he must have rolled up his sleeves or removed his shirt. One corner, behind the door, is free of most of the gore so obvious elsewhere. I suspect he removed his shirt, so as to keep it clean. But his boots must have been filthy."

He had retrieved his coat and hat from Lestrade while he made the report. He pointed at the cobblestones as he finished buttoning the coat.

"See!" He knelt down. "Here is a mark from his boot and another over there. He departed in that direction."

Lestrade stood before him, bursting with a single question.

"Was it Druitt?" he asked.

Holmes shook his head. "You know my beliefs on that score, Lestrade. Obviously, our killer meets his requirements: he is the same height, probably the same weight. But I have found no square toed boots in Druitt's possession that match these." He took another couple steps away from the door, allowing the coroner and his aides to enter.

"Why..." Abberline was forced to stop and force back the horror in his voice. He began again, his tone even and controlled.

"Why this? Why this charnel house?"

"In September, I showed how he lured Eddowes into a secluded building so he might kill and mutilate her without interruption" Holmes looked to the policemen. "Do we know her name?"

"We believe she is Mary Kelly," said Lestrade. "This was her room." He shuddered. "We cannot be sure at the moment."

Holmes could not argue with that assessment.

"He encounters her and she brings him back to her

room. He has the same plan as he had with Eddowes. He will kill her, perform the mutilations, then move the body out to display it." Holmes looked around the small court. There was a lone gaslight in one corner. "Over there, no doubt," he said, pointing it out.

"He begins his work, but is seized by a fit. This *compulsion*, for lack of a better word, takes over and he cannot control it. One mutilation leads to another until we reach the conclusion discovered in that room.

"Now, he cannot complete his ritual. He, himself, has prevented that from occurring. He cleans himself up as best he can and leaves."

"And you were looking for Druitt on the streets while this was occurring?"

"I lost him last night. I frustrated his attack on Miss Morstan and you see before you the result!" It was the detective's turn to be angry, though his ire was directed at himself and not his colleagues. He lowered his voice and leaned closer to the two policemen. "I swear I will not allow him to commit another murder. I will prevent it, if I must go to the dock myself!"

"Holmes," cautioned Lestrade. "Take care in what you say!"

"Care?" demanded Holmes. "This *monster* took no care with Miss Mary Kelly, gentlemen. By all that is holy, I shall take no more care with him!"

As he finished, the aides came out, carrying the remains on a covered stretcher. The coroner, ashen, held a hand over his mouth to contain the contents of his stomach. The detective returned to the door, looking at the now empty bed.

For all the blood and gore, the space beneath the body lay clean and dry. The rough outline of the woman was shown, a slight person in height and stature. The two policemen stepped past Holmes and into the interior. The detective spoke a last comment before departing.

“I have some plans to make. First, I must see Watson off to Cornwall and then make a report to my brother. I will join you at the Scotland Yard as soon as I can after that. Is that acceptable?”

Abberline nodded, and Holmes turned away from the butchery of Miller’s Court. He had the cabbie drive quickly, as if the speed of removing himself from such an horrendous vision would make it fade from his mind. The attempt was unsuccessful as he tried to quiet his racing brain. His every faculty was directed towards how he could end the wave of blood that was sweeping across Whitechapel.

Holmes arrived at Victoria Station before Watson’s train departed. Mary Morstan was already secure in their coach. The ex-Army surgeon, sturdy as ever, waited by the train door, his right arm in a sling. They were already calling the passengers to board, and the men had little time.

“Holmes!” Watson’s voice was filled with concern at the ashen image of his friend. The effects of Miller’s Court were obvious to see. “Is it that bad?”

“Yes, and worse,” returned Holmes. He lowered his voice “Do not tell Miss Morstan the terror she was spared. Do not let her see the newspapers! I am sure Mrs. Cecil Forrester will aid in that.”

"Undoubtedly! What is our next course of action?"

Holmes smiled, but it was grim and without heart.

"You shall see your lady to Cornwall, and spend two full days recovering." Watson opened his mouth in protest, but the detective would have none of it. "Two full days!" he scolded. "That is not enough time as it is, but I will expect your return to London on Monday, barring any complications from the wound." Watson nodded, accepting the orders in silence. "I am off to see Mycroft. Perhaps he can provide a plan where I can see none."

The conductor shouted for all to board, and the train, whistle blowing, began to move. Watson grabbed a rail and pulled himself onto the steps. He tried to wave to his friend, but the sling on his arm, plus a sudden reminder of pain, stopped him. He entered the coach and quickly made his way to the cabin. He sat down in the cushion seat and Mary laid herself against him, her head on his shoulder.

"And what of Mr. Holmes?" she asked

Watson thought he caught a glimpse of the detective, moving through the crowd in the station. Then the station was gone, the cityscape of London before them as the train moved to the southwest.

"It is this damnable case," he said, letting his arm slip around her waist and pulling her just slightly closer. "This case has no end and it is tearing him apart. I feel...I feel like I did when I went down to Baskerville Hall," he said.

"And how is that?"

"I feel as if I am abandoning him at the time he needs me most."

She shuddered, perhaps hurt by the comment.

"Ensuring my safety means less?"

"No, no, my dear," he soothed. "It means everything, which is why I am here!" They were leaving London now, catching glimpses of open country as the suburbs fell behind them "But as soon as you are safely settled with Mrs. Forrester, and I have spoken to the local constabulary, I must return."

"He seems a stern fellow," she observed. "I feel he would prefer to manage it all on his own."

"*Seems* is the word. For all his bluster," said Watson, thinking of his dear friend, "he is a gentle soul. And this case...this case will have the heart from him if we cannot bring it to a conclusion."

The detective pushed all thoughts of sentimentality from his mind. There was no longer room for it. He half considered taking the train to Blackheath and ending the investigation directly. Holmes found a cab and continued the thought on his way to the Diogenese club.

He had little fear of the police if he committed such a crime. True, Lestrade may suspect his hand in it, but Holmes had no doubts he could hide his involvement successfully. It was certainly easy enough to justify the act as nothing more than removing the danger of a mad dog.

The thought of a dog brought up the recent experience at Baskerville Hall and the demise of Stapleton. That idea held a certain appeal to the detective: remove Druitt to the bog and let nature take its course. He wondered what the London equivalent of the Grimpen Mire was and, at that same moment, the Thames came briefly into view.

There was a connection there, though he was not

completely sure yet what it was. Some ideas arrive with the suddenness of a thunderclap, while others build up piece by piece. He realized this would be the latter, so he left it in the back of his mind to work itself out.

He arrived at the Diogenese club and was shown up to his brother. Uncharacteristically, Mycroft was pacing the floor. He held a newspaper in his hand and shook it angrily at his brother as he entered.

"What is this?" he demanded.

"It is called slaughter," replied Holmes icily. "It is what this animal does!"

"And your suspect?"

"He escaped my surveillance last night. The police remain unconvinced he is the man."

Mycroft sat down, though his agitation continued to display itself in nervous movements.

"That is about to change!" returned the brother. "Warren has tendered his resignation."

The words carried a lot of venom, much more than Holmes was used to hearing from his aloof sibling.

"It will improve the bureaucracy," replied Sherlock, "but it will do little to help the poor lads working the streets."

"I do not care about that!" There was actual anger in Mycroft's voice. Sherlock Holmes could not remember the last time he had seen his brother angry. "What are *you* going to do about this?"

"Is it now my responsibility to clean up the East End?"

"If you will meddle in such matters, then yes! Your friend Watson has made you famous, so now the Home

Secretary thinks you possess some magical ability to resolve this."

"I am doing what I can."

The words sounded as hollow as he felt. There was always the struggle between what he knew compared to what he could prove. In this case, Holmes was completely blocked by that difference. His efforts were completely thwarted when it came to making a single provable connection between the barrister and the Whitechapel butcher.

Saturday, November 10 *Plans*

Holmes was swarmed by the press as he entered Scotland Yard that morning. The police managed to hide most of the horror of Miller's Court, but enough was escaping that the press was literally going wild.

His meeting with the police officials was unsuccessful. Abberline refused to believe Druitt was the guilty party. He could not allow that a barrister and teacher was so mentally unbalanced that he could commit a heinous crime on one day and function normally on the next. Abberline left the brief meeting angrily, the revulsion of the scene at Miller's Court having clearly left its mark on the police inspector.

"So what is next, Holmes?" asked Lestrade in resignation. Miller's Court had made a deep imprint on him as well.

"We need to monitor Druitt. Abberline may deny his involvement, but you cannot deny that as soon as I lost track of him this, this..." Words failed the detective. He swallowed and continued. "I must be sure he does not kill again, Lestrade."

"We can arrest him," offered the inspector. "But he is a

barrister. He will not remain in custody with the evidence we have."

"Abberline will never allow it, Lestrade! We will not be allowed to sully the man's reputation by connecting him to these murders without conclusive proof."

"Then find it!"

"I have tried!" protested Holmes. He lowered his voice. "I have used *unofficial* methods to investigate him, Lestrade. I can make no positive connection between him and the crimes. There are hints, there are indications, there are circumstances, but not one conclusive piece of evidence!"

"Then how is that possible if he is guilty? The perpetrator of these killings is insane! You expect me to believe a madman is capable of covering his tracks so well as to even thwart your skill?"

Holmes sat back, frustrated. How could he explain a matter he could only dimly perceive to those who did not sense it at all?

"Because he is mad does not rule out that he is also clever."

Lestrade was stymied by the situation. "What would you have me do?"

"We must keep him under observation at all times. I have engaged the rooms beneath his in Blackheath. A pair of inspectors to aid me and Watson would be invaluable."

Lestrade nodded. "I will convince Abberline on that score. It is only a prudent step."

"I will contact his brother again. Perhaps I can coerce him into getting Druitt committed, even if only for a short time."

"And if that does not work?"

"Then I will seek other means, Lestrade."

"You will end up in jail," pointed out the inspector. "Disgraced. Everything you have done will be forgotten."

"You would have me allow this to continue simply for the sake of my reputation?"

"I would have you address it legally, even if we can only manage a temporary solution."

Holmes smiled, remembering his meeting with the Bessarabian gang leader earlier in the week.

"Perhaps our friend Dosenovitch has it right."

"What is that?"

"That we are in need of a *permanent* solution, Lestrade." Holmes stood and walked to the door of the room. "By all that is holy, Lestrade, I will not allow this to happen again!"

Monday, November 12 *Everything Changes*

Watson returned to Baker Street early on Monday, the morning *Times* tucked under his left arm. As he entered the rooms, he was surprised to find Holmes in his chair, the room clouded with tobacco smoke.

"Watson! Welcome back!."

Watson removed his hat and coat and casually tossed the paper to his friend.

"I will not rest while the beast is still on the prowl in London." He nodded towards the newspaper. "You will find the front page interesting."

"They have announced Warren's resignation," stated Holmes flatly, without consulting the paper.

Watson's shoulders sank in disappointment. "You have heard already?"

Holmes consigned the morning edition into the growing stack of papers in the corner.

"In truth, Mycroft informed me on Saturday. I am more than glad to see him gone. He was utterly incompetent. First, he causes a riot in the spring through his inaction, and then destroys evidence in a capital crime in hopes of preventing a repetition." Holmes set down his pipe and stood, drawing his house coat about him. "He never acted except in his own interest. We are all best rid of him."

"What of Abberline and Lestrade? Will they be caught up in the backwash of Warren's departure?"

The doctor swayed uncertainly and the detective was immediately concerned.

"Have a seat, Watson. I can see you are not fully recovered from your injury!" snapped Holmes, clearing the doctor's chair for him. "They are quite safe," he assured his friend, retaking his seat across from him. "I made doubly sure of that with Mycroft. They have done everything humanly possible to run this killer to ground."

Watson withdrew his revolver from his suit pocket and laid it on the table next to him.

"Not everything," he replied, his words cold. "When shall we relieve the public of this maniac?"

The meaning was quite clear.

"In due time, old friend." He leaned closer, his voice taking sudden animation. "I have laid plans with Lestrade. We have the room below him in Blackheath. As of Saturday, he is watched constantly and can go nowhere without being followed." He looked at the clock on the mantle. "In fact, we are tasked with this evening's surveillance, but there is sufficient time to prepare."

"And the objective?" asked the doctor, unconvinced by this new tactic.

"Three fold, Watson. First, that we might apprehend him in the act of some criminal activity we can prove in a court. I believe he is also guilty of a number of minor break-ins and thefts, over and above the murders. That accounts for the additional 'trophies' and burglary tools we discovered in his room. If we can bring him before the dock, we can remove him to jail for at least some period.

"Second, I believe he grows less stable every day. If we catch him displaying signs of his insanity, we can lock him away in an asylum, which is infinitely preferable to jail. Once institutionalized, he will remain so for the remainder of his life. I have a meeting with his brother tomorrow to discuss such an alternative.

"Third, we will assure he cannot harm another person. The next time he boards the train for London, a dozen detectives will be waiting to follow him from the station."

"What if he eludes them?" asked Watson, still doubtful of the plan. "He escaped you the last time he came to London."

"Yes," returned Holmes slowly. "Yes, he did." His features remained somber as he concluded the brief treatise. "In that case," he explained, his eyes resting on the pistol. "In that case, I will resort to your solution and resolve the problem of Mr. Montague Druitt."

"Good!" spat Watson bitterly. "After Thursday, I will be more than happy to pull the trigger myself."

Holmes replied, his voice more somber still. "We must be certain, Watson."

The two men exchanged glances, the meaning clear and unspoken between them. They knew what solution was required, and they would not hesitate to exercise it. Watson stood, wincing slightly at the pain in his shoulder.

"Are you well enough to engage in this chase?" asked Holmes.

"I may be right-handed, Holmes, but I have been injured worse and still managed to use a pistol effectively."

"Ah," said Holmes. "Afghanistan."

"Indeed."

There was a pile of calling cards that had been accumulating over the last week. Mrs. Hudson had set them on the entry table and they caught Watson's eye. He started glanced through them, noting several repetitions.

"Have you looked at these?" he asked the detective. "There are several here from a Jameson Smythe of the Nonpareil Club."

"In truth, I have not bothered. Until we resolve this Whitechapel business, I cannot be distracted by another case."

"Well, if the number of his cards is any indication, this gentleman is persistent."

Watson picked his bag from the floor.

"I shall need some clean clothes if we are staying in Blackheath," he observed.

"Plan for two days," said Holmes. "We will trade with men from Scotland Yard."

Holmes headed for his own room. "In the meantime, I have some inquiries to make. Get some rest! I shall return in time for the afternoon train."

They reached the rooms in Blackheath in late afternoon, the sun sliding below the horizon in the deepening fall. They were greeted by Inspectors Gregson and Coulter as they entered the rooms.

"Good to see you again, Dr. Watson," greeted Gregson. He glanced towards the arm in a sling. "Nothing too serious, I trust."

"Nothing to keep me from the conclusion of this case."

They followed the detectives into the room, though Watson noticed Mrs. Marshall staring from a crack in her door.

"What have you to report?" asked Holmes.

"Nothing," said Gregson.

"Nothing?"

"He was here when we arrived on Saturday, and he did not leave until this early afternoon." The inspector hesitated, but then voiced his concern to the master detective. "In truth, Mr. Holmes, I believe you have it all wrong in this instance. While the nervous sort, he seems a quiet man."

"He went to his classes at Valentine's this afternoon?" asked the detective, ignoring Gregson's opinion on Druitt.

"Not today, sir," returned Gregson.

"What?"

"No, sir," concurred the younger Coulter. "He arrived at the school, a bit late actually. He was not there for more than half an hour. We followed him back here and he has remained upstairs since."

"Odd," observed Watson.

"Indeed," agreed Holmes. "None the less, we are here to relieve you gentlemen. You best be off."

"We will return in the morning," said Gregson.

He and the other inspector donned their coats and hats and left. Watson and Holmes sat in the room, neither saying anything for a long while. Holmes sat facing the closed door, while Watson was near the fire.

"What if he tries to sneak out?"

Despite himself, Watson's voice was a low, conspiratorial whisper. Holmes smiled, but his reply was equally low.

"I have adjusted the lamp across the hall," he said. He gestured towards the crack at the bottom of the door. "He cannot get by without casting a shadow."

"Good."

They sat and both men began reading their newspapers. After several minutes, Holmes stopped and looked to Watson.

"You may find this interesting."

He handed the newspaper to the doctor, the page folded to a short article. Two Englishmen who had been traveling with a woman had met with a tragic end in Budapest. They had been stabbed, and the Hungarian police were of opinion that they had quarreled and had inflicted mortal injuries upon each other. The names of Latimer and Kemp were mentioned towards the end, but of the woman, there was no word.

"So that is the end of Latimer," said the doctor after reading it.

"Yes, and it occurred on the continent, as I have told Abberline and Lestrade for the past month!" replied the detective. "There is the conclusion to the murder of Paul Kratides. It would appear his sister managed to achieve what the courts could not."

"Why did the police believe he was in London when he was still abroad I wonder?" said Watson.

"I have a theory," offered Holmes, "but with the principles dead, we will never know. I think it was a petty plot by Latimer. His confederates spread the word of his return while he remained safely in Europe."

"What would he gain by such a ploy?"

"It was probably an attempt to make me fret over his oath of vengeance," explained the detective. Holmes chuckled drily. "It would have irked him in great measure to know how little stock I placed in his threat! He could not know that the false rumor would influence the police in the Whitechapel murders. No doubt, creating the confusion would have pleased him."

Watson handed the paper back. "Good riddance!"

They lapsed back into silence. As his ears grew accustomed to the lack of sound, Watson heard the regular beat of pacing on the floor over their heads. Tirelessly, endlessly, the sound moved back and forth.

"He paces like a caged animal," noted the doctor.

Holmes glanced upwards, as if his penetrating gaze might actually see their quarry through the floor.

"No, Watson. More like an animal in his lair." Holmes withdrew his pipe and tobacco and returned to his scrutiny of the door. "He is not caged; he is cornered. That is when animals are most dangerous."

Tuesday, November 13 *Blackheath*

Holmes pulled out his watch, his eyes glancing at the ceiling above them. The pacing continued.

"He should be at the school this morning, before going to his chambers."

"That is odd," agreed the doctor.

There was a knock at the door and Gregson entered.

"Still here, Holmes?" he asked

"Yes, as is our quarry." Holmes gestured to the ceiling. "Watson and I have an appointment at his brother's residence shortly."

Gregson was confused. "I thought he had classes Tuesday mornings, then to London and his chambers in the afternoon?"

Watson shrugged, wincing at the pain in his shoulder from the slight action.

"We are confused as well."

Holmes collected his hat and gloves.

"This break in routine does not bode well, Gregson. Be cautious!"

* * * * * * *

The trip to the Druitt family home was not far. William Druitt inherited the bulk of the family estate, including the residence. It was a well-appointed house, with two of the sisters still living under the roof.

The elder brother took the two men into a sitting room, closing the door behind them to assure silence.

"His sisters do not know of Montague's situation. It would break their hearts to discover the truth of him."

"What truth is that?" asked Holmes.

"You do not know?" said the brother in surprise. ""He was dismissed from Valentine's on Monday! He came here quite distressed over the matter."

"Dismissed? Did he relate the cause?"

"He would not speak of the details," replied William Druitt. "What am I to do, Mr. Holmes?"

"That is what I came to discuss," the detective replied. "Can you move to have your brother committed? I am hoping we can restrict his movements for some period of time."

"He will not have it, Mr. Holmes," explained Druitt in utter resignation. "I have explained the family history."

"I am aware your mother is confined."

"As is her sister. A cousin committed suicide. Our eldest sister appears to be on the brink and may soon need to follow her mother into the asylum."

"A sorry record, sir," said Watson.

"Sorry indeed," agreed Druitt. "But that history obsesses Montague. He has stated he would rather die than be committed, and now he has lost his teaching position."

"We need the details of the cause," said Holmes. "May I have permission to act in your name and interview the headmaster at the school?"

"For what purpose?"

"To find information that may allow us to confine him," replied the detective.

"I don't know..."

Holmes let out a sigh of exasperation. "Mr. Druitt, you desire my assistance, and yet you seem determined to take no actions!"

"I am concerned for my brother!"

"As am I," returned Holmes. "But if he is guilty of these crimes, as we both fear, it will heap ignominy upon your family if it becomes known. You must help me prevent that!"

These words had the desired effect. The senior Druitt composed himself before answering.

"Yes," he agreed meekly. "Yes, I will do that."

"Good. I will see if the school can provide information on your brother's actions and if there is something we might use to confine him!"

The trip from the Druitt residence to the school was short. Holmes, however, fumed over the inaction of the brother during the short drive. It was an indication of his own frustration that he would complain so openly about a client. He composed himself, setting the anger behind him to conduct the interview of the headmaster.

Sir John Whitworth greeted them cordially. He was a well-cut older gentleman with a sterling reputation befitting his position managing the prestigious school.

"Mr. Holmes," he said, showing them to chairs in his office. "I am certainly pleased to meet someone of your renown! How may I be of service?"

"We are here at the behest of William Druitt. He is concerned for the welfare of his brother, and we need to inquire as to the reasons for his dismissal. My friend Dr. Watson is here to render a medical opinion, if required."

Whitworth was reticent to discuss the matter.

"I would prefer not to provide all the details, Mr. Holmes. I am concerned for both the reputation of the school as well as Mr. Druitt."

"Can you at least state the case in general, sir?"

Whitworth dropped his voice to a conspirator's whisper as he explained the situation.

"Truth be known, sir, Mr. Druitt has been odd this past term. Eccentric would be the charitable term, but this past Friday was beyond the pale."

Holmes and Watson exchanged meaningful glances. The importance of the previous Friday was not lost on them.

"Pray continue," urged the detective.

"Montague Druitt has been here for 6 years without a problem, and now suddenly this!" explained Whitworth. "He has shown erratic behavior, and telling strange stories to the class. But last Friday, he was extremely late and arrived in such a disheveled and confused state, I had to remove him from the classroom immediately. This will not do, not at all."

"What sort of stories?" inquired Watson.

"Reminiscences and regrets," Whitworth explained. "Angry stories about his father; fears for his mother and his own sanity. Not the sort of stories we want related to a roomful of impressionable boys!"

"Without doubt." Holmes probed further, hoping to find something conclusive. "Anything specific from Friday?"

"No, sir. More of the same, but to such degree he would not move on to the class materials! At length, one of the boys left the room and found me. His students were quite sad, actually. They like Montague." Whitworth spread his hands in submission. "I thought long and hard over the weekend and came to the conclusion there was no other solution. I dismissed him Monday morning but agreed to pay him for the entire term."

"Quite generous."

The headmaster missed the sarcasm in Watson's comment.

"I was not happy with the decision, but I do have responsibilities." He sighed. "If Mr. Druitt can compose himself and provide some assurance of his behavior, I am willing discuss his return. As I say, he is a popular teacher."

"Well, sir," said Holmes, "that is beyond the scope of my involvement, but I will surely relay it to his brother."

He stood and extended his hand.

"Thank you for your time, Sir John. I can assure you everything you have told us will be held in the strictest confidence."

Whitworth shook Holmes' hand, then that of Dr. Watson. His final statement was made to the physician.

"I do hope you can find help for the young man, doctor," returned Whitworth. "He has been such a pleasant chap to have around!"

"We are blocked at every turn!" said Holmes in frustration as they headed back to their rooms.

The doctor concurred. "There is nothing to allow us to either arrest or confine him!"

"Precisely." Holmes paused, his active brain connecting this interview from his thoughts on seeing the Thames on Saturday. "Druitt is deathly afraid of falling prey to his mother's disease."

"He already has in my opinion." The doctor's tone left no room for sympathy.

"Until this recent affair at the school, he has conducted his day to day life in such a manner that only his closest relation suspect there is something seriously wrong with him."

"It may be true," Watson conceded, "but how does that aid us?"

Holmes eyes narrowed, considering the possibilities before them.

"I am not completely sure," he admitted. "But it may provide us a means of turning that fear upon itself."

Wednesday, November 14 *The Nonpareil Club*

The man burst into their rooms early the next morning with Mrs. Hudson close behind.

"Sir!" She insisted. "You cannot come up here!"

"I will not be denied!" shouted the man. His clothes were well tailored, but his appearance was disheveled. He was small, with dark hair and slightly bug-eyed. His accent, though English, spoke of foreign origins. Watson stepped forward to help Mrs. Hudson usher the man from the premises, but Holmes refrained him.

"Come, Watson," he said soothingly, trying to introduce a note of calm. "This is undoubtedly Jameson Smythe from the Nonpareil Club. He has been trying to contact me these last several days."

"Indeed I am, sir," he said, twisting his arm away from Watson's grasp. "But I have sent letters and telegrams and left cards without a response! I come to you in this manner in desperation only because of something that threatens to ruin me if I cannot determine its roots."

Holmes waved him into a chair, while allowing Mrs.

Hudson to depart as well. He could not remember sleep. For him, everything seemed to begin with the moment he stepped into the room in Miller's Court. He wanted to dismiss the man out of hand, but somehow found the strength to maintain his civility.

"You must forgive us, Mr. Smythe, but we have all been under some strain of late dealing with matters in Whitechapel."

"Strain?" Smythe seemed incredulous anyone but he could know the meaning of the word. The reference to Whitechapel was missed entirely. "My reputation teeters on the brink these last few weeks, sir. I know something of strain!"

"That may well be, Mr. Smythe," interrupted Watson. "But we are investigating a series of murders!"

Smythe reached inside his code and withdrew an envelope, shaking it in front of the detective.

"Your own brother has given me a letter of introduction!"

"Mycroft?" Holmes snatched the letter from Smythe's hand, ripping it open as he spoke. "What can Mycroft have to do with a common gambling club?"

The detective read the words rapidly before thrusting the crumpled page towards Watson for his friend's review. The words were plain enough. The club was used as a meeting place for *sensitive* discussions.

"Given your connections, I can perhaps allow you to relate how I may be of service?"

Smythe nodded, removing his handkerchief to mop the sweat from his brow.

"I would not have come had your brother not suggested it. Your brother does not gamble often, but he always wins when he chooses to participate in a game."

Holmes smiled. "I can assure you, my brother does not gamble. Though I do not share my brother's interests, I am aware of your club's *reputation*."

Smythe was perplexed by the response. Holmes fought back a smile. This man was vain and self-centered. He had missed the point entirely.

"I am glad you are acquainted with my establishment," he replied at length, visibly proud a citizen of such fame was aware of his club.

"Yes," said Watson. "Very posh; very exclusive. But you have been in the papers recently," he observed. "There is a growing scandal regarding one of your foremost members as I recall."

Holmes seated himself and lit his pipe. For the moment, it was a relief to hear the man out rather than return to speculating on the Whitechapel case.

"I have seen the articles as well, Watson." He settled in comfortably, trying to remember the days before Whitechapel when he would meet men such as Smythe on cases that drew his curiosity. "Tell us your story then, Mr. Smythe."

The club owner sat on the edge of the chair. He began his story, his voice nervous. His hands continued to wring in his anxiety.

"It began about a year ago when Colonel Arthur Upwood joined the club."

"Upwood of the 66th?" interrupted Watson.

"You know him?" asked Smythe.

Holmes saw the question for what it was. This man Smythe was a snob and could not believe a man so common as Watson would know such a distinguished officer as Upwood.

"I do indeed," replied the doctor with some enthusiasm. "At the Battle of Maiwand, his troops covered our retreat. When the hospital was in danger of being overrun, he personally led the counter attack that drove the Ghazis back." He looked to Holmes. "It was during that action I was wounded in the leg. If not for his resolute defense, I might not have survived. I met him briefly and he is a truly impressive man."

"Yes," Smythe concurred, sufficient disdain in his tone to indicate he was well acquainted with such persons. "A man heaped with military honors and exactly the sort we wish to have as members of the Nonpareil."

"Then what is your issue with him?" Holmes asked.

Again, the club owner fidgeted. When he spoke, it was a flat and simple statement.

"He wins, Mr. Holmes."

Holmes smiled. "If patrons did not win at your club occasionally, I venture you would have no patrons."

"You do not understand, sir." Smythe's head shook. "He *always* wins. His losses are so few that everyone has remarked upon it."

Holmes drew slowly on his pipe. "It seems plain the man is cheating if he defies the odds so regularly."

"Holmes!"

Watson was enraged by the accusation. Smythe,

however, spoke to explain his case in more details.

"But it is true, Dr. Watson. The only possibility is that the Colonel is cheating, but we cannot determine how he does it. And like you, we cannot accuse a man of such distinguished character of a misdeed. I am trying desperately to avoid a scandal, as much for his sake as our own."

Holmes nodded his understanding. "So you desire me to discover his method."

"Precisely, Mr. Holmes." There was a note of condescension in his voice as if he were thankful the detective finally appreciated his situation. "I will rely on your discretion, but this must be resolved in the most secret fashion. If word of the scandal were made public…" Smythe did not need to complete the statement.

Holmes withdrew his watch and checked the time. "What time do you require us?"

Smythe stood. "We are open from noon until the last patron leaves. Colonel Upwood is there regularly from 1:00 pm until midnight."

"Is there a location where we might observe him without being too obvious?"

"Our private dining room looks into the gaming hall."

"Then arrange a well-placed table and we shall luncheon with you this afternoon."

Smythe rose, grabbing Holmes hand and shaking it profusely.

"Thank you, Mr. Holmes! Words cannot express the gratitude!"

He was gone as suddenly as he appeared. The men

waited until they heard the door to the street close behind him before Watson spoke.

"Is this wise?"

Holmes was heading for his dressing room. His face needed a shave and a quick bath would not be remiss before going to the club.

"Wise? What do you mean?"

Watson let out a deep breath. The detective saw he was tired, but it did not occur to link Watson's condition to himself.

"You have not slept since Thursday, Holmes." The doctor was genuinely concerned for his well being. Unfortunately, Holmes did not see it. "Is this the best time to be taking another case?"

The detective was enthralled by this new challenge. He knew he needed something to distract him from Whitechapel. It was not until later that he understood how the need clouded his judgment.

Lunch was pleasant for the two men. Smythe provided the establishment's best meal. Holmes, for his part, ate slowly while observing the object of his investigation.

Colonel Upwood was a man whose appearance matched his reputation perfectly. Tall, with broad shoulders and a ruddy complexion born from years of overseas service, his thick, grey hair complimented the magnificent mustache perched on his upper lip. The firm, square jaw was just the sort that directors wanted for plays dealing with military heroes. Colonel Upwood was the perfect embodiment.

True to his word, Smythe's table afforded an excellent view of the gaming room and the colonel. Upwood played whist against all challengers. For some, it was only a game; others would play an entire rubber. It was obvious to even Watson that the man was winning regularly.

Smythe came up to them as they were completing their meal to inquire as to the progress. Holmes carried on the discussion but did not remove his eyes from the game being played.

"You are correct, Mr. Smythe. I have observed the play and Upwood or his partner have won nine of the last ten hands. Further, they won by an average of 4 tricks, which is well above normal." He looked to his host with a question. "Is it standard in your club to have a dedicated dealer for whist?"

"No, sir, it is not. Several months ago, the colonel introduced a professional dealer to his games to assure everyone his winning streak was indeed a combination of skill and good fortune. There," said Smythe, pointing at a man who came from the back room. He walked over to the table and handed a number of small boxes to the dealer. In return, the dealer handed back the cards from the most recent games. "At the colonel's request, we also provide a new deck for every game so it is clear the cards cannot possibly be marked."

"I see." The detective pushed himself away from the table. "May I inspect the operations in your back room?

Smythe led them to the room behind the scenes, a place of considerable bustle and work compared to the gaming floor. Cash was counted and secured while the needs of the workers at the various tables were filled: new dice, card decks, and the tools of the games distributed.

Holmes was particularly interested in the cards. Smythe showed him with some pleasure.

"The cards are printed especially for us with our own unique backing. They come sealed from the printer, with the tax stamp across the package. My staff reviews each deck, assuring all the cards are present and in proper condition. They then return the cards to their package and seal it with our own stamp. There is no way for anyone to tamper with these cards."

"So it would seem. May I see two unused decks, and then some returned from Colonel Upwood's table?"

Smythe handed Holmes the sealed packages. The detective opened them and examined them minutely, both on the front and the back. He spread them across the table, face up.

"What do you make of this, Watson?" he asked.

"Two decks of playing cards in sequence," said Watson blandly.

"Precisely."

Smythe returned with the used cards from the table.

"We have checked the cards ourselves and can find no mark to distinguish them."

"I believe you, because I do not believe the cards are marked."

"Then how…"

Holmes held up a hand for silence. He reviewed the used cards, quickly sorting them to assure everyone that they were all present.

"Mr. Smythe, do you concur that this deck is complete

and undamaged?"

The club owner reviewed them quickly.

"Yes."

Holmes stacked and shuffled the deck quickly. He took the previously used cards and put them in the new package.

"Do this for several decks of cards."

"What difference..." protested the club owner.

"Please humor me," interrupted Holmes. He looked to his friend. "Watson, how are your skills at whist?"

Watson shrugged. "I know the rules and usually manage to hold my own."

"Good! Let's prepare to do battle!" He looked to the club owner. "Mr. Smythe, we shall play at the Colonel's table, but you must insist the doctor and I play as partners."

"I will arrange it."

"And also provide only decks that have been shuffled before being taken to the floor. Do not let the dealer or the colonel know."

"I will do as you say." Smythe's face clearly displayed his conflicted emotions. He finished his statement on a more cautious note. "Please be aware, however, the colonel expects to play for a minimum of a pound a trick."

"A pound!" said Watson.

"Don't worry, Watson. I will stand for your share."

Smythe walked off to pass on the detective's instructions. Watson moved closed, his voice low.

"What the devil are you playing at?"

"I know how he does it!"

Watson snorted. "I can see that! Why not discuss it with Colonel Upwood?"

"Discuss it? Before I have my proof?" Holmes was almost offended by the idea.

"This is a military man, Holmes!" The physician was not happy with the detective's approach to the matter. Holmes did not see the difference.

"We will play the game and prove my theory, Watson." Holmes rubbed his hands together in anticipation. "If I am correct, we will discuss his options when I have finished."

Smythe brought Holmes and Watson to the card table. To his amazement, the colonel stood and stepped to Watson, a broad smile on his face and his hand outstretched in friendship.

"Surgeon Captain Watson! I haven't seen you since Maiwand!" He took Watson's hand and shook it firmly and continually. "Good lord, man how are you? How's the leg?"

Watson took a moment to compose himself over the good natured greeting. "I am so pleased you remember me, colonel," he managed to reply.

Upwood laughed. "I'll never forget those few minutes I watched you, captain. Standing outside the tent and protecting your surgery, firing at the Ghazis with your revolver as calmly as if you were on the pistol range!" Upwood released his hand but still clasped the physician firmly by the shoulder.

"I always suspected there was more to his leg wound

than he would relate," interjected Holmes.

"More?" Upwood was genuinely surprised. "My god, man! That was the single bravest thing I ever saw in my life! Surgeon Captain Watson and two of his assistants standing between the surgery and an uncounted horde of blood-thirsty savages! He deserved a VC for his work that day, no mistake about it."

Watson was embarrassed by the outpouring of praise from his superior officer.

"As I recall, you are the one that received the VC," he said.

Upwood shook his head sadly. "True, but your omission was not from my lack of trying, I assure you," he said. "You are the only officer I ever recommended for the medal. I watched you hold your ground and protect those wounded men, even after you were struck yourself." He laughed aloud, the camaraderie of soldiers clearly on display for all to see. "Damn but I would have hated to stand before you that day! You must have taken two dozen before you were hit!"

"Not nearly so many, sir."

"More than your share, I assure you, Surgeon Captain."

Watson grabbed the opportunity to change the subject. "But what of you, Colonel? I would have expected you to still be in the service."

Upwood grabbed a cane lying against the edge of the card table and tapped it against his left leg. The hollow sound of wood on wood echoed in the room.

"I am dreadfully sorry, Colonel," said Watson, the

physician showing sudden concern. "I did not know. When did that occur?"

Upwood waived the two newcomers into their chairs as he sank into his usual seat.

"One of those bloody, stupid things that happen," explained Upwood. "It wasn't even in combat, which makes it damned embarrassing!" There was a whiskey and water on the table, and he took a sip before continuing. "I was on a tiger hunt with a rajah. One of the damned boys was acting as a loader and discharged a rifle into my leg." He smiled again, punctuated by another sip of whiskey. "It's not all that bad," he explained. "It doesn't hurt in bad weather, which I am sure is superior to your wound."

Watson was forced to chuckle at the thin jest. "True without a doubt, sir."

"The worst part is there is no pension for such a wound. I was paid off, but my pension is less than I would have hoped." He waved a hand about the room. "That is what has reduced me to setting my luck and skill against Mr. Sherlock Holmes."

He looked at the great detective, his gaze firm and unwavering. Holmes took the offered hand and shook it briefly.

"I am honored you consider me a worthy opponent."

"I never realized that your Dr. Watson was Surgeon Captain Watson," he said, casting a glance to the doctor.

Holmes smiled. Despite the serious nature of their business, Colonel Upwood was personable and engaging.

"It would seem Watson has been as steadfast as my companion as he was as an army surgeon."

Holmes looked about him. In addition to the participants at the table, several other people were gathered to observe the event. Word spread through the club that they were to witness a confrontation of giants at the table.

Holmes reached into his pocket and set a stack of notes on the table. “I am ready to proceed when you are, Colonel.”

Upwood occupied his favorite chair with Holmes at his left and Watson to the right. The dealer, a small man by the name of Richard Wilson, was the fifth man in the four-man game and sat between Holmes and Upwood.

As directed, Smythe brought a number of the prepared decks to the table and set them by the dealer. Wilson opened the cards and quickly shuffled them. He set the deck down on the table by Holmes when he was finished.

“Please cut the deck, Mr. Holmes.”

Holmes deftly did so. The dealer took the cards and passed them out to the four players, turning the last face up next to Colonel Upwood.

“Trump for this game is...spades,” he announced as he placed the three of spades next to Upwood. He seemed surprised at the card, almost as if he expected a different suit.

Holmes tossed down a card and collected the trick, as he did for the next round. Then Upwood collected a number in a row and the two men traded back and forth. The colonel won the hand, seven tricks to six.

“You see, Mr. Holmes,” the colonel observed in a good natured comment. "Even a man of your intellectual reputation cannot hope to defeat the Upwood luck!”

Holmes smiled, unconvinced. "We shall see, Colonel."

Play on the next hand was much the same. Again, Wilson showed a peculiar hesitance that caught even Upwood's attention when he announced the trump. As the round completed, Holmes had triumphed by taking eight tricks to the colonel's five.

"Well," said the colonel philosophically, "you can't win them all."

The colonel won the next hand, but Holmes took the following three rounds, the last by a convincing nine to four margin. While the retired officer remained stoic as the play continued, Wilson, the dealer, became more flustered with each passing hand.

Wilson opened the next pack of cards. He started to turn the faces toward him to check them, but Holmes grabbed his wrist.

"We all know there are fifty-two cards in the deck," observed the detective. "The colonel or myself will point out if there are any problems with the card counts."

The man was nervous and beads of sweat lined his forehead. "But..."

"But what, Mr. Wilson?" asked Holmes. He faced Upwood as he continued. "Perhaps the colonel does not want to continue under the present conditions?"

Upwood did not waiver from the detective's icy stare.

"I am unclear as to your meaning, Mr. Holmes," he said, summoning a measure of indignation.

Holmes took the deck from Wilson's hands and spread the cards, face up, on the table. The random mix of cards was evident to all. Wilson showed visible surprise, though for Upwood there was merely a tightening of the jaw.

"And I can assure you," said Holmes, the icy tone of his voice matching the hardness of his gaze. "All your future games will begin with such decks."

Wilson looked to Upwood, his eyes pleading. The colonel remained silent while his partner, a Mr. Evans, looked on in confusion. Watson, for his part, had his gaze directed downward in shame.

"Then I suppose," said Upwood, his voice even and controlled. "The jig is up?"

"So it would appear," replied Holmes, his tone conclusive.

Upwood pushed his chair back from the table. As he did, Mr. Smythe approached the table hesitantly. The colonel stood up, his height and figure imposing, even in the face of defeat.

"I shall expect Mr. Smythe will want to speak with me in his offices," he said. He took his whiskey and water from the table and finished it in one swallow. "I shall meet him there momentarily."

Upwood turned and left before Smythe reached them. The club owner looked as bewildered as the card dealer when he spoke.

"Mr. Holmes?"

"The fraud is revealed," he announced, his tone lone. He nodded to the dealer. "The colonel was not alone in his scheming."

Before another word was spoken, the quiet bustle of the room was overpowered by the crack of a gunshot.

"That was a revolver!" shouted Watson.

The doctor leapt to his feet, followed closely by the detective and Smythe. They were first to arrive at the cloak room, the smell and smoke of gunpowder hanging in the air. Upwood lay on the floor, his head destroyed by the single shot from the service revolver gripped in his hand. Watson turned, trying to hold the bystanders back.

"You need to summon the police, Holmes."

Holmes looked to Smythe. "Of course, Watson. It is unavoidable now."

Wilson sat in the chair before Smythe's desk while the proprietor sat and watched his employee in stern disapproval. The man quaked, whether from fear or simply as a result of the day's stress was unknown.

"I want to make it clear," he said, taking a drink of whiskey that Watson provided. "It was me that went to the colonel, not the other way 'round."

"Give us the whole story," urged Holmes.

"It's simple enough," continued Wilson. "I saw the colonel's lucky streak startin' to peter out. When I had a chance, I suggested to him that I should deal for him, to assure his opponents everything was on the up and up. I was the one who suggested on a new deck for every hand."

"I remember when he proposed it," affirmed Smythe, his voice unemotional.

Wilson shook his head, still unable to believe the day's occurrences. "I made sure the streak continued, that's all."

"And how long did it take the colonel to realize you were helping him?" asked Holmes.

"About a week," returned the dealer. "He confronted me one night, and I was forced to own up. But after I explained it all, he finally agreed to let it continue." Wilson turned to Smythe, his eyes streaming with tears and his voice pleading as he looked to Watson. "He was desperate, Dr. Watson. He could barely survive on the army pension. He owed money; money he didn't have."

Wilson turned from the doctor to the club's proprietor. "You know the colonel, sir! He never let me take too much from anyone! He always moved his partners about and made sure that things evened out in the end. It was only him and me that were making extra on the side!"

"Indeed!" snapped Smythe. "I expect you out of my club immediately, Wilson! And you can be sure you will not deal cards on this continent again!"

Wilson stood, ashamed at his actions. Head bowed, he turned and left the room. Watson stepped forward to stop him, but Holmes waved him back. After the dealer had left, Smythe let out a heavy sigh.

"There will be no keeping this from the press now," he announced. "The club will be ruined."

Holmes sat down in the seat vacated by Wilson. "I am sorry," he explained. "Had I the slightest notion Colonel Upwood would take his own life, I would have proceeded differently."

Smythe nodded, accepting the explanation. "No doubt, sir. No doubt." He paused, looking directly to the detective. "What I don't understand, though, is how Wilson did it!"

Holmes was stoic, but reached into his pocket and withdrew a deck of unopened cards. He explained as he displayed them to the other two men.

"The idea is simple, though I am not sure I can replicate it exactly. The cards, when first opened, are in exact order by suit and sequence."

He fanned the cards to display them before pushing them back into a stack.

"As I said, I am not sure I can do this exactly. Mr. Wilson gets so much more practice than I."

Holmes split the deck and shuffled them once. Before pushing the two stacks together, he turned it over for the others to see.

The cards were interleaved almost exactly one to one. There were only two instances where Holmes had missed the shuffle.

"Mr. Wilson is much more precise. I would wager he manages an exact shuffle ninety-nine in one hundred times."

"And what does that achieve?" asked Watson.

"Wilson was able to track each card in the deck after each shuffle. If you would observe him, he shuffled each hand exactly five times."

"Would not all the hands end up exactly the same?"

"He would introduce variations, though each deck would be very close to the same when he finished his work."

Watson shook his head, finding the concept hard to believe. "But he would have to know the sequence of every card in the deck!"

"Without a doubt he did," assured Holmes.

"But the cards were cut!" protested the doctor.

Holmes nodded. "The cards *were* cut, but that is an old magician's trick. Wilson can most likely tell within a card how many were in each side of the cut. "

Smythe was unconvinced. "Still, Holmes, to remember every card! It is too much."

"Obviously not for Wilson. It is only fifty-two cards, after all. After the cut, he would start to deal."

"Surely he could not control the sequence of the cards!" protested Smythe.

"Not precisely. He knew who got which cards and he could introduce variations by dealing from both sides of the deck. He could also control the trump suit, which is important." Smythe nodded his agreement to the statement. "In a round of Whist, it takes only two or three cards to tip the balance. Wilson influenced the cards sufficiently he could always tip the balance in favor of Upwood or the colonel's partner."

Smythe accepted the explanation. "It will make little difference," he said. "The word will spread and the club is finished."

Holmes took a deep breath and let it out. The situation had gotten beyond his control and he did not handle it. Even then, he could not admit the full extent of his culpability to the proprietor.

"People are much harder to control than cards, Mr. Smythe. It should have occurred to me that Colonel Upwood might exercise such an option."

"Yes," snapped Watson, unable to contain his comments further. "He was a man of honor and not a common criminal!"

Smythe was summoned away briefly and the detective turned to his friend. His words could not express what he knew of his failure.

The two men made their leave from the proprietor, walking onto the London streets as the last glimmer of day was fading. Watson hailed a cab and they boarded, giving orders for Baker Street. They rode in silence for several minutes before Watson could stand it no further.

"The man was an honored military hero, Holmes!" he growled. "What did you expect to happen if you exposed his deceit?"

Holmes could not reply immediately. It took him a minute or more to compose an answer to the doctor's question.

"You are right, of course," he said. The words were simple and bland. They did not truly reflect what he knew. "I did not think the matter through."

Watson snorted at the reply. "Do you realize that is not an uncommon occurrence?"

Holmes looked sadly at his friend. "More often than you might imagine, Watson." He placed a hand on Watson's knee. "I *am* sorry it came to such a conclusion. That was not my intention."

Watson nodded, looking out the window. His voice betrayed the pent up emotion he was endeavoring to conceal.

"I know, Holmes. I know." There was a long pause before he finished. "But you, of all people, should have known!"

Holmes stared out his window, noting they crossed Commercial Street on their return towards Baker Street. He caught a brief glance of Whitechapel as they darted across the road.

"I misjudged the colonel's sense of honor," he said. "I misjudged it badly." He paused, his brief glimpse of the East End lost as they were again surrounded by the buildings of London.

"If only our East End murderer had that same sense of honor," the doctor observed in a low tone before falling silent.

No other word was spoken for the remainder of their journey. They descended from the cab and Holmes paid the driver. As they entered their rooms, Holmes laid his hat down and hung up his coat.

"Come, Watson," he said. "I have an excellent Bordeaux I set aside for a special occasion. I will have Mrs. Hudson send it up, and you can tell me of your friend."

"I do not need your wine, Holmes!" Watson stepped from the coach and looked away from the door. "I require some time to clear my thoughts!"

Watson stepped off and Holmes watched his friend walk into the growing fog. There was only the click of his cane on the pavement to mark his steps and the detective watched him until he disappeared.

"Hey, Mate!" snapped the cabbie.

Holmes looked at the man and handed him a one pound note as he stepped down. With a comment of appreciation, the cabbie closed the cab door and started off. Holmes, for his part, just looked into the fog where his friend had disappeared.

Thursday, November 15 *The Sign of Eight*

The next morning, Holmes realized Watson's analysis was correct. Druitt needed a sense of honor, but it was totally lacking in the soulless horror. The question the detective could not answer was whether or not there was anything resembling principles remaining within the monster.

The train ride to Blackheath was in silence as Holmes considered these things. There was a heavy air between the two, the previous day's events a barrier. Holmes did not have the words to break the silence; Watson did not have the desire. But as they stepped onto the platform, the physician at last interrupted the reverie.

"You have the makings of a plan, Holmes. I see it in your expression."

"Perhaps," he returned. "The police cannot arrest him because they have no damning evidence. I have no direct evidence, so we cannot do anything short of appointing ourselves his executioner."

"If it will rid the world of this beast..." offered Watson.

Holmes considered turning his friend loose on the suspect, but the events of the previous day preyed on his thoughts and stayed his hand.

“I cannot, Watson,” he explained. “I can take no action until I am certain. In the interim, our goal is to prevent him from taking any more lives.”

“And what will make you certain, Holmes?” asked his friend in frustration. “Catching him over the body of another dead woman, a bloody knife in his hand?”

Holmes nodded. “At least finding the knife, Watson. If we can find it, the law can remove the menace.”

“You mean by incarceration and execution? And if you do not find it?”

“I will arrange a *medical* confinement.”

Watson let out a deep breath of annoyance. “You are back to the idea of having him committed? His brother has already said he will not submit to that!”

“Yes, his brother will not, but there may be an opportunity to drive him to perform the task himself.”

Their cab arrived outside of the Blackheath rooms. The physician opened his door, but the detective stopped him.

“Watson, remain with the coach. I need you to follow him. I must take care of some business inside after he and the police leave.”

The doctor did not require an explanation of the detective’s business. “As you wish, Holmes.”

Holmes descended and Watson had the coachman move the cab to a location where the doctor could watch the residence and wait for Druitt to appear. Since his dismissal from Valentine’s, Druitt had replaced his normal routine by taking a walk before leaving for his chambers in London. The detective felt he had enough time to accomplish his mission before the barrister returned. He quickly went inside and up to his rooms where Gregson and another officer had kept watch on Druitt for the past day.

"Any change, Gregson?" asked Holmes.

"No, sir," replied the inspector, gathering his few belonging. "Normal routine yesterday and he spent the night pacing in his quarters."

"Very good. Watson and I have the watch. Would you be so kind to deliver this to Lestrade for me?"

He handed the Scotland Yard detective a note. Gregson read it quickly, looking at Holmes in surprise.

"I don't rightly know if we can let you have photographs of the victims, Mr. Holmes!" he protested.

"Just take it on to Lestrade. He and Abberline can decide."

"Yes, sir."

Gregson touched his hat and the two detectives left. Holmes locked the door after them and waited for the sound of Druitt leaving his quarters. When he heard the front door close, he went to the window and watched the barrister make his way down the street. As the man turned the corner, Watson's coach drove slowly past the house in leisurely pursuit.

Holmes left his apartment and took quick, silent steps up to his neighbor's rooms. It took only a second to enter and close the door behind him. He relocked it from the inside to be sure he had some notice of an unexpected return.

He had only one interest. The small display he had

decided was a trophy trove was not in its previous location. He looked around and spied a footlocker under the bed that was not present on his first visit. He pulled it out using great caution to not disturb the rug or the bed. Only a minute's effort was needed to pick the padlock and open it.

The items he had seen before were still there, but two new objects were present: a woman's hairbrush and a salt shaker. He looked at them, trying to discern a pattern. If his deduction was correct and these were trophies from his crimes, did it mean he had now killed seventeen women or did it mean something else?

He stared for a long time, organizing and reorganizing the eclectic articles. At last, he thought he hit upon it. The copper ring, the bit of mirror, a necklace and the hairbrush with the blonde hair no doubt belonged to the Ripper's victims. Those were personal objects, either used by or carried by a person. The others were articles from a person's house or rooms: a fork, a bit of candle, the salt shaker.

The detective counted quickly: eight personal; eight household. But eight personal items meant he had killed eight victims and he knew of only six. *Were there eight victims or had he misread this pattern, also?*

Holmes was never one to vacillate once a decision with made, but the events of the previous day made him pause. He misjudged Upwood and it led to the man's suicide. He could not know the impact of any of his actions on someone as unstable as Druitt. The most insignificant change might result in more deaths. The eight objects before him marked the end of eight lives, or at least that is what he believed. He forced his uncertainties to the back of his mind.

He selected the eight items his deductions had concluded belonged to the murder victims. He started to close the lid of the footlocker when a thought occurred to him. He remembered the case from September and how Jonathon Small had announced his presence. He smiled to himself. Perhaps there was a reason for all the cases that had intervened, he decided.

Holmes pulled out his notepad and pencil. He drew two circles to make an "eight" shape on a blank sheet then added lines horizontally through the center of each circle and vertically through the entire figure. The shape was now divided into eight sections. Below it he wrote in careful lettering: *Sign of the Eight.* He set the paper into the blank space occupied by their quarry's trophies.

The detective conducted one last, quick search of the locker. The one item that continued to be missing was a knife, the weapon used to commit the crimes. The case contained no sign of the weapon, nor was there any indication of blood stains to show it had ever been there.

Holmes considered making a more thorough search of the rooms, but quickly decided against it. The barrister would be returning shortly, and he could not afford to be caught. Further, his previous visit had revealed no clue to the knife's location. Wherever the weapon was hidden, it would not be so obvious as Druitt's personal rooms.

Carefully, Holmes relocked the case and returned it to the original position. He moved back the way he had come, insuring he erased all traces of his visit. That would be announced soon enough, and he did not want the drama of the moment to be lost by Druitt suspecting too soon. He quietly walked down the stairs and left the building, waiting on an opposite corner.

It was not long before the barrister returned and he rejoined Watson in the cab. The doctor was eager with anticipation.

"Did you find anything?"

"A new trophy: a hair brush with blond hair."

"Mary Kelly."

"Most likely. I think I figured out the pattern of his trophies. Eight for robberies, eight for killings."

"Eight?" The blood drained from Watson's features. "But we only know of six!"

Holmes nodded gravely.

"Too true. I shall have Lestrade review any unsolved murders in Whitechapel in July."

Watson looked to the detective, genuine fear in his eyes.

"You don't think he has gotten to Cornwall?"

"Steady!" said Holmes, placing a reassuring hand on his friend's shoulder. "He has been under constant surveillance since Miss Morstan left for Cornwall. No, I believe these two were committed earlier, before he established his pattern. That is why they were overlooked."

"Good!"

The relief was almost palpable in the doctor's word. Watson turned his attention back to the residence looking for sign of Druitt. After another few minutes of silent watching, he continued their conversation from the train.

"You said we had another option besides getting his brother to commit him. Do you actually believe you can force him to commit himself?"

"Commit," repeated Holmes. "Or something more enduring."

Watson did not react to the implication of the statement. The physician obviously found that solution quite acceptable.

At length, Druitt appeared outside. He was hesitant and looking about with great agitation. He wore the same clothes he had in the morning, an unusual move for the normally neat and trim barrister. His hair was mussed, his eyes wild as he started the short walk towards the train station.

"Good Lord, Holmes! What did you do in his rooms? The man appears a complete muddle!"

Holmes smiled as their coach trailed the barrister.

"I left him a message he could neither overlook nor ignore. He now has no doubts his secrets are known. Whatever fears of discovery he had before, they are multiplied many fold."

Holmes and Watson arrived at the station, stepping from their cab a discrete distance from Druitt. The man was nervous and fumbling as he climbed onto the train.

"Whatever fires are consuming him, Holmes," Watson commented with some satisfaction, "you have succeeded in adding fuel to the flames!"

"Excellent!" returned the detective. "We shall see what impact that has on his colleagues in the Inner Temple!"

Friday, November 16 *Night Visit*

"I do say, Holmes! This is too much!" whispered Watson, a note of panic beneath the words.

The halls of the Inner Temple were dark. They had distracted the night watchman long enough to gain entrance and find their way to Druitt's chambers. It took only a moment to pick the lock and move silently into the room.

"He still has secrets to be discovered," justified the detective.

"Such as?"

"The knife, Watson!" hissed Holmes. "Where does he hide the knife? If we can find the weapon, we may be able to end this case more to your liking!"

Holmes was swift and sure, using his bulls eye lantern to a minimum and making sure they did nothing to alert the watchman out front. He found a locked drawer and opened it.

"Your light, Watson!"

The doctor pointed his lantern into the drawer as Holmes expertly went through the contents.

"What is it?"

"Clothes," replied the detective. "Shoddy clothes for Whitechapel."

He closed the drawer but did not bother to relock it. There was a case of law books on one wall and the desk in the center of the room. Chairs and a table completed the furnishings. None yielded any clues to the detectives.

"Hidden in a book?" asked Watson.

Holmes examined them quickly, pulling on each quickly.

"The weight seems correct for all of them. If one was hollowed out, it would be lighter. I doubt that anyway."

"Why?"

"What if a colleague came in to borrow that particular volume?"

Watson nodded, yielding the point.

"I do not believe the weapon is here," announced Holmes with irritation.

"Now what?"

The detective gestured towards the door, the action dimly visible in the darkened room.

"We leave as quietly as we came."

But as they were leaving, Holmes left a scrap of paper on the barrister's desk, the drawing of the two circles with four lines and the "Sign of Eight" printed beneath it.

The constables did the daily mail exchange in the morning, handing Holmes a short stack of letters to replace the bag he took away. Holmes thumbed through them quickly and pulled one from the stack.

"How odd!" he said, looking at the sender.

"What is that?" asked Watson from the table while sipping his coffee.

"A letter from Robert Lees!" He tore it open and read the two lines written upon it. "Extraordinary!" He handed the note to Watson.

It's in the cards, Holmes.
It is in the cards.
Lees

"What the devil does that mean?" snorted Watson.

"I do not have the slightest idea," replied Holmes. He chuckled at a stray thought. "Do you have any idea what my brother will say when he hears of this? If he believes I am regularly using the services of the psychic, he will have *me* committed!"

They laughed at the small joke. The bell rang on the door, followed by quick steps upon the stairs.

"Ah, Lestrade!" greeted Holmes as the inspector entered. "You are here early this morning!" Holmes pointed to the table. "Coffee? A bit of breakfast?"

"Don't mind if I do," said Lestrade.

He handed Holmes an envelope, then hung his coat on the rack. The inspector joined Watson at the table while the detective reviewed the contents of the envelope. They were photographs of the victims.

"Thank you, Lestrade," Holmes said, setting them aside. "I will put these to good use."

He took his place at the table, dishing out a few eggs and taking some bacon. "What have you done to this Druitt?" asked the police inspector as he ate. "My men say he is in a proper state! He was pounding on their door early this morning wanting to see you."

"I paid him another unofficial visit. I am pointing out the errors of his ways."

Lestrade snorted. "Cryptic as always! I trust you will exercise caution in these *unofficial visits*?""

He looked to Watson for some explanation but the physician could only shrug to show he was equally ignorant of the detective's plan.

"And what was this business at the Nonpareil the other day?" continued the policeman.

Holmes was surprised at the question but answered quickly.

"An unrelated inquiry, Lestrade." He tried to keep the resignation from his voice. "It was not resolved to my liking."

Watson snorted. The police inspector clearly sensed the friction between the men, but ignored it and commented further.

"It stirred up quite the hornets' nest at the Yard."

Watson ruffled his newspaper. "We would not want the Yard stirred up by any means," he said with heavy sarcasm.

Lestrade bristled at the tone of the response. Holmes changed the subject before an argument could ensue.

"I have a question, Lestrade." Holmes was very serious as he spoke. "Are there any other unsolved murders in Whitechapel? I am interested in any that occurred in July."

Lestrade chuckled at the irony.

"There are always unsolved murders in Whitechapel, Holmes. You know that. There are none that were committed with knives, I can assure you of that!"

"These may not have been stabbings," Holmes explained. "Are there any strangulation victims in July, committed on a Friday or Saturday night? Was it raining?"

Lestrade stopped eating and looked hard at the detective.

"That's bloody specific, Holmes! What do you know?"

Holmes was silent for the briefest moment, considering whether or not to voice his suspicions. But he had promised Lestrade and Abberline he would share all his information. This was no different.

"I have reason to believe he has committed two additional murders we have not identified. I think we overlooked them because they were simple strangulations and he did not display the bodies in the manner to we have now associated to the Ripper."

"Why do you believe this?"

"Druitt has mementos; objects I believe are belongings of his victims."

"Those are clues, Holmes! We could arrest him!"

Holmes shook his head sadly. "These are simple, nondescript articles you could never prove belonged to a particular victim. If that were possible, I would have had you arrest him a month ago!"

"I see. And these lead you to believe there are more than six women?"

"Two more. Since there are no victims since August that are slashed and displayed, I deduce there are earlier victims in July he merely strangled. When that did not meet his needs, his level of violence increased."

Lestrade pushed his plate away. The information robbed him of his appetite.

"I will have someone review the logs."

Sunday, November 18 *A Sunday Walk*

Saturday was spent listening to the barrister pace in his rooms. Druitt did not even leave to take meals from Mrs. Patrick. Early Sunday, a constable arrived with a letter from Lestrade. It contained two new names with pictures from the autopsies.

"Are these your missing victims?" asked Watson.

Holmes nodded. "The first case was a simple strangulation. She was killed on the fourteenth, only a week after Druitt's mother was committed. A prostitute and, according to Lestrade's research, it rained steadily that whole night."

"And the other?"

"Another prostitute, but there is no surprise there," commented Holmes. "This second case shows more violence, which is what I would suspect. It was the night of the twenty-seventh, and it rained intermittently. The woman was pushed into a wall before she was strangled."

"That would seem to indicate the Ripper's *modus operandi*," confirmed Watson.

"Exactly," agreed the detective. "The rising level of

violence with each killing dovetails neatly into the August murders."

Holmes looked at the pictures, the faces so like those of the known victims. He sat down to write on the back of a picture, but instead his attention was drawn to a creak on the stairs. It was followed by a shadow crossing their door. The quarry was on the move.

"Quick, Watson!"

The men grabbed hats and coats and followed Druitt to the street. They followed him on an odd, shifting pattern until he arrived at a private residence. A small sign proclaimed it the home of "Madame Sybil - Futures Foretold". Watson looked at the sign with contempt.

"Now *he* is consulting a fortune teller?"

"Apparently," said Holmes.

"If these people know so much of the future," observed Watson with some derision in his voice, "I would expect them to identify this beast for what he is!"

Holmes chuckled dryly. "A point well taken, Watson!" The detective pointed down the street. "Find a place in the park where you can watch the front of the house and I will observe the back!"

They moved off and found places where they could watch the exits from the house and still see one another. It was over half an hour before Druitt left, exiting at the rear of the house. Holmes kept himself out of sight, waiting until Druitt moved off. He waved for Watson to join him.

"Be careful not to be seen, Watson" said Holmes. "We shall see what he is about and it will not hurt for him to believe he has lost us."

Carefully, they followed the man who seemed to be doing nothing more than wandering the streets. But after an hour, Holmes noted they had circled the same block multiple times. Then the barrister stopped in front of a house, and looked about.

With no one obviously in sight, Druitt walked up to the front door and rang the bell. There was no answer and he knocked. When there was still no answer, he looked around again before reaching inside his coat pocket. He withdrew the bundle of cloth containing the burglary tools Holmes discovered on their first visit to his rooms.

"He is breaking into that house!" Watson was amazed at the cheek of the man to be making such an attempt in broad daylight.

"Quickly now!" said Holmes, stepping into the open and striding swiftly towards the threatened home.

Druitt spied the two men immediately, as was Holmes' intention. He instantly abandoned his effort to unlock the door and began walking again, though this time it was clearly in the direction of the apartment. Holmes waited outside the building until he saw Druitt through an unshuttered window.

The sound of pacing above them continued as they settled into their chairs. Holmes picked up the pictures of the newly identified victims and wrote on the back.

"What the devil is that?"

Holmes handed the photo to Watson.

"Something I learned from our friend Jonathon Small," explained the detective "The Sign of Eight."

"The what?"

"It shows him what I know, even if I cannot prove it. And every time he sees that symbol, he will think of the lives he has ended."

Watson shook his head sadly at the thought. "I would surely go mad under such a burden."

"That is my intention!"

The pacing above continued, but suddenly slowed and stopped. There were several minutes of perfect silence, followed by a sound that might be a groan or a growl. With that, the pacing started anew at an even faster rate.

Monday, November 19 *Stronger Measures*

"You saw the psychic!" chided Mycroft in the most outraged tone.

Holmes laughed aloud. He had rarely seen his brother in such a state. Throughout dinner, the elder Holmes would pause as if he were about to speak but then remember his surroundings and catch himself. As it was, they barely made it to the safety of the Stranger's Room before the comment burst forth.

"I knew you would find that amusing!" replied Holmes. "But to be fair, I did not consult him. He sent me unsolicited advice."

The two brothers were alone in the room. Mycroft had brandy and tobacco laid out before dismissing the waiters. Watson was absent seeing to the needs of a patient. In truth, it was a ruse created by the detective so he might consult his brother alone.

"So you have enticed Watson away for the evening. What might I tell you?"

Neither brother could surprise the other with feats of deduction. They may as well have been two magicians trying to impress each other with their tricks.

"The Home Secretary needs this Whitechapel business concluded."

"It proceeds at its own pace."

"But you watch the guilty party."

"I believe so."

"Then end it," said Mycroft. There was no doubt as to his meaning in the tone of his voice.

"As I said, Mycroft," returned Holmes. "It proceeds."

"That is not sufficient!" Mycroft let anger enter his voice.

"I believe it will resolve itself within two weeks."

"*Believe* is not sufficient!"Mycroft's voice rose to an authoritative roar, but it had little impact on his younger sibling. "The success of this empire is based on accomplishments, not beliefs!"

Holmes ignored the tirade, but still felt his doubts about Druitt. Even as he let the idea that he was mistaken about Druitt cross into his mind, he shook them off. Miller's Court was the decisive moment and he would no longer allow himself any room for doubt.

"And if I am incorrect?"

Mycroft calmed quickly, showing how much of the previous anger was feigned for effect.

"In truth, Sherlock, I have my doubts about this barrister. I have faith in your skills, but you have not connected him to the actual crimes except in the most circumstantial way."

"And that has prevented me from more direct measures, brother," replied Holmes. The detective rarely admitted his doubts, and Mycroft was the only one with whom he could openly discuss them. "In my profession, I am used to dealing in absolutes. I obtain my needed proof and proceed accordingly."

Mycroft, the stern bureaucrat, allowed his features to soften and regarded his brother with some sympathy.

"My profession rarely allows for absolutes," he explained. "You must gather the best information you can discover and make a decision. Sometimes, those decisions are wrong."

Mycroft opened the brandy and poured some into his glass. Holmes held his out and, with some effort, Mycroft leaned his bulky form forward and also poured a drink for Sherlock. He leaned back and replaced the stopper in the bottle.

"I must insist on a deadline, Sherlock. The end of the month is sufficient to conclude this matter if Druitt is indeed the guilty party. If radical measures are required, I can assure you of protection at the highest level. Any hint of your involvement will be quashed immediately."

"I have my own plans." He sipped the brandy, but did not expound on the cryptic comment.

"Involving?" probed Mycroft.

"I prefer to keep the details to myself and not let it be known in the halls of government," returned the detective. He sipped some more brandy, but knew he had no option but to relent to his brother on the deadline. "If my plan is not successful by December, I will consider *other* methods."

Tuesday, November 20 *Card Tricks*

"Why are we here in the middle of the week?" asked Watson. "You know his pattern now."

"We cannot trust the pattern any more," explained Holmes.

"Why not, Holmes? The next crisis should be at the end of the month."

Holmes shook his head. The sound of pacing above them confirmed their target was still in his rooms.

"Druitt is a man possessed by demons neither of us can fathom." He let out a heavy sigh, admitting a thought that had preyed upon him for weeks. "I fear the charnel house at Miller's Court was caused by us preventing a killing at the end of October. Those pent up urges exploded in the orgy of violence against Mary Kelly. Now he has become unstable and unpredictable, Watson. We must be on our guard at every moment."

"You say Gregson stopped him in London this morning?"

The detective, at Holmes' urging, found a reason to detain and search the barrister on his daily trip to London.

As before, the attempt was fruitless.

"Yes, but he did not have a weapon."

"But if he is searching for another victim, why do they not find a knife?"

Holmes nodded in confirmation. There was a great deal of frustration in Watson's comment and the detective felt it, too.

"That continues to be the final piece of the puzzle, isn't it? He had it the night of the eighth, but not since. So where is it? Where can he be keeping it that is so easily available but it so well hidden from us?" Holmes pointed towards the small table in their rooms and stepped over to it. "Let me change the conversation, Watson."

He pulled out a deck of cards and waved his friend into the chair opposite him. He shuffled the deck and had Watson cut it. He fanned the cards in his hand and held them before the position.

"Take a card."

Watson reacted in a pique. "Are we to amuse ourselves with card tricks while waiting to apprehend this beast?"

"This is in conjunction with the case," said Holmes. He pressed the cards forward. "A card please."

Watson pulled the card and looked at it. He laid the ace of spades on the table.

"Droll," said the doctor.

"Another."

"Queen of Hearts"

"Another."

"Eight of Diamonds"

It continued for three more cards, by which time Watson had drawn the three remaining eights.

"So what does it mean?" he asked.

"The eights are obvious," said Holmes. "I have been looking into cartomancy since we discovered our friend believes in fortune telling."

"And this has meaning?" asked Watson, his hands above the selected cards.

"The ace of Spades is a death card. I want him to foresee his own death. The Queen of Hearts is a water element. Whatever the connection is between his murders and rain, I want to strengthen it in what is left of his mind."

"You are becoming as mad as he is, Holmes," concluded the doctor.

Holmes chuckled.

"Perhaps, but remember Lees: *It is in the cards*." Holmes pulled out another new deck. "Come, I have to practice this again. I cannot afford to make a mistake when the opportunity to confront Druitt presents itself."

Wednesday, November 21 *Cartomancy*

The sound of Druitt's footsteps stopped. Holmes and Watson were prepared to follow him into the cool evening, but instead the detective was surprised by a knock on their door. The two men looked at each other in astonishment on this turn of events. Watson produced his service revolver while Holmes considered the situation. He pointed to the closest bedroom and the doctor stepped silently into it while he went to the door. Holmes opened the door cautiously, unsure what to expect. The young barrister stood there, waiting patiently.

Druitt's appearance had become more disheveled with each passing day. He had not shaved since the previous week and Holmes was convinced he had not bathed in that time. But the shock of standing face to face with his quarry left the detective at a loss for words.

"May we talk for a while?" asked Druitt pleasantly to open the conversation.

Holmes surveyed the situation quickly. The man's hands were clearly visible and there was no indication that he had any weapons. The investigator stepped aside and allowed Druitt to enter the room. He heard the tell tale click of Watson's revolver cocking from the other room, but

Druitt did not appear to notice.

"Have a seat, Mr. Druitt," said Holmes evenly. "Perhaps I should have Mrs. Patrick send up some tea?"

For all the wildness of his appearance, Druitt spoke with the utmost civility.

"Most kind, but that won't be necessary."

The barrister took a seat at the small table and the detective sat across from him.

"To what do we owe this visit?" asked Holmes.

"You torture me, sir, and I have come to inquire the purpose."

Druitt's tone was in complete sincerity. In truth, Holmes was somewhat taken aback by the frank manner of the young man. If he did not know better, he might actually be convinced of the man's innocence.

"The purpose is clear, Mr. Druitt. We both know you have committed these hellish crimes even if I cannot prove it to the satisfaction of the authorities. They must end."

Druitt looked at the table top, unable to match the detective's gaze.

"I am a barrister, an officer of the court…"

"We both know better," interrupted Holmes.

"If there were some way for me to stop these crimes…"

Again, the detective interjected his comments and did not allow Druitt to finish.

"But that is the very point, isn't it, Mr. Druitt?" he said. "You are unable to stop no more than you are able to stop breathing."

Druitt appeared a beaten man, but Holmes saw it was only a façade. The barrister could not admit culpability to himself any more than he could admit it openly to the detective.

"What can I do to make you give up this harassment?"

"You can confess."

Druitt laughed lightly. "To something for which I have no guilt?"

"You can have yourself committed," offered Holmes/

"I would kill myself before allowing it."

Holmes grinned wryly at the comment.

"There is also that option," he allowed.

Druitt's resolved stiffened at that comment. Holmes thought perhaps he had pushed the man too far.

"That is a horrid suggestion, sir, and unworthy of you!"

"Perhaps," conceded Holmes. He hoped his voice conveyed an honesty he did not feel. He decided it was time to change his approach.

"I know you consulted Madame Sybil last week," he said. He pulled out a deck of cards. "Perhaps you will trust a higher power?"

"And now you mock me!" he snorted.

Druitt's voice contained anger. Holmes felt he was losing control of the situation. Worse, he was afraid he was pushing the barrister into a more rational state of mind. If his plan was to succeed, he needed to maintain the confusion Druitt had displayed for the last two weeks.

"It was only an offer," he replied meekly. He took the deck of cards from the table. "Robert Lees suggested I trust the cards."

The mention of Lees had the desired effect. Druitt's eyes widened slightly at the reference.

"You know Lees?"

"I have had the privilege of meeting him. We have corresponded."

While technically true, Holmes was stretching the truth considerably with these statements. He felt little guilt at doing so if it achieved his ultimate objective. He opened the deck of cards and shuffled them.

"Let us see what results we get."

He slid the deck to Druitt and allowed him to cut the cards. With a quick sleight of hand, he returned the cards to their original order. Druitt missed the move and Holmes was glad he had spent time practicing. With a quick move, he produced a card and laid it before his guest.

"The eight of Spades. That would signify eight deaths, would it not?"

"Yes," stammered Druitt, admitting the point.

"Queen of Hearts," said Holmes as he laid down the next card. "Women and a water sign." Druitt could only stare while the detective laid down another card. "The ace of Spades. Another harbinger of death!"

"This…this is a trick!" protested the barrister.

Holmes leaned back from the table, collecting the cards.

"The cards speak for themselves," he said in all

innocence. He pulled out another fresh deck. "But I can understand your concern. Let us try this a different way."

Holmes opened the deck and precisely shuffled it again, allowing Druitt to plainly watch every move. When he allowed the deck to be cut, he made it plain the stack was reversed when he put them together. Instead of laying cards on the table, he fanned them and held them in front of Druitt.

"Select your own card."

Druitt's extended his hand and pulled a card. As he looked at it, his face went ashen and he dropped it to the table. It was the eight of Hearts.

"Another eight. Draw again," urged the detective.

Druitt was more cautious, drawing a card from towards one end. His eyes widened and he set the card down.

"Queen of Spades."

Holmes felt his throat tighten. It was supposed to be the queen of Hearts again, but the significance of women and death worked just as well.

"And another?" he offered.

Druitt's hand shook as he reached forward. He withdrew the card and looked at it. His hand went limp and it fell to the table.

"The ace of Spades again," said Holmes. He restacked the deck rather than push his luck any further. "Do you trust the cards, Mr. Druitt?"

Druitt was a long time responding.

"I do not know." The voice was weak, barely above a whisper.

Holmes went to the door and opened it.

"The path is clear, Mr. Druitt. You merely need the courage to walk it."

Druitt rose and walked slowly to the door.

"Thank you for your time, Mr. Holmes," he said.

He did not wait for a reply, but instead walked up the stairs. Holmes waited until he heard the door close above before closing and locking his own. He ran his hand across his face to relieve the stress he felt while he let out a long, involuntary sigh of relief.

"I thought that was supposed to be the eight of Diamonds," said Watson as he emerged from the bedroom and slowly lowered the hammer on the revolver.

"It was. And the Queen of Hearts instead of Spades."

"You need more practice," observed Watson, with more than a hint of sarcasm in his voice.

Holmes sat in his chair, relived the brief interview was past him.

"Either practice or allow Lees the point that it is all in the cards!" The comment did not feel as light and airy as he wanted. The detective filled his pipe with deliberate slowness to give his frustration time to ease. He lit the pipe, letting the cool smoke work into his lungs.

"At any rate, Watson, trust me when I say I will not be trying that again anytime soon!"

Thursday, November 22 *Losing Everything*

The pair was up early the next morning to follow Druitt to chambers. The barrister entered the building while they took up their observation positions. It was a day to trade off, and Gregson and Smithers arrived to replace them as they watched the Inner Temple.

"Good morning, Gregson," greeted the detective.

"Good morning, sir," replied the inspector with a touch of his cap. "Anything new to report?"

Holmes related a small part of Druitt's visit to the rooms previous night. The policeman needed to know in case Druitt decided to repeat the visit. But as he told the story, he saw Druitt come out of the building.

"There he is now!"

Druitt walked to the curb and stopped, his eyes downcast. He remained motionless, almost a statue that attracted the attention of the passers-by. After a long time, he hailed a cab.

"What is this, Mr. Holmes?" Gregson asked.

"I am not sure," replied the detective. "Get on his trail. Send a telegram if he does anything unexpected."

"Yes, sir."

Gregson waved for his companion and the two men quickly hailed a cab to follow the barrister as he rode away in the direction of Victoria Station. Watson approached, puzzlement on his features.

"What has happened?"

"I am not sure, though I have my suspicions. Come! Back to Baker Street!"

"Whatever for?"

"We must be properly dressed to deal with a solicitor!"

Holmes sent a telegram to Druitt's solicitor and arrived promptly at the appointed time. John Etheridge was an eager young man and greeted them warmly. He was more than pleased to meet Sherlock Holmes and have the famous detective use his services to find a barrister. He was surprised when Holmes asked for Druitt by name.

"Mr. Druitt, sir?" replied Etheridge with some hesitation. "Why Mr. Druitt specifically?"

"I am acquainted with William Druitt and he explained his brother was having difficulty with his practice. I have a family property matter than needs resolution, as well as some minor debt collection efforts. I thought I might engage his services as a way of helping him out."

"I am afraid Mr. Druitt is not currently available. He has left on a holiday."

Holmes suspected there was more to the story than that. He feigned innocence as he continued.

"A strange time of year for a holiday, surely!"

Etheridge leaned forward and lowered his voice.

"May I rely on you discretion, Mr. Holmes?"

"Naturally," agreed the detective.

"Frankly, sir, he has been asked to *not* show up at his Chambers. His presence is upsetting to everyone."

Holmes feigned surprise at the revelation. "Why ever would that be?"

Etheridge continued in a conspiratorial whisper. "Mr. Druitt is having a bad spell, sir. As you are a friend of the family, you are doubtless aware that he has lost a sister and that his mother was committed to an asylum this past summer."

"Yes," the detective answered gravely. "It has been a trying time for the Druitts."

"Montague…Mr. Druitt, that is…has not managed it well. It weighs upon him most heavily. Our head of chambers directed he take a holiday and use the time to come to terms with these issues."

"I see."

Etheridge straightened up and his voice returned to its normal tone.

"I have several other barristers who will be more than happy to help resolve your issues."

"Most kind of you, sir, but I am afraid I have wasted your valuable time," Announced Holmes, standing abruptly. "As I said, I specifically wanted Mr. Druitt's services to help him at this difficult time. Since he is unavailable, then I will just use my normal barrister."

He quickly shook the solicitor's hand and left the

office, giving Etheridge hardly a moment to make a protest before he was gone.

"What does this all means, Holmes?"

The doctor had remained silent through the entire meeting, but finally had to ask for an explanation as they rode back towards Baker Street.

"It means my plan is working."

The detective let out a heavy sigh. He had always worked strictly on the basis of the law. His efforts were directed to bringing criminals to account in the courts. Now, he was deliberately working to destroy a person, to cause him to collapse so utterly he could no longer function.

"This may be his last straw, Watson. He has lost his mother, his teaching position, and now he is turned out of chambers. We have denied him access to Whitechapel or anything from the darker side of his nature." The detective nodded, satisfying with the progression of events, even was he was unhappy with the method. "He has only himself and who wants to be trapped with the Whitechapel murderer?"

Saturday, November 24 *Stones*

For the next two days, their quarry did not stir from his residence. His presence was advertised by the incessant pacing in the room above, but Druitt did not leave it even for meals. Holmes was wondering if he had reached an impasse, a point at which he could push the barrister no further. But then late in the evening, he heard the door to Druitt's room open and the man's uneven tread upon the stairs.

The detective followed Druitt into the clear night, the young barrister walking aimlessly through the streets of Blackheath. He would pause on occasion and pluck something from the ground, then continue on his way. Holmes quickly determined he was picking up stones. For what purpose, he had no idea.

Druitt came to a small pond and stopped, his gaze across the still, cold waters. Holmes had Watson wait, while he moved closer, stopping ten feet away from the man. Holmes did not speak. He waited in silence for Druitt to take some action. It was several minutes before Druitt spoke.

"What am I to do?"

Holmes could not be sure if the words were meant for him or if the young man was simply speaking to himself. He answered, to try to force the barrister further along the path he had chosen for him.

"You are the only one who can bring this to an end."

Druitt remained motionless for several more minutes. When he finally moved, he spied another rock upon the ground. He bent over and picked it up, slipping it into his coat pocket.

Holmes waited for him to get ahead a ways before he and Watson fell in him behind to follow his endless trek.

"Why is he collecting stones?" asked Watson.

"In truth, I have no idea." Holmes shrugged his shoulders, settling his coat about him more closely in the cool night air. "He is truly mad, Watson. I cannot be sure what the machinations of his troubled mind are contemplating." Ahead, Druitt bent over and collected another stone and added it to the collection in his pockets. "But if he wants to collect stones for an unknown purpose, I am willing to allow it."

He paused to light a cigarette but kept his eyes firmly fixed on their quarry. Druitt seemed befuddled, as if he was unsure which way to proceed. He began walking again so Holmes and Watson slowly trailed him.

"I will add one thing to that comment, Watson."

"What is that, Holmes?" asked the doctor.

"If there is any indication that collecting these stones is giving him pleasure or comfort, then I will deny the stones to him as well."

Sunday, November 25 *Empty Steps*

"Pacing, pacing, pacing! Will it never cease?" Watson exploded in frustration. "He must have paced 500 miles these past two weeks!"

"True enough," agreed Holmes.

"Your week is up, Holmes. I should have ended this Wednesday night!"

Holmes lit his pipe. Like his friend, he was dissatisfied with their course of action. He was accustomed to being on his feet, looking for clues, and searching for suspects. This investigation was limited to following one suspect in search of a resolution.

"I know." He was unable to keep his own frustration out of the concession. "But I will not let you have his blood on your hands. We must keep the pressure on."

"Perhaps we can have the police maintain the watch for two or three days so we can return to Baker Street," offered Watson. "It would be a welcome break from following the every move of a madman."

"As much as I would like to do so, we cannot." Holmes looked at his friend, reminding him of facts he had to constantly repeat to himself. “Do not get complacent about his mental state. You must remember this man is smart. He has eluded the police to the point they do not even believe his guilt. He has eluded me twice with dire results.”

He knocked his pipe ash on the floor and refilled it.

“No, we cannot relent. He might return to his senses and we will never be able to use his crimes against him. We must press him, Watson, and never allow him to think it all the way through. He must always know we are at his very heels!”

Holmes fell silent, leaning back and trying to think of anything else he might do to hasten the conclusion of this case. Watson returned to his newspaper, but after a few moments his eyes drifted upwards as the sound of footsteps continued.

Monday, November 26 *Mme. Montpenseir*

It was a cold and damp without a hint of dawn. They were surprised Gregson arrived to relieve them much earlier than expected. He brought with them an urgent plea from Lestrade, so Holmes and his companion left as quickly as possible for London.

The two men stepped from the train and, though it was nearly seven in the morning, it was still dark. It was almost a month to the solstice, and the days continued to grow shorter. A familiar voice shouted to them and Lestrade waved to them from across the platform.

"Holmes!" He called, obviously in a state of great excitement. "Holmes, you must come quickly!"

"What is so important to call us down this early, Lestrade. Another murder in the East End?"

Lestrade shook his head. "No, Mr. Holmes, nothing to do with Whitechapel. It is another case entirely."

Watson breathed a sigh of relief. It would have been too much for the Ripper to strike again after all their precautions.

"Mr. Holmes, please! Only you can prevent an

innocent woman from being arrested."

"Why would you arrest her if she is innocent?" asked the detective, more than a little sarcasm in his question.

"I cannot prove her innocence," admitted Lestrade in a voice so filled with anguish it would have plucked at the heart strings of even the most hardhearted man. "To make matters worse, Athelney Jones has charge of the case."

"Not him again!" puffed Watson

"Sadly," agreed Lestrade. "Now he is preparing to arrest all the members of the household as conspirators."

"It is his trademark," observed Holmes.

"Please, Holmes. It is not far and I am sure you can shed light where I cannot." The little inspector was almost pleading.

"You want me to prove who is guilty?" he asked.

"No, Holmes," said Lestrade, his voice in the most pleading terms. "I need you to prove who is innocent."

Even the stern detective could not deny a friend who so desperately required his assistance. He relented and Lestrade led his companions to the waiting carriage. In moments, they were off to Camden in the still, black morning.

"What is the nature of the crime?" asked Holmes once Lestrade had provided the address. It was a sign of the stress he was under that the detective was breaking his own rule of never asking for facts before reaching the crime scene.

"A murder, Holmes. Or at least, we assume it is murder."

"You have no body then."

"Precisely. We know there was a terrible argument the night before, which would be Saturday. Yesterday morning, the presumed victim's bed was discovered, covered in blood, an equally bloody knife on the floor beside it. The staff can provide alibis but the mistress of the house cannot."

"Then you have your crime and you have your murderer," concluded Holmes.

The policeman was not willing to accept so obvious a conclusion.

"I do not believe Mme. Montpenseir is guilty and I need you to prove that fact." Lestrade's voice clearly betrayed more than a professional interest in the woman in question. He continued, anguish clear in every word as he spoke. "If you do not prove her innocence, she will surely be arrested by the end of the day and, as you say, the circumstantial evidence is sufficient to convict her."

"A woman, you say? And the victim?"

"Mlle. Carere is her companion. She is, or maybe was, a nineteen year old French girl."

"And Jones is in charge of the investigation?"

Lestrade answered, embarrassed at the response. "Ever since Norwood, we keep him away from all but the most basic cases, but he was the only inspector available. I was asked to review his work, to avoid any further humiliation in the press." Lestrade shook his head in annoyance. "You will see, Holmes. On the surface, it is all very cut and dry and so simple even Jones could not go wrong. But when you take into account the people involved, the very idea of a murder seems just ludicrous.

And Jones, of course, will listen to no other ideas but his own!"

Holmes shook his head in fatigue. He was clearly not in a mood to clear up a case mishandled by inspector Athelney Jones.

"Lestrade," he said wearily, relenting to the desperate request. "I have had a long night and want to get back to my rooms. I will do this as a favor, but do not expect me to show my normal patience if I must deal with Jones."

Holmes leaned back and closed his eyes. Watson smiled, and did the same. Lestrade looked to the two men, almost frantic.

"Watson!" he demanded in a hoarse whispered. "What does he mean by that? I have never known Holmes to show much patience."

Watson looked to his napping friend and chuckled. "Lestrade, you have never seen him truly impatient." Watson closed his eyes in an attempt to get a short nap before reaching their destination. "I am afraid this is going to be brutal."

The carriage stopped outside Mme. Montpenseir's and Holmes' was immediately awake.

"Watson! What time is it?"

Watson pulled out his watch and checked it while Holmes pulled on his gloves and set his hat.

"Seven thirty-five."

"Very well."

And like a runner starting a race, he was gone,

sweeping past the policemen standing at the door. Lestrade and Watson trotted to keep up with the rapid pace. Holmes was inside and tossed his hat, gloves, and walking stick to another constable before turning to face Lestrade.

"Upstairs?"

"Third room on the..."

But the detective was already gone, Lestrade and Watson following several steps behind.

"Ah ha!" Holmes exploded. He aimed for the door in a bee line, but was met by the squat figure of Athelney Jones before he could enter. "Inspector Jones!" He continued. "I am here at the request of Inspector Lestrade."

"But it is not Lestrade's case now, is it?"

Holmes smiled, the grin on his lips at odds with the coldness of his stare.

"As I recall, you did not follow my advice at Norwood, and it cost you dearly in the newspaper." He leaned closer to Jones and lowered his voice. "I have a reporter at the Central News Agency who will print this story in any manner I dictate. *I* am not giving you a choice!"

He pushed past the policeman and entered the room. The other two men followed but Holmes held them at the entrance.

"Please! Jones has already disturbed everything enough."

Holmes moved cautiously, so much more in his element than in the streets of Whitechapel or Blackheath. He clucked and chortled, then stood up and approached the bed. He had barely set eyes upon it when he gave out a shout.

"Jones!"

The inspector re-entered the room.

"Yes, Mr. Holmes?" The voice was innocent.

"This simply will not do, *inspector*!" scolded Holmes sharply. "Look at this bed!"

"Yes? Obviously, this is the scene of a grisly crime. The poor girl was stabbed in her sleep no doubt!"

Holmes rolled his eyes in frustration and clucked disapprovingly.

"Lestrade!" he prompted

The inspector stepped over. He looked at the empty bed for a moment before the answer dawned upon him.

"Of course," snapped Lestrade. Holmes' presence helped to serve as a catalyst and he saw the solution immediately. "The blood is in a large pool. If the girl were killed in the bed, the body would have left an outline, like at Miller's Court!"

"Bravo, Lestrade! And you are correct: just like Miller's Court." Holmes got down on one knee. "Here is where the knife fell. The shape of the blade is clear." His finger traced the outline of a butcher's knife, the brown, dried blood stains marking the location. "But it is equally clear there is nothing to indicate the handle." Holmes stood, shaking his head sadly at Jones. "If someone had sprayed as much blood about, surely some would have landed on the handle and it would have left as clear an imprint as the blade."

He turned to the door, snapping an order to his companion. "Watson, I trust Inspector Jones has the staff gathered in preparation for arrest. Please step down and have a word with the cook. Specifically, find out if that worthy person was planning to make black pudding for breakfast."

Watson looked at Holmes in surprise, but knew better than to question the master detective.

"At once, Holmes."

He was gone, heading down the stairs as quickly as he could manage. Meanwhile, Holmes looked about the room, spying the jewelry box on the dresser. He stabbed a finger in that direction.

"There is your clue! Lestrade, you have shown Mme. Montpenseir your sympathy. Take the jewelry case to her and see if she can determine if any items are missing. Also discover if Mlle. Carere had any gentlemen friends."

"Of course, Mr. Holmes."

Lestrade left as quickly as Watson. Inspector Jones stared after his colleague in distaste.

"He oughtn't be following your orders, Holmes," he protested. "This is my case, after all."

Holmes shook his head in distaste. He gestured to Jones, his index finger bringing him over to a spot on the carpet.

"Do you believe Mme. Montpenseir carried the body of the young lady from the room?"

"Well, no, Mr. Holmes. I cannot believe the lady could have carried the body."

"So! She would have dragged the girl's body?"

Jones clucked in his condescending manner. "Well, that would be obvious to anyone, wouldn't it now?"

As his friends had observed, patience was hardly Holmes' strong point. He was particularly pointed as he explained his observation to the inept Jones.

"Yes, but what is *not* obvious are the heel marks the body would have produced in the rug and carpet. They are nowhere to be seen! Should they not be *clearly* visible, inspector?"

Jones stared blankly at the carpet as Watson came slowly back up the stairs, puffing to catch his breath.

"Yes, Holmes," he announced. "Black pudding is her specialty."

"And her jar of blood was missing." To Holmes, it was not a question, merely a confirmation of a fact he had already deduced.

"Exactly." Watson glanced towards the blood covering the bed. "I believe I can see where the contents were emptied."

Holmes smiled, the genuine warmth showing in his eyes whenever one of his deductions held true.

"That explains the blood, Inspector Jones. And here comes Inspector Lestrade with answer to the remainder of the mystery."

Lestrade held the jewelry box above his head in triumph.

"A good dozen of the most expensive pieces are missing, Holmes, *and* there was an American lad with which Mlle. Carere was particularly smitten."

Holmes stretched widely and yawned. It was clear to almost everyone that his work was completed.

"There is your case, Jones," Holmes said, heading for

the stairs and taking his gloves back from the waiting constable.

"I don't know that I rightly follow," said Jones densely, his short legs unable to keep up with the long strides of the detective.

"For heaven's sake, man!" snapped Lestrade, his patience at the breaking point. "The girl has faked her own murder because of remaining anger over the argument on Saturday, and then ran off with this American. She has taken some jewels to finance her journey. Find the lad and find the girl!"

Holmes nodded in Lestrade's direction. "Exactly."

They had reached the ground floor and the detective retrieved his hat, gloves and walking stick from the constable.

"Watson! Time!"

"Eight ten, Holmes."

"A personal best by five minutes." He stopped and looked to Lestrade. "Tell me, Lestrade. You saw the evidence and yet you did not believe Madame Montpenseir was guilty."

The Scotland Yard man shuffle uncomfortably, embarrassed. "I can't rightly explain it, Mr. Holmes. I can only say I know Madame Montpenseir is a lady, refined and truthful. I would stake my honor on that."

Holmes looked from one of his companions to the other.

"I cannot believe this!" He tried to sound disapproving, but could not hide his amusement. "You have both found wives because of my successful solution of cases." He turned back towards the carriage. “Come, Watson. If we hurry, we may still have time for Mrs. Hudson’s breakfast before some sleep and our return to Blackheath.”

Tuesday, November 27 *Alone in the Night*

Holmes sat in his chair. The room was dark, lit by the embers of the fire and the glimmer from the bowl of his pipe. He would take a draw, and the orange glow of the pipe would cast his face in a demonic shade.

"So how much longer do we keep doing this?" whispered Watson from his chair. "He hasn't moved in two days!"

"Not too much longer," said Holmes.

"How can you know that?"

Holmes pointed at the ceiling with the stem of his pipe. Watson listened. No longer did the sound of pacing track back and forth across the room. At first, the physician thought everything was in total silence. But then, imperceptibly, he heard the sound Holmes wanted him to notice.

Faintly, the sounds of sobbing drifted through the darkness.

Thursday, November 29 *Ultimatum*

Holmes answered his brother's summons for a meeting at Baker Street. Gregson and Smithers had the duty to keep up the surveillance on Druitt, so the detective could make the meeting. He dispatched Watson to his club for the evening so that he and Mycroft would have the privacy they needed for the conversation.

Mycroft appeared on time, his slow, distinctive tread on the stairs announcing his arrival. He entered the rooms breathing heavily, and let his weight drop onto the sofa.

"You really need to do something about those stairs, Sherlock!" he said, taking a brandy snifter from his brother.

The detective did not banter and went straight to the object of the visit.

"I know it is then end of the month, Mycroft."

"The case remains open," replied the elder Holmes. "And why do you waste your time with these other trifling affairs?"

"Because friends requested it," Holmes returned without apology. "And I must have something to keep my mind active while I observe this cursed barrister."

Mycroft's response was blunt. "You know how to end it."

"If you have an assassin to assign to the task, you may do so! My plans are continuing and are showing results."

Mycroft's walking stick tapped the floor rapidly in irritation.

"When?"

Holmes shifted, uncomfortable that his brother was demanding a timetable. Still, it was an expected requested and the detective had an answer prepared.

"I am close, closer than you can imagine. Within the week."

"Very well." Mycroft set down the snifter and painfully lifted his bulk to the standing position. "Seven days, Sherlock. Not one day more!"

Friday, November 30 *Endgame*

Rain rattled against the windows of the rooms in Blackheath. Their long vigil continued and Watson felt the need to comment.

"It is raining again, Holmes. Will he try to make a move tonight?"

"He wants to, Watson." He gestured towards the ceiling. The silence was as obvious as the sound of the continual pacing had been. "He is like a caged animal coiled in the corner and waiting to jump upon the zookeeper."

Watson withdrew his revolver and rechecked it. It was not the first time that evening he had done so.

"Is it still loaded?" asked Holmes.

Watson set it on the table between them so it was within easy grasp.

"Yes, and as I am one of the zookeepers, I am quite prepared to use it!"

Holmes smiled at the continuation of the analogy.

"It promises to rain all weekend," said Holmes. "I believe we are at the crisis."

Watson nodded and the two men sat in silence for a long time. There was little to be said between them. Almost three month's work had brought them to this point, waiting on a man they suspected of killing eight women. Holmes had handled cases that held the fate of nations and kings in his hands. This case had rocked the core of an empire that stretched around the entire world.

"Why doesn't he move?"

"Steady, old fellow," replied the detective. "He knows we are watching. Everything is present for him to satisfy his urge, but he cannot. He will not make a move until he believes he can lose us again."

Watson shuddered, remembering the close call on November eighth.

Holmes stepped over to the table and wrote out a telegram.

"What is that?"

"A notice to Lestrade. We can send it from the station. There will be no time to compose it once our prey is in motion."

"Write two copies," said the doctor.

Holmes nodded in a agreement, seeing Watson's idea immediately.

"Excellent thought, Watson. We will both be able to send it when needed."

He completed the sheets and returned to his seat after handing Watson his copy. And as he sat, the sound of footfalls reached them from above.

"He grows tired of waiting."

Holmes reached into his pocket and withdrew his own pistol. He checked the chambers and set it down on the table next to Watson's.

"Is it still loaded?" asked Watson with a grin.

Holmes tapped the reassuring metal of the revolver.

"Both zookeepers need to be prepared."

Saturday, December 1 *At Large*

The rain rattled against the windows of their Blackheath rooms. Holmes pulled out his watch and checked the time again.

"He must leave soon or he will miss the last train."

"You are sure it is tonight?"

Holmes knew too well the difficulty in predicting how people reacted. In this case, he was attempting to divine the thoughts in a troubled mind. It was almost a month since Miller's Court and Druitt had kept his desires under control for the entire time. Everything pointed to this night as the time when his inner demons would take control again.

"He has been silent since nightfall. It has been raining all day. He must break tonight and give in to his urges."

"And we will catch him in the act?"

Holmes rubbed the side of his nose with a finger. He would not let Watson know his actual plans for the evening. Whatever transpired, Druitt would not be returning from his next trip to Whitechapel.

"Yes. We will catch him in the act."

There was a creak on the stairs followed immediately by the sound of the front door closing. Holmes flew to the window and looked into the rainy night.

"Blast! He managed to steal past us!"

Watson was already on his feet and tossed Holmes his Inverness and deer stalker. They pulled their coats about them as they ran down the stairs and into the street.

"After him on foot! Keep an eye open for a cab!"

Holmes was already trotting down the street in the direction of the rail station. Ahead, he could see Druitt running. A cab appeared and Druitt called it over, and drove into the darkness leaving the detective and his companion behind.

"Holmes!"

Watson had flagged down another cab and was already climbing into it. Holmes climbed in, slamming the doors closed.

"To the station without delay!" snapped the detective, handing a one pound note up to the cabbie.

It was a wild and bouncing ride to the train station. The conductors were already making their boarding calls as the two men jumped from the cab.

"Holmes!" snapped Watson, "get on the train I'll send the telegram! I will grab a cab if I am too late for the train!"

"We will meet at Commercial and Whitechapel Road!" returned the detective as he looked about for Druitt.

There were few people on the platform and the conductor was making the final boarding calls. Holmes leapt onto the last car and worked his way forward as the train began to move. It became obvious Watson had missed the train and would be forced to take a cab to Whitechapel.

Car by car, the detective moved towards the front of the train, his eyes checking each compartment as he passed. Somewhere ahead, his quarry was waiting. But as he entered the final car, there was still no sign of the barrister. With a sinking feeling, Holmes retraced his steps.

The detective reached the final car and sank slowly into the last row of seats. He had been bested again. Druitt had continued on in his cab. It was not that much longer a trip by cab and the ruse had worked completely. Holmes felt overwhelmed with despair, wondering why he had not exercised Mycroft's option during the past month.

He tried to push the feelings aside, but they washed across him again. His mind returned to the night of the eighth when Druitt had eluded him and the dreadful consequences of his failure. But as he recalled that night, he also remembered Watson's stern admonishments. He straightened, and his mind began to work again, concentrating on the problem.

He had not completely lost the advantage: he was traveling by train and would arrive in Whitechapel before Druitt. Watson had sent the telegram to Lestrade so he could expect the inspector to be waiting for him at the station. He would have a little time to organize the police forces. His mind raced through his options as the train rolled into the night.

Holmes jumped off the train while it was still moving. Lestrade was already waiting with a few men and rushed up to him.

"Where is he?" demanded the inspector.

"I'll explain on the way to Whitechapel!" returned Holmes.

Lestrade led him to a waiting police coach and they were off with the bell ringing.

"He did not get on the train," said Holmes. "He must be on the way to Whitechapel by cab!"

They clattered through the streets of Westminster, trying to get past the slower moving traffic.

"Then all is lost!"

"No!" Holmes grabbed Lestrade's shoulder. "There is one more piece missing, something he has to collect."

"What?"

"The knife, Lestrade! The knife! It is the one thing I have been unable to discover, but I now believe I know where it is."

Lestrade was unconvinced. "Why should he bother? He can pick up another blade from a street vendor for a few pence!"

"No, he cannot." Holmes' mind raced at breakneck speed, and he forced himself to slow down as he explained. "He cannot use just any knife. The weapon is as important to him as the murder and the display of the body." Rain splashed against the coach windows. "And the rain. They are all parts of the whole and he must have them all if his ritual is to be complete."

The policeman looked at him, unsure and unimpressed.

"Then where is he hiding the knife?"

“The one place we could never look for it! In Whitechapel itself!”

Lestrade was skeptical of the revelation. “How can he be sure no one will find it?”

“I cannot be sure, but I will know when I find the hiding place."

Holmes had spent his time on the train well, drawing up definite plans to search the warren for their killer.

“It is a miserable night. That will help reduce the number of people and potential victims on the streets. Dispatch your men. Have them chase the prostitutes to safety, even if it is into a pub! If they see Druitt, chase him!”

“Chase him where? What chance have we of finding him within Whitechapel? What if…”

Holmes cut Lestrade off.

“We must proceed without hesitation once we reach the streets, Lestrade. There can be no doubts or questions! Your men need to spread the word quickly. And when we do give chase, tell them to force him south, out of Whitechapel and towards the river.”

“I don’t…”

“The river, Lestrade! Always towards the river! If you have never had faith in me before, you must act without questions this night! ”

The coach rattled into the night, towards the address given by the detective. As they passed Commercial and Whitechapel Road, Holmes leaned across the inspector and opened the door. He barely caught sight of Watson, but the doctor also spied him and headed towards a cab. The carriage lurched into the night, but Holmes was confident his friend was not far behind.

The coach slowed to a stop, but Holmes did not wait. While Lestrade issued his orders, he grabbed a lantern from a constable and moved to Leman Street. The police inspector found him shining his light on the walls of the alley.

"What are you looking for?" he asked.

"I am not entirely sure," replied the detective, "but this must be the place. This is where we lost him on the eighth. It was his only opportunity to get the knife."

Holmes was still searching when a few minutes later when Watson arrived. "What are we doing here?" asked the physician.

At almost the same instance, Holmes' light revealed a hole in the wall and he rushed over to it.

"It is just a rat hole," said Lestrade.

Holmes stuck his cane into the opening for a considerable length. When he withdrew it, his hand showed the depth was almost a foot. Holmes turned his attention to the ground, the light from the lamp darting quickly about. It froze on a scrap of clothe marked by dark brown stains. The detective snatched it up, and held it close to the light.

"Dried blood?" asks Watson

"Probably."

The outline of a blade and handle were clear. Holmes' finger traced the pattern.

"You see! Just the sort of blade we expected!"

He looked back at the spot where the cloth was laying and picked up a piece of broken brick. Taking the scrap back, he quickly fitted it into the hole.

“So that is where he keeps the knife!” said Watson

“Indeed. And why would one think to search all of Whitechapel for it?”

“How did you know?” asked Lestrade.

“He was searched; his rooms were searched; his chambers were searched. He did not have it on the seventh, but he had it on the eighth. He has not had it since, not until now.”

“And he ran in here on the eighth!” realized the doctor

“Precisely. Process of elimination. He hid the one truly incriminating piece of evidence as far away from himself as he could manage, yet he had to be sure it was safe. But he had to retrieve it before he could go on the hunt.”

“And he has it now!”

Watson’s words were chilling, even in the cold December air.

Holmes straightened, his fingers snapping with realization.

“I know where he is!”

He left at a run, with Watson yelling after him in the pursuit. “Where?”

“Where it all went wrong for him!” returned the detective. “Miller’s Court!”

The three men ran into the mist.

Sunday, December 2 *Absolution*

It was five blocks to Miller's Court. The men arrived quickly, but Watson and Lestrade were bent over, their hands on their knees as they gasped for breath.

"Why here, Holmes?" asked Watson between huffs. "Why do you say it went wrong here?"

Holmes head darted about, checking all directions. He was alert, like a cat sensing its prey.

"He planned to kill Mary Morstan that night, except we thwarted his efforts. He returned here and found poor Mary Kelly. But he lost control; he abandoned his ritual. He did not just kill and display the wretched woman. He literally tore her apart. And that is what has been driving him mad these past weeks!"

Holmes pointed his companions down two different alleys.

"Be prepared!" He slipped his police whistle into his mouth. He took out his revolver and cocked it. "As Watson's wound shows, he will not hesitate to defend himself. Have no qualms about firing!"

The men moved cautiously into the night. The rain

was letting up, changing over to a heavy mist, and even that was showing signs of diminishing. Their footfalls, despite their efforts at silence, echoed in the night. And as they emerged from the alley onto Commercial Road, they heard a scream.

Holmes looked to his right and there were two dark forms in the shadow between two street lamps. He shouted and ran in that direction. One figure slumped to the ground, the other darted off, the detective in close pursuit.

Watson reached the woman who lay prostrate, gasping for air. He grabbed her roughly, checking her throat for any signs of a wound. Lestrade knelt beside him and he allowed the inspector to take her.

"She is scared and half throttled, but is breathing normally! I must help Holmes!"

He did not wait for a reply and dashed into the night after his friend.

It was a moment before a constable arrived in response to the commotion. Lestrade left the newcomer in charge of the woman, and ran into the darkness after Holmes and Watson.

Holmes considered himself a fast runner, but he was not able to draw closer to the athletic Druitt. Still, his rapid pursuit did not allow the barrister to escape, and the two men ran south, south until they approached the Thames. Druitt ran into an alley between two warehouses and Holmes stopped, taking time to catch his breath. As with everything in London, he knew this place. The alley led to a dock, and the dock sat on the river. At last, their prey was cornered, for there were no exits.

Watson came up, gasping desperately for air. Holmes placed a hand on his shoulder to steady him. A few moments later, the police inspector joined them.

"Druitt is on the wharf. There is no way out, other than this entrance. I will go speak with him, but do not let him see either of you. Is that clear?"

Lestrade, still badly out of breath, did not understand the situation.

"Why do we not arrest him?"

"That is not my purpose, Lestrade." Holmes' words were as cold as the night.

"We have our man, gentlemen," he continued. "But whatever should happen, you will not allow Druitt to leave this wharf. Watson?"

The physician nodded, withdrawing his service revolver. The doctor's visage was grim and tight lipped. He held the weapon loosely at his side in preparation. Lestrade looked at the two men. He still did not comprehend the import of their actions, but the realization was dawning.

"You can't, Holmes…"

The detective cut his protest short. "Can you possibly obtain a conviction with the evidence I have made available?"

"No, but…"

"Then we use other methods. This *ends* tonight, Lestrade!"

Holmes was fierce, his features firm and terrifying. The

Scotland Yard inspector quailed in his presence. The detective left no doubts as to the outcome of the night's work.

"If you are unable to assist us, I suggest you return to the yard, *inspector*."

Holmes did not wait for a reply. He walked towards the wharf, disappearing into the shadows and growing fog as a light mist moved past. Watson looked to Lestrade, and hefted the reassuring weight of his pistol. Drawing his collar up to fend off the December weather, he followed Holmes as quietly as he could manage. After watching the two leave, Lestrade cast a glance about in confusion. His resolve stiffened. He prepared his own firearm and followed them into the gloom.

Holmes left the space between the warehouses. At the end of the dock, the dark outline of his quarry was visible against rain blurred lights across the river. He approached, not worrying about stealth. His footfalls rang crisply in the cold, wintry air of London. As he drew closer, Druitt's shape sharpened from the mists. The young barrister was wild eyed and unblinking. His clothes were disheveled, his face unshaven and hair unkempt. The features were tightly drawn. He turned to face his tormentor, his bright, wild eyes evident even on the unlit wharf.

"You task me, sir," he said in a surprisingly even voice. "You task me and I shall not have it!"

Holmes was unruffled by the confrontation. "That has been my intention, Mr. Druitt, and your desires are of no concern to me."

"I get no rest, no privacy! Everywhere, I am followed."

His voice rose, breaking towards the end. "I matter, Holmes. I have made the whole world see that I matter!"

"The opinion of the world matters even less to me than your desires," replied the detective. "That your crimes have piqued the gruesome imaginations of the masses means nothing."

"I have shown them…"

Holmes cut off the reply.

"You have only shown them the cruel inhumanity one person can display to another, an inhumanity that is only magnified by the pages of the newspaper and the size of the typeface!"

Holmes stepped closer, looking past the killer at the dark waters of the Thames. "You shall not be allowed a moment's peace as long as we both draw breath."

"Then that is our impasse," responded Druitt.

A silence rose between the two men for a few moments. Druitt's hand was in his coat pocket and Holmes noted a slight clicking sound.

"Mr. Druitt, you have brought your stone collection with you?"

Druitt withdrew his hand, displaying a fist sized stone. He returned hand and stone to the pocket, but made no comment. Instead, his gaze remained fixed on the cold, swift waters before him.

"Why do you have the stones?"

"They are solid and reassuring."

The barrister's voice was light, as if he were speaking to the air around him instead of another person. His eyes, though directed towards the detective, were unfocused.

"I perceive all you pockets are filled with the same." commented Holmes. "They are quite heavy, are they not?"

Druitt looked at the stone in his hand. "Yes. They slowed me down or you would never have caught me."

"You were not escaping me this night," returned Holmes.

It was difficult to see everything in the dim light, but the detective finally saw the bulge in back of Druitt's coat that indicated the final prize. He reached over to the man, and found the handle beneath the collar. Holmes withdrew the knife, the long, narrow blade glinting slightly from the lights on the other side of the river.

"All your pockets save this one. I shall relieve you of this."

Druitt's eyes centered on him, but did he not answer immediately. Instead, he turned back towards the river. At length, he replied in a low voice and the detective strained to understand him.

"The waters are peaceful, are they not? Peaceful, clean, and pure."

Holmes stepped closer to respond. "As much peace as you might wish." He drew alongside the man, his eyes directed towards the darkly rushing river. "Why do you wish peace, Druitt?"

"The faces..." Druitt stammered but collected himself and continued. His voice had more animation and contained a hint of fear. "The faces come to me in the night."

"How many faces, Druitt? How many faces do you see

in the night?"

"Too many, Holmes. Too many."

The detective's voice lowered even further, carrying the edge of loathing he had contained for the past three months. "Whose faces do you see, Druitt? Whose?"

Holmes reached into his pocket and withdrew the photographs.

"Catherine Eddowes? Annie Chapman?"

As he said each name, he held a picture in front of Druitt. He let them drop to the dock until all but one lay at Druitt's feet. The last he held in front of Druitt and the young man's eyes fixed on the photograph.

"And worst of all, Mary Kelley," accused Holmes.

He pressed Druitt. For weeks, the barrister had evaded any direct reference to the murders, now the detective was able to confront him directly. The police photograph showed her mutilated body lying on her bed, the still human eyes staring balefully from the stiff paper. Druitt took the sheet, not recognizing what it was.

He raised the photo to his listless eyes and, as recognition struck, his face grew even paler. He turned it over, and the Sign of Eight was marked on the back. The hand holding the picture dropped back to his side and he released it to fall into the rushing waters below the dock.

"So many faces, Holmes. So many."

"Too many, Druitt. Too many faces, too many helpless cries in the night!"

Druitt faced the great detective. His eyes had transformed from listless to pleading. His words quavered as he spoke.

"Do you know, Holmes, that you have been my best and only friend these past four weeks? You are the only person who has shown any understanding of me at all!"

Holmes felt revulsion at the admission. His chosen profession had steeled him to face many things, but this was not one of them.

"I am not your friend," he answered. "I am but a harbinger to bring you to this."

He gestured across the expanse of water beyond them. Druitt nodded, sad realization in the empty eyes.

"What is to be done?"

Holmes placed a firm hand on the man's shoulder. "You know the answer to that question, Druitt. You filled your pockets with stones to weigh yourself down. You brought yourself here to where the waters are peaceful and clean. You know what must happen."

Druitt faced back to the river. His back stiffened. "Yes, I know what must happen. I do not know if I can do it."

"Yes, Montague." Holmes words were gentle, soothing, and hypnotic. "You must do it. Only you can make the faces go way."

Watson remained in the shadows. The forms at the end of the dock were visible only as silhouettes. Even then, occasional wisps of fog obscured his vision of the two men. He heard the first words between the two clearly, but then their voices were lowered. No amount of straining brought the conversation to his ears. He thought of moving closer, but kept his position as Holmes instructed. He heard a slight sound behind and turned his head to find

Lestrade had pressed forward.

"What are they saying?" he asked in a hushed whisper that was scarcely audible.

Watson held a finger to his lips. No sound came from the wharf where the two men still stood.

"I can not hear," he replied.

"Perhaps…" ventured Lestrade, but he was allowed to speak no further.

Watson placed a hand to the other's mouth, his eyes still intent on the dark figures. Another wisp of fog engulfed them and they disappeared momentarily in the mist. And as the shapes disappeared, there was a loud splash, the sound of something falling into the river. Concern overtook him and Watson stepped from his hiding place and started down the dock with his gun at the ready. Lestrade was close on his heels.

The doctor had barely taken a step when a form hardened and emerged from the fog. His finger tightened on trigger, prepared to carry out Holmes instructions to prevent Druitt from leaving the wharf. But he did not need to see the shape clearly to recognize the form and movement as Sherlock Holmes.

"Holmes!" snapped Watson. His gaze moved past the detective to the empty space beyond. He started forward, but Holmes held up his cane to block him.

"It is done, Watson. None but us shall leave this wharf this night."

Lestrade lagged behind, intent on moving to the waters edge.

"Lestrade!" chided Holmes. "There is nothing to be

done there!"

"But what of Druitt?"

"He is gone, Lestrade. Destroyed. Consumed by his own guilt" The words were bitter and merciless. Watson had often remarked how his companion was little more than a calculating machine, a mechanism designed to discover and resolve crime. He had never seen that mechanism so steeled and directed.

Holmes gestured ahead with his cane. "Might we find Inspector Abberline at the Yard?"

Lestrade fell into step behind, walking quickly to catch up. "He spends most nights there these past several weeks. Our chances are good to find him there."

"Then we are off to the Yard," announced the detective, the cold tone yielding to a slight animation. "I shall make my report there."

Lestrade took the two men into Scotland Yard and the offices occupied by 'H' Division. It was well past three o'clock, and the rooms were deserted except for a dim light in the back. The detective brought Holmes and Watson to Abberline's office, where the chief inspector sat behind his desk, his head in his hands.

A bottle of scotch sat on the desk, near a half empty glass. Abberline looked up at the three intruders, his vision blurred by the spirits. When he spoke, his words were slow, though not slurred.

"And what brings you gentlemen here at such an hour?" he asked.

"A conclusion in Whitechapel, Inspector," announced

Holmes.

It took several seconds for Abberline's dulled senses to register the import of the statement. "A conclusion, you say? You have captured the murder?"

Homes shook his head ruefully. "I am sorry to say this conclusion is not so clearly clean cut, Inspector."

Abberline became more focused as the discussion progressed. He sat upright in his chair, reaching over to turn up the gas. Light glared in the room, and Watson blinked at the sudden increase in intensity.

"If there is no capture, then how is the case concluded?"

Holmes took a deep breath before explaining the events of the evening. Even as he did, the details he related were sketchy. He was not going to tell the Chief Inspector anything more than he needed.

"Montague Druitt is dead by suicide. His body will doubtless be discovered in the Thames within the next few days. With him dead, there will be no more 'Ripper' murders."

Abberline considered the comments. He picked up his glass for another sip of whiskey before replying. "You are so sure he is the guilty party?"

Holmes did not hesitate in his reply. "*Was* the guilty party, Inspector. *Was*." The detective placed his hands on the desk and leaned closer to Abberline. "I am as sure Druitt was the Ripper as I can be of anything I have not witnessed with my own eyes."

He reached into his inside pocket and withdrew the knife. He laid it on Abberline's desk.

“I took this from him before he entered the water.”

Watson and Lestrade stared at the weapon. Holmes made no mention of it on their trip to the yard. The doctor recognized the type of blade immediately.

“A post mortem knife!” The observation burst forth, a hushed and surprised whisper.

“It was the correct man, in the correct place, with the correct weapon. I did not need to watch him wield it to know he was the one.”

Abberline picked up the knife, looking at it in a mixture of loathing and wonder. Lestrade moved to his chief’s side to view the final piece of evidence in the string of heinous crimes.

Holmes straightened and pulled on his gloves. None of the men had removed their hats or coats, but this was the detective’s signal the interview was concluded.

“You will have to watch Whitechapel to get past the period ending on December 10th, and then again at the end of the month. Nothing will happen and you can shut down the investigation. The killings have stopped, Abberline."

"What will we tell the public, Holmes?" asked Lestrade.

“You shall tell them you believe the murderer is dead and you shall seal the files. You have done it before.” He looked to his companion. “Come, Watson. We have taken enough of the inspector's time this evening.”

The ride to Baker Street was in silence. Holmes was obviously deep in thought and Watson did not want to intrude. At length, however, the doctor could not remain silent any longer.

"Are you positive Druitt was Jack the Ripper? You have staked your reputation at Scotland Yard upon that fact. If you are wrong, they will not remember the hundreds of case where you were correct."

"I have no care of that. I have my deductions and the knife. What more do I need?"

"A confession?"

"He would not confess, Watson. Even in those final moments, he could admit to no one he was Jack the Ripper."

"And if there is another killing?"

Holmes yielded the point. "Then I am proved wrong, if just this once. I believe Druitt the right man and the official police had no way to bring the killings to an end. I have, yet again, filled their deficiencies."

The cab clattered to a halt in front of 221B.

"We will sleep. In the morning, we will make a final trip to Blackheath."

"Whatever for?"

"We must reclaim our meager belongings from those rooms and pay Mrs. Patrick for a final week's rent. I will make one last visit to Druitt's rooms to insure he left no incriminating evidence behind."

"Posh!" spat Watson. "What do we care if that beast is implicated in the killings?"

Holmes was tired. He could not recall ever being so exhausted at the conclusion of a case as he was this night.

He found the strength to explain to his friend.

"I do not do it for him, Watson. He has a brother and two remaining sisters who are innocent of any wrong doing. A public revelation will ruin them all. Given their family history, it may well drive the sisters to their deaths."

Watson nodded, the explanation clear to him once it was made.

"You are right, of course," relented Watson. "There is no need to add more sorry blood to those hands."

The doctor reached for the latch and opened the door on the cab. But he did not move, for he had one more question. It was difficult to force the words from his lips.

"I must know, Holmes." He struggled, finding it nearly impossible to finish his query. Still, he managed to speak. "Did Druitt jump into the river or did you push him?"

Holmes had stepped down from the hansom as Watson spoke. He stopped, frozen in position, as the words came. He moved again, more slowly now, and stepped aside so Watson could exit the coach as well.

"We shall need a spot of hot tea this morning, Watson, to drive out the cold." He walked to the door and opened it quietly. "Perhaps, like Inspector Abberline, we might allow ourselves something more substantial."

Tuesday, January 1, 1889 *Epilogue*

"Here are two articles for you."

Holmes handed the first *Times* of the year to Watson. A short column at the bottom of the first reported the circumstances under which Druitt's body found by Thornycroft's. The second revealed that Mlle. Carere, the young lady who was Mme. Montpenseir's ward, had been found alive and married in New York.

"It says Druitt had fourteen hundred in notes on him!" Watson was amazed at the sum. "Where could he have gotten so much money?"

Holmes shrugged and, as usual, lit a pipe.

"It probably attests to his success as a burglar," he returned. "It seemed he excelled at that craft better than the bar."

Watson let out a heavy sigh of frustration as he let the paper fall across his lap.

"I still do not understand," he confessed. "He was a man of gentle means. He had two good professions, a life of comfort, if not outstanding success, before him. Why commit these atrocities?"

Holmes shook his head. He went over to the writing table and began to pen a letter.

"You still look for motive, Watson. Stapleton had motive, and you saw that. The ease of solving Mme. Montpenseir's case was because she had no motive whereas Mlle. Carere had the motive of revenge for faking her death. Even Colonel Upwood's motives were apparent, for it was not the money but respect that he sought."

The pen scraped across the paper as the detective wrote quickly. He signed with a flourish and looked back to his friend.

"You may contrast those with Druitt, a man driven by internal fires were can scarcely imagine. His motives...his motives existed within him, and we will never truly understand such desires and cruelty. " He paused, adding a final observation. "If there is justice in the universe, he is in another type of fire at this point."

"I am a Christian, Holmes, and I trust he is burning in eternal damnation!"

Holmes addressed and sealed the letter he had written.

"What is that?"

"Instructions to William Druitt for Montague's inquest. What to say and what not to say." Holmes thought for a second. "I shall have Lestrade attend, I think. Thanks to your stories, he has his own notoriety, but he will not draw the attention that Abberline or I would."

Watson nodded. At this point, their best efforts were directed towards protecting the family. Still, there was one aspect of the case he could not reconcile. "You made yourself the judge and jury in other cases, Holmes. I have even gone along with you in those instances."

The doctor's point was plain.

"But in this case, you believe I am also the executioner," he said.

"Exactly."

There was disapproval in Watson's voice. The tone stung even the normally cold heart of the detective.

"I am too well aware of that, old boy." He tried to sound apologetic, hoping his friend would eventually understand his dilemma. "Too well aware," he repeated.

Holmes set the letter down next to the partial mailbag that sat on the floor. The volume of mail had dropped steadily over the past eight weeks as no new murders occurred. The detective decided this would be the last of his mail he would let the police review.

"When are you and Miss Morstan to be married?" he asked as he took his violin.

"In April," replied Watson. "Hopefully, it will be warmer by then."

"I will be sorry to see my roommate leave," observed Holmes. "But for now, my dear Watson, we have had some weeks of severe work. This evening, I think, we may turn our thoughts to more pleasant channels. I have a box for 'Les Huguenots' and we can stop at Marcini's for a dinner on the way."

"Of course, Holmes," agreed the doctor.

But the heavy thoughts of the past weeks played across Watson's features. He ignored the breakfast Mrs. Hudson had laid out and instead got his coat and walking stick.

"I think I need to take some air."

Holmes watched him leave the rooms. The detective saw his abandoned violin in the corner. He could not remember the last time he had played it. He picked it up and stepped to the window.

On the street below, Watson walked into the crisp January air. The doctor looked up at the rooms and his eyes met Holmes'. The master detective tried to read the look that passed between them, but it was unclear. Something had changed between them that November night in Camberwell. Watson did not hold the gaze long and, turning up his collar to the cold, walked down the street.

Holmes watched him, wondering if their friendship would ever be the same. He placed the violin beneath his chin and began to play, but even the music could not replace what had been lost since he examined that first body in Whitechapel.

Author's Postscript

This is a work of fiction and not an historical document. To that end, I must point out the variances between the "facts" of the story and the facts known about Jack the Ripper. While I have tried to follow the evidence of the Ripper killings as closely as possible, it is necessary to add information in the story to reach a conclusion. After all, if the investigators actually had all the clues made available to Holmes, they would have stood a good chance of catching the killer. Since Holmes gets the benefit of our modern understanding of serial killers, it is only fair to point out what changes were made to the evidence available to the great detective as opposed to the police who actually worked on the case in 1888.

It is generally accepted that the Ripper killed five women, starting with Annie Chapman and ending with Mary Kelly. The two earlier victims noted are included by some writers as Ripper killings, but do not seem to follow the pattern. Still, the Martha Tabram murder on August 7th *does* fit the pattern in a two regards: 1) the date fits the arbitrary date pattern of Ripper killings and 2) she was stabbed to death. Most evidence indicates she was killed by a soldier, and, indeed, she was last seen in the company of a soldier. But that observation is not conclusive and, despite turning out all the troopers who may have been involved, none were discovered. She may have been the first Ripper killing, and her timing and style of death work well as a "practice" killing for the serial killer of the story. For this plot reason, I let Holmes keep her as a victim.

The two strangulations in July are purely fictional. The Ripper shows a clear trend of increasing violence in the known murders, as do serial killers in general. It helps the plot of the story to introduce "practice" crimes as an antecedent to the better publicized cases to maintain the pattern. Of course, if any Ripperologist out there is aware of strangulations in Whitechapel in the months preceding the appearance of the Ripper, I would be interested in the details.

Regarding Druitt as the culprit, what we know of the man seems to best fit the profile of a serial killer of all the main suspects. Still, there is little actual evidence to point to him as the Ripper. I believe his death so soon after Mary Kelly and the ending of the Ripper murders at the same time is more than coincidental. Death by suicide is not an uncommon end for serial killers who can no longer stand the duality of their compulsions.

It is for this reason, the very "commonness" of the man, that I have always felt he was the best candidate as the Ripper. Other writers that send Holmes on the trail of the Ripper lean towards a Royal Family or a "high society" resolution to the case. While these stories are entertaining, I feel they are more reflective of a prejudice against the upper class than a real attempt at solving the crime. A socialite in the streets of Whitechapel would have been noticed by everyone, particularly the squads of police dispatched to catch the killer: tall hats and tails were hardly common in Whitechapel. The pattern of killings fits those of other serial killers better than a grandiose conspiracy hatched in the bowels of Masonic ritual. I wanted to treat this as a "normal" serial killer case (if there is such a thing) and present Holmes with the challenges faced by police officers who regularly deal with those types of crimes.

Of course, Montague Druitt was a barrister, not a doctor. Donald Rumbelow ascribes 1881 as a time when Druitt *may* have studied medicine, or he may have been a medical student at the time of the killings since his legal career was not progressing. His father was a doctor, and it may be that he learned some of the skills from him. But there is no evidence to support the idea that Druitt had any medical training and there are aspects of the Ripper killings that indicate the murderer had medical knowledge. I kept both these aspects in the story to explain the apparent surgical skills of the Ripper, but there are no records to support the contention.

Druitt's brother *did* bring him to the eyes of the police. When testifying at Druitt's inquest in January, William stated he was the only living relative, thus protecting the sisters from any scandal that might erupt. This seems to indicate some thought of guilt on the part of his brother and certainly many of the police at the time had him high on their list of potential Rippers. But again, there is no more *hard* evidence to support Druitt as the killer than any of the other suspects put forward by the police at the time or the scores of researchers since.

William Druitt's description of Montague as "sexually insane" is another indicator of guilt, but what does "sexually insane" mean in Victorian times? Did Druitt like looking at women's ankles when they stepped out of carriages? With no further comment on why this diagnosis was made, we are left to our own devices, and I allow Holmes to flesh out the accusation to arrive at his own conclusion. This is based on what is known of modern serial killers, but cannot, in truth, be applied to Druitt except in a work of fiction.

Another fascinating aspect is that the Ripper killings were also the first "mass media" crime. Telegraph, transatlantic cables, and newspapers made the killings a world wide event, followed throughout the British Empire. The Ripper played to the world audience like any actor of the modern screen. There were other serial killers in operation at the time, but these virtually unknown today. The difference is that Jack played to the press, the others did not.

There is suspicion the two "red ink" Jack the Ripper post cards were written by an American. I supply Tallman to fill that void. There was no known reporter that actually fits this description. The "William Randolph Hearst" connection is merely an historical fiction that meshes well with the times.

I also feel the need to explain to all the true Holmes fans who read this that the Holmes chronology used was that assembled by William S. Baring-Gould in "The Annotated Sherlock Holmes". I believe Baring-Gould supports his chronology very well by cross referencing aspects and comments in the stories. This is not intended to disparage any of the other chronologies of Holmes adventures. All similar chronologies are made with careful attention to the dates and activities of the time.

I started from the idea of interweaving the Ripper killings with whatever cases happened to fall into the August-November 1888 time frame. To find not one but *three* of the master's most famous cases occurred in the fall of 1888 was just too much to overlook. Further, the demands of those cases helps explain the length of time needed by Holmes to come to a successful Ripper resolution. Certainly, the references in "The Hound of the Baskervilles" to Holmes' delay in London because of "the pressure of another case" can only be a reference to the Whitechapel murders, despite Conan-Doyle's allusion to "black mailing". I trust I have not stepped too far out of line with my retelling of the three tales in this work.

The two additional cases (the Nonpareil and Mme. Montpenseir) are included because Watson specifically references them in "Hound of the Baskervilles". His final discussion of the case comes in early December, and Holmes refers to these two cases as occurring in the interim. Since it is known Druitt committed suicide in early December, these two cases had to occur by then. I hope my creation of these cases was entertaining and apply to the overall plot.

I corrected the obvious inconsistency where "The Sign of Four" starts in July, and ends in September. I accept Mr. Baring-Gould's conclusion that the July start is a misprint in the original. "The Greek Interpreter" was moved forward a few days for dramatic purposes and removes the need to repeat the story in its entirety.

An apology to our English friends for the American spelling...

Finally, I hope both the "Baker Street Irregulars" and the amateur "Ripperologists" out there have found this reading experience accurate and enjoyable.

ABOUT THE AUTHOR

Donald Joy is a native Nebraskan. He and his wife Teresa still reside in Nebraska and are big Husker fans. Don has written stories since he was a child and started writing his first book in high school. He is a graduate of the University of Nebraska at Omaha Writer's Workshop with a Bachelor of Fine Arts in Creative Writing.

"Murder in Whitechapel" combines a life long love of Sherlock Holmes stories with an interest in the darker side of humanity displayed by Jack the Ripper. It is his first published novel.

www.ingramcontent.com/pod-product-compliance
Lightning Source LLC
Chambersburg PA
CBHW051429260626
47162CB00001B/18

9780615808840